Passionate Pregnancies

MAYA BANKS

First Published in Great Britain 2017
By Mills & Boon, an imprint of HarperCollins*Publishers*
1 London Bridge Street, London, SE1 9GF

PASSIONATE PREGNANCIES © 2017 Harlequin Books S. A.

Enticed By His Forgotten Lover, *Wanted By Her Lost Love* and *Tempted By Her Innocent Kiss* were first published in Great Britain by Harlequin (UK) Limited.

Enticed By His Forgotten Lover © 2011 Maya Banks
Wanted By Her Lost Love © 2011 Maya Banks
Tempted By Her Innocent Kiss © 2012 Maya Banks

ISBN: 978-0-263-92967-6

05-0617

Our policy is to use papers that are natural, renewable and recyclable products and made from wood grown in sustainable forests.The logging and manufacturing processes conform to the legal environmental regulations of the country of origin.

Printed and bound in Spain
by CPI, Barcelona

Maya Banks has loved romance novels from a (very) early age, and almost from the start, she dre of writing them, as well. In her teens she filled coun notebooks with overdramatic stories of love and pass Today her stories are only slightly less dramatic, but less romantic.

She lives in Texas with her husband and three childre and wouldn't contemplate living anywhere other tha the South. When she's not writing, she's usually hunting, fishing or playing poker. She loves to hear from her readers, and she can be found on Facebook or you can follow her on Twitter (www.twitter.com/maya_banks). Her website, www.mayabanks.com, is where you ca find up-to-date information on all of Maya's upcoming rel

Maya's current and
eleases.

ENTICED BY HIS
FORGOTTEN LOVER

BY
MAYA BANKS

To Jane Litte because she loves this trope above all others. ;)

To Charles Griemsman for all his words of encouragement and his never-ending patience.

One

Rafael de Luca had been in worse situations before, and he'd no doubt be in worse in the future. He could handle it. These people would never make him sweat. They'd never know that he had absolutely no memory of any of them.

He surveyed the crowded ballroom with grim tolerance, sipping at the tasteless wine to cover the fact that he was uneasy. It was only by force of will that he'd managed to last this long. His head was pounding a vicious cadence that made it hard to down the swallow of wine without his stomach heaving it back up.

"Rafe, you can pack it in," Devon Carter murmured next to him. "You've put in enough time. No one suspects a thing."

Rafael swiveled to see his three friends—Devon, Ryan Beardsley and Cameron Hollingsworth—standing protectively at his back. There was significance there. Always at his back. Ever since they were freshmen in college, determined to make their mark on the business world.

They had come when he was lying in the hospital, a yawning black hole in his memory. They hadn't coddled him. Quite the opposite. They'd been complete bastards. He was still grateful for that.

"I've been told I never leave a party early," Rafe said as he tipped the wine toward his mouth again. As soon as the aroma wafted through his nostrils, he lowered the glass, changing his mind. What he wouldn't give for a bloody painkiller.

He'd refused any medication. He despised how out of control painkillers made him feel. But right now, he'd gladly take a few and pass out for several hours. Maybe then he'd wake up without the god-awful pain in his temples.

Cam's lips twisted in a half snarl. "Who gives a damn what you typically do? It's your party. Tell them all to—"

Ryan held up his hand. "They're important business associates, Cam. We want their money, remember?"

Cam scowled as he scanned the room.

"Who needs a security team with the three of you around?" Rafael drawled. He joked, but he was grateful for people he could trust. There was no one else he'd admit his memory loss to.

Devon leaned in quickly and said in a low voice, "The man approaching is Quenton Ramsey the third. His wife's name is Marcy. He's already confirmed for the Moon Island deal."

Rafael nodded and took a step away from the shelter of his friends and smiled warmly at the approaching couple. A lot rode on making sure their investors didn't get nervous. Rafael and his business partners had located a prime spot for their resort—a tiny island off the coast of Texas just across the bay from Galveston. The land was his. Now all they had to do was build the hotel and keep their investors happy.

"Quenton, Marcy, it's wonderful to see you both again. And may I say how lovely you look tonight, Marcy. Quenton is a very lucky man."

The older woman's cheeks flushed with pleasure as Rafael took her hand and brought it to his lips.

He nodded politely and pretended interest in the couple, but his nape was prickling again, and he squelched the urge to rub it. His head was lowered as if he were hanging on to every word, but his gaze rapidly took in the room, searching for the source of his unease.

At first his gaze flickered past her but he yanked his attention back to the woman standing across the room. Her stare bore holes through him. Unflinching and steady even when his eyes locked with hers.

It was hard for him to discern why he was so arrested by her. He knew he generally preferred tall, leggy blondes. He was a total sucker for baby blues and soft, pale skin.

This woman was petite, even in heels, and had a creamy olive complexion. A wealth of inky black curls cascaded over her shoulders and her eyes were equally dark.

She looked at him as if she'd already judged him and found him lacking. He'd never seen her before in his life. Or had he?

He cursed the gaping hole in his memory. He remembered nothing of the weeks before his accident four months ago and had gaps in his memory preceding the weeks that he remembered nothing of. It was all so…random. Selective amnesia. It was complete and utter bull. No one got amnesia except hysterical women in bad soap operas. His physician suggested that there was a psychological reason for the missing pieces of his memory. Rafael hadn't appreciated such a suggestion. He wasn't crazy. Who the hell *wanted* to lose their memory?

He remembered Dev, Cam and Ryan. Every moment of the past decade. Their years in college. Their success in business. He remembered most of the people who worked for him. Most. But not all, which caused him no end of stress in his offices.

Especially since he was trying to close a resort development deal that could make him and his partners millions.

Now he was stuck not remembering who half his investors were and he couldn't afford to lose anyone at this stage of the game.

The woman was still staring at him, but she'd made no move to approach him. Her eyes had grown colder the longer their gazes held, and her hand tightened perceptibly on her small clutch.

"Excuse me," he murmured to the Ramseys. With a smooth smile, he disengaged himself from the group who'd assembled around him and discreetly made his way in the direction of his mystery woman.

His security team followed at a short distance, but he ignored them. They didn't shadow him for fear of his safety as much as his partners feared it getting out that he'd lost his memory. The security team was an annoyance he was unused to, but they kept people at arm's length, which served him well at the moment.

The woman didn't pretend to be coy. She stared straight at him and as he approached, her chin thrust upward in a gesture of defiance that intrigued him.

For a moment he stood in front of her, studying the delicate lines of her face and wondering if in fact this was their first meeting. Surely he would have remembered.

"Excuse me, but have we met?" he asked in his smoothest voice, one that he knew to be particularly effective on women.

Likely she'd titter and then deny such a meeting. Or she'd blatantly lie and try to convince him that they'd spent a wonderful night in bed. Which he knew couldn't be true, because she wasn't his type.

His gaze settled over the generous swell of her breasts pushed up by the empire waist of her black cocktail dress. The rest of the dress fell in a swirl to her knees and twitched with sudden impatience.

She did none of the things he'd supposed. When he glanced back up at her face, he saw fury reflected in the dark pools of her eyes.

"*Met? Have we met?*" Her voice was barely above a whisper, but he felt each word like the crack of a whip. "You sorry bastard!"

Before he could process the shock of her outburst she nailed him with a right hook. He stumbled back, holding his nose.

"Son of a—"

Before he could demand to know if she'd lost her damn mind, one of his guards stepped between him and the woman, and in the confusion accidentally sent her reeling backward. She stumbled and went down on one knee, her hand automatically flying to the folds of her dress.

It was then, as she cupped her belly, that the realization hit him. The folds had hidden the gentle curve of her body. Had hidden her pregnancy and the evidence of a child.

His guard went to roughly haul her to her feet.

"No!" Rafael roared. "She's pregnant. Do not hurt her!"

His guard stepped back, his startled gaze going to Rafael. The woman wasted no time scrambling to her feet. Her eyes flashing, she turned and ran down the marble hallway, her heels tapping a loud staccato as she fled.

Rafael stared at her retreating figure, too stunned to do or say anything. The last time she'd looked at him, it wasn't fury he'd seen. It wasn't the fiery anger that prompted her to hit him. No, he'd seen tears and hurt. Somehow, he'd hurt this woman and damned if he knew how.

The vicious ache in his head forgotten, he hurried down the hallway after her. He burst from the hotel lobby, and when he reached the steps leading down to the busy streets, he saw two shoes sparkling in the moonlight, the silvery glitter twinkling at him. Mocking him.

He bent and picked up the strappy sandals and then he

frowned. A pregnant woman had no business wearing heels this high. What if she'd tripped and fallen? Why the devil had she run? It certainly seemed as if she wanted a confrontation with him, but at first opportunity, she'd fled.

At least she'd had the common sense to ditch them so she wasn't running down some street on a pair of toothpicks.

"What the hell is going on, Rafe?" Cam demanded as he hurried up behind him.

In fact, his entire security team, along with Cam, Ryan and Devon, had followed him from the hotel into the crisp autumn air. Now they gathered around him and they looked as though they were concerned. About him.

He blew out his breath in frustration and then shoved the pair of sparkly, ultra-feminine shoes at Ramon, his head of security.

"Find the woman who wore these shoes."

"What would you like me to do with her when I find her?" Ramon asked in a sober voice that told Rafael he'd definitely find the woman in short order. Ramon didn't typically fail in any task Rafael set him to.

Rafael shook his head. "You aren't to do anything. Report back to me. I'll handle the situation."

He was treated to a multitude of frowns.

"I don't like it, Rafe," Ryan said. "This screams setup. It's not impossible that your memory loss hasn't already been leaked to the press or even a few confidential sources who haven't yet gone wide with it. A woman could manipulate you in a thousand ways by using it against you."

"Yes, she could," Rafael said calmly. "There's something about this woman that bugs me, though."

Cam's brow lifted in that imperious way that intimidated so many people. "Do you recognize her? Is she someone you knew?"

Rafael frowned. "I don't know. Yet. But I'm going to find out."

*   *   *

yony Morgan stepped from the shower, wrapped a towel
around her head and then pulled on a robe. Even a warm
shower hadn't stopped the rapid thump of her pulse. Try as
she might, she hadn't been able to let go of her rage.

Have we met?

His question replayed over and over until she wanted to
throw something. Preferably at him.

How could she have been so stupid? She wasn't typically
one to lose her mind over a good-looking man. She'd been
immune to a good many with charm and wit.

But from the time Rafael de Luca had stepped onto her
island, he'd been it for her. No fighting. No resisting. He was
the entire package. Perfection in those uptight business suits
he wore. Oh, she'd managed to get them off of him. By the
time he left the island, his pilot hadn't even recognized him.

He'd gone from a sober, uptight, type A personality to
laid-back, relaxed and well vacationed.

And in love.

She closed her eyes against the sudden surge of pain that
swamped her.

He obviously hadn't been in love. Or anything else. He
came. He saw. And he conquered. She was just too hopelessly
naive and too in love herself to consider his true motives.

That may well have been the case, but it didn't mean he
was going to get away scot-free with his lies and deception.
She didn't care what she had to do, he wasn't going to develop
the land she'd sold him into some ginormous tourist mecca
and turn the entire island into some playground for bored,
wealthy jet-setters.

It had taken all her courage to crash his party tonight, but
once she'd learned the purpose—a gathering of his potential
investors for the project he planned to ruin her land with—
she'd been determined to confront him. Right there in their

midst. Daring him to lie to her when the entire room k̶ of his plans.

She hadn't counted on him denying that he'd ever met h̶ But then how better to paint her as the village idiot? Or some crazy do-gooder granola bar out to halt "progress."

The force of just how wrong she'd been threatened to flatten her. She sighed heavily and shook her head. She had to calm down or her blood pressure was going to skyrocket.

Slowly she unclenched her jaw. Her teeth were ground together with enough force to break them.

Where was room service? She was starving. She rubbed her belly apologetically and made a conscious effort to let all the anger and stress flow out of her body. It couldn't be good for the baby to have her mother so pissed off all the time.

She gritted her teeth before she realized that she'd done so again. Forcing her jaw to relax once more, she performed the arduous task of combing out her hair and blow-drying it.

She was finishing up when a loud knock sounded at her door.

"Food. Finally," she murmured as she turned off the hair dryer.

She hurried to the door and swung it open. But there was no food cart or hotel employee. Rafael stood there, her abandoned shoes dangling from his fingertips.

She stepped back and tried to slam the door, but he stuck his foot in, preventing her from shutting it.

As indomitable as ever, he pushed his way in and stood in front of her. She hated how small and vulnerable she felt against him. Oh, she hadn't always hated it. She'd loved how protected and cherished he'd made her feel when she curled her much smaller body into his.

She bared her teeth into a snarl. "Get out or I'll call hotel security."

"You could," he said calmly. "But as I own this hotel, you might have a hard time having me thrown out."

Her eyes narrowed. Of course he'd own the hotel she'd chosen to stay in. What were the odds of that?

"I'll call the police then. I don't care who you are. You can't force yourself into my hotel room."

He raised an eyebrow. "I came to return your shoes. Does that make me a criminal?"

"Oh, come on, Rafael! Stop playing stupid games. It's beneath you. Or it should be. I get it. Believe me—I get it! I got it as soon as you looked right through me at the party. Though I have to say, the 'have we met?' line? That was priceless. Just priceless. Not to mention overkill."

It was all she could do not to hit him again, and maybe he realized just how badly she wanted to because he took a wary step back.

She advanced, not willing for a moment to allow him to control the situation. "You know what? I never took you for a coward. You played me. I get that. I was a monumental idiot. But for you to hide from the inevitable confrontation like you've done makes me physically ill."

She stuck a finger into his chest, ignoring the baffled look on his face. "Furthermore, you're not going to get away with your plans for *my* land. If it takes every cent I own, I'll fight you. We had a verbal agreement, and you'll stick to it."

He blinked, then looked as if he was about to say something.

She crossed her arms, so furious she wanted to kick him. If it wouldn't land her on her ass, she'd do it.

"What? Did you think you'd never see me again? That I'd hide away somewhere and sulk because I learned you don't really love me and slept with me to get me to agree to sell to you? You couldn't be more mistaken," she seethed.

Rafael reacted as though she'd hit him again. His face paled and his eyes became hard, cold points. If she weren't so angry, what she saw in his gaze would probably scare the bejesus out of her. But Mamaw had always said that common sense was the first thing to go when someone got all riled up. Boy, was that the truth.

"Are you trying to insinuate that you and I have slept together?" he asked in a dangerously low voice that—again— should have frightened her. But she was way beyond fear. "I don't even know your name."

It shouldn't have hurt her. She'd long since realized why Rafael had chosen her. Why he'd seduced her and why he'd told her the lies he told. He couldn't shoulder the entire blame. She'd been far too easy a conquest.

But still, that he'd stand there before her and categorically deny even knowing her name sliced a jagged line through her heart that was beyond repair.

"You should go," she said in a barely controlled tone. Damn the tears, but if he didn't leave now, she wasn't going to keep her composure for long.

His brow furrowed and he cocked his head to the side, studying her intently. Then to her dismay, he swept his hand out and smudged a tear from the corner of her eye with his thumb.

"You're upset."

Sweet mother of God, this man was an idiot. She could only pray their child inherited her brains and not his. She nearly laughed aloud but it came out as a strangled sob. How could she hope for the poor baby to inherit any intelligence whatsoever when it was clear that both his parents were flaming morons?

"Get. Out."

But instead he cupped her chin and tilted it upward so he could stare into her eyes. Then he wiped at the dampness on her cheek in a surprisingly gentle gesture.

"We can't have slept together. Besides the fact that you aren't my type, I can't imagine forgetting such an event."

Her mouth gaped open and any thoughts of tears fled. She

wrenched herself from his grasp and gave up trying to get the man out of her room. He could stay. She was going.

She gripped the lapels of her robe and stomped around him. She made it into the hall before his hand closed around her wrist and he pulled her up short.

Enough was enough. She opened her mouth to let out a shriek, but he yanked her against his hard body and covered her mouth.

"For God's sake, I'm not going to hurt you," he hissed.

He muscled her back into the hotel room, slammed the door and bolted it shut behind them. Then he turned and glared at her.

"You've already hurt me," she said through gritted teeth.

His eyes softened and grew cloudy with confusion.

"It's obvious you feel as though I've wronged you in some way. I'd apologize, but I'd have to remember you and what I supposedly did in order to offer restitution."

"Restitution?" She gaped at him, stunned by the difference in the Rafael de Luca she fell in love with and this man standing before her now. She yanked open her robe so that the small mound of her belly showed through the thin, satin nightgown underneath. "You make me fall in love with you. You seduce me. You tell me you love me and that you want us to be together. You get my signature on papers agreeing to sell you land that has been in my family for a century. You feed me complete lies about our relationship and your plans for the land. But that wasn't enough. No, you had to get me pregnant on top of it all!"

His face went white. Anger removed all the confusion from his features. He took a step toward her and for the first time, fear edged out her fury. She took a step back and braced her hand against the TV stand.

"Are you saying that we slept together and that I am the father of your baby?" he demanded.

She stared wordlessly at him, hurt still crowding viciously

into her chest. "Are you trying to say we didn't? That I imagined the weeks we spent together? Do you deny that you left me without a word and never looked back?"

Sarcasm crept into her voice but there was also deep pain that she wished wasn't so evident. It was enough that he'd betrayed her. She didn't want to be humiliated further.

He flinched and closed his eyes. Then he took a step back and for a moment she thought he was finally going to do as she'd demanded and leave.

"I don't remember you," he said hoarsely. "I don't remember any of it. You. Us. That." He gestured toward her belly.

He trailed off and something about the bewilderment in his voice made her stop in her tracks. She crossed her arms protectively over her chest and swallowed.

"You don't remember."

He ran a hand through his hair and swore under his breath. "I had an...accident. Several months ago. I don't remember you. If what you're saying is true, we met during the period where my memory is a complete blank."

Two

Rafael watched as all the color leeched from her face and she swayed unsteadily. With a curse, he reached to grasp her arms. This time she didn't fight him. She was limp in his hands and he felt the slight tremble beneath his fingers.

"Come, sit down, before you fall," he said grimly.

He led her to the bed and she sat, her hands going to the edge to brace herself.

She glanced up at him, her eyes haunted. "You expect me to believe you have *amnesia?* Is that the best you could come up with?"

He winced because he felt much the same about the idea of amnesia. If all she'd said was true and their positions were reversed, he'd laugh her out of the room.

"I don't ask this to make you angry, but what is your name? I feel at quite a disadvantage here."

She sighed and rubbed a hand wearily through her thick hair. "You're serious about this."

He made a sound of impatience and she pinched the bridge of her nose between her fingers.

"My name is Bryony Morgan," she said quietly.

She bowed her head and black curls fell forward, hiding her profile. Unable to resist, he ran his finger over her cheek and then pushed the hair back behind her ear.

"Well, Bryony, it would seem you and I have a lot to discuss. I have many, many questions as you can well imagine."

She turned her head to stare up at him. "Amnesia. You're seriously going to stick to this insane story?"

He tried to remember how skeptical he'd be in her shoes, but her outright disbelief was ticking him off. He wasn't used to having his word questioned by anyone.

"Do you think I like being punched in the face at a public gathering by a woman claiming to be pregnant with my child when to my knowledge it's the first time we've met? Put yourself in my shoes for a moment. If a man you'd never seen before or had no memory of walked up to you and said the things to you that you're saying to me, don't you think you'd be a little suspicious? Hell, you'd probably have already called the cops you keep threatening me with."

"This is crazy," she muttered.

"Look, I can prove what happened to me. I can show you my medical records and the doctor's diagnosis. I don't remember you, Bryony. I'm sorry if that hurts you, but it's a fact. I have only your word that we were ever anything to each other."

Her lips twisted. "Yeah, we can't forget I'm not your type."

He winced. Trust her to remember that remark.

"I'd like for you to tell me everything. Start from the beginning. Tell me when and where we met. Maybe something you say will jog my memory."

A knock sounded at the door and he scowled. "Are you expecting someone at this hour?" he asked when she rose to answer it.

"Room service. I'm starving. I haven't eaten all day."

"That can't be good for the baby."

She didn't look as though she appreciated the remark. Gathering her robe tighter around her, she went to the door and a few seconds later, a room service attendant wheeled in a cart bearing covered plates. She signed the bill and offered a halfhearted smile of thanks to the man.

When Rafael and Bryony were alone again she pushed the cart the rest of the way to the bed. "Sorry. Obviously I wasn't counting on company. I only ordered enough food for one."

He lifted a brow as she began uncovering the dishes. There was enough food to feed a small convention.

"Sit down and relax. We can talk while you're eating."

She settled in the armchair catty-corner to the bed and curled her feet underneath her. As she reached for one of the plates, he studied the face of the woman he'd forgotten.

She was beautiful. No denying that. Not the kind of woman he usually gravitated toward. She was entirely too outspoken for his liking. He preferred women who were gentle and, according to his close friends, submissive.

Quite frankly it made him sound like a jackass. But he couldn't deny he did like his women a bit more biddable. He found it fascinating that he'd supposedly met and fallen in love with Bryony Morgan, the antithesis of every woman he'd dated for the past five years.

Okay, so he bought that he'd been attracted to her. And yeah, he could buy sleeping with her. But falling in love? In a span of a few weeks?

That was a giant hole in the fairy tale she'd spun.

But she was also a woman, and women tended to be emotional creatures. It was possible she thought he was in love with her. Her hurt and betrayal certainly didn't seem feigned.

And then there was the fact she was pregnant with his child. It would probably make him seem even more of a bastard, but it would be stupid not to insist on paternity testing. It wasn't out of the realm of possibility that she'd made the entire thing up after learning of his memory loss.

He had the sudden urge to call his lawyer and have him tell him whose signature was on the real estate contract for the land he'd purchased sometime during the weeks he'd lost. He hadn't seen the paperwork since before his accident. He paid people to keep his business running and his affairs in order. Once he scored the deal, there was no reason to look back.

Until now.

Damn but this was a mess. And yeah, he was definitely calling his lawyer first thing in the morning.

"What are you thinking?" she asked bluntly.

"That this is a huge cluster f—"

"You're telling me," she muttered. "Only I don't see what's so bad from your perspective. You've got more money than God. You're not pregnant, and you didn't just sign away land that's been in your family for generations to a man who's going to destroy it to build some tourist trap."

The pain in her voice sent an uncomfortable sensation through his chest. Something remarkably like guilt ate at him, but what did he have to feel guilty about? None of this was his fault.

"How did we meet?" he asked. "I need to know everything."

She toyed with her fork, and her lips turned down into an unhappy frown.

"The first time I saw you, you were wearing an uptight suit, shoes that cost more than my house and you had on sunglasses. It annoyed me that I couldn't see your eyes, so I refused to speak to you until you took them off."

"And where was this?"

"Moon Island. You were asking about a stretch of beach-front property and who owned it. I, of course, was the owner, and I figured you were some guy from the city with big plans to develop the island and save all the locals from a life of poverty."

He frowned. "It wasn't for sale? I remember it being for sale before I ever went down there. I wouldn't have known about it otherwise."

She nodded. "It was. I…I needed to sell it. My grandmother and I could no longer afford the property taxes. But we agreed we wouldn't sell to a developer. It was bad enough that I was forced to sell land that's been in my family for generations."

She broke off, clearly uncomfortable with all she'd shared.

"Anyway, I figured you for another stiff suit, and so I sent you across the island on a wild-goose chase."

He sent a glare in her direction. For the first time, a smile flirted on the edge of her lips.

"You were so angry with me. You stormed back to my cottage and banged on my door. You demanded to know what the hell I was doing and said I didn't act like someone who desperately needed to sell a piece of land."

"That sounds like me," he acknowledged.

"I informed you that I wasn't interested in selling to you and you demanded to know why. When I told you of my promise to my grandmother that we'd only sell to someone willing to sign a guarantee that they wouldn't commercially develop the stretch of beach, you asked to meet her."

An uncomfortable prickle went up his nape. That didn't sound like him. He wasn't one to get personal. Everyone had their price. He would have simply upped his offer until he found theirs.

"The rest is pretty embarrassing," she said lightly. "I took you to meet Mamaw. The two of you got along famously. She invited you to stay for supper. Afterward we took a walk on the beach. You kissed me. I kissed you back. You walked me back to my cottage and told me you'd see me the next day."

"And did I?"

"Oh, yes," she whispered. "And the day after, and the day after. It took me three days to talk you out of that suit."

He lifted a brow and stared.

Her cheeks turned red and she clamped a hand over her mouth. "Oh, God, I didn't mean it like that. You wore that suit everywhere on the beach. You stuck out like a sore thumb. So I took you shopping. We bought you beachwear."

This was starting to sound like a nightmare. "Beachwear?"

Her head bobbed up and down. "Shorts. T-shirts. Flip-flops."

Maybe the doctor had been right. He lost his memory because he *wanted* to forget. Flip-flops? It was all he could do not to stare down at his very expensive leather loafers and imagine wearing flip-flops.

"And I wore this…beachwear."

She raised an eyebrow. "You did. We bought swim trunks, too. I don't know of anyone who goes to an island and doesn't pack something to swim in, so we got you some trunks and I took you to my favorite stretch of the beach."

So far her version of the weeks missing from his memory was so divergent from everything he knew of himself that it was like listening to a story about someone else. What could have possessed him to act so out of character?

"How long did this relationship you say we had go on?" he croaked.

"Four weeks," she said softly. "Four wonderful weeks. We were together every day. By the end of the first week, you gave up your hotel room and you stayed with me. In my bed. We'd make love with the windows open so we could listen to the ocean."

"I see."

Her eyes narrowed. "You don't believe me."

"Bryony," he said carefully. "This is very difficult for me. I'm missing a month of my life and what you're telling me sounds so fantastical, so utterly out of character for me, that I can't even wrap my head around it."

She pressed her lips together but he could still see them tremble. "Yeah, I get that this is difficult for you. But try to see things from my perspective for just a few moments. Imagine that the person you were in love with and thought was in love with you suddenly can't remember you. Imagine what kind of doubts you have when you discover that everything he told you was a lie and that he made you promises he didn't keep. How would you feel?"

He stared into her eyes, gutted by the sorrow he saw. "I'd be pretty damn upset."

"Yeah. That about covers it."

She stood and pushed the serving cart back so that she could step around it. Her hand crept around the back of her neck and she rubbed absently as she stood just a short distance from where he sat on the edge of the bed.

"Look, this is…pointless. I'm really tired. You should probably go now."

He shot to his feet. "You want me to go?" It was on the tip of his tongue to ask her if she was out of her damn mind, but that wouldn't win him any more points with her. "After dumping this story on me, after telling me I'm going to be a father, you expect me to just walk away?"

"It's what you did before," she said wearily.

"How the hell can you say that? How do you know what I did or didn't do when *I* don't even know? You said you loved me and that I loved you. I've just told you I can't remember any of it. How do you get that I walked away from you? That I somehow betrayed you? I was in an accident, Bryony. What was the last day you saw me? What did we do? Did I dump you? Did I tell you I was leaving you?"

Her face was white and her fingers were balled into tiny fists at her sides.

"It was the day after we closed on the land. You said you

had to go back to New York. It was some emergency you had to attend to personally. You said it wouldn't take more than a day or two. You told me you'd be back, that you couldn't wait to come back, and that once you'd returned, we'd discuss what we'd do with the land," she said painfully.

"What day was it? The date, Bryony. The exact date."

"June third."

"The day of my accident."

She looked stricken. Her hand flew to her mouth. She looked so unsteady that he thought she might fall. He reached out, snagged her wrist and pulled her down to sit beside him. She didn't fight. She just stared at him numbly.

"How? What happened?"

"My private jet went down over Kentucky," he said grimly. "I don't remember a lot. I woke up in a hospital and had no idea how I'd come to be there."

"And you remember nothing?" she asked hoarsely.

"Only those four weeks. I have some other gaps but it's mostly people I'm supposed to know or remember but don't. I didn't initially remember the circumstances surrounding my decision to fly down to Moon Island, but that's easy enough to figure out since I bought a piece of property while I was there."

"So you just forgot *me,*" she said with a forced laugh.

He sighed. "I know it's not easy to hear. Try to understand that I'm having the same difficulty believing all you've told me. I may not remember you, Bryony, but I'm not a complete bastard. It doesn't bring me any satisfaction to see how much this hurts you."

"I tried to call," she said bleakly. "At first I waited. I told myself all sorts of excuses. It was a bigger emergency. You're a really busy guy. But then I tried to call the number you'd given me. No one would let me speak to you. There were always excuses. You were in a meeting. You were out of town. You were at lunch."

"There was a pretty tight security net around me after the accident. We didn't want anyone to know of my memory loss. We were afraid it would make investors lose their confidence in me. Any sign of weakness will make many people pull out of a deal."

"It looked—and felt—like a brush-off, and it pissed me off the more time that passed because you didn't have the balls to tell me to my face."

"So why now? Why did you wait so long to come here and confront me?"

She stared warily at him as if determining whether he was suspicious of her motives. And maybe he was. It certainly made sense that if she'd been that angry—and pregnant—she wouldn't have waited four months to confront him.

"I didn't find out I was pregnant until I was nearly ten weeks along. And Mamaw was having health problems so I was spending a lot of time with her. I didn't want to upset her by telling her that I suspected you'd seduced me and lied to me—to us—about your plans for the land. It would have broken her heart. Not just about the land. She knew how much I loved you. She wanted me happy."

Well, damn. He felt about two inches tall.

He ran a hand through his hair and wondered how the hell someone's life could change so drastically in a single day.

"We have some decisions to make, Bryony."

She turned and tilted her head in his direction. "Decisions?"

He met her gaze. "You've told me that I was in love with you. That you were in love with me. You've also said that you're pregnant with my child. If you think I'm just going to walk out of your hotel room and not look back, you're insane. We have a hell of a lot to work out and it isn't going to be resolved in a single night. Or day. Or week even."

She nodded her agreement.

"I want you to come with me."

Her eyes widened. Her mouth parted and her tongue swept nervously over her bottom lip.

"Where exactly are we going?"

"If everything you say is true, then a hell of a lot of my life and future changed on that island. You and I are going to go back to where it all started."

She stared in bewilderment at him. Had she expected him to walk away? He wasn't sure if he was angry or resigned over that fact.

"We're going to relive those weeks, Bryony. Maybe being there will bring it all back."

"And if it doesn't?" she asked cautiously.

"Then we'll have spent a lot of time getting reacquainted."

Three

"Have you lost your mind?" Ryan demanded.

Rafael stopped pacing and leveled a stare at his friends, who'd gathered in his office.

"Let's not talk about who's lost their mind," Rafael said pointedly. "I'm not the one mounting a search for the woman who screwed me over with my brother."

Ryan glared at him then shoved his hands into his pockets and turned to stare out the window.

"Low blow," Devon murmured.

Rafael blew out his breath. Yeah, it had been. Whatever the reason for Ryan trying to track down his ex-fiancée, he didn't deserve Rafael acting like an ass.

"Sorry, man," Rafael offered.

Cam leaned back in Rafael's executive chair and placed his feet up on the desk. "I think you're both certifiable. No woman is worth this much trouble." He clasped his hands behind his head and leveled a stare in Rafael's direction. "And you. I don't even know what to say to your crazy idea of going back with her to Moon Island. What do you hope to accomplish?"

That was a damn good question. He wasn't entirely certain. He wanted his memory back. He wanted to know what had made him go off his rocker and supposedly fall in love with and impregnate a woman in a matter of weeks.

He was thirty-four years old, but from all accounts, he'd acted like a teenager faced with his first naked woman.

"She says we fell in love."

He nearly groaned. Just saying the words made him feel utterly ridiculous.

The three other men stared at him as if he'd just announced he was taking a vow of celibacy. Though at the moment, it didn't sound like a bad idea.

"She also claims the child she's pregnant with is yours," Devon pointed out. "That's a lot of things she's claiming."

"Have you talked to your lawyer?" Ryan asked. "This entire situation makes me nervous. She could do a lot of damage to this deal if she goes public. If she spills her tale of you being a complete bastard, knocking her up and hauling ass before the ink on the contracts was dry, it's not going to make any of us look good."

"No, I damn well haven't spoken to Mario yet," Rafael muttered. "When have I had time? I'm calling him next."

"So how long are you going to be gone on this soul-searching expedition?" Cam asked.

Rafael shoved his hands into his pockets and rocked back on his heels. "As long as it takes."

Devon glanced down at his watch. "As much as I'd love to stick around and be amused by all this, I have an appointment."

"Copeland?" Cam smirked.

Devon curled his lip in Cam's direction.

"The old man still adamant that you marry his daughter if you want the merger?" Ryan asked.

Devon sighed. "Yeah. She's...flighty, and Copeland seems to think I'd settle her."

Rafael winced and shot his friend a look of sympathy.

Cam shrugged. "So tell him the deal's off."

"She's not that bad. She's just young and...exuberant. There are worse women to marry."

"In other words, she'd drive a stick-in-the-mud like you crazy," Ryan said with a grin.

Devon made a rude gesture as he headed toward the door.

Cam swiveled in Rafael's chair and let his feet hit the floor with a thud. "I'm off, too. Make damn sure you give us a heads-up before you head off to find yourself, Rafe."

Rafael grunted and claimed his chair as Cam followed behind Devon. Ryan still stood at the window and he turned to Rafael once they were alone.

"Hey, I'm sorry for the crack about Kelly," Rafael said before Ryan could speak. "Have you been able to find her yet?"

Ryan shook his head. "No. But I will."

Rafael didn't understand Ryan's determination to hunt down his ex-fiancée. The whole fiasco had taken place during the four weeks Rafael had lost, but Devon and Cam had told him that Kelly had slept with Ryan's brother. Ryan had tossed her out and had seemingly moved on. Only now Ryan had hired an investigator to find her.

"You don't remember Bryony?" Ryan asked. "Nothing at all?"

Rafael slapped a pen against the edge of his desk. "No. Nothing. It's like looking at a stranger."

"And you don't think that's odd?"

Rafael made a sound of exasperation. "Well, of course it's odd. Everything about this situation is odd."

Ryan leaned back against the window and studied Rafael. "You'd think if you'd fallen head-over-ass for this woman, spent every waking moment for four weeks with her and managed to knock her up in the process that there would at least be some serious déjà vu."

Rafael tossed the pen down and spun in his chair until his foot caught on the trash can next to his desk. "I get where you're going with this, Ryan, and I appreciate your concern. Something happened on that island. I don't know what, but there is a gaping hole in my memory and she's at the center. I've got to go back, if for no other reason than to disprove her story."

"And if she's telling the truth?" Ryan asked.

"Then I've got a hell of a lot of catching up to do," Rafael muttered.

Bryony stood outside the high-rise office building and stared straight up. The sleek modern architecture glistened in the bright autumn sun. The sky provided a dramatic backdrop as the spire punched a hole in the vivid blue splash.

An orange leaf drifted lazily onto her face, brushing her nose before fluttering to the ground. It joined others on the sidewalk and skittered along the concrete until it was crunched beneath the feet of the many passersby.

She was jostled by someone shouldering past her and she heard a muttered "Tourist" as they hurried on by.

The city frightened and fascinated her in equal parts. Everyone was so busy here. No one stopped even for a moment. The city pulsed with people, cars, lights and noise. Constant noise.

How did anyone stand it?

And yet she'd been ready to embrace it. She'd known that if she were to have a life with Rafael, she'd have to grow used to city life. It was where he lived and worked. Where he thrived.

Now she stood in front of his office building feeling hesitant and insecure. There was a seed of doubt and it grew with each breath. She couldn't help but wonder if she wasn't being an even bigger fool this time.

"Fool me once, blah blah," she muttered. "I must be insane to trust him."

But if he were telling the truth. If his utterly bizarre and improbable story were true, then he hadn't betrayed her. He hadn't dumped her. He hadn't done any of the things she'd accused him of.

Part of her was relieved and the other part had no idea what to think or believe.

"Bryony, is it?"

She yanked her gaze downward, embarrassed that she was still standing in front of the building looking straight up like a moron, and saw two of the men she'd seen with Rafael at the party.

She took a wary step back. "I'm Bryony, yes."

They were both tall. One had medium brown hair, short and neat. He smiled at her. The other one had blond hair with varying shades of brown. It was longish and unruly. He frowned at her, and his blue eyes narrowed as though she were a nasty bug.

The smiling one stuck out his hand. "I'm Devon Carter, a friend of Rafael's. This is Cameron Hollingsworth."

Cameron continued to scrutinize her so she ignored him and focused on Devon, although she had no idea what to say.

"Nice to meet you," she murmured.

"Are you here to see Rafe?" Devon asked.

She nodded.

"We'll be happy to take you up."

She shook her head. "No, that's okay. I can make it. I mean I don't want to be a bother."

Cameron shot her a cool, assessing look that made her feel vastly inferior. Her chin automatically went up and her fingers balled into a fist at her side. She really wasn't a violent person. Truly. But in the past few days, she'd had her share of violent fantasies. Right now she visualized Cameron Hollingsworth picking himself up off the pavement.

"It's no bother," Devon said smoothly. "The least I can do is see you to the elevator."

She frowned. "You think I'm incapable of finding the elevator? Or are you just one of those really nosy friends?"

Devon's smile was lazy and unbothered. He looked at her as if he knew exactly how wound up she was and that her stomach was in knots. Maybe she had that beautiful look of a woman about to puke.

"Then I'll bid you a good day," Devon finally said.

She swallowed, wishing she hadn't been quite so rude. It was a fault of hers that she went on the offensive the minute she felt at a disadvantage. She wasn't going to win any friends acting like a bitch.

"Thank you. It was nice to meet you."

She injected enough sincerity into her tone that even she believed herself. Devon nodded but Cameron didn't look impressed. She forced herself not to scowl at him as the two men walked to the street and got into a waiting BMW.

Taking a deep breath, she headed to the revolving door and entered the building. The lobby was beautiful. A study in marble and exposed beams. The contrast between old and modern should have looked odd, but instead it looked opulent and rich.

There was a large fountain in the middle of the lobby and she paused to allow the sound of the water to soothe her. She missed the ocean. She didn't venture off the island often, and it made her anxious now, in the midst of so much hustle and bustle, to return to the peace and quiet of the small coastal island she'd grown up on.

Her throat tightened and pain squeezed at her chest. Because of her, her family's land was now in the hands of a man determined to build a resort, golf course and God knew what else. Not that those were bad things. She had nothing against progress. And she certainly wasn't opposed to free enterprise and capitalism. A buck was a buck. Everyone wanted to make a few. Not that Rafael seemed to have any problem in that area.

But Moon Island was special. It was still untouched by the heavy hand of development. The families that lived there had been there for generations. Everyone knew everyone else. Half the island fished or shrimped and the other half had retired to the island after working thirty years in cities like Houston or Dallas.

There was an unspoken agreement among the residents that they wanted the island to remain as it was. A quiet place of splendor. A haven for people wanting to get away from life in the fast lane. Things just moved slower there.

Now because of her, that would all change. Bulldozers and construction crews would move in, and slowly the outside world would creep in and change the way of life.

She bit her lip and turned in the direction of the elevator. It hurt to think how naive she'd been. And now that she had distance from the whirlwind relationship she'd jumped into with Rafael, she knew how stupid she'd been. But at the time... At the time she hadn't been thinking straight. She'd been powerless under his onslaught, his magnetism and the idea that he was as caught up as she was.

She angrily jabbed the button for the thirty-first floor then stepped back as others crowded in. It wasn't as if the thought hadn't occurred to her to add in a legal clause to the contract, but she'd imagined that it would seem as though she didn't trust him. Sort of like demanding a prenuptial agreement before marriage. Yeah, it was smart, but it was also awkward and brought up questions she hadn't wanted at the time.

He'd absolutely sold her on the idea that he wanted to buy the land for personal use. It hadn't been a corporation name on the closing documents. It had been his and only his. Rafael de Luca. And she'd believed him when he'd said he'd be back. That he loved her. That he wanted them to be together.

She was so deeply humiliated over her stupidity that she couldn't bear to think about it. Now, when she'd come to New York to confront Rafael over his lies, she was confronted by his extraordinary claim that he'd lost his memory. It was so damn convenient.

But she couldn't help whispering, "Please let him be telling the truth." Because if he was, then maybe the rest wasn't as bad as she thought. And that probably made her an even bigger moron than she'd already proved herself to be.

When she got off the elevator, there was a reception desk directly in front of her. As Bryony walked up, the receptionist smiled. "Do you have an appointment?"

An appointment? It took her a moment to collect herself and then she nodded. "Rafael is expecting me."

Her voice sounded too husky and too unsure, but the receptionist didn't seem to notice.

"Are you Miss Morgan?"

Bryony nodded.

"Right this way. Mr. de Luca asked that you be shown right in. Would you like some tea or coffee?" With a glance down at Bryony's belly, she added, "We have decaf if you prefer."

Bryony smiled. "Thank you, but I'm fine."

The receptionist opened a door, and Rafael looked up from his desk. "Mr. de Luca, Miss Morgan is here."

Rafael rose and strode forward. "Thank you, Tamara."

"Is there anything you'd like me to get for you?" Tamara inquired politely.

Rafael shook his head. "See that I'm not disturbed."

Tamara nodded and retreated, closing the door behind her.

Bryony stared at Rafael, such a short distance away. She could smell him he was so close. She was at a complete loss as to how to act around him now. She could no longer maintain the outraged, jilted-lover act because if he couldn't remember her, he couldn't very well be blamed for acting as though she didn't exist for the past months.

But neither could she just take up where they'd left off and throw herself into his arms.

The result was tension so thick and awkward that it made her want to fidget out of her shoes.

He stared at her. She stared at him. One would never guess that they'd made a child together.

Rafael sighed. "Before this goes any further, there is something I have to do."

Her brows came together and then lifted when he took a step toward her.

"What?" she asked.

He cupped her face and stepped forward again until their bodies were aligned and his heat—and scent—enveloped her.

"I have to kiss you."

Four

Bryony took a wary step back but Rafael was determined that she wouldn't escape him. He caught her shoulders and pulled her almost roughly against him, swallowing up her light gasp just before his lips found hers in a heated rush.

He wasn't entirely certain what he'd expected to happen. Fireworks? His memory miraculously restored? Images of those missing weeks to flash into his head like a slide show?

None of that happened, but what did shocked the hell out of him.

His body roared to life. Every muscle tensed in instant awareness. Desire and lust coiled tight in his belly and he became achingly hard.

And hell, but she was responsive. After her initial resistance, she melted into his chest and returned his kiss with equal fervor. She wrapped her arms around his neck and clung to him tightly, her lush curves molded perfectly to his body. A body that was screaming for him to pin her to the desk and slake his lust.

He pulled back as awareness returned. For the love of God, what was he thinking? She was pregnant with his child, he couldn't remember her and yet he was ready to tear both of their clothes off and damn the consequences.

Well, at least she couldn't get pregnant again....

He ran a hand through his hair and turned away, his heart thudding out of control and his breaths blowing in ragged spurts from his nose.

Not his type? He shook his head. He'd never met a woman in his life with whom he shared such combustible chemistry.

When he turned back around, Bryony stood there looking dazed, her lips swollen and her eyes soft and fuzzy. It was all he could do not to haul her back into his arms to finish what he'd started.

"I'm sorry," he began before breaking off. "I just had to know."

Her eyes sharpened and the haze lifted away. "Know what?"

She crossed her arms over her chest and tapped her foot in agitation as she stared him down.

"If I could remember anything," he muttered.

Her lip curled into a snarl, baring her teeth. He was reminded of a pissed-off cat, and remembering that she'd decked him the night before, he took a step back.

"And?"

He shook his head. "Nothing."

She threw him a disgusted look and then turned to stalk out of his office.

"Wait a damn minute," he called as he started after her.

She made it to the door before he caught her arm and turned her around to face him.

"What the hell is your problem?"

She gaped at him. "My problem? Gee, I don't know. Maybe I don't appreciate being mauled as some sort of experiment.

I get that this is difficult for you, Rafael, but you aren't the only one suffering here. You don't have to be such an ass."

"But—"

Before he could protest, she was gone again, and he watched her walk away. At least she was wearing sensible shoes she wouldn't trip in.

He stood there arguing with himself over whether to go after her, but what would he say when he caught up? He wasn't sorry he kissed her even if it hadn't been a magic cure-all. It had told him one important thing. He couldn't get close to her without erupting into flames, which meant the likelihood of her carrying his child...?

Pretty damn good.

He strode back to his desk and picked up the phone. A few seconds later, Ramon answered with a curt affirmative.

"Miss Morgan has just left my office. See that she gets back to her hotel safely."

Bryony got off the elevator and exited the office building, no longer caring whether she and Rafael had dinner plans. Her jaw ached from the tight set of her teeth and tears stung the corners of her eyes.

She'd hoped for any sign of the Rafael de Luca she'd fallen in love with. Maybe she had also hoped that their kiss would spark...something. Or that maybe he would embrace the possibility that he'd felt something for her...once.

But there had been no recognition in his eyes when he'd pulled away. Just lust. Lust that any man could feel. A man could have sex with any number of women, but it didn't mean he harbored any deeper feelings for her.

The crisp air ruffled her hair and she started down the sidewalk, no clear direction in mind. It seemed colder than before and she shivered as she walked. Around her, horns honked, people jostled as they passed, dusk was settling and streetlights had started to blink on.

There was still plenty of light for her to walk the few blocks back to her hotel and she needed to let off some steam. She was flushed from Rafe's kiss and she was furious that he'd been so cold and calculating about it.

She'd felt like…a plaything. Like she hadn't mattered. Like she was just a set of boobs for his amusement.

But then that's likely all she'd ever been from the start.

She couldn't afford to be stupid a second time. Not until she had his guarantee—his *written* guarantee—that he wouldn't develop the land would she allow herself to think that his intentions toward her had been sincere.

She hugged her arms to her chest and stopped at a pedestrian crossing. A man knocked into her and she turned with a startled "Hey!"

He mumbled an apology about the time the light turned and the crowd surged forward. With her attention diverted she didn't feel the tug at her other arm until it was too late.

Her purse strap fell and her arm was nearly yanked from its socket as the thief started to run.

Anger rocketed through her veins and, reacting on instinct, she grabbed ahold of the strap with her other hand and tugged back.

The man was close to her own unimpressive height and nearly as slight, but grim determination was etched into his grimy face. He slammed into her, sending her sprawling to the pavement. She hit with enough impact to jar her teeth, but the strap was wrapped around her wrist now.

He jerked again and this time dragged her a few feet before he let out a snarl of rage and backhanded her. Her grip loosened and out of the corner of her eye she saw a flash of silver.

Fear paralyzed her when she saw the knife coming toward her. But her attacker slashed at the strap, sending her flying backward as the tension was released. He was gone, melting into the crowd as she lay sprawled on the curb holding her eye.

It had only taken a few seconds. Under a minute, surely. She heard someone shout and then someone knelt next to her.

"Are you okay, lady?"

She turned, not recognizing the person who'd spoken, and she was too stunned to respond. Then she saw a sleek black car screech to a halt in front of her and a huge mountain of a man rushed out to hover protectively over her.

He moved with a grace that belied his enormous size and he knelt in front of her, his hand cupping her chin as he turned her this way and that to examine her eye.

He barked rapidly into his Bluetooth but she was too muddled to know what he said or to whom he had spoken. She hoped it was the police.

"Miss Morgan, are you all right?" he asked urgently.

"H-how do you know my name?"

"Mr. de Luca sent me."

"How would he know what happened?" she asked in a baffled tone.

"He wanted to make sure you made it to your hotel safely. I didn't catch you in time to give you a ride. I was looking for you when I saw what happened."

"Oh."

"Can you stand?" he asked.

She slowly nodded. She'd certainly try. As he gently helped her to her feet, she clutched at her belly, worried that her fall had hurt her child.

"Are you in pain?" the man demanded.

"I don't know," she said shakily. "Maybe. I'm just scared. The fall…"

"I'm taking you to the hospital at once. Mr. de Luca will meet us there."

She didn't protest when he ushered her into the backseat of the car. He got in beside her and issued a swift order for the driver to take off. They were away and into traffic in a matter of moments.

She sank back into the seat, her hands shaking so badly that she clenched them together in her lap to try and quell the movement.

The giant beside her took up most of the backseat. He leaned forward and rummaged in an ice bucket in the console and a moment later held an ice pack to her eye.

She winced and started to pull away, but he persisted and held it gently to her face.

"Are you feeling any pain anywhere else?" he queried.

"I don't think so. I'm just shaken up."

His expression was grim as he pulled away the ice pack to examine her eye.

"You're going to have one heck of a bruise. I think it's a good idea to have a doctor check you out so you can be sure the baby wasn't harmed."

She nodded and grimaced when he put the ice pack back into place.

"Thank you," she murmured. "For your help. Your timing was excellent."

His face twisted with anger. "No, it wasn't. If I had been there a moment earlier, he wouldn't have hurt you."

"Still, thanks. He had a knife."

She swallowed the knot of panic in her throat and drew in steadying breaths. She could still see the flash of the blade as it slashed out at her. A shiver stole up her spine and attacked her shoulders until she trembled with almost violent force.

"I don't even know your name," she said faintly.

He looked at her with worried eyes as if he thought his name was the last thing that should be on her mind.

"Ramon. I'm Mr. de Luca's head of security."

"I'm Bryony," she said, before realizing he already knew her name. He'd called her Miss Morgan earlier.

"We're almost there, Bryony," he said in a steady, reassuring voice.

Was she about to melt down on him? Was that why he was staring at her with such concern and speaking to her as if he was trying to talk her down from the ledge?

She leaned her head back against the seat and closed her eyes. He followed with the ice pack and soon it was smushed up against her face again.

A few seconds later, the car ground to a halt and the door immediately opened. She opened her eyes as Ramon removed the ice pack and hurriedly got out of the car. He reached back to help her out and they were met by an E.R. tech pushing a wheelchair.

Astonished by the quickness in which they got her back to an exam room, she stared with an open mouth as she was laid on one of the beds by two nurses and they immediately began an assessment of her condition.

Ramon hung by her bedside, watching the medical staff's every move. As if sensing Bryony's bewilderment, Ramon leaned down and murmured, "Mr. de Luca is a frequent contributor to this hospital. He called ahead to let them know you'd be arriving."

Well, that certainly made more sense.

"The on-call obstetrician will be in to see you shortly," one of the nurses said. "He'll want to make sure all is well with the baby."

Bryony nodded and murmured her thanks.

The nurse went over a series of questions as she did her assessment. Bryony was a little embarrassed over all the fuss. Near as she could tell, all she'd suffered was a black eye and a bruised behind. But she wouldn't turn down the opportunity to make sure all was well with her baby.

She'd leaned back to close her eyes when the door flew open and Rafael strode in, his expression dark and his gaze immediately seeking out Bryony.

He hurried to her bedside and took her hand in his. "Are you all right?" he demanded. "Are you hurt? Are you in any pain?" He took a breath and dragged a hand through his hair in agitation. "The…baby?"

Before she could respond, his gaze settled on her face and his eyes darkened with fury. He tentatively touched her cheek and then he turned to Ramon, his jaw clenched.

"What happened?"

"I'm fine," Bryony said in answer to the barrage of questions. But Rafael was no longer concentrating his efforts on her. He was interrogating his head of security.

"Rafael."

When he still didn't stop his tirade of questions, she tugged at his hand until finally he turned back to her.

"I'm okay. Really. Ramon showed up just in time. He took good care of me."

"I should not have let you leave my office," Rafael gritted out. "You were upset and in no condition to be out on the streets. I'd thought Ramon would give you a ride home."

She shrugged. "I walked. He didn't catch up with me until after…."

Rafael looked hastily around and then dragged a chair to her bedside. He perched on the edge and stared intently at her.

"Has the doctor been in yet? What has he said about the baby? Are you hurt anywhere else? Did the bastard hit you?"

She shook her head at the flurry of questions and blinked at the fierceness in his voice and expression. This wasn't a side of Rafael she'd ever seen before.

"The nurse said the on-call obstetrician would be in to see me shortly and that he would conduct an assessment to make sure all was well with the baby. And no, I'm not hurt anywhere else."

She raised her hand to her eye and winced when she pushed in on the already swelling area.

Rafael captured her hand and pulled it away from her eye.

"It's unacceptable for you to be walking the streets of New York City alone. I don't even like you staying in that hotel alone."

She smiled in amusement. "But it's your hotel, Rafael. Are you suggesting it isn't safe?"

"I'd prefer you were with me, where I know you are safe," he said through gritted teeth.

Her brows came together as she studied him. "What are you saying?"

"Look, we were going to be leaving together for Moon Island in a few days anyway. It's only reasonable that you'd stay with me until we depart. It will give us additional time to...reacquaint ourselves with one another."

She stared hard into his eyes, looking for... She wasn't sure what she was looking for. What she saw, however, was burning determination and outrage that she'd been harmed.

He may not remember her, but his protective instincts had been riled, and whether he fully accepted that she carried his child, he was certainly concerned about both mother and baby.

Wasn't that a start?

"All right," she said softly. "I'll stay with you until we leave for the island."

Five

Rafael would have carried her into his penthouse if she'd allowed it. As it was he argued fiercely until she rolled her eyes and informed him that she was perfectly okay and that no one got carried around because of a black eye.

The reminder of her black eye just infuriated Rafael all the more. She was a tiny woman and the idea that some street thug had manhandled her—a pregnant woman—made his jaw clench. Even though the doctor had assured him that all was well with her pregnancy.

He wasn't sure what to do with himself. He was in new territory for sure. Bryony was the first woman he'd ever brought up to his penthouse and it felt as though his territory had been invaded.

"Would you like me to order in dinner?" he asked when he'd settled her on the couch. Surely it wasn't a good idea for her to go out and it was late.

"I'd like that, thanks," she said as she leaned her head back against the sofa.

He frowned when he saw the fatigue etched on her face. "You must be tired."

Her lips twisted ruefully and she nodded. "It's been an eventful couple of days."

Guilt crept up his nape until he was compelled to rub the back of his neck. He hadn't made things easier for her. She'd traveled a long way and then... Then things had gone all to hell.

He stood, irritated with himself. Why should he feel guilty about anything? He couldn't remember. God knew he'd tried. He went to bed frustrated every single night, hoping when he woke the next morning that everything would be restored and he could stop wondering about the holes. Stop wondering if he'd done something ridiculous like seduce and fall in love with a woman in the space of a few weeks.

It sounded so incredible that he couldn't wrap his head around it.

No, he shouldn't feel guilty. None of this had been his fault.

Except for the fact that he'd upset her and caused her to flee his office and she'd wound up being mugged as a result.

He studied her from across the room as he picked up the phone to call in their food order. She already looked as if she was asleep and he battled with whether to even bother waking her for dinner.

His gaze drifted to her belly and he swiftly decided against allowing her to sleep through the meal. It had likely been hours since she'd eaten anything.

He returned to her a moment later and settled on the chair next to the couch where she lay sprawled. "Would you like something to drink while we wait for the food?"

She stirred and regarded him lazily through half-lidded eyes. "Do you have juice? I feel a little light-headed."

He bolted to his feet. "Why didn't you say anything before now?"

She shrugged. "Quite frankly all I wanted was a comfortable place to sit and relax. Having all those people around me was making me crazy."

He strode to the kitchen and rummaged in the fridge for orange juice. After checking the date on the carton, he poured a glass and went back into the living room.

This time he sat on the couch next to her and handed her the glass. She drank thirstily until half the contents were gone and then handed him back the glass.

"Thanks. That should do the trick."

"Is this something that happens regularly or is it just the excitement of the day?" he asked suspiciously.

"I'm borderline hypoglycemic. My blood sugar gets too low every once in a while. Pregnancy sort of messes with that and I have to be careful to eat regularly or I risk passing out."

Rafael swore under his breath. "What if you were to pass out when you were alone?"

"Well, the point is to make sure I don't pass out."

He scowled and then checked his watch. Only five minutes had passed since he'd placed the order.

"I'll be fine, Rafe," she said softly. "My grandmother is a diabetic. I'm well acquainted with how to handle low or elevated blood sugar."

The shortened version of his name, only used by his closest friends, slipped from her lips as if she'd used it a thousand times before. Coming from her, it sounded…right. As if he'd heard it before or maybe even encouraged her to use it.

He put a hand to his nape and looked away. Why couldn't he remember? If he had truly been involved with this woman, and if, like she'd said, they'd formed some romantic attachment—he couldn't quite bring himself to say *love*—then why would he shove her as far from his memory as he could?

She kicked off her shoes and then curled her feet underneath her on the couch before grabbing one of the cushions to snuggle into. It occurred to him that if they were a real couple he would have sat beside her and…cuddled. Or maybe offered her a foot rub. Weren't pregnant women supposed to have swollen ankles or something?

Which further proved to him that the idea of him falling in love and spending four weeks wrapped up in one woman was just…ludicrous. He dated. He even had relationships, but they were on his terms, which meant that his female companions didn't come to his penthouse. If they had sleepovers, it was done in one of his hotels. He certainly didn't engage in cuddling or cutesy things that a man would do for the woman he loved.

But then she glanced up and their eyes met. There was something in her gaze that peeled back his skin and squeezed his chest in a manner he wasn't familiar with. She looked… tired and vulnerable. She looked as if she needed…comfort.

Hell.

"Rafe, he got away with my purse," she said quietly.

He nodded. The police had come to the hospital to take her statement but it was doubtful they'd find her attacker.

"I didn't think…I mean everything happened so fast, and then at the hospital…" She lifted her hand in a helpless gesture that only made his desire to comfort her stronger.

"What is worrying you, Bryony?"

"I need to cancel my credit cards. My bankcard. God, he's probably already emptied all my accounts. My driver's license was in it. How am I supposed to get back home? I can't fly without identification."

The more she spoke, the more agitated she became. He slid onto the couch beside her and awkwardly put his arms around her.

"There's no need to panic. Do you have the telephone numbers you need?"

She shook her head and then laid it on his shoulder, her hair brushing across his nose.

"I can look them up on the internet if you have a computer."

He snorted. "Do I have a computer... I'm never without an internet connection of any kind."

She lifted her head and stared into his eyes. "You were when you were on the island."

His brow crinkled. "That's impossible. I wouldn't have just dropped off the map like that. I have a business to run."

"Oh, you kept in touch," she said. "But you often made your calls or answered emails in the morning or late at night. During the day you left your BlackBerry at my house while we explored the island."

He sighed. "See this is why I have such a hard time with the story you tell. I would never do something like that. It isn't me."

Her lips turned down in a frown and she leaned away from him.

To cover the sudden awkwardness, he stood and went to his briefcase to pull out his laptop. He stood for a long moment with his back to her just so he could compose himself and keep from turning and apologizing. He didn't want to hurt her, damn it. But one of them was crazy, and he didn't want it to be him.

He finally went back to the couch, opened the laptop and set it on a cushion next to her.

"If you have any problems canceling your cards or ordering new ones, let me know. I've typed up my address so you can have them overnighted here."

"And my license?" she asked in a tight, frustrated voice. "How am I going to get home?" She dragged her fingers through her hair, which only drew attention to the dark bruise marring her creamy skin.

"I'll get you home, Bryony. I don't want you to worry. Can you call your grandmother to fax a copy of your birth certificate? It's my understanding you can fly with the birth certificate but you'll be subjected to closer scrutiny by security."

"Couldn't we take your jet? Oh, I guess… Sorry." She broke off, seemingly embarrassed at her slip.

"I have more than one," he said dryly.

She continued to stare at him. "Then why aren't we taking it? Wouldn't it be easier to fly without identification if we were on a private jet?"

He cleared his throat and then rubbed the back of his neck. "Let's just say I have a newly developed phobia of flying on small planes."

She frowned. "I must sound so insensitive. I'm just… This has been a rotten trip all the way around."

"Yes, I suppose it has been for you," he murmured.

He eased back onto the couch beside her as she tapped intently on the keys. He hated how unsure of himself he was around her. But it was himself he was angry at. Not her.

If she was to be believed, her life had been completely upended. By him.

More and more he had an uneasy feeling that she was telling the truth. No matter how bizarre and unlikely such a scenario seemed. And if she was telling the truth, then he had to figure out what the hell he was going to do with the woman he supposedly loved and the child she carried. His child.

Six

"This reminds me of the nights we spent at my house," Bryony said as she forked another bite of the seafood into her mouth.

He paused, fork halfway to his own mouth, resigned to hearing more about his uncharacteristic behavior. But she said nothing and resumed eating, her gaze downcast, almost as if she knew how ill at ease he was.

But his curiosity was also piqued because, damn it, *something* had happened between them and she was the only key he had to recover the missing pieces of his memory.

He forced himself to sound only mildly inquisitive. "What did we do?"

A faraway look entered her eyes and she stared toward the window at the night sky. "We used to sit cross-legged on the deck and eat the dinner I'd cooked. Then I'd lay my head in your lap and you'd stroke my hair while we listened to the ocean and watched the stars."

Her voice lowered, catching on a husky note. "Then we'd

go inside and make love. Sometimes we didn't make it to the bedroom. Sometimes we did."

The dreamy quality of her voice affected him fiercely. His body ached and he hardened at the images she provoked. It was suddenly very easy for him to see her spread out before him, his mouth on her skin, her fingers clinging to him as he brought them both pleasure.

He shook his head when he realized he was staring and that he was so tense that his muscles had locked. Part of him wanted to just get it over with. Take her to bed, have sex with her until they both forgot their names. His body was eager enough, but his mind was calling him a damn fool.

And she'd likely think it was some damn experiment after he'd basically admitted earlier that his kiss had been nothing more than that.

An experiment.

He wanted to laugh. Could he call desire so keen that his eyes had crossed when he'd looked at her an experiment?

Whether he wanted to admit it or not, they had compelling—uncontrollable—chemistry. Maybe he'd gotten so wrapped up in her that he'd lost all common sense. Maybe he'd made her rash promises in the heat of the moment. If her outrage was anything to go on, he at least hadn't been stupid enough to sign anything.

He needed her cooperation. He needed this deal. He had too many investors committed. Money had exchanged hands. Construction was on a tight deadline, and the last thing he needed was her making noises over him reneging on a deal.

She'd lifted her gaze and was now studying him so intently that he found her scrutiny uncomfortable. He studied her in return, finding himself mesmerized by her dark eyes. The delicate lines of her face called to him. He wanted to trace his fingers over her cheekbone and down to her jaw and then over the softness of her lips.

Had this been the way he'd felt when he'd first seen her?

Logic told him it had to have been. How could his reaction now have been any different than the first time he'd laid eyes on her?

"Why are you staring at me?" she asked in a low voice.

"Maybe I find you beautiful."

Her reaction wasn't what he expected. She lifted her nose in scorn and shook her head.

"I thought I wasn't your type."

"What I said was that you aren't my *normal* type."

Her lips twisted. "That isn't what you said. To quote you exactly, you said, 'You aren't my type.' That pretty much tells me you don't find me remotely appealing."

"I don't care what I said," he growled. "What I meant was that you aren't the type of woman I normally…date."

"Have sex with?" she asked mockingly. "Because we did, you know. We had lots and lots of sex. You were insatiable. In fact, unless you are the best damn actor in the world and can fake, not only an erection, but an orgasm as well, I'd say you're either lying now about me not being your type, or you're not terribly discerning when it comes to the women you sleep with."

He'd just been insulted but he was so distracted by the sparks shooting from her eyes and how damn gorgeous she looked when she got sassy that he couldn't formulate a response.

"See, the problem is, a woman can get away with faking sexual attraction," she continued. "We can pretend all manner of things. Men? It's kind of hard to pretend attraction to a woman if your penis isn't cooperating."

"Holy hell," he muttered. "I think we've established that it's pretty damn obvious I'm sexually attracted to you. Whatever I may have thought in the past about my preferences in women obviously doesn't apply to you."

"So then you're willing to concede that you slept with me and that the child I'm carrying is yours?"

"Yes," he said through gritted teeth. "I'm willing to concede it's possible, but I'm not stupid enough to believe it's absolutely true until either I regain my memory, or we have DNA testing done."

Her top lip curled a moment and it looked as if she wanted to light into him again, but instead, she took a calming breath. "As long as you're willing to accept the possibility, I can work with that," she muttered.

"Were you always this...charming with me when we spent all this time together?"

She lifted one eyebrow. "What's that supposed to mean?"

"Just that I tend to like my women a little more..."

"Stupid?" she challenged.

He scowled.

"Weak? Mousy? Unchallenging?" she continued. "Or maybe you prefer them to simply nod and say 'yes, sir' to your every whim."

She broke off in disgust and regarded him as if he were some annoying bug she was about to squash.

He finally decided remaining silent was his best option so he didn't dig his hole any deeper.

She laid down her fork and raised her haunted gaze to his. He was surprised to see tears shimmering in her eyes, and his throat knotted. Damn. He hadn't wanted to upset her again. He wasn't *that* big of a jerk.

"Do you have any idea how hard this is for me?" she asked in a quiet, strained voice. "Do you know how difficult it is for me to see you again and not touch you or hug you or kiss you? I came here expecting to confront a man who scammed me in the worst possible way. I had resigned myself to it and there was nothing I wanted more than to wash my hands of you. But then you tell me this story about losing your memory and what am I supposed to do then? Now I have to consider that maybe you didn't lie to me, but I'm scared to death of believing that and then being wrong. Again. I have to put everything on hold until you regain your memory, and that sucks because I just don't know how to feel anymore."

He stared at her, frozen, an uncomfortable sensation coiling in his chest.

"I can't exactly walk away. It's what I accused you of and there's a part of me that thinks, 'What if he's telling the truth? What if he regains his memory tomorrow and remembers he loves you? What if it's all some horrible misunderstanding and we have a chance to get back what we had on the island?'"

She shoved her plate away and looked down as she visibly tried to collect herself.

"But what if I was right?" she whispered. "What if me sticking around hoping makes me an even bigger fool than falling for your lies to begin with? I have a child to consider now."

Before he could think twice about what he should say or do, he found himself reaching for her. It was impossible not to want to touch her, to offer her comfort. The pain in her expression was too real. Her eyes were clouded with moisture and hurt shimmered in their depths.

He pulled her into his arms and leaned back against the couch. For a moment she lay there stiffly, so still that he wondered if she held her breath.

He inhaled the scent of her hair and felt keen disappointment that it stirred nothing to life in his memories. Wasn't smell supposed to be the most powerful memory trigger?

Gradually she relaxed against him, her fingers curling into his chest as her cheek rested on his shoulder.

He dropped his mouth to the top of her head and stopped himself a moment before brushing his lips across her hair. It seemed the most natural thing to do and yet he knew tenderness wasn't a usual characteristic. It seemed too personal. Too intimate.

But the need to show her a more gentle side of himself was a physical ache.

"I'm sorry," he said truthfully. He had no love for seeing this woman hurt. He didn't like to see anyone needlessly suffer. The fact that he was the source of her pain made him extremely uncomfortable.

"Just let me stay here a minute and pretend," she said. "Just don't say…anything."

He carefully laid his hand over her dark curls and did as she asked. He sat there, her head on his shoulder, one arm wrapped around her, his hand wrapped in her hair, and silence descended on them.

But the silence felt awkward to him, as if he should fill the gaps. Or ask questions. Something…

He glanced down at the soft curls splayed out over his chest. He could just feel the swell of her belly against his side.

Was this his reality? And if it was, why wasn't he running as hard as he could in the other direction?

It wasn't as if he was commitment-phobic. Okay, maybe a little, but it wasn't as if he'd endured some trauma in the past that made him leery of women. Nor was he some patsy who was afraid of allowing a woman to hurt him.

He hadn't ever committed because… Well, he wasn't entirely certain. Men in relationships lacked a certain amount of control. They could no longer make solo decisions, and Rafael was used to making decisions in a split second— without conferring with someone else.

It wasn't a fluke that he owned his own business, not to mention had a partnership with three of his friends. His work took a lot of time. Time he wouldn't have if he had to worry about being home every night for dinner.

He liked being able to jet off at a moment's notice. He looked forward to business meetings—considered them a challenge. While he didn't have a lot of downtime, he did enjoy taking it at his leisure. He met Ryan, Devon and Cam at least once a year for golf, lots of alcohol and other pursuits only available to men who were not otherwise involved in a relationship.

Simply put, he'd never met a woman who made him want to give up all that. He damn sure couldn't imagine meeting her and giving up his life in a matter of four weeks. That kind of decision would have to be made over the course of years. Maybe never.

But on the other hand.

There was always a *but*.

As he stared down at the woman curled trustingly in his arms, something pulled at him. Some desire he hadn't ever acknowledged, one that would normally have horrified him— *should* horrify him.

He found himself wishing he could remember all the things she'd described to him, because all of a sudden, they sounded appealing.

And if that didn't scare the hell out of him, he wasn't sure what would.

Seven

"Rafael! Rafael! Wake up! Hurry!"

Rafael came awake with a start, his arms flying out as he pushed himself up from his bed. Bryony stood at his bedside, fully dressed, hopping around like her feet were on fire.

He threw his feet over the side and leaned forward. "What is it? Is it the baby? Are you hurt?"

She frowned a moment, shook her head and then grinned like a maniac. He rubbed his eyes and ran his hand through his hair.

"Then what the hell are you shouting about?" He glanced over at his bedside clock. "For God's sake, it's early!"

"It's snowing!"

She grabbed at his hand and started to pull. The covers fell away from his hips and they both went still. Her gaze dropped about the time his did and it was then he remembered he hadn't worn anything to bed, and worse, his penis was making its presence known in a not very subtle way.

He yanked the covers back over him as she stepped hastily

back, pulling her sweater around her like a protective barrier. Hell, it wasn't as if he was bursting into *her* room trying to maul her.

"Sorry," she said. "I'll just go down by myself."

She turned and he scrambled out of bed, pulling the sheet with him.

"Wait a minute," he ordered. "What are you doing? Where are you going?"

Her eyes came alive again, brimming with excitement. The sparkle was infectious.

"Outside, of course! It's snowing!"

He glanced toward his window but he was too bleary-eyed to make sense of the weather. "Haven't you ever seen snow before?"

She shook her head.

"Are you serious?"

She nodded this time. "I live on an island off the Texas coast. We don't exactly get snow there, you know."

"But you've been off the island. Haven't you ever been anywhere it snowed before?"

She shrugged. "I don't leave much. Mamaw needs me. I go to Galveston to do our shopping, but I do a lot of it online."

He saw her cast sidelong glances at the window as if she were afraid the snow would disappear at any moment. Then he sighed. "Give me five minutes to get dressed and I'll go down with you."

Her smile lit up the entire room and he was left with the feeling that someone had just punched him in the stomach. She nearly danced from his bedroom and shut the door behind her.

Slowly he dropped the sheet to the floor and stared down at his groin. "Traitor," he muttered.

He went into the bathroom, splashed water on his face and surveyed his unshaven jaw with a grimace. He never left his apartment without looking his best. There wasn't time for even a shower. The lunatic was probably already outside dancing in the snow.

He brushed his teeth and then went to his closet to pull out a pair of slacks and a sweater. He realized that since she'd never seen snow, she'd hardly be dressed for it, so he pulled a scarf and a cap from the top shelf.

Any of his jackets or coats would swallow her whole so he'd simply have to limit her snow gazing to a short period of time.

After donning his overcoat, he walked out of his bedroom to find Bryony glued to the window in the living room. Big flakes spiraled downward and her smile was like a child's at Christmas.

"Here," he said gruffly. "If you're going to go out, you need warmer things."

She turned and stared at the scarf and cap he held out and then reached for them, but he waved her hand off and looped the scarf around her neck himself, pulling her closer.

"You probably don't even know how to put one on," he muttered.

After wrapping the scarf around her neck, he arranged the cap over her curls and stepped back. She looked…damn cute.

Before he could do something idiotic, he turned and gestured toward the door. "Your snow awaits."

Bryony walked into the small courtyard that adjoined the apartment building, surprised that it was empty. How could everyone just stay inside on such a beautiful day? As soon as one of the flakes landed on her nose, she turned her face up and laughed as more drifted onto her cheeks and clung to her lashes.

She held out her hands and turned in a circle. Oh, it was marvelous and so pretty. There was just a light dusting on the patio surface, but along the fence railing and the edges of the stone planters, there was enough accumulation for her to scoop into a ball.

She scraped her hands together until she had a sizeable amount of snow and then she turned to grin at Rafael. He regarded her warily and then held up his hand in warning.

"Don't even think…"

Before he could finish, she let fly and he barely had time to blink before the snowball exploded in his face.

"…about it," he finished as ice slid down his cheek.

He glared at her but she giggled and hastily formed another snowball.

"Oh, hell no," Rafael growled.

As she turned to hurl it in his direction, a snowball hit the side of her face and melting ice slid down her neck, eliciting a shiver.

"I see you couldn't resist," she said with a smirk.

"Resist what?"

"Playing. But who could resist snow?"

He scowled. "I wasn't playing. I was retaliating. Now come on. You've seen the snow. We should go back inside. It's cold out here."

"Well, duh. It *is* snowing," she said. "It's supposed to be cold."

Ignoring his look of exasperation, she hurled another snowball. He ducked and she ran for cover when she saw the gleam in his eyes. She hastily formed another snowball then peered around one of the hedges in time to get smacked by his. Right between the eyes.

"For someone who doesn't play in the snow, your snowball fighting is sure good," she muttered.

She waited until he went for more snow and she nailed him right in the ass. He spun around, wiping at his expensive slacks—but who wore slacks to play in the snow for Pete's sake?—and then lobbed another ball in her direction.

She easily dodged this one and nailed him with another on the shoulder.

"I hope you know this means war," he declared.

She rolled her eyes. "Yeah, yeah. I made you lose that stuffy attitude once. I'll do it again."

His eyes narrowed in confusion and she used his momentary inattention to plaster him in his face.

Wiping the slush from his eyes, he began to stalk toward her, determination twisting his lips.

"Uh-oh," she murmured and began backtracking.

There wasn't a whole lot of room for evasion in the small garden, and unless she wanted to run back inside, there wasn't anywhere to go. Since it was probably his plan to herd her back indoors, she decided to meet him head-on and weather whatever attack he had in mind.

She began scooping and pelting him with a furious barrage of snow. He swore as he twisted and ducked and then he made a sound of resignation and began scooping snow from the stone benches and hurling it back at her as fast as he could.

Unfortunately for her, his aim was a lot better and after six direct hits in a row, she raised her hands and cried, "Uncle!"

"Now why don't I believe you?" he asked as he stared cautiously at her, his hand cocked back to blast her with another snowball.

She gave him her best smile of innocence and raised her empty hands, palms up. "You win. I'm freezing."

He dropped the snowball and then strode forward to grasp her shoulders. He swept that imperious gaze up and down her body, much like he'd done the first time they'd met. This time it didn't rankle, for she knew that beneath that boring, straight-laced hauteur lay a fun-loving man just aching to get out. She just had to free him. Again.

She sighed at the unfairness of it all. It was like some sick joke being played on her by fate. Karma maybe. Though she was sure she'd done nothing so hideous as to have the love of her life and father of her child regard her as a complete stranger.

She shivered and Rafael frowned. "We should go inside

at once. You aren't dressed for the weather. Did you bring nothing at all to wear for colder weather?"

She shook her head ruefully.

"We'll need to go shopping then."

She shook her head again. "There isn't a point. We'll be leaving to go back to Moon Island and it's still quite warm there."

"And in the meantime you'll freeze," he said darkly.

She rolled her eyes.

"You at least need a coat. I'll send out for one. Do you have a preference? Fur? Leather?"

"Uh, just a coat. Nothing exotic."

He made a dismissive gesture with his hands as if deciding that consulting with her was pointless. "I'll have it arranged."

She shrugged. "Suit yourself." He always did.

"When the doorman told me you were out playing in the snow, I asked him if the real Rafael had been abducted by aliens."

Bryony and Rafael both swung around to see Devon Carter leaning against one of the light posts just outside the door leading back into the apartment building.

"Very funny," Rafael muttered. "What are you doing here?" He took Bryony's hand in his.

Devon raised one lazy brow. "Just checking in on you and Bryony. I heard there was some excitement yesterday."

Bryony grimaced and automatically put her other hand to the bruise she'd forgotten about until now.

"As you can see, she's fine," Rafael said. "Now if you'll excuse us, we're going up so she can change into some warmer clothing."

"Actually I was checking on you," Devon said with a grin. "Bryony strikes me as someone who can take care of herself."

Bryony cleared her throat as the moment grew more awkward. Devon wasn't worried about her. He was worried about Rafael in her clutches. Her face warm with embarrassment, she extricated her hand from Rafael's grasp.

"I'll just go up and leave you to, uh, talk. Did you leave the door unlocked?" Or whatever it was they did in these kinds of apartments. Rafael fished in his pocket and then held out a card. "You'll need this for the elevator."

She tucked it into her hand and hurried toward the door after a small wave in Devon's direction.

The two men watched her go and then Rafael turned to his friend with a frown. "What was that all about?"

Devon shrugged. "Just checking in on you, like I said. You've had a lot to digest over the past couple of days. Wanted to see how you were holding up and whether you'd remembered anything."

Rafael grimaced and then shoved Devon toward the door. "Let's at least go inside. It's cold out here."

The two men stopped in the coffee shop off the main lobby and Rafael requested the table by the fire.

"Things are fine," Rafael said after they were seated. "I don't want you worrying, nor do I want you plotting with Ryan and Cam to protect me for my own good."

Devon sighed. "Even if I think this idea of yours to jet off to this island is a damn foolish idea?"

"Especially then."

Devon sipped at his coffee and didn't even attempt to sugarcoat his question. But then that wasn't Devon. He was blunt, if anything. Cut and dried. Practical to a fault.

"Are you sure this is what you want to do, Rafe? Do you really think it's a good idea to go off with this woman who claims to be pregnant with your child? It seems to me, the smarter thing to do would be to call your lawyer, have paternity testing done and sit tight until you get the results."

Rafael's lips were tight as he stared back at Devon. "And what then?"

Devon blinked. "Well, that depends on the outcome of the tests."

Rafael shook his head. "If it turns out that I'm the father, if everything she claims is true, then I will have effectively denied her for the entirety of the time I wait for the test results. If she's telling the truth, I've already dealt her far too much hurt as it is. How can I expect to mend a rift if I have my lawyer sit on her while we wait to see if I'm going to be a father?"

Devon blew out his breath. "It sounds to me like you've already made up your mind that she's telling the truth."

Rafael dragged a hand through his hair. "I don't know what the truth is. My head tells me that she couldn't possibly be telling the truth. That the idea of me falling head-over-ass for her in a matter of weeks is absurd. It sounds so ludicrous that I can't even wrap my head around it."

"But…?"

"But my gut is screaming that there is definitely something between us," Rafael grimly admitted. "When I get near her, when I touch her… It's like I become someone else entirely. Someone I don't know. I hear the conviction in her voice when she talks of us making love by the ocean and I believe her. More than that I *want* to believe her."

Devon let out a whistle that sounded more like a crash-and-burn. "So you believe her then."

Rafael sucked in his breath. "My head tells me she's a liar."

"But your gut?"

Rafael sighed because he knew what Dev was getting at. Rafael always went with his gut. Even when logic argued otherwise. And he'd never been wrong.

"My gut tells me she's telling the truth."

Eight

"Do you feel well enough to travel?" Rafael asked Bryony over dinner.

Bryony looked up from the sumptuous steak she was devouring to see Rafael studying the bruise on her face.

"Rafael, I'm fine."

"Perhaps you should see an obstetrician before we leave the city."

"If it makes you feel any better, I'll go see my doctor as soon as we get to the island, but I'm certainly capable of traveling. Unless you have matters to attend to here? I can go ahead of you if you can't get away yet."

Rafael frowned and put down his fork. "We'll go together. It's important we retrace all our steps and follow the same pattern we did when I was there before. Perhaps the familiarity will bring back my lost memories."

Bryony cut another piece of her steak, but paused after she speared it with her fork. "What does your doctor say?"

Rafael became visibly uncomfortable. Even though the

table they'd been seated at provided complete privacy from the other patrons, he glanced around as if the idea of anyone overhearing his personal business caused him no end of grief.

His lips pursed in distaste and then he finally said, "He thinks there's a psychological reason behind my memory loss. If I was so happy and in love then why would I want to forget? It makes no sense."

She was unable to control the flinch. Her fingers went numb as she realized how tightly she gripped the fork.

"I didn't say that to hurt you," he said in a low voice. "There's just so much I don't understand. I want to go back because I want to find the person I lost while I was there. The man you say you loved and who loved you is a stranger to me."

"Apparently we're both strangers to you," she said quietly. "Maybe that man doesn't exist. Maybe I imagined him."

Rafael's gaze dropped down her body to where her belly was hidden by the table. "But neither of us imagined a child. He or she is all too real, the one real thing in this whole situation."

She couldn't keep the sadness from her expression. The corners of her mouth drooped and she shoved her plate aside, her appetite gone.

"Our baby isn't the only real thing in our relationship. My love for you was real. I held nothing back from you. I guess we won't know whether you were real when you were with me. You deny that you could be that person. You deny it with your every breath. And I'm supposed to forget all of this denial if you suddenly remember you did and do love me."

She dropped her hands into her lap and wound her fingers tightly together as she leaned forward.

"Tell me, Rafael, which man would I believe? The man who tells me I'm not his type and that he couldn't possibly have loved me, or the lover who spent every night in my arms while we were on the island? No matter what you remember tomorrow, or the next day, I'll always know that a part of you rebels at the mere thought of being with me."

She could tell her words struck a chord with him. Discomfort darkened his features and regret simmered in his eyes. He splayed his hand out in an almost helpless gesture.

"Bryony, I…"

She gave a short, forceful shake of her head. "Don't, Rafael. Don't make it worse by saying you didn't mean it. We both know you did. At least you've been honest. You just need to remember that you're not the only victim in this."

"I'm sorry," he said, and she knew he meant it.

He reached across the table and slipped his hand over hers. For a moment he stroked his thumb across her knuckles and then he gently squeezed.

"I really am sorry. I'm being a selfish bastard. I know this has to hurt you and that none of this is easy for you. Forgive me."

Her heart squeezed at the sincerity in his eyes. It was all she could do not to throw herself into his arms and hold on for all she was worth. She wanted to whisper to him that she loved him. She wanted to beg him never to let her go. But all she could do was stare across the table in helpless frustration.

"What if you never remember?" she asked, voicing her greatest fear.

"I don't know," he said honestly. "I hope it doesn't come to that."

She leaned back in her seat, slipping her hand from underneath his. The heaviness in her chest was a physical ache, one that clogged her throat and made it hard to breathe.

"What have you packed?" she asked lightly, forcing a smile.

He looked confused by the abrupt shift in conversation. "I haven't yet."

She raised an eyebrow. "We leave in the morning and you

don't know how long you'll be gone. Aren't you leaving it to the last minute?"

He grimaced. "I wasn't sure what to pack. You mentioned things like swimwear and flip-flops."

She laughed as some of the tension in her chest eased. "Well, it's too cold to swim. The weather is still quite warm but the water is chilly. But we can buy you shorts and flip-flops like we did before. We can't have you wearing suits all the time, and your expensive loafers will just get ruined."

"I'm trusting you," he muttered. "Since you swear I did this before."

"And it didn't kill you," she teased. "When I was done with your makeover, you looked more relaxed and less like a stuffed shirt."

"You're implying I'm stuffy?" he asked in mock outrage.

"Oh, you were. Totally stuffy."

"I don't want to stand out this time. I'd like to keep my… problem…as private as possible."

"Of course," Bryony murmured.

He sat back in his chair and fiddled with his wineglass, though he didn't pick it up to drink. He turned in the direction of the band playing soft, mellow jazz and then back to her, his expression thoughtful.

"Tell me, Bryony. Did we ever dance?"

Caught off guard by the question, she shook her head mutely.

He stood and held his hand out to her. "Then dance with me now."

Mesmerized by the husk in his tone, she slipped her hand into his and allowed him to pull her to her feet. He led her onto the dance floor and slid his palm over her back as he pulled her into his embrace.

She closed her eyes and sighed as she melted against him. His warmth wrapped tantalizingly around her and his scent brushed over her nose. She inhaled deeply, holding his essence in the deepest part of her.

Oh, how she'd missed him. Even when she'd hated him, when she'd thought the absolute worst, she'd lain awake at night remembering the nights in her bed when they'd made love with the music of the ocean filling the sky.

She was acutely aware of him as they swayed in time to the sultry tones. He cupped her to him possessively, as if telling the world she belonged to him. It was nice to get lost in the moment and her daydreams.

As he turned her, she tilted her neck and gazed up at him as he tucked her hand between them, his thumb caressing the pulse at her wrist.

"You are an interesting dilemma, Bryony."

She raised her brows. "Dilemma?"

"Conundrum. Puzzle. One of the many things I can't seem to figure out lately."

She cocked her head to the side in question.

"I swear I have no memory of you. I look at you and draw a blank. But when you get close to me, when I touch you…" His voice dropped to a mere whisper and it sent a shiver racing down her spine. "I feel as though…"

"As though what?" she whispered.

He had a slightly bewildered look on his face as if he were searching for just the right word. Then finally he sighed and stared down at her, his gaze stroking over her skin.

"We fit," he said simply. "I have no explanation for it, but it just feels…right."

Her heart sped up. Hope pulsed in her veins, the first real hope she'd had since hearing his fantastic story. She didn't know whether to squeeze him or kiss him, so she stood there as they swayed with the music and smiled so brilliantly that her cheeks hurt.

"Amazing that such a simple thing could make you so happy," he murmured.

"We do fit," she said, her voice catching as her throat throbbed with a growing ache. She reached up to frame his face and then she leaned up on tiptoe to brush her lips across his.

She meant it to be a small gesture of affection. Maybe a reminder of what they'd once shared. Or maybe to just reaffirm the sensation to him that they fit. But he didn't allow her to stop there.

Cupping his hand to the back of her head, he wrapped his other arm around her waist and hauled her up until her lips were in line with his.

There was nothing tentative about his kiss. No hesitancy as he attempted to find his way back. It was as if they'd never been apart. He kissed her like he'd kissed her so many times before, only this time… There was something different she couldn't quite put her finger on. More depth. More emotion. It wasn't just sexy or passionate. It was…tender.

Like he was apologizing for all the hurt. For the separation and misunderstanding. For what he couldn't remember.

She sighed into his mouth, sadness and joy mixing and bubbling up in her heart until she was overwhelmed by it all. When he finally drew away, his eyes were dark, his body trembled against hers, and as he eased her down, his hand slid up her arms to cup her face.

"Part of me remembers you, Bryony. There's a part of me that feels like I've come home when I kiss you. That has to mean something."

She nodded, unable to speak as emotion clogged her throat. She swallowed several times and then finally found her voice.

"We'll find our way back, Rafe. I won't let you go so easily. When I thought you didn't want me, that you'd played me, it was easy to say never again. But now that I know what happened, I won't give up without a fight. Somehow I'll make you remember. It's not just your happiness at stake. It's mine, too."

He smiled and stroked a thumb over one cheekbone. "So fierce. You fascinate me, Bryony. I'm beginning to see how it could be true that I was so transfixed by you from the start."

Then he leaned down and kissed her again, the room around them forgotten. "I want to remember. Help me remember."

"You'll get it back," she said fiercely. "We'll get it back. Together."

Nine

The flight back to Houston was much better than her trip to New York. On the way she'd been squeezed between two men who she swore had to be football players. She hadn't been able to move and had spent the entire time being miserable.

She and Rafael occupied the first two seats in first class, and once they'd taken off, she'd reclined without guilt, since there was plenty of room between the rows.

By the time they landed in Houston, she actually felt rested and ready for the drive from the airport.

Apparently Rafael had ideas of having a driver take them to the island.

"My car is here. There's no reason for us not to take it," she insisted as they stood in baggage claim.

"We would both be more comfortable if you let me see to the travel arrangements."

"And what am I supposed to do without my car? We'll need it on the island. It's small but everything isn't in walking distance."

As their luggage piled up, Rafael sighed. "All right. We'll take your car. But it's senseless for you to drive when we've already been traveling half the day."

She rolled her eyes and bit her lip to keep from making a remark about spoiled men.

She grabbed a cart for their luggage and Rafael piled it up and pushed it as she led him to the parking garage.

"Where is the damn parking lot?" he demanded. "In Galveston?"

"It's a bit of a walk," she admitted. "But it's all indoors and then we'll take the elevator to the top level."

"Why did you park on the roof?"

She shrugged. "I just kept going around and around and then suddenly I was on the roof. It's the same as parking anywhere else."

He shook his head as they trudged down the long corridor. When they finally got to the elevator, Bryony breathed in relief. A few moments later, they were on the roof and she took out her keys to remotely unlock the car.

"What the…"

She cast him a puzzled look.

"That's your car?" he asked.

She looked toward the MINI Cooper and nodded. "Is something wrong?"

"You expect to fit me *and* the luggage in this tin can?"

"Quit being so grumpy," she said mildly. "We'll manage. It does have a luggage rack. I'm sure I have a bungee cord in the trunk."

"Who the hell carries around bungee cords?"

She laughed. "You never know when they'll come in handy."

They filled the trunk and then piled suitcases into the back until the bags were stacked to the roof of the car.

"There," she said triumphantly as she shut the door. "We didn't even have to use the bungee cords."

"Unfortunately we didn't push the passenger seat back before we stored all the luggage," he said dryly.

Bryony winced when she saw him fold his legs to get into the front seat. His knees were pushed up into the dash and he didn't look at all comfortable.

"Sorry," she mumbled as she got into the driver's seat. "I wasn't thinking. No one who ever rides in my car has such long legs."

"How do you plan to drive the baby around after he or she is born?"

Bryony reversed out of the parking space and then drove toward the exit. "In a car seat, of course."

"And where do you think the car seat will fit in here? Even if you crammed it in, if you got into a wreck, neither of you would likely survive. Someone could run right over you in this thing and probably not even realize it."

"It's what I have, Rafael. There's not a lot I can do about it. Now let's talk about something else."

"How far of a drive is it?"

She sighed. "An hour to Galveston from the airport. Then we take a ferry to Moon Island. It's about a half-hour ferry ride so we should be there in under two hours barring any traffic issues."

It was a bad thing to say. Thirty minutes later, they were completely stalled on I-45. Bryony cursed under her breath as Rafael fidgeted in his seat. Or at least tried to fidget. He couldn't move much and he looked as if he was ready to get out and walk. It would probably be faster since traffic hadn't moved so much as an inch in the past five minutes.

"I know what you're going to say," she said when she saw him turn toward her. "We should have left my car at the airport. Yeah, I know that now, but really, traffic jams are a fact of life in Houston."

A smile quirked at the corners of his mouth. "I was actually going to say it's a good thing I went to the bathroom before we left the airport."

She heaved a sigh. "Just be grateful you aren't pregnant."

He arched an eyebrow. "Want me to take over?"

She shook her head. "You'd never be able to drive with your knees jammed to your chin. Let's find something to talk about. Music would just irritate me right now."

He seemed to think for a moment and then he said, "Tell me what you do. I mean, do you work? You said you took care of your grandmother but I wasn't sure if that was a full-time task or not."

Bryony smiled. "No. Mamaw is still quite self-sufficient. I wouldn't say I take care of her as much as we take care of each other. She's been sicker lately, though. As for what I do, I'm sort of a Jill of all trades. I do a little bit of everything. I'm the go-to gal on the island for whatever needs doing."

He looked curiously at her.

"Basically I'm a consultant if you want a posh name for my job. I'm consulted on all manner of things, though nothing you'd probably think was legitimate," she added with a laugh.

"You have me curious now. Just what exactly are some of the things you do?"

"One day a week I take care of the mayor's correspondence. He's an older gentleman, and he's not fond of computers. Or the internet for that matter. He likes old-school things like actual newspapers, print magazines, watching the news on the local channel instead of surfing to CNN. That sort of thing. He doesn't even have cable if you can believe it."

"And this guy got elected?"

Bryony laughed. "I think you'll find that our island is pretty tolerant of being old-fashioned. It's a bit of a throwback. While you can certainly avail yourself of all the modern conveniences such as internet, cable TV and the like, a large percentage of our population is quite happy in their technology-challenged world."

Rafael shook his head. "I'm shuddering as you speak. How can anyone be happy living in the Dark Ages?"

"Oh, please. You enjoyed it well enough yourself once I finally weaned you off your BlackBerry and your laptop. You went a whole week without using either. A week!"

"Surely a record," he muttered.

"Oh, look, traffic is moving!"

She put the MINI Cooper into gear as cars began to crawl forward. She checked her watch to see that they'd already lost an hour; it would be close to dark by the time they arrived on the island.

Still, the delay couldn't dim her excitement. It was foolish of her to get her hopes up, but she wanted so badly to relive her time with Rafael on the island. Take him through all the steps they'd taken before.

She wanted him to remember. Because if he didn't, things would never be the same for them. He'd resisted the idea of being with her. Her only hope was for him to remember and then…

Then just as she'd told him the night before, she'd forever have to live with the fact that at least some part of him recoiled at the idea of them being lovers.

"Penny for your thoughts?"

She grimaced as she navigated her way down the interstate. "They aren't worth that much."

"Then don't think them."

To her surprise, he leaned over, curled his hand around her nape and massaged lightly, threading his fingers through her thick hair. It was tempting to close her eyes and lean her head all the way back but then they'd have a wreck and never get off this damn interstate.

"I'm nervous, Rafael," she admitted.

She bit her lip, wondering if she shouldn't just shut up, but she'd always had this habit of being completely honest. It wasn't in her makeup to shy away from the bald truth, no matter how uncomfortable. She always figured if people talked more about their issues then there wouldn't *be* so many issues.

Rafael—the old Rafael—hadn't minded her speaking her mind. They'd enjoyed long conversations and she'd always told him what was occupying her thoughts.

But now, she had a newfound reservation against being so forthright. She hated feeling so unsure of herself.

"Why are you nervous?" he asked softly.

"You. Me. Us. What if this doesn't work? I feel like this is my only chance and that if you don't remember, I've lost you."

"Regardless of whether I regain my memory, we still have a child to think about. I'm not going to disappear just because I can't remember the details of his conception."

"You sound like you've accepted that I'm carrying your child."

He shrugged. "I've embraced the very real possibility. Until I'm proven wrong, I choose to think of it as my child."

Her heart did a little squeeze in her chest. "Thank you for that. For now it's enough. Until we figure out everything else, it's enough that you accept our baby."

"And you."

She turned to glance quickly at him before returning her gaze to the highway.

He lowered his hand from her neck to cover her hand that rested on his leg. "There is definitely something between us. If I accept that we made a child together, surely I have to accept that we were lovers, that you meant something to me?"

"I hope I did," she said softly.

"Tell me, Bryony, do you still love me?"

There was a note of raw curiosity in his voice. Almost as if he wasn't sure how he wanted her to answer.

"That's unfair," she said in a low voice. "You can't expect

me to lay everything out when there's a real possibility we'll never be what we once were to each other. You can't expect me to admit to loving a man who thinks of me as a complete stranger."

"Not a stranger," he corrected. "I've already admitted that it's obvious we were something to each other."

"Something. Not everything," she said painfully. "Don't ask me, Rafael. Not until you remember me. Ask me then."

He reached up to touch her cheek. "All right. I'll ask you then."

Ten

After what seemed an interminable time, Bryony drove her little car onto the ferry and was immediately sandwiched by vehicles twice the size of hers.

Rafael had serious reservations about her driving around with a newborn in something only a little larger than a Matchbox car.

To his surprise, she opened her door and started to climb out.

"Where are you going?"

She ducked down to look at him through the window and flashed a wide smile. "Come on. It's a beautiful sunset. We can watch it from the railing."

Her exuberance shouldn't have surprised him by now. He'd gotten a taste of it in bits and pieces, but now that they'd left the city, she seemed to be even more excited, as if she couldn't wait to go back....

There was no doubt that he wanted to regain his memory. Having a gaping hole in his mind wasn't at all acceptable to someone like him, who was used to control in every aspect of his life. Now he was dependent on someone else to guide him and it made him extremely uncomfortable.

But in addition to knowing what happened during those lost weeks, he found himself hoping. Hoping that Bryony was right even if it meant a drastic change for him. He wasn't at all sure he was ready for fatherhood and a relationship. Love. If Bryony was to be believed… Love. It baffled him and intrigued him all at the same time.

He didn't want to hurt her. At this point he'd do anything to keep from hurting her and so he hoped that some miracle had occurred on this island and that he'd be able to find that same miracle again.

He climbed out of the car and stretched his aching legs. He inhaled deeply, enjoying the tang of the salty air. A breeze ruffled his hair, but he noted it was a warm breeze despite the coolness of the evening. The air was heavier here but… cleaner, if that made sense.

Bryony, in her impatience—which he was fast learning was an overriding component of her personality—grabbed his hand and tugged him toward the rail where others had gathered. Some had chosen to remain inside their vehicles, but others, like he and Bryony were leaning over the side and staring at the burst of gold on the horizon. Pink-and-purple hues mixed with the strands of gold, and spread out their fingers until the entire sky looked as if it were alive and breathing fire.

"It's beautiful, isn't it?"

He glanced down at Bryony and nodded. "Yes, it is."

"You don't see too many sunsets," she said smugly.

"What's that supposed to mean?"

She shrugged. "You mentioned before when we used to sit out on my deck that it wasn't something you ever had time to do. You usually worked late and were always in too big a hurry. So I was determined to show you as many as I could while you were here. Looks like I get to do it all over again. Oh, look! Dolphins!"

He looked to where she was pointing to see several sleek, gray bodies arc out of the water and then disappear below the surface.

"They follow the ferry quite a bit," she said. "I look for them every time I make the trip to Galveston."

He found himself caught up in the moment and before he knew it, he was pointing as they resurfaced. "There they are again!"

She smiled and hooked her arm through his, hugging him close. It seemed the most natural thing in the world to extricate his arm and then wrap it around her. They stood watching as the dolphins raced through the water, with her tucked up close to his side.

He shook his head at the absurdity of it all. Here he was without his phone or an internet connection. He'd left his BlackBerry in the car. He was on a ferry, of all things, watching dolphins play as he held the mother of his child.

Much was said about near-death experiences and how they changed a person. But it would appear that he'd begun his great transformation act *before* his accident.

It was little wonder Ryan, Dev and Cam were so worried about him. They were probably back in the city researching mental hospitals in preparation for his breakdown.

He rubbed his hand up and down Bryony's arm and then pressed a kiss to the top of her head. Then he sighed. He had to admit, he was actually looking forward to being on the island and spending time with Bryony and not just because he was anxious to recover his memory.

She wrapped her arms around his waist and squeezed. Her hug warmed him all the way through but not in a particularly sexual way. It was comforting. It was like holding a ray of sunshine.

As strange as it might sound, he felt comfortable around

her. A complete stranger. Someone, who before a few days ago, he hadn't remembered, and for all practical purposes had never laid eyes on.

Yeah, his statement the night before had been a little—okay, a *lot* corny—but it was absolutely true. They fit. She fit him. And he had absolutely no explanation for it, other than somehow, he'd lost his heart and soul on that island and then the entire event had been wiped from his mind.

Okay. He accepted it. Hell, he embraced it. He wasn't fighting it. He was ready for whatever lay ahead. So why couldn't he remember?

He held her tightly to him, his face buried in her fragrant, dark curls. Tentatively he slid his hand down to cup her belly, the first time he'd made an overt gesture to acknowledge the life inside her womb.

She stiffened momentarily and then slowly turned her face up so she could look at him.

He rubbed in a gentle back-and-forth motion, exploring the firmness of the swell. Something he could only define as magic tightened his chest and flooded his heart.

This was his child.

Somehow he knew it.

He was going to be a father.

The realization befuddled him and at the same time, he felt such a sense of awe. He hadn't planned on fatherhood. In fact, he'd always been extremely careful in his sexual relationships. Extremely careful. He'd bordered on phobic about an accidental pregnancy.

Had he purposely discarded protection with Bryony? Had he considered the fact that they could make a child? Had she entertained such a possibility?

He frowned as he remembered her outrage and anger that it hadn't been enough that he'd screwed her over, but that he'd made her pregnant, too. No, that didn't strike him as the reaction of a woman who'd embraced such a thing.

Evidently it hadn't been something either of them had planned, but it was also obvious he hadn't gone to great lengths to prevent it.

He kissed her upturned lips and she smiled as she snuggled closer to him. Then she sighed in regret and carefully pulled away.

"We're nearly there. We should go back to the car."

Bryony turned on her headlights as they rounded the sharp turn and began the drive north toward her cottage. She frowned when she saw several vehicles parked on the highway near her driveway.

Her heart began to pound as fear gripped her. Had something happened to Mamaw? She'd spoken to her grandmother just hours earlier when she and Rafael had landed in Houston. She'd sounded fine then and eager to see Bryony again.

She recognized one of the vehicles as belonging to Mayor Daniels. What would he be doing here?

She pulled into the gravel driveway and turned off the ignition. Her grandmother stepped out onto the front porch followed by Mayor Daniels, who wore a frown, and Sheriff Taylor, who didn't look any happier.

She opened her door and scrambled out. "Mamaw, is everything all right? Are you okay?"

"Oh, honey, I'm fine. Sorry if we worried you. The mayor and the sheriff had some questions." Her grandmother eyed Rafael as he got out of the passenger seat. "We all do."

Bryony frowned and looked over at Mayor Daniels. "It couldn't wait? We've been traveling all day and got stuck in a traffic jam on the interstate."

The mayor picked up his finger and began to shake it, as he did every time he was upset over something. The sheriff put a hand on his shoulder.

"Easy, Rupert, give her a chance to explain."

"Explain what?" Bryony demanded.

"Why a ferry full of construction equipment landed on our island yesterday and why they're set to start building some fancy new hotel on the land you sold to Tricorp Investment," the mayor said as he shook an accusing finger at Bryony.

She shook her head adamantly. "There must be some mistake, Mayor. I've been in New York City all week to straighten out this mess. Rafael would have told me if construction was already scheduled to begin. And I didn't sell to Tricorp. I sold to Rafael."

The sheriff grimaced. "There's no mistake, Bry. I questioned the men myself. Asked to see their permits. Everything is all legal. I even asked to see the plans. That whole stretch of the beach is going to be turned into a resort, complete with its own helicopter pad."

Her mouth dropped open and she turned to Rafael, dread and disappointment nearly choking her. "Rafael?"

Eleven

Rafael bit out a curse as he faced four accusing stares. Bryony's was confused, though, and a little dazed. Pain and bewilderment made their way across her face and the look in her eyes made him wince.

"Now see here," the mayor began as he stepped forward.

Rafael brought him up short with a jerk of his hand. He stared hard at the other man and the mayor took a hasty step back, nearly pulling the sheriff in front of him for protection.

"This is a matter between Bryony and myself," he said in an even voice. "As she said, we're tired. We've traveled all day, she's pregnant and she's dead on her feet. I won't stand here arguing with you in her driveway."

"But—" The mayor turned to the sheriff. "Silas? Are you going to let him get away with this?"

The sheriff sighed and adjusted his hat. "What he's doing isn't illegal, Rupert. It might be unethical, but it isn't illegal. He owns the land. He can do what he likes with it."

"Rafael? Did you approve this? Is it true they're starting construction?" Bryony asked in a strained voice.

Her grandmother stepped to her side and wrapped her arm around Bryony's waist. Her grandmother was a frail-looking woman and it irritated Rafael to no end that it was Bryony who looked the more fragile of the two at the moment.

"We'll discuss this in private," he said tightly.

"Do you want him here, Bry?" the sheriff asked.

Bryony raised a hand to her temple and rubbed as if she had no idea what to say to that question. Hurt crowded her eyes, and then deep fatigue, as if all her energy had been sapped in a single instant.

Knowing if he didn't take control of the situation, he'd likely be carted off to some second-rate jail cell, Rafael moved to Bryony's side and gently pried her away from her grandmother. He wrapped his arm around her waist and cupped his hand over her elbow.

"We'll talk inside," he murmured.

She stared up at him as if she searched for some shred of truth or maybe deceit. He couldn't be entirely sure what she was thinking.

Then she stiffened and looked toward the two men. "He's staying here, Silas. I appreciate your concern."

"And the construction?" Rupert asked in agitation. "What am I supposed to tell everyone? It wasn't me who sold the land to the outsider but it happened on my watch. I'll never win reelection if it becomes known that the island went to hell during my term."

"Rupert, shut up," Bryony's grandmother said sharply. "My granddaughter is upset enough without you yammering on about your political career."

"Come on, Rupert. Nothing good can come of us standing in her driveway at this hour. There'll be plenty of time to sort this out tomorrow," Silas said as he herded the older man toward his vehicle.

As he left, he tipped his hat to Bryony. "Let me know if you need anything, young lady."

Bryony gave him a tight smile and nodded her thanks. When the two men were gone, Bryony's grandmother hugged her.

"I'm glad you're home. I worry when you travel. Especially to a city like New York."

If Rafael had expected the older woman to turn on him in anger he was wrong. Instead she gently enfolded him in a hug and patted his cheek.

"Welcome back, young man. I'm glad you found your way back here."

With that, she walked down a narrow stone path in the grass that led to the adjoining yard.

"Will she be okay?" Rafael asked with a frown. "Should we take her home?"

Bryony sighed. "She lives next door. Just a few steps from my front door."

"Oh. Right. Sorry."

"Yeah, I know, you don't remember."

This time her tone lacked the patience and understanding she'd exhibited until now. There was an undercurrent of hurt that cut into him and pricked his conscience.

Hell. He'd once have argued that he didn't have a conscience when it came to business. Business was business. Nothing personal. Only now…it was definitely personal.

"Come on," she said. "We need to get all this luggage inside."

He put his hand on her arm. "You go in. I'll bring in the luggage. Don't argue. Go get something to drink or eat if you're hungry. I'll be in in just a moment."

She shrugged and walked to the steps leading onto the porch. A moment later, she disappeared into the house, leaving Rafael standing in the driveway staring at his surroundings with keen eyes.

So this is where he'd spent so many days and nights. This is where his life had supposedly undergone such a drastic change. He didn't feel anything other than that he was distinctly out of his comfort zone and in way over his head.

He carried the luggage in two trips to the front porch and then propped her door open and began lugging the bags into the living room.

As he stepped in, he stared around, absorbing the look and feel of the place Bryony called home. It reflected her personality to a T. Sunny, cheerful, a little cluttered, as if she were always in too much of a hurry to keep it spotless. It looked lived-in, nothing like his sterile apartment, which a cleaning lady made spotless every day regardless of whether he was in residence or not.

She stood with her back to him, staring out the French doors that led onto the deck. Her arms were wrapped protectively around her chest and when she turned, he could see the barricade she'd erected as surely as if it were a tangible shield.

"Did you know about the construction? Did you order it to begin?" she asked.

He sighed. "Do you want me to lie, Bryony? I won't. I've been nothing but truthful to you. Yes, I ordered construction to begin. I would have started much sooner but my accident delayed me significantly. My investors are anxious. They want to see progress in return for the money they've shelled out."

"You promised," she choked out.

He ran a hand through his hair and wished he could make this go away. At least until they had matters between them sorted out.

"You know I can't remember," he said. "As far as I knew, the land was bought, the deal closed, the property to do with as I liked. There was nothing in the contract that stipulated how I could use the land. I wouldn't have signed such a contract. The land is useless to me unless I develop it."

Damn it. Why couldn't he remember? Surely he wouldn't have made her such a promise. It defied all logic. Why on earth would he have bought the land and promised not to develop it?

He closed the distance between them and slid his hand over her shoulder. She flinched and lifted her shoulder away, but he kept his hand against her skin.

"Bryony, again, I'm not doing this to hurt you. I don't remember. You say I made you a promise, but I have no proof of that. What I do have is proof of sale. I have your signature on the closing documents as well as a copy of the bank draft issued to you from my bank."

She turned to face him again, her eyes red-rimmed. She looked to be fighting tears with every bit of her power.

"I made it clear from the start that I wouldn't sell to you unless you promised it wouldn't be developed on a large scale. Obviously I can't control what a new owner does with the land, but I'd hoped for something in keeping with the integrity of our community here. You looked me in the eye and you promised me that you had no such plans. That was a lie, Rafael. It's an obvious lie because clearly you had investors lined up, plans drawn, a schedule planned. You yourself just said that your accident delayed the groundbreaking significantly."

Rafael swore because one of them had to be lying and he didn't want it to be him. He didn't want it to be her.

"Damn it, Bryony, I refuse to feel guilt for something I can't remember."

"We should get some sleep," she said dully. "There's little point in arguing over this when we're both tired and I'm upset. I'll show you to the guest room. It has its own bathroom. There are towels and soap, everything you should need."

And just like that, she was dismissing him. She'd withdrawn and he was treated to the cold, angry woman she'd been the first night in New York when she'd confronted him at his event.

He drew in a breath, feeling like a fool for what he was about to say, but it rushed out before he could think better of it, before he could question his sanity.

"I'll put a temporary halt to construction. Tomorrow. I'll go to the site myself. Until we sort things out between us and I regain my memory, I'll halt the groundbreaking."

She blinked in surprise, her mouth forming a silent O. From all appearances it was the last thing she'd expected him to say, and he was suddenly glad of it. Fiercely glad that he'd caught her off guard.

"Really?"

He nodded. "I'd go tonight but no one will be at the site and I have no idea where they're staying, but if I'm there at dawn in the morning, I'll make sure nothing is done until I give the okay to begin."

Once again she surprised him by launching herself into his arms and hugging him so tight he struggled to breathe. For such a small woman, she possessed amazing strength.

"Every time I think you've let me down, you do something to completely change my mind," she whispered fiercely. "Every time I think I've lost the Rafael I fell in love with, you do something to make me realize he's still there and I just have to find him again."

He wasn't sure he liked the sound of that. As if he was some sort of Dr. Jekyll and Mr. Hyde. Hell, maybe he *was* crazy. It was the only explanation behind the past few months of his life.

Most men bought a flashy sports car, had an affair or hooked up with a girl barely out of school in their midlife crisis. Apparently he did bizarre things like fall in love and throw away a multimillion-dollar deal.

Ryan, Dev and Cam were going to kill him.

Twelve

"You did *what?*"

Rafael held the phone away from his ear and winced at the string of expletives that flooded the airways.

"I'm coming down there. We all are," Devon said. "This is precisely what I was afraid of happening. You get down there and she has you by the balls. Make me the bad guy. I don't care, but construction has to begin immediately. We're already months behind schedule."

Rafael paced back and forth over the slight bluff over-looking the beach while Bryony waited in the car. The crew hadn't been happy that they were being asked to stand down, until Rafael informed them they'd be paid full wages during the temporary layoff. He'd stressed *temporary* and hoped like hell that he would have this resolved in a few days' time.

He didn't offer that little tidbit to Devon. Devon would really lose his composure if he knew Rafael was footing the bill for a crew of construction workers to sit around and enjoy beach life for the next few days.

"You stay your ass in New York," Rafael said. "I don't need you and Cam and Ryan to babysit me. It's the right thing to do, Devon. Until I know what the hell I promised or didn't promise or whatever else happened while I was down here the first time, the right thing to do is wait."

"Since when have you ever been concerned with doing the right thing?" Devon asked incredulously. "We're talking about the king of get-it-done, it's business, not personal, whatever it takes, score the deal. Are you getting soft in your old age or has she messed with your head so much that you no longer know up from down?"

Rafael scowled. "You make me sound like a complete bastard."

"Yeah, well, you are. Why should that bother you now? It's what's made you so successful. Don't go growing a conscience on me now."

Rafael frowned even harder. "What do you know about this deal, Devon? What aren't you telling me?"

There was a long silence. And then his friend said, "Look, I don't know what happened down there. What I do know is that before you left New York, you said quite clearly that you'd come back with a signed bill of sale and you didn't give a damn what you had to do to achieve it."

"Son of a bitch," Rafael muttered. "That's not helping my case here."

"Why do you want it to help your case? You've got the land. You've got our investors on board. The only thing standing in our way right now is you."

Rafael stared back at the car to see that Bryony had gotten out and leaned against the door. Her hair blew in the morning breeze and it was a little chilly. She hadn't worn a sweater.

"Yeah, well, for now I'm not moving," he said quietly. "I'll accept full responsibility for this."

"Damn right you will," Devon said in disgust. "We've all made sacrifices, Rafael. We're on the verge of being huge.

With this resort deal and the merger with Copeland hotels, we'll be the largest luxury resort business in the world. Don't screw it up for all of us."

Rafael sighed. Yeah, he knew they'd made sacrifices. Devon was even marrying Copeland's daughter to cement this deal. They were close to having everything they'd ever wanted. Success beyond their wildest imaginations.

And he'd never felt worse or more unsure of himself in his life.

"Trust me on this, Dev. Give me some time, okay? I'll make it right. I've never not come through before. But this is my future we're talking about here."

Rafael heard the weary sigh through the phone. "One week, Rafe. One week and if ground isn't broken, I'm coming down there and I'm bringing Ryan and Cam with me."

Rafael ended the call and shoved the phone into his pocket. One week. It seemed a ridiculous amount of time to decide the fate of his entire future. And Bryony's future. The future of his child.

He blew out his breath and walked away from the beach toward Bryony's car. She was probably tired. He'd bet that neither of them had slept much the night before. He'd seen dark circles under her eyes when they'd left her cottage before sunup to drive to the construction site.

With a week's reprieve, it was time to concentrate on the most important issue at hand—regaining his memory and figuring out his relationship with Bryony Morgan.

As Rafael strode back toward the car, Bryony regarded him warily. He looked angry and determined. Whatever phone call he'd made, it hadn't been pleasant. She could hear his raised voice all the way inside the car, though she couldn't make out what it was he said.

True to his word, he'd given the order to suspend ground-breaking. It hadn't taken long for her cell phone to start ringing. Rupert had been first, congratulating her on keeping

Rafael de Luca in line. Bryony had rolled her eyes and bitten her tongue. As if anyone could leash Rafael de Luca. No, whatever reason he had for agreeing to postpone construction, it hadn't been because she'd asked him to.

Her pride had already taken enough of a beating. She wasn't going to beg him.

Then Silas had called to confirm that construction had indeed been halted and then expressed his concern that the workers were now on the island with nothing to do for the next however many days. He worried about the implications. As if Bryony had any experience with enforcing the law.

Still, she had to remember that a lot of people counted on her to keep things running smoothly. It was what she did. Never mind that her life was in shambles. She didn't offer any guarantees about keeping her own affairs straight.

When Rafael arrived, he didn't say anything. He took the keys from her and guided her around to the passenger side.

When he got in, she eyed him sideways. "Everything okay?"

"Fine."

He started the engine and drove over the bumpy dirt path back to the main road and then accelerated.

"Feel like some breakfast?"

It sounded like he grunted in return, but she couldn't be sure. Still, he hadn't said no, so she took it as an affirmative.

"I'll make your favorite."

He glanced sideways at her. "My favorite?"

"Eggs Benedict."

"Yeah, it is," he mumbled. "I guess I told you that before."

"Uh-huh."

Clearly he wasn't in a talkative mood. He looked downright surly. She was more of a morning person, but Mamaw wasn't, and she often told Bryony she was too cheerful for her own good before noon. Mamaw didn't have any compunction about telling her to shut up and go away, but Bryony guessed Rafael was too polite to do the same.

Funny, but she hadn't noticed him being particularly grumpy in the mornings before, but then more often than not, they'd slept late after a night of making love.

Just the memory of them waking in bed, wrapped around each other, had her cheeks warming and a tingle snaking through her body.

She missed those nights. And the mornings. Most of the time she'd cooked for them both, but at least twice, Rafael had risen while she still slept and brought her breakfast in bed.

So instead of saying anything further, she reached over and took his hand, squeezing it before lacing her fingers through his.

He looked surprised by the gesture, but he didn't make any effort to extricate his hand from hers.

"Thank you."

He cocked his head.

"For doing that. It means a lot not just to me, but also to the people on this island."

He looked uncomfortable. "You need to understand that this is only a temporary solution. I can't suspend operations indefinitely. There are a lot of people counting on me. They've trusted me with their money. My partners are heavily invested with me. This is… This is huge for us."

"But you understand I would have never sold you the land if you hadn't given me your promise," she said. "The result would be the same. It's not as though I sold you the land under false pretenses."

Rafael sighed but then squeezed her hand. "For now let's not talk about it. There's no simple solution to all this whether I regain my memory or not."

For the first time she weighed his position in the matter.

If all he'd said were true, then it couldn't have been easy for him to call off the operation.

Regardless of whether he'd lied to her before, he'd done the honorable thing now and it was costing him dearly.

She leaned over and brushed her lips across his cheek. "I realize this isn't easy, but we all appreciate it. I've already gotten calls from the mayor and the sheriff. I'm sure there will be more before the day is out. You can expect to be courted by the locals while you're here. They'll want to present their case."

"Are they angry with you?" he asked. "The mayor didn't seem pleased with you last night. Do they all blame you?"

She blew out her breath. "They think I'm young and gullible. Some of them blame that and not me directly. They're too busy feeling sorry for me for being taken by a suave, debonair man. Others put the blame solely on my shoulders, as they should."

Rafael's face grew stormy. "It's your land. You can't allow others to guilt you into keeping it just because they don't want their way of life to change."

She shrugged. "I grew up here. They consider me a part of their family. Family doesn't turn their backs on each other. A lot of them think I did just that. Maybe I did. I knew that if you and I were going to be together that I wouldn't stay here. I knew I'd have to make the move because your business is based in the city. At the time I didn't care."

He slowed to pull into her driveway and stopped the car. For a long moment he stared out the windshield before finally turning to face her.

"So you were willing to give up everything to be with me."

"Yes," she said simply. Throwing his words back at him, she continued. "I don't say that to hurt you. It's simply the truth and we've both been honest and blunt. I'm not trying to make you feel guilty."

"I don't know what to say."

She smiled. "Let's not say anything. Let's go eat instead. I'm starving. After breakfast we'll go buy you the things you need for your stay and then maybe we'll sit on the deck. Enjoy the day."

Strangely enough, it sounded blissful.

Suddenly, after a not-so-great start to the day, he found himself quite looking forward to the rest.

Thirteen

Bryony tugged Rafael from shop to shop in the town square where she made him try on more casual clothing. Jeans. Lord but the man looked divine in jeans. They cupped his behind in all the right places and molded to his muscular legs.

And a T-shirt. Such an unremarkable item of clothing but on him… A simple white T-shirt displayed his lean, taut body to perfection.

He looked uncomfortable when he came out of the dressing room. He had on the jeans and the shirt she'd picked out and he was barefooted. Barefooted.

She was standing there drooling over a barefooted man in jeans. And she wasn't the only one.

"Oh, my," Stella Jones breathed. "Honey, that is one fine specimen you've got there. He looks hot in the *GQ* stuff, don't get me wrong, but he fills out a pair of jeans like nobody's business."

Bryony shot the saleswoman a glare but had to admit she was right.

"Will this make you happy?" Rafael asked wryly as he turned, hands up.

"Oh, yeah," Bryony murmured. "Me and every other female on this island."

Stella chuckled. "Shall I bag up a few more pair like that one?"

"And T-shirts. Lots of T-shirts. I'm thinking white and maybe a red one."

"Green wouldn't be bad with those dark eyes and hair," Stella advised.

Rafael rolled his eyes. "I'm going back in to change while you ladies sort it out."

"No! No!" Bryony said in a rush. "Just let me pull off the stickers. No reason to change out of them. Stella will ring them up. You'll be more comfortable."

"And so will the rest of us," Stella said over her shoulder as she sashayed off to get the rest of the clothing.

Rafael grinned and sauntered toward Bryony. "So you like me in jeans?"

"I think *like* is perhaps too mild a word," Bryony muttered.

Although Bryony had been openly affectionate with Rafael the entire day, taking his hand, hugging him or twining her arm through his, he hadn't made any overt gestures of his own. But now he slid his arms around her and pulled her into his embrace.

He rested his hands loosely at the small of her back and then slid his fingers into her back pockets, pulling her closer until she was pressed against his chest.

"I like you in jeans, too," he said with a sly grin.

Her heart fluttered as she curled her arms around his shoulders.

"Yeah, but I'm wearing baggy jeans with an elastic maternity waist."

"They fit your behind just fine."

To emphasize his point he moved his fingers to where they were snug in her back pockets.

"We'll have the whole island talking," she murmured.

He snorted. "As if they aren't already? I think everyone who lives here has been out to either look at us or tell me what a wonderful thing I did by stopping the construction. And I think it's a widely known fact that it's my child you're carrying. What else could they possibly talk about beyond that?"

"Okay, you have a point," she said wryly.

He leaned down and kissed her softly. "Why don't we take our jeans-clad selves back to your cottage and I'll fix us some lunch."

She raised her eyebrows. "What have you got in mind?"

"I don't know. It depends on what you have in your pantry. You cooked breakfast for us and you've taken me around town all morning. The least I can do is pamper you awhile. Are your feet tired?"

She laughed even as her heart squeezed at the concern in his voice.

"My feet are fine, but I wouldn't turn down a massage if you're offering."

He gave her a smile filled with genuine warmth. "I think that could be arranged."

She flung her arms around him and buried her face in his chest. "Oh, Rafael. Today has been perfect. Just perfect. Thank you."

When she pulled away, he had a befuddled expression on his face as if he didn't know quite how to respond to her outburst.

"I had no idea shopping for jeans made you so happy," he teased.

She flashed him a cheeky grin. "Only when I get to see you wear them."

He patted her affectionately on the behind and then gestured for her to go ahead of him. "Let's go then. All this shopping has worked up my appetite."

She laced her fingers with his, delighting in the sense of closeness that had quickly built between them. Whether he remembered or not, the moment they'd arrived, Bryony had sensed a change in Rafael. He'd reverted to the more relaxed, easygoing man with whom she'd fallen in love.

He may not see himself as someone who would get away from the stress of the business world, or someone who would leave his cell phone off or his computer put away for a period of days, but Moon Island had changed him. She'd like to think that his relationship with her had changed his priorities. Maybe it was fanciful and naive for her to think such things, but it didn't stop her from hoping that he'd rediscover the island—and her.

They drove back to the cottage but Bryony directed him to pull into her grandmother's driveway instead of her own.

"I want to check in with her and see how she's doing. I've only talked to her on the phone for the last week. I don't often leave her for long periods of time."

Rafael nodded. "Of course. Would you prefer I go ahead to your cottage and begin lunch?"

"Only if you want to. I don't mind if you come unless you're uncomfortable. I'm only going to talk to her a minute or two. Make sure everything's okay."

"Then I'll go with you," Rafael said. "I'd like to get reacquainted. You two seem to be very close. Did I spend a lot of time with her before?"

Bryony smiled. "You got along famously. You'd drop in on her every other day or so whether I was with you or not. You spoiled her by bringing her favorite flowers and a box of goodies from the bakery."

"I sounded…nice," he said, as though the idea were ridiculous.

She paused in the act of opening her car door and turned

her head so she looked directly at him. "You say that as if you aren't…nice."

He shrugged. "*Bastard* has been used on more than one occasion to describe me. This morning being the most recent. I've been called a lot of things. Ruthless. Driven. Ambitious. Son of a bitch. You name it. But nice? I can't say that being thoughtful was ever a priority. It's not that I intended to be a jerk, but I was never really concerned about it."

"Well, you were wonderful to my grandmother and I loved you for it," she said. "You were wonderful to me, too. Maybe you don't associate with the right people."

He laughed at that. "Maybe you're right. I guess we'll see, won't we?"

Bryony's grandmother appeared on the front porch and waved for them to come in. Bryony reached over and squeezed Rafael's hand. "Stop worrying so much about what you were or weren't. No one says you have to stay the same forever. Maybe you were ready for a change. Here you could be whoever you wanted because no one knew you before. You got to have a fresh start."

He raised her hand and pressed a kiss to her palm. "What I think is that you're a special woman, Bryony Morgan."

She smiled again and opened her car door. As she got out, she waved at her grandmother. "We're coming!"

Mamaw smiled and waved, then waited with the screen door open while Rafael and Bryony made their way up the steps.

"Good afternoon to you," Mamaw said cheerfully.

She pulled Bryony into a hug and then did the same with Rafael, who looked a little dumbstruck by the reception.

"Come in, come in, you two. I just sweetened a pitcher of tea and it's ready to pour. I'll get us some glasses. Have a seat on the back porch if you like. It's a beautiful day and the water is gorgeous."

Bryony tugged Rafael to the glass doors leading onto a

deck that was similar in build to her own. The wood was older and more worn but it added character. The railings were dotted with potted plants and flowers. Colorful knickknacks and decorative garden figurines were scattered here and there, giving the deck an eclectic feel.

Bryony often thought it resembled a rummage sale, but it so fit her grandmother's personality that it never failed to bring a smile to Bryony's face.

Mamaw didn't much believe in throwing things away. She wasn't a hoarder and she *would* part with stuff after a while, but she liked to collect items she said made her house more homey.

"It's beautiful out here," Rafael said. "It's so quiet and peaceful. There aren't many stretches of private beach like this. It must be amazing to have this all to yourself."

Bryony settled into one of the padded deck chairs and angled her head up to catch the full sun on her face. "It is," she said, her eyes closed. "The whole island is like this. It's why we're so resistant to the idea of commercially developing parts of it. Once the first bit of 'progress' creeps in, it's like a snowball. Soon the island would just be another tourist stop with cheesy T-shirts and cheap trinkets."

"What I purchased was just a drop in the bucket for an island this size. Surely you don't begrudge any development. You could have the best of both worlds. The majority of the island would remain unspoiled, a quiet oasis, while a very small section would be developed so that others could be exposed to your paradise."

She dropped her head back down, opening her eyes to look at him. "You sound just like a salesman. The truth is, the whole sharing-our-paradise-with-others spiel is precisely what we don't want to do. Call us selfish but there are numerous other islands that tourists can go to if they want sun and sand. We just want to be left alone. Many of the people who live here retired to this island precisely because it was private and unspoiled. Others have made their whole lives here and to change it now seems grossly unfair."

"Having one resort wouldn't ruin the integrity of the island and it would boost the economy and bring in an influx of cash from those tourists you all despise."

She smiled patiently, unwilling to become angry and frustrated and ruin a perfect day. Besides, biting his head off didn't serve her purpose.

"We don't need an influx of cash into our economy," she said gently.

He arched a disbelieving eyebrow. "Everyone can always use a boost in capital."

She shook her head. "No, the thing is, many of the people who retired here left high-paying corporate jobs. Hell, some of them were CEOs who sold their companies or left the management to their sons and daughters and came to Moon Island to escape their high-pressure jobs. They have more money than they'll ever spend."

"And the rest? The ones who've lived here all their lives?"

She shrugged. "They're happy. We have shrimpers who are third- and fourth-generation fishermen. We have local shop owners, restaurant workers, grocery store clerks. Basically everyone's job fulfills a need on the island. Selling souvenirs to tourists isn't a need. Neither is providing them entertainment. We have a comfortable living here. Some of us don't have much but we make it and we're happy."

"There is a certain weirdness to this whole place," Rafael said with an amused tone. "Like stepping into a time warp. I'm shocked that you have internet access, cable and cellular towers."

"We keep up," she said. "We just don't particularly care about getting ahead. There is a certain je ne sais quoi about our lifestyle, our people and our island. In a lot of ways it can't be described, only experienced. As you did for those weeks you were here."

"And yet you were going to walk away from your life here. For me."

She went still. "Yes, I've already said so. I mean I assumed I would have to make changes. You run a business. You have a home in New York. I could hardly expect you to give all that up and live here. I expected it to be an adjustment but I thought it—you—would be worth it."

"Given your passion for this island and the people here, I'm a little awed that you thought I was worth that kind of sacrifice."

"You sell yourself short, Rafael. Don't you think you're worth it? That someone could and should love you enough to give up important things to be with you?"

He averted his gaze, staring out over the water as if he had no answer. His body language had changed and he held himself stiffly. His jaw tightened and then he made an effort to relax.

"Maybe I've never met anyone who thought that much of me," he finally said.

"Again, you're associating with the wrong people. And you've definitely been dating the wrong women."

The mischievous tone in her voice wrung a smile out of him.

"Why do I get the feeling that I probably tried like hell to keep you at arm's length and you were having none of that?"

She frowned. "Not at all. You seemed…" Her expression grew more thoughtful. "You were definitely open to what happened between us. You certainly did your share of pursuing. Put it this way. I didn't have to try very hard to get past that stuffy exterior of yours."

He shook his head. "I'm beginning to think I have a double running around impersonating me. I know I keep saying this, but the man you describe is so far out of my realm of understanding that he seems a complete and utter stranger. If

I didn't know better, I'd say I suffered the head injury before I arrived here. Not after."

"Does it appall you that much?"

He jerked his gaze to her. "No, that's not what I'm saying at all. It's not that I'm shamed or angry. It's hard to explain. I mean think for a moment of things you would never do. Think of something so not in line with your personality. Then imagine someone telling you that you did all those things but you can't remember them. You'd think they'd lost their mind, not that you'd lost yours."

"Okay, I can understand that. So it's not that you can't accept the person you were."

"I just don't understand him," Rafael mused. "Or why."

"Maybe you took one look at me and decided you had to have me or die," she said impishly.

He leaned sideways until their mouths were hovering just a breath apart. "Now that I can understand because I find I feel that way around you with increasing frequency."

She closed the remaining distance between them and found his lips in a gentle kiss. He kissed the bow of her mouth and then each corner in a playful, teasing manner, and every time she felt a thrill down to her toes.

"I have tea, but I can see you're not that interested," Mamaw said with a laugh.

Bryony pulled back and turned to see her grandmother standing outside the glass doors holding two tea glasses. "Of course I want your tea. It's the best in the south."

"Do I like it?" Rafael asked, a hint of a smile on his face.

Mamaw walked over and handed him a glass. "You sure do, young man. Said it was better than any of that fancy wine you drink in the city."

He gave her a smile that would have made most women melt on the spot. "Well, then if I said it I must have meant it." He took the glass and took a cautious sip.

Bryony took her own glass and sent Rafael an amused

look. "It isn't spiked. I promise. You're looking at it like you expect it to be poisoned."

He took another sip. "It's good."

Mamaw beamed at him as if it were the first time she'd heard the compliment.

"Have a seat, Mamaw. We came to see you, not to be alone."

Her grandmother pulled up a chair and sat across from Bryony and Rafael. "Bryony tells me you were in a plane crash. That must have been traumatic for you."

Rafael nodded. "I don't remember much about the crash. I do have a few memories. Mostly of the aftermath and feeling relief that I was alive. But the rest is a blur. Including the weeks before the crash as I'm sure Bryony has told you."

Mamaw nodded. "It's a shame. Bryony was so upset. She was sure you'd pulled a fast one on her and left her alone and pregnant."

Heat crept up Bryony's neck. "Mamaw, don't."

"No, it's fine," Rafael said to Bryony. "I'm sure she has anger toward me just like you did. There's no need for her to pretend differently."

Mamaw nodded. "I like a man who's honest and straight-forward. Now that you're back and are trying to work things out with my granddaughter, I think we'll get along just fine."

He smiled. "I hope so, Ms.…." He stopped in midsentence and looked to Bryony for help. "What do I call her? I don't remember you telling me her name."

Bryony laughed. "That's because to everyone she's just Mamaw."

Mamaw reached forward and patted Rafael's leg. "There now, if that makes you uncomfortable, you can call me Laura. Hardly anyone does. Just the mayor because he thinks it's unseemly for a man of his position to be so familiar with one of his constituents. His malarkey, not mine. He's a bit of an odd duck, but he's a decent enough mayor."

"Laura. It suits you. Pretty name for an equally pretty lady."

To Bryony's amusement, her grandmother's cheeks bloomed with color and for once she didn't have a ready comeback. She just beamed at Rafael like he'd hung the moon.

"Are things okay with you, Mamaw?" Bryony asked. "How have you been feeling and do you need us to get you anything while we're out?"

"Oh, no, child, I'm good. Silas came by while you were gone and took my grocery list to his nephew. He's got a job delivering groceries now. Just got his driver's license and he's excited to get to be driving everywhere. I keep expecting to hear of him getting into an accident with the way he zips around these roads but so far nothing's happened and not one of my eggs was broken, so I guess he's got it under control."

"You're taking your medicine every day like you're supposed to?"

Mamaw rolled her eyes and then looked toward Rafael. "One would think she was the grandmother and I was the ditzy young granddaughter. Mind you, it wasn't me who got herself pregnant. I know how to take *my* pills."

"Mamaw!"

She shrugged. "Well, it's true."

"Oh, God," Bryony groaned. "You're on fire today, aren't you. I should have just gone home."

Rafael chuckled and then broke into steady laughter. Bryony and her grandmother stared as he laughed so hard he was wiping at his eyes.

"You two are hilarious."

"Easy for you to say. She wasn't taking you to task for not using a condom," Bryony said sourly.

"It was next on my list," Mamaw said airily.

Rafael shook his head. "At least I can claim I have no memory of the event."

"It broke," Bryony said tightly.

"Now see, if you were taking your pills like you were supposed to, a broken condom wouldn't be an issue," Mamaw said.

Bryony stood and tugged at Rafael's arm. "Okay, I've had enough of let's embarrass the hell out of Bryony today. It's obvious Mamaw is feeling her usual sassy self, so let's go home. I'm starving."

Rafael laughed again and climbed out of his chair. He bent down to kiss Mamaw on the cheek. "It was a pleasure to reacquaint myself with you."

Fourteen

"Comfortable?" Rafael asked as he plumped a pillow behind Bryony's back.

Bryony reclined on the wicker patio lounger. She smiled up at Rafael and sighed. It was an absolutely beautiful day as only a fall day could be on the island. Still quite warm but without the oppressive heat and humidity of summer. The skies were brilliant blue, unmarred by a single cloud, and the salt-scented air danced on her nose as the soft music of the distant waves hummed in her ears.

"You're spoiling me," she said. "But by all means keep on. I'm not opposed in the least."

He sat at the opposite end of the lounger and pulled her feet into his lap. He toyed with the ankle bracelet and then traced a finger over the arch of her foot.

"You have beautiful feet."

She shot him a skeptical look. "You think my feet are beautiful?"

"Well, yes, and you draw attention to them and your ankles

with this piece of jewelry. I like it. You have great legs, too. A complete package."

"I don't think I've ever had my feet propped on a gorgeous guy's lap while he does an analysis of my legs and ankles before. It makes me feel all queenly."

He began to press his thumb into her arch with just enough force to make her moan.

"Isn't that how a man should make the mother of his child feel? Like a queen?"

"Oh, God, you're killing me. Sure, in theory, but how many guys really do? Of course, I've never been pregnant before so how would I know?"

He laughed. "I think you're supposed to pick up on the fact that I'm embracing this child as our child. Our creation. Together. I know it seems I've ignored his or her presence. We haven't discussed your pregnancy much, but I've thought of little else since I found out. It's kept me up at night. I lay there thinking how ill-prepared I am to be a father and yet I have this eager anticipation that eats at me. I start to wonder who the baby will look like. Whether it will be a son or a daughter."

Tears crowded her eyes and she felt like an idiot. But there was no doubt the longing in his voice hit her right in the heart and softened it into mush.

"Why do you think you're ill-prepared to be a father?" she asked softly.

He closed both hands around her foot and rubbed his thumbs up and down the bottom, pressing and massaging the sole, then moving up to her arch and on to the pads below her toes.

"I work to the exclusion of all else. I never go anywhere that I don't bring work with me. Most of my social events are work-related. There are times I sleep at my office. Just as many times I sleep on a plane en route to a meeting or to scope out a location for a new development. A child needs the attention of his parent. He needs their love and support. All I can really do is provide financially."

"I said this once already but you don't have to stay the same person just because that's who you've always been. Parents make changes for their children all the time. I'm not any more prepared for parenthood than you are. I always imagined I'd wait until I was older."

He arched a brow. "Just how old are you? You make it sound like you're some teenager."

She laughed. "I'm twenty-five. Plenty old to have children but since until a few months ago I haven't had a serious relationship, and by serious I mean thinking of marriage and commitment, et cetera. I knew that having children was still some years away."

"It would seem we're both going to be handed parenthood before we thought we were ready."

"But would we really ever say we were ready? I mean who just announces one day, 'Okay, I'm ready for children'? I think even people who plan their pregnancies still have to be a little unprepared for the changes that occur with the arrival of a child."

"You're probably right. I think you'd make a great mother, though."

She cocked her head, flushed with pleasure at the compliment. "That means a lot that you'd say that, Rafael, but what makes you think so? I haven't exactly shown a lot of responsibility to this point."

"You are a loving and affectionate woman. Warm, spontaneous. Loyal and generous. And you're direct. You had no qualms about taking me on when you thought I'd wronged you. I can only imagine how fierce you would be in protection of our child."

"Do you know why I think you'd make a great father?"

His hands stilled on her foot and he glanced up at her.

"Because you admit your shortcomings," she said gently.

"You know your faults. You acknowledge them. You're well aware of the areas where you'd need to change. Most people aren't that self-aware. I have no doubt that you'd be sensitive to your child's needs and make adjustments. There's nothing you can say to convince me that you wouldn't absolutely put your child first in your priorities."

He slid one hand up her leg to snag her fingers and then he squeezed. "Thank you for that."

"I still love you, Rafael."

The words slipped out. They were an ache in her heart that she had to let loose. Here in this moment, it was more than she could take, even though she'd sworn she wouldn't make herself vulnerable again until they had resolved his memory loss and their relationship. She simply had to tell him how she felt.

His eyes darkened. His hands were no longer gentle as he roughly pulled her up and toward him. She sprawled indelicately across his lap as he framed her face in his grasp. For a long moment, he stroked her cheek as he stared into her eyes.

Then he leaned his forehead against hers in a surprisingly tender gesture as he gathered her hand in his, trapped it between their chests.

"I had no idea how I'd feel when I asked you if you still love me yesterday. It was an idle curiosity. I had no idea the impact those words would make. I can't even explain it. How can I?"

"I had to tell you," she whispered. "I've been honest. I don't want to hold anything back. It's hard for me. I'm unused to being reserved. You deserve to know the truth. You're here. You're making the effort. The least I can do is meet you halfway. It was my pride that held me back before. I didn't want to humble myself or make myself vulnerable to you again, but holding back the words doesn't change anything."

He lowered his head and kissed her, forgoing his earlier

gentle and playful smooches. His lips moved heatedly over hers, dragging breath from her then returning it, demanding it.

He tasted of the lemonade he'd served with the lunch he'd prepared. Tart and sweet and so hot. He licked over the seam of her mouth then plunged inward again as if determined to taste every part of her.

Always before, his lovemaking had seemed practiced and deliberate. Smooth and seductive. Now there was a desperation to his every caress and kiss, like he couldn't wait to touch her or to have her. Even as the differences plagued her, she gave herself over to this seemingly new man. It felt different. He was different.

"I want to make love to you, Bryony, but I want it to be for the right reasons. I want you to know I want you for the right reasons. Right now I couldn't care less about the past or what I do or don't remember. What I know is that right here, right now, I want to touch you and kiss you more than I want anything else."

As gracefully as she could manage when her legs and hands were shaking, she got off his lap to stand before him. Then she reached down for his hand and slid her fingers through his.

"I want you, too," she said simply. "I've missed you so much, Rafe."

He rose unsteadily, his eyes dark and vibrant with desire. His usually calm composure seemed shaken and he raised a trembling hand to her cheek.

"Be sure of this, Bryony. Whatever happens today, whatever has happened in the past, what I remember or don't remember—it's not going to matter if you give yourself to me again. Now. If we do this now, we're starting over. New page. Fresh beginning."

She rubbed her cheek over his hand and closed her eyes. "I'd like that. No past. Just today. Here and now. You and me."

He wrapped an arm around her and urged her toward the door. They stumbled inside the cottage and she guided him toward her bedroom. Past the guest room where he'd slept the night before. Back to the place where they'd spent so many hours making love in the past.

He closed the door and she stood in front of him, suddenly shy and unsure. Though she'd made love with him countless times before, it seemed new. He seemed different. Maybe she herself was even different.

And then she laughed.

Her laughter startled him. He looked up and cocked his head to the side. "What's so funny?"

She closed her eyes and shook her head ruefully. "I was standing here thinking that this felt like the first time and I'm so terribly nervous but then I thought how ridiculous that was when I'm pregnant with your child, a testament to the fact that it's far from the first time for us."

His expression softened and he pulled her gently into his arms. "In a lot of ways this is our first time. I think we should treat it as such. I know I plan to reacquaint myself with your body. I want to touch and see every part of you. There'll be no rushing. I want to savor every moment and draw it out until we're both crazy."

She swayed toward him, feeling light-headed, as if she were a little drunk. He caught her to him and carefully walked her back until she met with the edge of the bed.

Silently he began to unbutton her shirt, taking his time as he worked down her body. When he was done, he carefully parted the lapels and pushed back and over her shoulders so that the material fell away and she stood in her jeans and bra.

"Pretty and delicate," he said as he fingered the lace that cupped the swell of her breast. "A lot like you. It suits you. I like you in pink."

"You don't fancy a siren in red or black?" she asked with a grin.

"No. Not at all. I like the softness of pink and how feminine it looks on you. Very girly."

He lowered his head to kiss the bare expanse of skin that peeked above the cup and then nuzzled lower, pushing down the lace ever so slightly until he was just a breath from her taut nipple.

Then he drew away. "I like girly."

"You are a tease," she said in a strained voice.

He reached down to unbutton her pants, loosening them and then pulling them down just enough to bare the swell of her belly.

To her utter shock, he went to his knees and molded her stomach with both hands. He gently caressed the bump and then pressed a kiss to her flesh.

It was an exquisitely tender moment and an image she'd never forget as long as she lived. This proud, arrogant man on his knees in front of her, lavishing attention on their baby—and her.

She gazed down, lovingly running her fingers through his dark hair. He stared up at her and the look in his eyes made her catch her breath.

Then he tugged at her jeans and slowly rolled them over her hips and down her legs. When they pooled at her feet, he lifted one leg, his hands sliding up and down in a sensual caress. He tugged the material free and then lifted her other foot to completely remove the jeans.

"Matching lacy pink," he said just before pressing a kiss to the V of her underwear. "I like it. I like it a lot."

Her legs trembled and butterflies fluttered through her veins, around her chest and up into her throat.

She wasn't self-conscious about her pregnant body as many women were. In fact, she liked the newfound lushness of her curves. In a lot of ways she'd never looked better. Her skin glowed with a healthy sheen. Her breasts had grown larger and she was fascinated by the shape of her expanding abdomen.

She hadn't really considered being worried over Rafael's reaction to the changes in her body. If she had, she would have worried in vain because he seemed entranced. Nothing in his actions told her he found her anything but desirable.

"You're beautiful," he said in a raw voice, almost as if he'd been privy to her thoughts.

Slowly he rose, sliding his hands up her body as he straightened to stand in front of her. Then he tangled his fingers in her hair and fit his mouth to hers.

She struggled for air but wouldn't retreat long enough to take a breath. She took every bit as much as he did, demanding more in return.

There was something markedly different between them. Their lovemaking had always been casual. Fun, a little flirty and laid-back. The Rafael who stood before her now was… different. It was in the way he looked at her, so dark and forbidding, as if he were set to devour her. As if he wanted her more than he'd ever wanted another woman.

Fanciful but there was definitely nothing casual about the way he touched and kissed her.

She liked the new Rafael. He was commanding and yet gentle and loving. Reverent.

He cupped one hand around her nape, his fingers pressing possessively on her neck as he pulled her into another bone-melting kiss. Then he nibbled a path down her jaw to her ear and sucked the lobe into his mouth. Each tug sent pulsating waves of desire low into her pelvis. Her muscles clenched and she tensed as a whispery sigh floated from her lips.

His mouth never leaving the sensitive column of her throat, he slipped his arms underneath hers and hoisted her upward so he could lift her onto the bed. He lowered her then hovered over her, his denim-clad knee sliding between her thighs.

He kissed her again, then reached up to brush the hair from

her forehead, his touch so light and caressing that it sent a thrill coursing through her veins.

Once more he brushed his mouth across hers as if he hated to leave her even for the time it would take him to undress. But he stepped back and the fact that his hands shook as he pulled at his T-shirt endeared him to her all the more.

He stripped the shirt off, the muscles rippling across his chest and shoulders. He tossed it aside and then began undoing the fly of his jeans. She nearly moaned when he pulled both jeans and underwear down in one impatient shove.

The man was sexy. Cut like a flawless gem. Toned. Fit. Lean but not too lean. He had enough bulk that told of his workout regimen.

Her gaze drifted downward to his groin and she sighed her appreciation as his erection jutted upward. Impatient for him to return to her, she shifted and leaned up on her elbows so she could better see him.

But then he was crawling back onto the bed, straddling her body. He put the flat of his palm on her chest and gently pushed her down onto the mattress. Then he carefully slipped the straps of her bra off her shoulders, nudging until the cups released her breasts.

He lifted her just enough that he could fit one hand underneath to unhook her bra and then he pulled it away and tossed it onto the floor.

For a long moment he stared down at her, his gaze drifting up and down her body then focusing on her, their eyes catching and holding.

"I'm burning the image of you into my memory," he said in a husky voice. "I don't want to ever forget again. I can't imagine how I ever did to begin with. What man when presented with such beauty could possibly let such a memory of it escape?"

Her heart went all fluttery again. It was hard to breathe around him. When he wasn't sending shivers of delight over her flesh with his touch, he sent ripples of pleasure through her heart with his words.

"Kiss me," she begged softly.

"Just as soon as I've taken the last of your pink girly underwear off," he said with a smile.

His fingers danced down her sides and hooked into the lacy band of her panties and he tugged, moving backward as he pulled them down her legs.

This time he moved up the side of her and curled his arms around her, pulling her against him so her naked flesh met his. It was a shock. A delicious, decadent thrill. His hardness was cupped intimately in the V of her legs and her breasts pressed against the slightly hair-roughened surface of his chest.

As he kissed her, his hand roamed possessively down her back and over the swell of her buttocks and then around to cup her belly before drifting lower into the damp, sensitive flesh between her legs.

She moaned and arched forward as his fingers found her most sensitive points. His erection slid between her slightly parted legs, burning, rigid, branding her flesh.

She wanted him inside her, a part of her, after being so long without him. She stirred restlessly, clinging to him, spreading her legs wider to encourage him to take her.

He smiled against her mouth. "So impatient. I'm not nearly finished yet, little love. I want to make you crazy with pleasure before I make you mine again. So crazy that you'll scream my name when I slide into your warmth."

"I want you," she whispered. "So much, Rafe. I missed you. Missed holding you like this. Missed having you touch me."

He drew away and regarded her, his expression so serious that it touched something deep inside her. "I think somehow that I've missed you, too, Bryony. A part of me has. I don't think I could be so happy so quickly with you if we hadn't known each other before, if we hadn't been…close. Lovers.

You feel so perfect next to me. I feel like I've opened the door into someone else's life because this feels nothing like mine and yet I want it so badly I can taste it. I can feel it."

She reached up and tugged him down into a kiss, so moved by his words that her heart felt near to bursting.

"I don't want to wait. I need you now, Rafe. Please. Be inside me. Let me feel you."

He leaned over her body, pressing into her, his heat enveloping her. She savored the sensation of being mushed beneath him, of inhaling his scent so deeply that she could almost taste him.

"Are you sure you're ready, Bryony?"

Even as he spoke, he slid one finger inside her and rolled his thumb across her clitoris. She closed her eyes and gripped his arms until her fingers felt bloodless.

"Please," she whispered again.

He positioned himself and pushed the tiniest bit forward until he was barely inside.

"Open your eyes. Look at me, Bryony. Let me see you."

Her eyelids fluttered open and she met his gaze, so dark and sensual.

He slid forward again, just a bit, stroking her insides with fire. He seemed determined to draw out their reunion, to make it last.

She let her hands wander down his sides and she caressed up and down, encouraging him to complete the act.

He leaned down until their noses brushed and then he angled his mouth over hers just as he slid the rest of the way inside her welcoming body.

Tears burned her eyes. The knot in her throat was such that she couldn't speak. She didn't have words anyway to describe the sensation of being back with the man she loved after having thought she'd lost him.

He withdrew and thrust again, his mouth never leaving

hers. He breathed her. She breathed him. Their tongues tangled, stroked and coaxed.

He let his body descend on her and planted his forearms into the mattress so that she wasn't completely bearing his weight as his hips rocked against hers.

It was much like the ocean waves, rolling forward then receding. Gentle and yet building in intensity. He was patient, much more patient than he'd ever been.

"Tell me if I hurt you," he said against her mouth. "Or if I'm too heavy for you."

In answer she wrapped both arms around him and hugged him tight. She slid one hand down to cup his firm buttocks as he undulated his hips against her.

"Tell me what you need," he whispered. "Tell me how to please you, Bryony."

Her hands ran up his back to his shoulders and then one slid to his nape, her fingers thrusting upward into his hair.

"You're doing just fine," she said dreamily. "I feel like I'm floating."

He dropped his head to suck lightly at her neck and then he nibbled to the curve of her shoulder and sucked again, harder this time until she was sure he'd leave a mark.

She hadn't had such a mark since she was a teenager, but strangely it thrilled her that she would have a reminder of his possession.

He groaned. "I'm sorry, Bryony. I can't— Damn it." He issued several more muffled curses that ended in a long moan as he increased his pace.

As soon as the intensity changed, the orgasm that had begun as a lazy, slow build escalated into a sharp coiling burn low in her abdomen. It rose and spread until she gasped at the tension.

She dug her fingers into his back, not knowing how else to handle the mounting pressure. She arched her buttocks off the bed, pushing him deeper inside her. He tensed and shuddered against her, reaching fulfillment while she was still reaching blindly for her own.

He pulled from her body, rolled to the side and slid his hand between her legs, caressing and stroking her taut flesh. He lowered his head to her breast and sucked her nipple into his mouth, laving it with his tongue as he pressed another finger inside.

His thumb rolled over her clitoris, his fingers worked deep and his mouth tugged relentlessly at her breast. Her surroundings blurred and the coiling tension suddenly snapped, unraveling at super speed.

"Rafael!"

Her back came off the mattress and her hand went to his hair, gripping, her fingers curling into his nape as she went rigid underneath him.

Her release was sharp. It was sweet. It was intense. It was one of the most shattering experiences of her life. She was left clinging to him, saying his name over and over incoherently as she came down.

He continued to stroke her, more gently than before, sweetly and comfortingly as she settled beneath him, her body quivering and shaking like she'd experienced a great shock.

Her mind couldn't quite put it all together yet. All she knew was that it had never been this way between them before. She was…shattered. There was no other way to put it. And completely and utterly vulnerable before him. Bare. Stripped.

He gathered her close, holding her tightly as they both fought for breath. His hands seemed to be everywhere. Caressing. Touching. Soothing. He kissed her hair, her temple, her cheek and even her eyelids.

The one thing that seemed to penetrate the haze that surrounded her was that however undone she was, he'd been equally affected.

She wrapped herself around him as tightly as he was

wound around her, snuggled her face into the hollow of his neck and drifted into a fuzzy sleep, so sated that she couldn't have moved if she wanted to.

Fifteen

Bryony woke to warm kisses along her shoulder and hands possessively stroking her body.

"Mmm," she murmured as she lazily stretched.

"Oh, good, you're awake. I'd hate to think I was taking advantage of a sleeping woman."

She laughed. "Oh, I bet."

"I have a lot to make up for," he said.

He slid his mouth down the midline of her chest and then over the swell of one breast.

"You do?"

He traced the puckered crest of her nipple with his tongue and then sucked gently. He let go and looked up to meet her gaze. In the soft glow of her bedside lamp, she could see regret simmering in his eyes.

"Evidently I have no control when it comes to you. I wanted to make it good for you. I wanted it to last. I didn't take care of you very well. I guess it goes along with my selfish-bastard ways."

She rolled her eyes and lifted her palm to caress the side of his face. "If I had been any more satisfied I think I would have died. I like that I drove you a little wild."

He arched one eyebrow. "A little? I'm not sure that accurately describes the mind-numbing experience I had. I don't ever remember losing it like that with any other woman. Was it like that between us before?"

"No," she said softly. "Not like that."

"Better?"

"Definitely better."

"Ah, good then. I was starting to feel threatened by the self I couldn't remember."

She laughed and then so did he. It felt good for once to joke about an event that had altered the courses of both their lives.

"I'm hungry."

He lowered his mouth to her breast again. "So am I."

Laughing, she smacked his shoulder. "For food! It's been… What time is it anyway?"

He shrugged underneath her palm that had stilled on his shoulder. "Sometime in the wee hours of the morning. We slept a long time. You wore me out."

"Let's eat in bed and then…"

He arched an eyebrow as he stared lazily back up at her. "Then what?"

She smiled wickedly. "Then I'm going to have dessert."

"In that case—" he scrambled up, covers flying "—you stay here. I'll get us something to eat and be back in a minute."

She pulled the covers to her chin and snuggled into the pillows, smiling as he strode naked out of the bedroom. He didn't look at all abashed by his nudity. Confidence in a man was so sexy. She sighed and stretched, a dreamy smile spreading across her face.

Fifteen minutes later, Rafael returned with a tray holding

two saucers. Piled on each was two grilled-cheese sandwiches. There were two glasses of leftover lemonade from lunch.

She sat up as he placed the tray over her lap and her mouth watered at the smell of the buttery grilled bread and melted cheese.

"Oh, this is perfect."

"Glad you approve. It was all I could think of that would be done this quickly," Rafael said as he climbed onto the bed. He sat cross-legged in front of her and reached for one of the sandwiches.

They ate, stealing glances, their gazes meeting and then ducking away. She was mesmerized by this unguarded side of Rafael. If possible she was more in love now—after only a few days—than she'd been before. It seemed like he was freer with her now.

She left half of one of the sandwiches and drank the lemonade down then waited patiently for him to finish his own food.

When he would have gotten up to remove the tray, she leaned forward and wrapped her hands around his wrists, holding him motionless. Then she shoved the tray off the bed. It landed with a clatter, the saucers and glasses rolling this way and that.

She kissed him. Not a sweet, nice-girl kiss. She gave him the naughty version that said *I'm about to have my wicked way with you*.

"Oh, hell," he groaned.

"Oh, yes," she purred just before she gave him a shove.

He fell back, sprawled on the bed, his eyes glowing with fierce excitement as she threw one leg over his knees and straddled him.

She reached down and wrapped her fingers around his straining erection and smiled. "I think it's time for dessert."

"Oh, damn…"

She lowered her mouth and ran her tongue around the tip

of his penis. His breath hissed out, the sound explosive in the silence. His fingers tangled in her hair and he arched his hips.

"Bryony," he whispered.

She took him hard, loving and licking every inch of him. She wanted to give him as much pleasure as he'd given her. She wanted to show him her love—her heart.

She settled between his legs, her hair drifting down over his hips. His fingers gentled against her scalp and stroked lovingly as she continued making love to him.

He made low sounds of appreciation and of pleasure and he began thrusting upward, seeking more of her mouth. Finally it seemed to be too much for him to bear.

He grasped her shoulders and hauled her up his body until she straddled him.

She scooted up until his erection was against her belly and she carefully wrappped her fingers around his length. Instinctively she glanced back up, seeking direction. He held out his hands for her to grab and when she did, he pulled her toward him.

"Take me," he whispered. "I made you mine again. Now make me yours."

Oh, how seductive his husky words were. Prickles of anticipation licked over her skin like flames to dry wood. She rose up, using his hands to brace herself with. Their fingers slid together, twining, symbolic of their joining. She arched over him and he let one of her hands go long enough to position himself at her opening.

As soon as she began the delicious slide downward, he laced their fingers back again and she began the delicate mating dance of a woman reclaiming her man.

Before she'd never felt bold enough to take the initiative in their lovemaking. Rafael had always been the one to take control, had always seen to her pleasure before his own. And yet she preferred this man who wanted her so badly that he found his release before her, who was so lost in passion that he couldn't control his response. This man seemed more… real.

Now she delighted in teasing him, pleasuring him, taking control and driving him crazy with desire.

It was a heady, intoxicating feeling that only heightened as she watched him through half-lidded eyes.

He squeezed her hands and then took his away from hers. He caressed her hips then slid his palms up her sides to cup her breasts, toying and teasing her nipples as she undulated atop him.

His eyes glittering and his mouth tight, he lowered one hand, splayed it over her pelvis and dipped his thumb between their bodies to rub gently over her clitoris.

She flexed and spasmed around him and they both gasped. He stroked harder, finding a rhythm she responded to, and with his other hand, he caressed and plucked at her nipples, alternating until she was nearly mindless.

How quickly he'd turned the tables. Though she was on top, taking him in and out of her body at her leisure, his hands worked magic, finding all her sweet spots.

"Come for me, Bryony," he said. "I want to feel your heat around me as you come apart."

Her head fell back. Her entire body trembled. Her knees shook where they dug into the mattress. Beautiful, intense, vicious tension coiled low in her belly, spread to the spots he so expertly stroked and then it gathered and burst in all directions.

The force of her orgasm was staggering. She fell forward, but he was there to catch her. She braced her hands on his chest, not wanting to leave him, not wanting to stop until he found his own release, but she couldn't be still.

She writhed uncontrollably. All the while he held her and stroked his hands over her body as he whispered her name over and over in her ear.

She heard a sob, an exclamation of pleasure and knew it was herself, but it sounded so distant that it seemed impossible it could have come from her.

When her strength sagged from her, he simply held her hips and took over, thrusting upward into her still quivering body until he went tense underneath her.

Then he wrapped his arms around her, pulling her down until there was no space separating them. He thrust one last time and then they both went limp on the bed.

She was sprawled atop him. She probably resembled a dishrag, but she couldn't muster the energy to care.

He rubbed his hand up and down her back, down over her buttocks and then back up to tangle in her hair. He kissed her forehead and then ran his fingers through her hair again.

"That was incredible."

"Mmm-hmm," she agreed.

He stroked her arm in a lazy pattern. "What happened here, Bryony? It sure as hell wasn't just sex. I've had just sex before. This doesn't qualify."

"No," she said in a low voice. "It wasn't just sex."

"Then what was it?"

She raised her head and stared down into his eyes. "It was making love, Rafael. I love you. You loved me. I'd like to think that didn't just go away. Some things the heart knows even if the mind hasn't accepted it or has blocked it out."

"It scares the hell out of me that something this huge could be forgotten. I haven't loved anyone before."

"Never?"

He shook his head. "I'm sure I loved my parents in the beginning. I don't hate them now. I just don't think about them, the same way they don't think about me. I was an inconvenience. They were merely the people who gave me my DNA. It sounds cold, but it is what it is. I'm not saying that because I'm harboring some horrible psychological defect because my mommy doesn't love me. I'm merely saying that

I've never deeply loved anyone and now that I supposedly have, I forgot it? It and nothing else?"

"Maybe finally falling in love was so traumatic for you that you blocked it out," she teased.

"I can't believe you can joke about this," he grumbled.

"Well, it's either laugh or cry and crying gives me a headache. Besides, you'll remember. I think you're already starting to. A lot of things are instinctive to you. You don't treat me like a stranger even though for all practical purposes I am. If you really thought I was unknown to you would you be in my bed sharing your deep, dark secrets?"

"Probably not," he admitted.

She leaned down to kiss him and then rested her head on his shoulder again. "One day at a time, Rafe. It's all we can do and hope that each day brings us closer to the time you remember us."

He tightened his arm around her and kissed her forehead. "I'm not sure I deserve your sweetness or your patience, but I'm damn grateful for both."

Sixteen

When his BlackBerry rang first thing the next morning, Rafael knew by the ring tone who it was and he ignored it. Devon had called Cam in. Cam was calling to curse and yell at him that he was a moron who was thinking with his dick.

Cam was predictable if nothing else.

When his phone immediately began to ring again, Rafael cursed and leaned down as far as he could without loosening his hold on Bryony. He managed to drag his pants closer and fish the BlackBerry out. He hit the ignore button first and then hit the power button second.

His business could run without him for a couple of days. He paid many people very good money to think on their feet and be able to handle any situation that arose. It was time to give them the freedom to do what he'd hired them to do.

Oddly, in the past such an idea would make the control freak in him break out in hives. Now, he reasoned that he parted with good money so that he could occasionally enjoy a break.

Maybe Bryony was right. He didn't have to be the person he'd always been. Furthermore, she was right in that he would make sacrifices for his son or daughter.

He didn't want to be an absentee father. He didn't want to be like his own father, who thought being a provider was his only obligation to his family.

There was a hell of a lot more to parenthood than providing all the material necessities. Rafael wanted to be there for all the school plays, the soccer games. He wanted to be the one to put money under his kid's pillow when he lost a tooth and pretend that it was the tooth fairy.

He wanted to be a father. The best father he could be.

He gazed down at Bryony, whose head was pillowed on his shoulder. The morning sun shone on her skin, giving it a translucent, angelic glow. She looked at peace. She looked content. She looked...loved.

Then his mind kicked in with a screaming *whoa*.

No way was he falling for this woman after only a few days.

But had it been just a few days? Or was he responding to the weeks they'd spent together before?

It could be she was right. On some level he remembered her, recognized her as the woman he'd chosen. But the woman he'd fallen in love with?

He'd always considered that love was like being struck by lightning. This odd sort of contentment didn't match with what he considered falling in love might feel like. He damn sure hadn't thought it could be so...easy.

Easy. Yeah. Love was complicated, wasn't it? No one managed to pull it off in a few days. It was the good sex talking.

But, no. Bryony had been right about one thing. It wasn't just sex. Calling it that cheapened it on some level. Reduced it to the level of flirtatious, sex-only relationships he'd had in the past. A quick romp in bed, send the woman on her way. Move on to the next.

Nothing about his past experiences came even close to the way he felt about Bryony or the way he felt about making love to her.

Last night had felt like something he'd been anticipating forever. A sense of homecoming that was so keen, it had nearly flattened him. He'd been ridiculously emotional, like he wanted to go around blurting out how he felt and crap. The mere idea should have humiliated the hell out of him, but it didn't.

Being forthright with Bryony just felt natural. She'd played it completely straight with him. He'd played it straight with her even when it had meant admitting or saying something that had hurt her.

It was weird being this honest and open with a woman— hell, with anyone. He trusted Ryan, Dev and Cam, but he never talked about intensely personal issues with them. Not that they wouldn't listen, but that wasn't the nature of their relationship.

His thoughts flickered back to the woman in his arms. Yeah, she did odd things to him. Made him want to do stuff, different stuff. Stuff that should have him running the other direction.

He sighed. This was a woman a man kept. Maybe he'd known that when he met her. Maybe it was true that a man just knew when he'd met the woman who would change everything for him.

Bryony was the marrying kind. Not the bed-'em-and-leave-'em-with-a-smile kind of woman. She had permanent written all over her sweet face.

She was…his. And hell if he was going to let her go. He didn't care if he ever remembered. He had enough pieces of the puzzle to know that she belonged with him. They had a lot to work out—what new couple didn't? They'd jumped ahead a few steps in the relationship with her being pregnant, but it wasn't anything they couldn't work out.

The more he settled the matter in his mind, the more convinced he became that this was right. She was right. Bryony. Their baby. Him. A family. He could have it all.

The resort.

He grimaced. It hung over him like a dark cloud. It was the one thing standing between him and Bryony. She swore he had promised her he wouldn't develop the land, which made absolutely no sense. Why buy it at all? He certainly didn't have need of a private expanse of beach for personal use.

A hell of a lot rode on this deal.

There had to be some way to convince her and the rest of the people on the island that one resort wouldn't change their way of life.

It was either that or he had to go back to his partners—and friends—and investors and pull the plug on the entire thing. He would lose a hell of a lot of money, but worse than that, he'd lose credibility, future backing and his standing in the business community.

All because of a promise he couldn't remember making.

Bryony stirred in his arms and his grip tightened possessively around her. Before she could open her eyes, he pulled her close and kissed her lingeringly.

She sighed as her eyelashes fluttered, then her warm brown eyes found his and she smiled. "That's a nice way to wake up."

"I was thinking the same thing," he murmured.

"What time is it?"

"Seven."

She yawned and snuggled closer to him. "Plenty of time."

"Plenty of time for what?"

"To do whatever we want or nothing at all."

He chuckled. "I like your attitude."

"Any idea what you'd like to do today?"

"Yeah, actually. I thought you could take me around the island. Private tour. Show me what makes it so special to everyone who lives here. I can't remember the last time I went to a beach just to see and enjoy the sights and sounds."

She leaned her head back and frowned. "You work entirely too hard. Maybe your accident was a blessing in disguise. If it causes you to slow down and reevaluate then it's a good thing."

"I wouldn't have put it that way exactly. I'm not sure nearly dying is the kind of wake-up call anyone wants," he said dryly.

She touched his cheek. "But would you be thinking the way you're thinking now if it hadn't happened?"

He sighed. "Maybe not. Maybe you're the reason for my reevaluation. Ever think of that?"

She smiled and leaned up to kiss him. "I'll take that explanation. I prefer it over thinking about you dying anyway."

"You and me both," he muttered.

"Tell you what. You hit the shower. I'll cook breakfast. Then I'll take my bath and we'll head out. The weather is supposed to be gorgeous all week. We can pack a picnic and eat out on the beach."

"I've got a better idea. How about we shower together then I'll help you cook breakfast. I cook a mean piece of bacon."

She laughed and he sucked in his breath at the love shining in her eyes as she stared up at him. No one had ever looked at him like that.

Then her expression grew serious as she stroked her palm over his unshaven jaw. "I love you, Rafe. I don't want to make you uncomfortable. I don't expect anything in return. But now that I've told you I can't not keep saying it. I look at you and it just bursts out."

He captured her hand and pulled it to his mouth, his heart thudding against the wall of his chest. "I like you saying it," he said hoarsely. "It means… It means everything to me right now."

She pulled away, joy lighting her eyes. Eyes he could drown in. Her eyes were so expressive. They reflected her mood so perfectly. Sad, angry, happy. You only had to look into her eyes to know exactly what she was thinking.

She crawled over him, giving him a good view and feel of her soft curves. It was all he could do not to haul her back and make love to her all over again.

When her feet hit the floor, she turned back and held out her hand. "How about that shower?"

He stared at her profile for a long moment, committing to memory just how she looked bathed in morning sunlight, her gently rounded abdomen, the swell of her breasts and the wild curls that spilled down her back.

This was his. His woman. His child.

"Do you have any idea how beautiful you are?"

She flushed, her face grew pink, but her eyes lit up until they were as bright as the sunlight pouring into her room.

"I do now."

He grinned at her cheeky response. "Let's go hit the shower."

Seventeen

"You've done a good thing, Mr. de Luca," Silas Taylor said as they stood on the patio of Laura's house.

Bryony's grandmother had invited everyone over for tea and lemonade and for some of her famous peanut butter cookies. And by everyone, she meant whomever happened to wander by.

Such a thing baffled Rafael, who was used to strict guest lists and checking invitations at the door. Laura didn't seem to mind. In fact, the more guests that meandered through, the more delighted she seemed to be.

There was no entertainment. Conversation drifted from one mundane topic to the next or people just stood around, enjoying the day and inquiring as to the health of yet another islander who was either family, friend or both.

"My investors probably wouldn't agree," Rafael said dryly as he turned his attention back to the sheriff.

Silas shrugged. "They'll find something else to invest in. Those kind always do. People are always looking for places to put their money and there are always people willing to take it. Seems to me it wouldn't be that hard to figure it out."

Rafael wanted to laugh. Or shake his head. Months of financial analysis, blueprints being drawn up, investors courted, endless planning on his and Ryan, Devon and Cam's parts all reduced to a few words so casually tossed out.

"That may be so, but I lose credibility and respect in the process," Rafael said evenly. "Next time I want their backing, they won't be so willing to give it."

"And what will you gain?" Silas asked as he looked in Bryony's direction. Bryony, who stood in a small group of people looking so damn beautiful that it made Rafael's teeth ache. "Seems to me you gain far more than you lose." With that, Silas slapped him on the shoulder.

"Something to think about, my boy."

Then he walked away, leaving Rafael to shake his head again. Boy. He wanted to laugh. Granted the sheriff was at least thirty years older than Rafael, but no one had called him a boy since he'd been a boy.

Time was running out. His BlackBerry was full of voice-mail notifications and missed calls, and his inbox was bursting. His week would soon be up, and Dev would come down with Ryan and Cam to kick Rafael's ass.

For the past several days, Rafael had willfully ignored everything but Bryony and their time together. They'd spent every waking moment walking the beach, cooking together, laughing together, talking of nothing and everything.

They made love, they ate, they made love some more. There was an urgency he couldn't explain, almost as if he wanted to cram a lifetime into as few days as possible because he feared it would all slip away from him.

Tomorrow decisions had to be made. He couldn't hold them off any longer. He still had no idea what he would do, but he couldn't—wouldn't—lose Bryony over a resort. Over money.

"Can I get you something, Rafael?"

Rafael turned to see Bryony's grandmother smiling at him. He smiled back and shook his head. "No, I'm okay. Don't let me keep you from your guests."

"Oh, they're fine. Besides, you're a guest, too. How are you liking your stay so far?"

Again Rafael's gaze found Bryony. This time she lifted her head as if sensing that he watched her and her face lit up with a gorgeous smile.

"I'm enjoying it very much. I'm only sorry I can't remember when I was here before."

Laura stared thoughtfully at him for a long moment and then put her hand on his shoulder. "Maybe it's better that you don't."

She patted him and after offering those cryptic words, she turned to talk to another group of people.

Rafael shoved his hands in his pockets and turned to stare out over the water. He hadn't ever been someone who practiced avoidance, but he knew that was precisely what he was doing. Here, it was as if he existed in a bubble. Nothing could intrude or interfere, but the outside world was still there, just waiting. The longer he put off the inevitable, the more he dreaded it.

"Rafael, is something wrong?"

Bryony's soft voice slid over him at the same time her hand slipped through his arm and she hugged herself up to his side.

He disentangled his arm from her grasp just long enough to wrap it around her waist and then pulled her in close again.

"No, just thinking."

"About?"

"What has to be done."

Instead of pressing him for answers as he thought she might, she said, "Why don't we take off, go for a long walk?

Mamaw won't mind. She's having fun being the center of attention. She won't even notice we've gone."

Unable to resist, he leaned down to kiss her brow. She was so in tune with his moods. It shouldn't have surprised him that she could read him so easily. He'd found that he could pick up on the nuances of her moods just as quickly. He anticipated her reactions much like she did his own.

It was something he imagined a couple doing after years of marriage.

When he drew away, she took his hand and tugged him toward the stone path leading through the garden and down the dune onto the sand.

Sand slid over his toes but he found he didn't mind as much as he had when he first started wearing these ridiculous flip-flops.

They ventured closer to the water that foamed over the sand. Soon the cool waves washed over their feet, and Bryony smiled her delight as they danced back to avoid a larger one from getting them too wet.

Soon Laura's and Bryony's cottages were distant points behind them as they approached the land that he'd purchased from her.

"My father used to bring me here," she said. "He used to tell me that there was nothing greater than owning a piece of heaven. I feel like I've let him down by selling it."

Rafael grimaced feeling even guiltier over his part in the whole thing. It didn't matter that if it hadn't been him it would have been someone else. She could no longer afford the taxes and if someone hadn't bought it, eventually the land would have been seized for taxes owed. Either way it would no longer belong to her.

But you have the power to give it back to her.

The thought crept through his mind, whispering to him. It was true. He owned the land. Not his company. Not his partners. He'd purchased the land outright. The building of the resort and development of the land was what he'd brought investors in for.

"I love you," she said as she squeezed his hand.

He looked curiously at her, startled by her sudden affection.

She smiled. "You just looked like you needed that today."

He stopped and pulled her into his arms, brushing a thick strand of her hair from her eyes as the wind blew off the water. "I did need that. I shouldn't be surprised that you always know just what to say." He took in a deep breath. "I love you, too, Bryony."

Her eyes went wide with shock and then filled with tears. Her body trembled against him. "You remember?" she whispered.

He shook his head. "No, but it doesn't matter. You said I loved you then. I know I love you now. Isn't now all that matters?"

Wordlessly she nodded.

"The whole story doesn't seem so crazy anymore," he admitted. "I couldn't accept that I fell in love with you in a matter of weeks and yet here I am in love with you after only a few days."

"Are you sure?"

He smiled but his heart clenched at the hope and fear in her eyes. She seemed so worried that he'd change his mind or that he wasn't really sure of himself or his feelings.

He tipped her chin up and leaned down to brush a kiss across her lips. "I've handled this whole thing so clumsily. I don't have any experience with telling a woman I love her. I imagine there were more romantic ways of doing it but I simply couldn't *not* say it any longer."

"Oh, Rafe," she said, her eyes bright with love and joy. "You've made me so happy today. I've been so afraid and unsure. I hate being uncertain more than anything else. The not knowing just eats at you until you're a nervous wreck."

"I'm sorry. I don't want you to worry. I love you."

She wrapped her arms around his neck and hugged him to her. "I love you, too."

He slowly pulled her arms away until he held her in front of him. She looked a little worried at the sudden seriousness of his expression and he tried to soften his features to reassure her. But he couldn't really offer her any reassurance. Not yet.

"I need to leave tomorrow," he said grimly.

Her expression went blank and her mouth opened but nothing came out. "Wh-why?" she finally stammered out.

"I need to go back and work things out with my partners and our investors. I've avoided it for as long as I can. I can't do so any longer. I wanted you to know how I felt before I leave. I don't want you to have any doubts that I'll come back this time."

Uncertainty flickered across her face and her eyes went dim. He could tell she didn't entirely trust him and he couldn't blame her. Not after what had happened last time.

"You could come with me," he said. He was grasping at straws, anything to allay her fears. "We wouldn't have to be gone long. A few days at most. I know you don't like to be away from…here."

She reached for him, her hands clutching at his arms as she looked up at him, her eyes so earnest. "I don't like to be away from *you,* Rafe. You. Not here. Or there. Or anywhere."

"Then come with me. I won't lie to you, Bryony. I don't know if I can fix this. All I can do is promise to try."

She let her hands slide down to grip his, so tight that her knuckles went white. "I believe in you."

He crushed her to him and buried his face in her hair. She made him want to be the man she was so convinced he already was.

"You'll come with me?"

"Yes, Rafe. I'll come with you."

She pulled away and he laced their fingers together, holding their hands between them.

"No matter what happens, Bryony, I love you and I want this to work out between us. I need for you to trust in that."

"I do trust you. You'll fix this, Rafe. I know you will."

He smiled then, feeling some of the anxiety lift away. He could breathe easier. The idea of expressing his feelings had given him a sense of uneasiness, but now that he'd done it, he realized it had been harder not to tell her what was in his heart even if his head still screamed that this was all wrong.

He'd spent a lifetime of listening to his head and being ultra-practical. Maybe it was time he threw a little caution to the wind and let his heart lead for once.

Eighteen

Bryony's phone rang in the middle of the night. She pried herself from Rafael's arms and reached blindly for the phone on her bedside table.

"Hello?"

"Bry, it's Silas. You need to come to the hospital. It's your grandmother."

Bryony scrambled up, shaking the fuzz of sleep from her eyes. "Mamaw? What happened?"

"She had one of her spells. Blood sugar dropped. She called me and I couldn't understand a word she was saying so I rushed over and took her to the hospital."

Dear Lord, and she and Rafael had slept through it all.

"Why didn't someone come over and tell me?" she demanded.

"There wasn't a need to alarm you if it turned out to be nothing. I still think it's nothing but the nurse insisted I contact you so you could come down and sign some paperwork. They just want the insurance stuff squared away. You know these damn hospitals. Always wanting their money," Silas grumbled.

"Of course, I'll be right there."

Bryony hung up to see Rafael sitting up in bed, a look of concern on his face.

"Is Laura all right?"

Bryony grimaced. "I don't know. She's a diabetic and she doesn't always take care of herself. Sometimes she doesn't always take her insulin and at other times she doesn't eat when she should. I never know if she's in insulin shock or on the verge of diabetic coma."

"I'll go with you," he said as he hurried from the bed.

Twenty minutes later, they strode into the small community hospital. Silas met them in the main hallway.

"How is she?" Bryony asked anxiously.

"Oh, you know your grandmother. She's as mad as a wet hen at having to stay overnight. She didn't even want to go to the hospital. I made her drink some orange juice at the house and she came right around but I thought she ought to be checked out anyway. She's not speaking to me as a result."

Bryony sighed. "Where is she now?"

"They moved her out of the emergency room to observation. They won't release her until they know for sure they have someone to watch over her for the next twenty-four hours."

"Take us to her," Bryony said.

As Silas predicted, Mamaw was in a fit of temper and ready to go home. The doctor was attempting to lecture her on the importance of not missing a meal and Mamaw's lips were stretched tight in irritation.

She brightened considerably when Bryony and Rafael walked through the door but glowered in Silas's direction.

Bryony went to the bed and kissed her grandmother's cheek. "Mamaw, you scared me."

Mamaw rolled her eyes. "I'm fine. Any fool can see that. I'm ready to go home. Now that you're here, they should let me go. They seem to think I need a babysitter for the next little while."

"Glad to see you're all right, Laura," Rafael said as he bent to kiss her cheek.

Mamaw smiled and patted Rafael's cheek. "Thank you, young man. Sorry to drag you and my granddaughter out of bed at this hour. Pregnant women need their rest, but no one but me seems to be concerned with that little tidbit."

"Is she okay to go home, Doctor?" Bryony asked, directing her attention to the physician standing to the side.

The doctor nodded. "She knows what she did wrong. I doubt it'll do any good to tell her not to do it again, but she's fine otherwise. You'll need to keep an eye on her for the next twenty-four hours and check her blood sugar every hour. Make sure she eats properly and takes her insulin as directed."

"Don't worry. I will," Bryony said firmly. "Can we take her home now or does she need to stay?"

"No, as long as she goes home with someone, she's free to leave as soon as we get her discharged. That'll take a few minutes so make yourself comfortable."

Mamaw shooed the doctor away with a scowl and then stared pointedly at Silas, who still stood by the door. With a sigh, Silas nodded in Bryony's direction and walked out.

Bryony shook her head in exasperation. "When are you going to stop being such a twit to him, Mamaw? He's crazy about you and you know darn well you're just as crazy about him."

"Maybe when he stops treating me like I'm incapable of taking care of myself," she grumbled.

Bryony threw up her hands. "Maybe he'll stop when you prove that you can. You know better than to skip meals, especially after taking your insulin."

Rafael picked up Mamaw's hand and gave her a smooth smile. "You cannot fault a man for wanting to ensure the safety of the woman he loves. It's a worry we never get over. We always want to protect her and see to her well-being."

Mamaw looked a little gob-smacked. "Yes, well, I suppose…" She cleared her throat and glanced at Bryony again. "I thought you two were leaving in the morning."

"Rafael will have to go without me," Bryony said brightly. "You come first, Mamaw. I'm not leaving you alone after promising the doctor I'd look after you."

Rafael slid his hand over Bryony's shoulder. "Of course, you should stay. Hopefully my business in the city won't take long and I'll be back to see my two favorite women again."

"You have a smooth tongue, young man," Mamaw said sharply. Then she smiled. "I like it. I like it a damn lot. If Silas were that smooth, I'd probably have already said yes to his marriage proposal."

Bryony's mouth popped open. "Mamaw! You never told me Silas has asked you to marry him. Why haven't you said yes?"

Mamaw smiled. "Because, child, at my age I'm entitled to a few privileges. Making my man stew a little is one of them. If I said yes too quickly he'd take for granted my affection for him. A man should never take his woman for granted. I aim to make sure he always knows how lucky he is to have me."

Rafael broke into laughter. "You are a very wise woman, Laura. But do me a favor. Let Silas off the hook soon. The poor guy is probably miserable."

"Oh, I will," Mamaw said airily. "At my age I can't afford to wait too long."

Bryony squeezed her grandmother's hand. "I'll stay over with you at your house. I know you don't like to be away from your home for very long."

Mamaw's expression became troubled. "I don't want to interfere in your plans. You two have had enough problems without me adding to them."

Rafael put a finger to his lips to shush her. "You're no burden, Laura. I'll be back before either of you know it and then Bryony and I can plan our future together."

Bryony's heart pounded a little harder. It was the first time he'd spoken of their future—as in a life—together. He'd told her he loved her. She believed him. But she'd been greatly unsure of where that put them. There were still a lot of obstacles to overcome.

The fact that he seemed committed to them being together long-term sent relief through her veins.

Just then a nurse walked in with discharge papers and began the task of taking Mamaw's IV out and discussing the doctor's orders with her.

A half an hour later, they had Mamaw bundled into the car and were on their way back to her cottage.

Once Bryony got her grandmother into bed, she walked back into the living room where Rafael waited. She went into his arms and savored the hug he gave her.

"Crazy night, huh?" he said.

She drew away. "Yeah. Sorry I won't be able to go with you. I don't think I should leave Mamaw even if she says she's fine."

"No, of course you shouldn't," he agreed. "I'll call you from New York and let you know how things are going. Hopefully I can be back in a few days. I have motivation to get this done."

She arched a brow. "Oh?"

He smiled. "Yeah, a certain pregnant lady will be waiting for me to return. I'd say that's pretty powerful incentive to get everything wrapped up so I can get my butt back on a plane."

"Yeah, well, Rafael? This time don't get into an accident. I'd really like not to have to wait months to see you again."

He tweaked her nose. "Smart-ass. If it's all the same, I have no desire to ever crash again. Once was enough. I know how lucky I am to be alive. I plan to stay that way for a long time to come."

She leaned into him and wrapped her arms around him. "Good. Because I have plans for you that are going to take a very, very long time to fulfill."

He gave her a questioning look. "Just how long are we talking about?"

"As long as you can keep up with me," she murmured.

"In that case, it's going to be a very long time indeed."

She kissed him and then reluctantly pulled away. "You should probably go back home so you can shower and get packed. It'll be light soon and you'll need to be down to catch the ferry. Rush-hour traffic going into Houston is a bitch and you're going to be hitting it at a bad time."

"You sure you're okay with me driving your car?"

She laughed. "The question should be whether it's going to hurt your pride to drive my MINI. I could always have Silas drive you to Galveston and you could get a car service to the airport."

He shook his head. "Your car is fine. Right now my only concern is that it gets me there so I can hurry up and return to you."

She rested her forehead on his chest. "I'll miss you, Rafe. I won't lie, the idea of you leaving panics me because I keep thinking of the last time I said goodbye to you thinking I'd see you again in a few days."

He cupped her face and tilted her head back so she looked up at him. "I'm coming back, Bryony. A plane crash and the loss of my memory didn't keep us apart last time."

"I love you."

He kissed her. "I love you, too. Now go get some rest. I'll call you when I land in New York."

Nineteen

"It's about damn time you got your ass up here," Cam said grimly as he got out of his car in passenger pickup at LaGuardia and strode around to help Rafael with his bags. "Devon's been in a snit ever since you left. Your delaying the groundbreaking just pissed him off even more. Copeland has got him over a barrel with this whole marrying-his-daughter thing. Ryan has been stewing over private investigator reports. I swear no one's head is where it should be right now. Except mine. It's obvious that any time a woman's involved disaster follows," he said sourly.

"Cam?" Rafe said mildly as he opened the door to the passenger side.

Cam yanked his gaze up and stopped before climbing into the driver's seat. "What?"

"Shut the hell up."

Cam got into the car grumbling about flaky friends and vowing all the while never to mix business and friendship again. Rafael rolled his eyes at his friend's consternation, considering that the four had always done business together.

"So what the hell is going on, Rafael? Dev says you've gotten cold feet."

"I don't have cold feet," Rafael growled. "I just think there has to be another way of making this deal go through that doesn't involve using the property on Moon Island."

Cam swore again. He went silent as traffic got snarled and he expertly weaved in and out, making Rafael white-knuckle his grip on the door handle.

Anyone riding with Cam deserved hazard pay. Not that he drove often. Cam almost always had a driver and it wasn't because he was too good to drive himself. Quite simply he was so busy that he utilized every moment of his time to conduct his business affairs and if he had a driver, he had that much more time to work.

Rafael figured Dev must have leaned on him pretty hard to get him to drive himself to the airport to pick up Rafael.

"So you still don't remember anything?" Cam asked when they'd cleared one particularly nasty snarl.

"No. Nothing."

"And yet you believe her? Have you even started the process for paternity testing yet?"

"It doesn't matter what happened before. I love her now," Rafael said quietly.

There was dead silence in the car. Only the sounds of traffic and car horns penetrated the thick silence inside the car.

"And the resort deal?" Cam finally asked.

"There has to be something we can work out. It's why I'm here. We have to fix this, Cam. My future depends on it."

"How nice of you to be so concerned about your future," Cam muttered. "Nothing about the rest of ours, though."

"Low blow, man," Rafael bit out. "If I didn't give a damn about you and Ryan and Dev, I wouldn't be here. I would have just called off the whole damn thing and told all the investors to go to hell."

Cam shook his head. "And you wonder why I've sworn off women."

"Planning to play for the other team?" Rafael asked for a grin.

Cam shot him the bird and glowered. "You know damn well what I mean. Women are good for sex. Anything more and a man might as well neuter himself and be done with it."

Rafael chuckled. "You know I look forward to the day that I get to shove those words down your throat. Even better, I can't wait to meet the woman who does it for you."

"Look, I just don't understand what's changed. Four months ago you were on top of the world. You got what you wanted. And now suddenly it's not what you want."

They pulled to a stop in front of Rafael's apartment building. Rafael turned to Cam. "Maybe what I want has changed. And how the hell would you know that I got what I wanted four months ago? I didn't see you until I woke up in a hospital bed after the plane crash."

Cam shook his head. "You called me the day before you left. You were all but crowing. Said you'd closed the land deal that day and that next were going to be on a plane back to New York. I asked if you'd had a good vacation since you'd been gone for four damn weeks. You told me that some things were worth the sacrifice."

Rafe went still. Suddenly it was hard to get air into his lungs. His chest squeezed painfully as pain thudded relentlessly in his head.

"Rafael? You okay, man?"

Still images flashed through his head like photos. The pieces of his lost memory shot out of a cannon. Random. Out of order. It all hurled at him at supersonic speed until he was dizzy and disoriented.

"Rafe, talk to me," Cam insisted.

Rafael managed to open the car door and stumble out onto the curb. He put a hand back toward Cam when his friend would have gotten out, too.

"I'm fine. Leave me. I'll call you later."

He hauled his luggage out of the trunk and then walked mechanically toward the entrance. His doorman swung open the glass doors and offered a cheerful greeting.

Like a zombie, Rafael got into the elevator, clumsily inserted his card and nearly fell when the elevator began its ascent.

Memories of the first time he saw Bryony. Making love— no, having sex with her. The day at the closing agent's office when Bryony had signed over her land and he'd given her the check. Of the day he'd told her goodbye.

It all came back so fast his head spun trying to catch up. He was going to be sick.

The elevator doors opened and it took him a full minute to force himself inside his apartment. Leaving his luggage inside the doorway, he staggered toward one of the couches in the living room, so sick, so devastated that he wanted to die.

He slumped onto the sofa and lowered his head to his hands.

Oh, God, Bryony would never forgive him for this.

He couldn't forgive himself.

"Mamaw, would it really be so terrible if they built a resort here?" Bryony asked quietly as the two women sat on Mamaw's deck.

Mamaw glanced over at Bryony, her eyes soft with love. "You're taking on too much, Bryony. You have to decide what's best for you. It's not your responsibility to make the entire island happy. If this resort is coming between you and Rafael, you have to decide what is the most important to you. Is it making everyone here happy? Or is it being happy yourself?"

Bryony frowned. "Am I being unreasonable to hold him to a promise he made? It seemed so simple then, but apparently he has business partners—close friends of his—and investors counting on him. This is how he makes his living. And I'm asking him to give all that up because we're all afraid that our lives will change."

Mamaw nodded. "Well, that's something only you can answer. We've been lucky for a lot of years. We've been overlooked. Galveston gets all the tourists. We stay over here and no one ever comes calling. But we can't expect that to last forever. If Rafael doesn't build his resort, someone else will eventually. We'd probably be better off if Rafael builds it because he at least has met the people here and he knows where they're coming from. If some outsider comes in, he won't give a damn about you or me or anyone else here."

"I don't want everyone to hate me," Bryony said miserably.

"Everyone won't hate you," Mamaw said gently. "Rafael loves you. I love you. Who else do you want to love you?"

Suddenly she felt incredibly foolish. She closed her eyes and slapped her head to her forehead. "You know what? You're right, Mamaw. It's my land. Or it was. Only I should have the right to decide who I sell it to and what they do with it. If the other people here wanted things to remain the way it was so badly then they could have banded together to buy the land. It was okay when they didn't have to foot the tax bill. They were more than happy to tell me what I could or couldn't do with my own land."

Mamaw chuckled. "That's the spirit. Get angry. Tell them to piss off."

"Mamaw!"

Her grandmother laughed again at Bryony's horrified expression.

"You've tied yourself in knots for too long, honey. First

you were upset that he left. Then you were convinced he left you for good. Then you found out you were pregnant and you grieved for him all over again. Then he came back and you were happy. Don't give it up this time. This time you can do something about it."

Bryony leaned forward and hugged her grandmother. "I love you so much."

"I love you, too, my baby."

"Don't think I'm not going to turn these words back on you about Silas."

Her grandmother laughed and pulled away. "You leave Silas to me. He knows I'll come around sooner or later and he seems content to wait until I decide to quit making him miserable. I'm old. Don't begrudge me my fun."

"I don't want to be away from you. I want you to see your great-grandchild when he's born."

Mamaw sighed in exasperation. "You act like we'd never see each other anymore. Your Rafael is as rich as a man can get. If he can't afford to fly you to see me, then what good is he? You should ask for a jet as a wedding present. Then you can go where you want and when you want."

Bryony shook her head. "You're such a mess. But you're right. I'm just being difficult because I hate change."

Mamaw squeezed her hand. "Change is good for all of us. Never think it isn't. It's what keeps us young and vibrant. Change is exciting. It keeps life from getting stale and predictable."

"I suppose I should call Rafael and tell him to go ahead with the resort. It'll be such a load off him I'm sure."

"Better yet, why don't you get on a plane and go see him," Mamaw said gently. "Some things are better said in person."

"I can't leave you. I promised the doctor—"

"Oh, for heaven's sake. I'll be fine. I'll call Silas over to drive you to the airport. If it makes you feel any better, I'll have Gladys come over and stay with me until Silas comes back."

"Promise?"

"I promise," Mamaw said in exasperation. "Now get on the internet and figure out when the first available flight is to New York."

Twenty

Bryony got into the cab and read off the address to the driver. She was nervous. More nervous than she'd ever been in her life. How ridiculous was it that she had to get Rafael's address from the papers from the sale of the land. She hadn't known. It hadn't been covered in ordinary conversation.

She was truly flying solo because Rafael hadn't answered his cell phone or his apartment phone. A dreaded sense of déjà vu had taken hold but she forced herself not to descend into paranoia. He had every reason the first time not to answer her calls given that he was in the hospital recovering from serious injuries.

Still, old feelings of helplessness and abandonment were hard to get rid of and the more times she tried to call with no response, the more anxious she became.

The ride was long and streetlights blinked on in the deepening of dusk. The city took on a whole different look at night. It seemed so ordinary and horribly busy during the day. People everywhere. Cars everywhere. Not that there wasn't an abundance of both at night, but the twinkling lights on every building lit up the sky and gave the skyline a beautiful look.

When the cab pulled up in front of Rafael's building she got out, paid the fare and then stood staring at the entrance. She shivered. Of course she'd forgotten a coat. It still hadn't been ingrained in her that while it was warm where she lived, it was cold in other places. And she'd been in such a hurry to get to Rafael, she hadn't bothered with more than an overnight bag and a few necessities.

She started toward the door when a man brushed by her. She frowned. He looked familiar. Ryan? One of Rafael's friends. Ryan Beardsley. Maybe he could at least get her inside since Rafe wasn't answering his phone.

"Mr. Beardsley," she called as she hurried to catch him before he disappeared inside.

Ryan stopped and turned, a frown on his face. When he saw her, the frown disappeared but neither did he smile.

"I don't know if you remember me," she began.

"Of course I remember you," he said shortly. "What are you doing here? And for God's sake, why aren't you wearing a coat?"

"It was warm when I left Texas," she said ruefully. "I came to see Rafael. It's important. He hasn't been answering his phone. I need to see him. It's about the resort. I wanted to tell him it was okay. I don't care anymore. Maybe I never should have. But I don't want him to mess things up for you or his investors or his other friends."

Ryan looked at her like she was nuts. "You came here to tell him all that?"

She nodded. "Do you know if he's home? Have you heard from him? I know he's busy. Probably more so now than ever, but if I could just see him for a minute."

"I'll do you one better," Ryan muttered. "Come on. I'll

take you up to his apartment. Devon should already be here. We haven't heard from him since he arrived."

Bryony's eyes widened in alarm.

"Now don't go looking like that," Ryan soothed. "Cam dropped him off and he was fine. He's probably just busy trying to dig himself out of this mess he's gotten himself into."

He took Bryony's arm and tugged her toward the door.

"What the hell have you done to yourself?" Devon asked in disgust.

Rafael opened one eye and squinted, then made a shooing gesture with his hand. "Get the hell out of my apartment."

"You're shit-faced."

"I always said you were the smart one in this partnership."

"Mind telling me what prompted you to tie one on when you should be salvaging a business deal you seem determined to flush down the toilet?"

"I don't give a damn about the resort. Or you. Or anyone else. Get lost."

Rafael closed his eye again and reached for the bottle he'd left on the floor by the couch. Damn thing was empty. His mouth felt like he'd ingested a bag of cotton balls and his head ached like a son of a bitch.

Suddenly he was jerked off the couch, hauled across the floor and slammed into one of the armchairs. He opened his eyes again to see Devon's snarling face just inches from his own.

"You're going to tell me what the hell is going on here," Devon demanded. "Cam said everything was fine when he picked you up. Then suddenly you go radio silent and I come up here to check on your ass and you're so liquored up you can't see straight."

Pain splintered Rafael's chest, and worse, shame crowded

in from every direction. He'd never been so ashamed in his life.

"I'm a bastard," he said hoarsely.

Devon snorted. "Yeah, well, what else is new? It never bothered you before."

Rafael lunged to his feet, gathered Devon's shirt in his fists and got into Devon's face. "Maybe it bothers me *now*. Damn it, Devon, I remember everything, okay? Every single detail and it makes me so sick I can't even think about it."

Devon's eyes narrowed but he made no move to remove Rafael's hands from his shirt. "What the hell are you talking about? What do you remember that's so bad?"

"I used her," Rafael said quietly. "I went down there with the sole intention of doing whatever it took to get the land. And I did. God, I did. I seduced her. I told her I loved her. I promised her whatever she wanted to hear. All so I could make this deal happen. And it was all a lie. I left there with the intention of never going back. I had what I wanted. The sale was closed. The paperwork was filed. I had won."

A wounded cry from the doorway made Rafael jerk his head around. He went numb from head to toe when he saw Bryony standing there, white as a sheet, Ryan right beside her, supporting her with an arm when she'd stumbled back.

It was a nightmare. His worst nightmare come to life. What was she doing here? Why now?

He let go of Devon's shirt and started toward her. "Bryony." Her name spilled from his lips, a tortured sound that reflected all the shame and guilt that crowded his soul.

She took a hasty step back, shaking off Ryan's arm. She was so pale that he worried she'd fall right over.

"Bryony, please, just listen to me."

She shook her head, tears filling her beautiful eyes. It was a sight that staggered him.

"Please, just leave me alone," she begged softly. "Don't

say anything else. There isn't a need. I heard it all. Leave me with some of my pride at least."

She turned and fled into the elevator, the sound of her quiet sobs echoing through his apartment.

Rafael stood, feeling dead on the inside as he watched the elevator close. "Go after her," he croaked out to Ryan. "Please, for me. Make sure she's okay. She doesn't know anyone here in the city. I don't want anything to happen to her."

With a curse, Ryan turned and jammed his finger over the call button. Behind Rafael, Devon got on the phone and called down to the doorman with muttered instructions to stall Bryony until Ryan arrived.

"Why aren't you going after her yourself?" Devon asked after Ryan got into the returning elevator.

Rafael dropped back into the armchair and cupped his head between both hands. "What am I supposed to say to her? I lied to her. I played her. I used her. Everything she feared I had done, I absolutely did."

Devon sat on the edge of the couch and eyed his friend. "And now?"

"I love her. And knowing what I did to her, what I felt while I was doing it, sickens me. I'm so ashamed of the person I was that I can't even think about it without wanting to puke."

"No one says you have to be that person now," Devon said quietly.

Rafael closed his eyes and shook his head. "Do you know she's been telling me that all along? She kept saying that I didn't have to be the person I always was and that just because something has always been didn't mean it always had to be."

"Sounds like a smart woman."

"Oh, God, Devon, I messed this up. How could I have done what I did? How could I have done something like that to her? She's the most beautiful, loving and generous woman I've ever met. She's everything I've ever wanted. Her and our child. I want us to be a family. But how can she ever forgive me for this? How can I ever forgive myself?"

"I don't have the answers," Devon admitted. "But you won't find them here. You're going to have to fight for her if you love her and want her. If you give up, that just tells her that you are the man you used to be and that you haven't changed."

Rafael raised his head, his chest so heavy that it was a physical ache. "I can't let her go. I have no idea how I'm going to make her understand, but I can't let her go. No matter what I did then, no matter how big of a bastard I was then, that's not who I am now. I love her. I want another chance. God, if she'll just give me another chance, I'll never give her reason to doubt me again."

"You're convincing the wrong person," Devon said. "I'm on your side, man. Even if you are the biggest jackass in North America. And hey, whatever happens with this resort deal, I'm behind you one-hundred percent, okay? We'll figure something out. Now go get your girl."

Twenty-One

Bryony walked off the elevator in shock. Her limbs were numb. Her hands were like ice. She was on autopilot, her mind barely functioning.

Rafael's harsh words played over and over in her mind.

I used her.

I seduced her.

She flinched and wobbled toward the door, where the doorman stepped in front of her and put a hand on her arm. "Miss Morgan, if you would wait here, please."

She looked up at the man in confusion. "Why?"

"Just wait, please."

She shook her head and started to walk out the door only to have him take her arm and steer her back into the lobby again.

Anger was slowly replacing her numb shock. She yanked her arm away from the older man and retreated. "Don't touch me." She backed right into another person; she turned to excuse herself but found herself looking up at the mountain who worked as Rafael's head of security.

"Miss Morgan, I had no idea you were in the city." He frowned. "You should have let Mr. de Luca know so I could have met you at the airport. Did you come with no escort?"

The doorman looked relieved that Ramon was there and he hastily resumed his position by the door, leaving her to stand by the security man.

"I'm not staying," she said tightly. "In fact, I'm on my way back to the airport now."

Ramon looked puzzled, and then Ryan Beardsley was there, inserting himself between her and Ramon.

"That will be all, Ramon. I'll take Miss Morgan where she needs to go."

"The hell you will," Bryony muttered. She turned and stalked toward the door.

Ryan caught up to her as soon as she stepped outside. He took her arm, but his hold was gentle. So was the look on his face. The sympathy burning in his eyes made her want to cry.

"Let me give you a ride," he offered gently. "It's cold and you really shouldn't take a cab if you have no idea where you're going. You probably don't even have a hotel, am I right?"

She shook her head. "I was planning to stay with Rafael." She broke off as tears brimmed in her eyes.

"Come on," he said. "I'll take you to my place. It's not far. I have a spare bedroom."

"I want to go back to the airport," she said. "There's no point in staying here."

He hesitated and then cupped her elbow to lead her out of the building. "All right. I'll take you back to the airport. But I'm not leaving you until you get on a plane. You probably haven't even eaten anything, have you?"

She looked at him, utterly confused by how nice he was being to her.

"Why are you doing this?" she asked.

He stared at her for a long moment, brief pain flickering in his own eyes. "Because I know what it's like to have the rug completely pulled out from under you. I know what it's like to find out something about someone you cared about. I know what it's like to be lied to."

Her shoulders sagged and she wiped a shaking hand through her hair. "I'm just going to cry all over you."

His smile was brief but he turned her and motioned to a distant car. "You can cry all you want to. From what I heard, you're entitled."

"You can go now," Bryony said in a low voice, as Ryan hoisted her only bag onto the scale at the airline check-in desk.

"You've got a little time. Let's go get something to eat. You're pale and you're shaking still."

"I don't think I can." She placed her hand on her stomach and tried to will the queasiness away.

"Then a drink. Some juice. I'll make sure you get back to security in enough time to catch your flight."

She sighed her acceptance. It was much easier to just cede to Ryan's determination, though for the life of her she couldn't figure it out. In a few moments he had her seated at a little round table outside a tiny bistro, a tall glass of orange juice in front of her.

Her eyes watered as she stared sightlessly at it. Her fingers trembled as she touched the cool surface.

"Ah, hell, you aren't going to cry again, are you?"

She sucked in steadying breaths. "I'm sorry. You've been nothing but kind. You don't deserve to have me fall apart all over you."

"It's okay. I understand how you feel."

"Oh?" she asked in a shaky voice. "You said you knew what it felt like. Who screwed you over?"

"The woman I was supposed to marry."

She winced. "Ouch. Yeah, it sucks, doesn't it? At least Rafael never promised to marry me. He certainly hinted about it but he never went that far in his deception. So what happened?"

Ryan's mouth twisted and for a moment, Bryony thought he'd say nothing.

"She slept with my brother just weeks after we became engaged."

"That'll do it," she said wearily. "I'm sorry that happened to you. Sucks when people you put all your faith into gut you in return."

"That about sums up my feelings on the subject," Ryan said with an amused chuckle.

She drained the juice and set the glass back down on the table.

"Let me get you something to eat. Can you keep it down now?"

Ryan's concern was endearing and she offered a half-hearted smile. "Thanks. I don't feel hungry, but you're right. I should probably eat."

He got up and a few minutes later returned with a selection of deli sandwiches and another glass of orange juice. As soon as she took the first bite, she realized just how hungry she was.

Ryan studied her for a long moment, sympathy bright in his eyes. "What will you do now?"

She paused midchew and then continued before swallowing. She took a sip of the juice and then set the glass back down.

"Go home. Have a baby. Try to forget. Move on with my life. I have my grandmother and the people on the island. I'll be fine."

"I wonder if that's what Kelly did," he mused aloud. "Went on with her life."

"Is that her name? Kelly? Your ex-fiancée?"

He nodded.

"So she didn't hang around? With your brother I mean? I suppose that would be awkward at family get-togethers."

"No, she didn't hang around. I have no idea where she went."

"Probably just as well. If she was the kind of person who'd sleep with the brother of the man she's going to marry, she isn't worth your idle curiosity."

"Maybe," he said quietly.

Silence fell and Bryony picked at her food, getting down what she could. She kept hearing Rafael's damning words over and over in her head. No matter what she did, she couldn't turn it off, couldn't make it go away.

She was humiliated. She was angry. But more than anything, she was destroyed. Twice she'd allowed him to manipulate her and to make her love him. Worse, she'd fallen even deeper in love the second time around. She'd been ready to capitulate and give him what he'd wanted all along. What he didn't even *need* from her because he had no intention of ever honoring his promise to her.

She was twice a fool for believing him and for not being smart enough to get the agreement in writing.

She was an even bigger fool for loving him.

A tear slid down her cheek and she hastily wiped it away but to her dismay another fell in its place.

"I'm sorry, Bryony. You didn't deserve this," Ryan said quietly. "Rafael is my friend, but he went too far. I'm sorry you got caught in the middle of this deal."

She wiped away more tears and bowed her head. "I'm sorry, too. I wanted so much for it all to be real even when my head knew that something wasn't right. I should have never come to New York to confront him. I should have trusted my first instinct. He used me to get what he wanted. I knew that and I couldn't leave it alone. If I had just stayed home, I'd be over it by now and I would have never gotten involved with him a second time."

"Would you be over it?" Ryan asked gently.

"I don't know. Maybe… I definitely wouldn't be sitting here crying my eyes out, thousands of miles from home."

"True," Ryan conceded. He checked his watch and grimaced. "We should get you to security. Your flight leaves soon." His phone rang, and he looked down then frowned. He hesitated a moment and then punched a button to silence the ring. Then he looked back up. "You ready?"

She nodded. "Thank you, Ryan. Really. You didn't have to be this nice. I appreciate it."

Ryan smiled as he took her arm and they began the walk toward the security line. When they reached the end, she turned and blew out a deep breath. "Okay, well, this is it."

Ryan touched her cheek and then to her surprise pulled her into his arms for a tight hug.

"You take care of yourself and that baby," he said gruffly.

She pulled away and smiled up at him. "Thanks."

Squaring her shoulders, she eased into the security line. In a few hours she'd be back home.

Twenty-Two

Rafael dragged himself into the shower, washed the remnants of his alcohol binge from his fuzzy brain and proceeded to punish himself with fifteen minutes of ice-cold water. He'd been trying to call Ryan to find out where the hell Bryony was, but Ryan wasn't answering. He had to get his act together and prepare to plead his case to her. This was the most important deal of his life. Not the resort. Not the potential merger with Copeland Hotels. Not his partnership with his friends.

Bryony and their child were more important than any of that. He was furious that he could have been such a cold, calculating bastard with her before. But if she'd listen to him, if she'd just give him another chance, he'd prove to her that nothing in this world was more important to him than her.

By the time he got out, his mind was clear, he was freezing his ass off and he had only one clear purpose. Get Bryony back.

He dressed and strode into the living room, surprised to see Devon and Cam both sprawled in the armchairs.

"You two look like hell," he commented on his way to the kitchen.

Cam snorted. "You're one to talk, alcohol boy. When was the last time you went on a bender like that? Weren't we in college? Hasn't anyone told you we're too old for stuff like that now? It's a good way to poison yourself."

"Tell me something I don't know," Rafael muttered.

"So what's the plan?" Devon drawled.

"I've got to get her back," Rafael said. "Screw the deal. Screw the resort. This is my life. The woman I love. My child. I can't give them up over some ridiculous development deal."

"You're serious," Cam said.

"Of course I'm serious," Rafael snarled. "I'm not the same bastard who would do anything at all to close a deal. I don't *want* to be that man any longer. I don't know how you stood him for as long as you did."

Cam grinned. "Well, okay then. Don't get pissy about it."

"Have either of you heard from Ryan? I sent him after her, but the son of a bitch won't answer his phone."

Devon shook his head. "I'll try him. Maybe he's just not answering *your* calls."

Like that was supposed to make Rafael feel any better. But at this point, he didn't care how he had to get to Bryony. Just as long as he did.

Just as Devon put the phone to his ear, the elevator doors chimed and Rafael jerked around, holding his breath that by some miracle Bryony had come back. He let it all out when he saw Ryan stride in.

Rafael strode forward to meet him. "Where the hell is Bryony? I've been calling you for the last couple of hours. Where have you been?"

Ryan glared back. There was condemnation in his eyes. And anger. "I just spent the past couple of hours listening to Bryony cry because you broke her heart. I hope to hell you're happy now that you've destroyed the best thing that's ever happened to you."

"Whoa, back off," Devon said as he stood. "This isn't any of our business, Ryan. He's already beaten himself up enough without you piling on."

"Yeah, well, you didn't have to listen to her cry."

"Where is she?" Rafael demanded when he found his voice. The image of Bryony crying sent staggering pain through his chest. "I need to see her, Ryan. Where did you take her?"

"To the airport."

Rafael's heart dropped. "The airport? Has she already left? Do I have time to catch her?"

Ryan shook his head. "She's probably already in the air."

Rafael cursed. Then he turned and slammed his fist into the wall. He leaned his forehead against the cabinet and fought the rage that billowed inside him.

When he looked up, an odd sort of peace settled over him. He looked at his friends—his business partners—and knew that this could very well be the end of their relationship.

"I have to go after her," he said.

Devon nodded. "Yeah, you do."

"I'm canceling the deal. I'm pulling the plug. I don't give a damn how much it costs me or if it costs me *everything*. It already has. I'm going to give back that damn land. Bryony will never believe that I love her as long as it stands between us. I have to get rid of it and make it a nonissue."

Slowly Cam nodded. "I agree. It's the only way you're going to get her to believe that you love her now."

To his surprise, all three of his friends nodded their agreement.

"You're not pissed? We had a lot riding on this."

"How about you let us deal with the resort plans," Devon said. "You go after your woman. Settle down. Have babies. Be nauseatingly happy. I'm going to see what I can do to salvage the resort proposal. Maybe we can find another location."

"I'm not even going to ask," Rafael said. "Tell me about it later. I owe you. I owe you big."

"Yeah, well, don't think I won't collect. Later. After you've kissed and made up with Bryony," Devon said with a grin.

"Need a ride to the airport?" Ryan asked. "My driver's still outside. I told him I wouldn't be long."

"Yeah. Just let me get my wallet."

"Not going to pack a bag?" Cam asked.

"Hell, no. Bryony can buy me more jeans and flip-flops when I get down there."

"After she kicks your ass you mean?" Devon asked.

"I'll let her do whatever she wants just as long as she takes me back," Rafael said.

"Good God," Cam said in disgust. "Could you sound any more pathetic?"

Devon laughed and slapped Cam on the back. "Apparently that's what falling in love does to a guy. Take my advice. Marry for money and connections, like I am."

"I think the best idea is to never marry," Cam pointed out. "Less expensive that way. No costly divorces."

Rafael shook his head. "And you all called me the bastard. Come on, Ryan. I've got a plane to catch."

"Bryony!"

Bryony turned to see her grandmother waving to her from her deck. Silas stood beside her, watching as Bryony stood close to the water's edge.

She'd been there for a couple of hours, just watching the water, alone with her thoughts. She knew her grandmother and Silas were both worried. She'd given them an abbreviated version of everything that had happened. No sense in them knowing the extent of Bryony's stupidity.

They knew enough that Rafael had made a fool of her and would develop the land, but then Bryony had been prepared to give up that fight. So the outcome would be the same, only Bryony wouldn't have the man she loved.

Bryony waved but turned back to the water, not ready to deal with them yet. Mamaw and Silas had both fussed over her ever since she'd gotten back home. She was exhausted and what she really wanted was to go to sleep for about twenty-four hours, but every time she closed her eyes, she heard Rafael's words. They wouldn't go away, she couldn't make herself stop hearing them no matter how hard she tried.

And she was damn tired of crying. Her head ached so badly from all the tears she'd shed that it was ready to explode.

Her cell phone rang in her pocket and she picked it up, just as she'd done the other twenty times that Rafael had tried to call her. She hit the ignore button and a few seconds later, heard the ding signaling that she had a voice mail. One of the many he'd left her.

What else was there left for him to say? He was sorry? He hadn't meant to deceive her? Was she supposed to forgive him just because he forgot what a jerk he had been? How could she be sure he hadn't made it all up just to get her to shut up and not make noises that would scare off his precious investors?

If he kept her quiet enough for long enough then the deal would be sealed.

She didn't like how cynical she'd grown. It would never occur to her before that anyone would be so devious, but Rafael had taught her a lot about the world of business and the lengths that some people would go for money.

She hoped he made a ton off his precious resort and she hoped it kept him warm at night. She hoped it made up for all the sweet baby kisses he'd miss.

The thought depressed her. Money was just paper. But a child was something so very precious. Love was precious. And she'd offered it to Rafael freely and without reservation.

She felt like the worst sort of naive fool.

Finally her feet got cold enough from the surf that she

could no longer feel her toes, so she turned to trudge back up to her grandmother's deck. She'd say her goodbyes, assure Mamaw that she'd be just fine and then she'd go home and hopefully sleep for the next day.

As she got close, she saw Rafael standing on the deck and Mamaw and Silas were nowhere to be found. How the hell had he gotten down here so fast? Why would he even bother? She didn't react to his presence. She wouldn't give him the satisfaction.

She walked up the steps, past him to collect her sweater and then she started down the walkway that led to her own cottage.

"Bryony," he called after her. "Wait, please. We have to talk."

She picked up her pace. She knew he followed her because she could hear his footsteps behind her, but she blindly went on. When she reached to open her door, his hand closed around her wrist and gently pulled her away.

"Please listen to me," he begged softly. "I know I don't deserve anything from you. But please listen. I love you."

She went rigid and closed her eyes as pain crashed over her all over again. When she reopened them she was grateful that no tears spilled over her cheeks. Maybe she'd finally cried herself out.

"You don't know how to love," she said in a low voice. "You have to possess a heart and a soul, and you have neither."

He winced but didn't let go of her wrist. "I'm not going to lie to you, Bryony. Neither am I going to sugarcoat what I did."

"Well, good for you," she said bitterly. "Does that ease your conscience? Just leave me alone, Rafael. You got what you wanted. You don't have to deal with me anymore. Just make this easier on both of us. If you're wanting absolution, see a priest. I can't offer you any. You should be happy. You got the land. You'll build your resort. Everyone gets what they want."

"Not you," he said painfully. "And not me."

"Please, Rafael," she begged. "I'm tired. I'm worn completely out. I just want to sleep before I fall over. Please, just go. I can't do this with you right now."

He looked so much like he wanted to argue, but concern darkened his eyes and slowly he eased his fingers from her wrist.

"I love you, Bryony. That's not going to change. I don't want it to change. Go get some sleep. Take care of yourself. But this isn't finished. I'm not letting you go. You think I'm ruthless? You haven't seen anything yet."

He touched her cheek and then let it slide down her face before falling away. Then he turned and walked back down the path to her grandmother's house.

She closed her eyes as pain swelled in her chest and splintered in a thousand different directions. She wanted to scream. She wanted to cry. But all she could do was stand there numbly while the man she'd given everything to walked away.

Twenty-Three

"It's been a week," Rafael said in frustration. "A week and she still won't acknowledge me, much less talk to me. As much as I loathe the man I used to be, at least he would have no qualms about forcing the issue."

Rafael stood on Laura's back deck having a beer with Silas and brooded over the fact that Bryony still refused to see him. He was about to go crazy.

Silas chuckled. "You've got stamina, son. I have to give that to you. Most men would have tucked tail and left by now. I'm still amazed that you managed to talk Laura down from killing you and actually got her to side with you. I can't figure out if you're the dumbest man alive or just the luckiest."

Bryony had holed up in her cottage and while Laura went over daily to check in on her, Bryony hadn't ventured out except to walk on the beach. The one time Rafael had confronted her on the sand, she'd retreated inside. He hadn't bothered her since because he wanted her to have that time outside without worrying that she'd encounter him.

"I'm not leaving," Rafael said. "I don't care how long it takes. I love her. I believe she still loves me, but she's hurting. I can't even blame her for that. I was a complete and utter bastard. I don't deserve her but she's the one who kept telling me I didn't have to be the same man. Well, damn it, I'm choosing to be different. I want her to see that."

Silas put his hand on Rafael's shoulder. "Around here we have a saying. Go big or go home. I'm thinking you need to go big. Really big."

Rafael frowned and turned to the other man. "What did you have in mind?"

"It's not what I have in mind. It's what you ought to be thinking about. You've already promised me and Laura that you have no intention of developing that land, but does she know that? Does the rest of the island know that? Seems to me you're missing an opportunity to make a grand gesture and prove once and for all you're a changed man."

"Okay, I'm with you," Rafael said slowly.

"No, I don't think you are. Call a town meeting. I'll let it leak out that you have a big announcement about the resort. Folks will show up because they'll want to launch their objections and nothing gets people out to a town meeting more than getting to air their grievances. Trust me, after twenty years of being the sheriff here, I know what I'm talking about."

"That doesn't help me when Bryony refuses to leave her cottage," Rafael pointed out.

"Oh, Laura and I will make sure she's there. You just worry about how you're going to humble yourself before everyone," Silas said with a grin.

Rafael sighed. He had the feeling this wasn't going to be one of his better moments. He might have no desire to be the unfeeling bastard he'd been before but it didn't mean he wanted to air his personal life in front of a few hundred witnesses.

But if it would get him in front of Bryony so she'd be forced to listen, he'd swallow his pride and do it.

"Are you crazy?" Bryony sputtered out. "Why would I want to go listen to his spiel about his plans for the resort?"

"Now, Bry, I didn't imagine you for a coward," Silas said in exasperation. "By now everyone knows what happened. They don't blame you."

"I don't care what they think," Bryony said in a low voice. "I was prepared to be the brunt of their censure when I went to New York to tell Rafael to go ahead with the plans, that I wouldn't fight him."

"Then what's the problem?" Mamaw asked.

"I don't want to see him. Why can't either of you understand that? Do you have any idea how much it hurts to even look at him?"

"The best thing you can do is show up with your head held high. The sooner you get it over with, the sooner you can start coming out of that cottage of yours. It's just like a bandage. Better to rip it off and have it done with than to delay the inevitable."

Bryony sighed. "Okay, I'll go. If I do, then will you please leave me alone and let me deal with this my own way? I know you're worried but this isn't easy for me."

Mamaw squeezed her into a big hug. "I think things will be a lot better after today. You'll see."

Bryony wasn't as convinced but she allowed Silas and Mamaw to drag her to the municipal building where the meeting would be held. It took everything she had not to run back out the door when Silas led her to a front-row seat.

Talk about being a masochist. She'd have a front-row seat in which to listen to the man she loved announce his plans for a resort made possible by her stupidity.

She sighed and sank into one of the folding chairs. Mamaw and Silas took the spots on either side of her. Several people stopped by to talk to Silas. Some even shot sympathetic looks in her direction.

Yep, it was clear everyone knew what a naive fool she'd been.

At least no one was yelling at her for allowing the outsider to come in and develop the island. Yet.

Rupert strode in a minute later, an uncharacteristic smile plastered on his face. It wasn't his politician smile. It was a genuine one filled with delight. He looked, for lack of a better word, giddy.

He held up his hands for quiet and then frowned when the din didn't diminish. He cleared his throat and scowled harder. He was forever complaining to Bryony that he wasn't given enough respect by his constituents.

Finally Silas stood, held up his hands and hollered, "Quiet, people. The mayor wants your attention."

Rupert sent Silas a disgruntled look when everyone hushed. Then he looked over the audience and smiled. "Today we have Rafael de Luca of Tricorp Investment Opportunities, who is going to talk about the piece of property he recently acquired here on the island. Give him your undivided attention, please."

It took all of Bryony's self-restraint not to swivel in her seat to see if he was here. Many of the assembled people began to murmur, and then Bryony heard footsteps coming up the aisle.

Rafael stepped to the podium and Bryony was shocked by his appearance. First, he was wearing jeans. And a T-shirt. He looked tired and haggard. His hair was unkempt and it didn't look like he'd shaved that morning.

There were hollows under his eyes and a gray pallor to his skin that hadn't been present before.

He cleared his throat and glanced over the audience before his gaze finally came to rest on her.

He looked…nervous. It didn't seem possible that this ultra-confident businessman was nervous. But he seemed uneasy and on edge.

She watched in astonishment as he fiddled with something on the podium and when he looked up again, there was a rawness to his eyes that made her chest tighten.

"I came to this island for one thing and one thing only. I wanted to buy property that Bryony Morgan had put up for sale."

Several muttered insults filtered around the room, but Rafael continued on, undaunted.

"When it became clear that she would attach stipulations to the sale of the land, I conspired to seduce my way into her heart. Basically I was willing to do whatever necessary to convince her I'd do as she asked without having to commit her conditions onto paper."

Bryony would have bolted to her feet, but Mamaw gripped her arm with surprising strength.

"Sit. You need to listen to this, Bryony. Let him finish."

Rafael held up his hands to quiet the angry murmurs of the crowd. Then his gaze found Bryony's again. She slowly slid back into her seat, caught by the intensity in his stare.

"I'm not proud of what I did. But it was part and parcel of the kind of man I was. I left here, never intending to return until it was time for groundbreaking. But my plane crashed. It took weeks to recover and I lost all memory of the time I was here. I'm so grateful for that accident. It changed my life."

The room went completely silent on the heels of his last statement. Everyone seemed to lean forward in anticipation of what he'd say next.

"I came back here with Bryony to try to regain my memory. What I did was fall in love with this island and with Bryony. For real this time. She's told me on multiple occasions that I don't have to always stay the person I was, that I can change and be whoever I want to be. She's right. I don't want to be the person I was any longer. I want to be someone I can be proud of, someone *she* can be proud of. I want to be the man Bryony Morgan loves."

Tears crowded Bryony's eyes and her fingers curled into tight little fists in her lap. Mamaw reached over to take one of her hands and rubbed it reassuringly.

"I'm giving Bryony back the land I bought from her. It's hers to do as she likes. If she wishes, she can make it a gift and deed it to the town. Turn it into a park. Make it a private sanctuary. I don't care. Because all I want is her. And our child."

He stopped speaking and seemed to be battling to keep his composure. His fingers curled around the edges of the podium, but she could see that they still shook.

Then he walked around the podium, down the single step that elevated the stage. He came to a stop in front of her and then dropped to one knee. He reached for her hand and gently pried her fingers open and then he laced them with his, something he'd done a hundred times before.

"I love you, Bryony. Forgive me. Marry me. Say you'll make me a better man than I was. I'll spend the rest of my life *being* that man for you and our children."

A sob exploded from her throat at the same moment she launched herself from her seat and threw her arms around him. She buried her face in his neck and sobbed huge, noisy sobs.

He gripped her tight, holding one hand to the back of her head. He shook against her, almost as if he were dangerously close to breaking down himself.

He kissed her ear, her temple, her forehead, the top of her head. Then he pulled back, framing her face in his hands before peppering the rest of it with kisses.

Around them there were sighs and exclamations, even a smattering of applause, but Bryony tuned them all out as she held on to the one thing she needed most in this world.

Rafael.

"Give me your answer, please, baby," he murmured in her ear. "Don't torture me any longer. Tell me I haven't lost you for good. I can be the man you want, Bryony. Just give me the chance."

She kissed him and stroked her hands over his face, feeling the stubble on his jaw and drinking in the haggardness of his appearance. He looked as bad as she'd felt over the past week.

"You already are the man I want, Rafael. I love you. Yes, I'll marry you."

He shot to his feet and lifted her up, twirling her round and round with a whoop. "She said yes!"

The crowd burst into cheers. Mamaw sniffed indelicately and when Silas handed her a handkerchief, she blew her nose loudly and then sniffed some more.

Slowly he allowed her to slide down his body until her feet touched the floor, but he kept his arms tight around her as if he didn't want to let her go even for a moment.

"I'm sorry, Bryony," he said sincerely. "I'm sorry I lied to you, that I hurt you. If I could go back and change it all I would."

"I'm glad you can't," she said. "As I sat here and listened to everything you said, I realized that if things hadn't happened exactly as they had, you wouldn't be here now. What's important is that you love me now. Today. And tomorrow."

"I'll love you through lots of tomorrows," he vowed.

Bryony glanced around as the townspeople began filtering out of the building. Mamaw and Silas had discreetly made their exit, leaving Bryony and Rafael alone at the front of the room.

"What are we going to do, Rafe? What are you going to do? I came to New York because I was going to tell you that you should go ahead with the resort deal. But if you don't go through with it, what will it mean for your business?"

Rafael sighed. "Ryan, Devon and Cam support me. You

support me. That's all I need. When I left, they were trying to work out a way to salvage the deal. I'm guessing they'll look for an alternative location. I really don't care. I told them I wasn't going to lose you and my child over money. You and our baby mean more to me than anything else in the world. I mean that."

"After the spectacle you just made of yourself, I believe you," she teased.

"I'm tired," he admitted. "And so are you. Why don't we go back to your cottage, climb into bed and get some rest. I can't think of anything better than having you back in my arms."

She leaned into his embrace, wrapped her arms around him and closed her eyes as the sweetness of the moment floated gently through her veins.

Then she tilted her head back and smiled up at him, feeling the weight and grief wash away. For the first time in days, the thick blanket of sadness lifted, leaving her feeling light and gloriously happy.

She took his hand and tugged him down the aisle to the doorway leading to the outside. As they stepped out, sunlight poured over them, washing the darkness away.

For a brief moment, she paused and tipped her face into the sun, allowing the warmth to brush over her cheeks.

She looked up at Rafael, who was staring intently at her. His love was there for the entire world to see, shining in his eyes with brightness that rivaled the sun.

It was a look she'd never grow tired of in a hundred years and beyond.

"Let's go home," she said.

Rafael smiled, took her hand and pulled her toward the waiting car.

* * * * *

WANTED BY HER
LOST LOVE

BY
MAYA BANKS

To the kidlets for being so helpful and understanding
when mom has to work

One

"Almost enough to make you believe in the fine institution of marriage, isn't it?" Ryan Beardsley said as he watched his friend, Raphael de Luca, dance with his radiant new bride, Bryony.

The reception was taking place inside Moon Island's small, nondescript municipal building. It wasn't exactly where Ryan imagined any of his friends would host a wedding reception, but he supposed it was fitting that Rafe and Bryony would marry here on the island where so much of their relationship had been forged.

The bride positively glowed, and the swell of her belly added to her beauty. They stood in the middle of the makeshift dance floor, Bryony tucked into Rafe's protective hold, and they were so focused on each other that Ryan doubted the world around them existed. Rafe looked like he'd been handed the universe, and maybe he had.

"They look disgustingly happy," Devon Carter said next to him.

Ryan chuckled and looked up to see Dev holding a glass of wine in one hand, his other shoved into the pocket of his slacks.

"Yeah, they do."

Dev's mouth twisted in annoyance and Ryan chuckled again. Devon himself wasn't very far away from a trip down the aisle, and he wasn't taking it with good grace. Still, he couldn't resist needling his friend.

"Copeland still putting the screws to you?"

"And how," Devon muttered. "He's determined for me to marry Ashley. He won't budge on the deal unless I agree. And now that we've relocated the resort and begun construction, I'm ready to get on with the next step. I don't want him to lose confidence over this blown deal. Problem is, he's insisted on a dating period. He wants Ashley to be comfortable around me. I swear I think the man believes he lives in the eighteen hundreds. Who the hell arranges a marriage for their daughter anymore? And why the hell would you make marriage a condition of business? I can't wrap my head around it."

"There are worse women to marry, I'm sure," Ryan said, thinking of his own narrow escape.

Devon winced in sympathy. "Still no word on Kelly?"

Ryan frowned and shook his head. "No. But I only just started looking. She'll turn up."

"Why are you looking for her, man? Why would you even want to go back down that road? Forget about her. Move on. You're better off without her. You're out of your mind for pursuing this."

Ryan curled his lip and turned to look at his friend. "I have no doubt I'm better off. I'm not looking for her so I can welcome her back into my life."

"Then why did you hire an investigator to find her, for God's sake? You'd be better off letting the past stay in the past. Get over her. Move on."

Ryan was silent for a long moment. It wasn't a question he could entirely answer. How could he explain the burning desire to know where she was? What she was doing. If she was all right. He shouldn't care, damn it. He should forget all about her, but he couldn't.

"I want some answers," he finally muttered. "She never cashed the check I gave her. I'd just like to know that nothing has happened to her."

The excuse sounded lame even to him.

Devon raised an eyebrow and sipped at the expensive wine. "After what she pulled, I'd imagine she's feeling pretty damn stupid. I wouldn't want to show my face either."

Ryan shrugged. "Maybe." But he couldn't shake the feeling that it was something more. Why was he even worried? Why should he care?

Why hadn't she cashed the check?

Why couldn't he get her out of his mind? She haunted him. For six months, he had cursed her, lain awake at night wondering where she was and if she was safe. And he hated that he cared, even though he convinced himself he'd worry about any woman under the same circumstances.

Devon shrugged. "Your time and your dime. Oh, look, there's Cam. Wasn't sure Mr. Reclusive would actually crawl out of that fortress of his for the event."

Cameron Hollingsworth shouldered his way through the crowd, and people instinctively moved to get out of his way. He was tall and broad chested, and he wore power and refinement like most other people wore clothing. The stone set of his demeanor made him unapproachable by most. He could be a mean son of a bitch, but he could usually be counted on to relax around his friends.

The problem was, the only people he counted as friends were Ryan, Devon and Rafe. He didn't have much patience for anyone else.

"Sorry I'm late," Cameron said as he approached the two men. Then he glanced over the dance floor and his gaze stopped when he came to Rafe and Bryony. "How did the ceremony go?"

"Oh, it was lovely," Devon drawled. "All a woman could hope for, I'm guessing. Rafe didn't give a damn as long as the end result was Bryony being his."

Cam emitted a dry chuckle. "Poor bastard. I don't know whether to offer my condolences or my congratulations."

Ryan grinned. "Bryony's a good woman. Rafe's lucky to have her."

Devon nodded and even Cameron smiled, if you could call the tiny lift at the corner of his mouth a true smile. Then Cam turned to Devon, his eyes gleaming with unholy amusement.

"Word is you're not far from taking a trip down the aisle yourself."

Devon muttered a crude expletive and flipped up his middle finger along the side of his wineglass. "Let's not ruin Rafe's wedding by talking about mine. I'm more interested in knowing whether you were able to acquire the site for the new location of our hotel since Moon Island is now officially a bust."

Cam's eyebrows went up in exaggerated shock. "You doubt me? I'll have you know that twenty prime acres of beachfront property on St. Angelo is now ours. And I got a damn good deal. Better yet, construction will commence as soon as we can move crews in. If we really dig in, we'll come close to hitting our original deadline for the grand opening."

Their gazes automatically went to Rafe, who was still wrapped around his bride. Yeah, the man had caused them a major setback when he pulled the plug on the Moon Island venture, but it was hard for Ryan to get up in arms about it when Rafe looked so damn happy.

Ryan's pocket vibrated, and he reached down to pull his phone out. He was about to hit the ignore button when he saw who was calling. He frowned. "Excuse me, I need to take this."

Cameron and Devon waved him off and returned to their bantering as Ryan hurried out of the building. As soon as he stepped outside, the sea breeze ruffled his hair and the tang of salt filled his nose.

The weather was seasonable but by no means hot. It was about as perfect a day as you could ask for, especially for a wedding on the beach.

He turned to look at the distant waves and brought the phone to his ear.

"Beardsley," he said by way of a terse greeting.

"I think I've found her," his lead investigator said with no preamble.

Ryan tensed, his hand gripping the phone until his fingers went numb. "Where?"

"I haven't had time to send a man to get a visual confirmation yet. I only just got the information in a few minutes ago. I felt strongly enough about her identity to give you a heads-up. I should know more by tomorrow."

"Where?" Ryan demanded again.

"Houston. She's working in a diner there. There was a mix-up originally in her social security number. Her employer reported it wrong. When he put in the correction, she popped on to my radar. I'll have photos and a full report for you by tomorrow afternoon."

Houston. The irony wasn't lost on him. He'd been close to her all this time and never known it.

"No," Ryan interjected. "I'll go. I'm already in Texas. I can be in Houston in a couple of hours."

There was a long silence over the phone. "Sir, it might not be her. I prefer to get confirmation before you take a needless trip."

"You said it was most likely her," Ryan said impatiently. "If it turns out not to be, I won't hold you responsible."

"Should I hold off my man then?"

Ryan paused, his lips tight, his grip on the phone even tighter. "If it's Kelly, I'll know. If it's not, I'll inform you so you can continue your search. There's no need for you to send anyone down. I'll go myself."

Ryan drove through Westheimer in the blinding rain. His destination was a small café in west Houston where Kelly was waitressing. It shouldn't surprise him. She'd been waitressing in a trendy New York café when they'd met. But the check he'd written her would have prevented her from needing to work for quite some time. He figured she would have returned to school. Even when they'd become engaged, she'd expressed the desire to finish her degree. He hadn't understood it, but he'd supported her decision. The selfish part of him had wanted her to be completely reliant on him.

Why hadn't she cashed the check?

He had hopped the ferry to Galveston immediately after giving Rafe and Bryony his best wishes. He hadn't told Cam or Dev that he'd found Kelly, just that he had an important business matter to attend to. By the time he'd gotten to Houston it had been late in the evening, so he'd spent a sleepless night in a downtown hotel.

When he'd gotten up this morning, the skies had been gray and overcast and there hadn't been a single break in the rain since he'd left his hotel. At least the weather had been beautiful for Rafe's wedding. By now the happy couple would be off on their honeymoon—someplace where there was an abundance of blue skies.

He glanced over at his GPS and saw he was still several blocks from his destination. To his frustration, he hit every single red light on the way down the busy street. Why he was in a hurry, he didn't know. According to his investigator, she'd worked here for a while. She wasn't going anywhere.

A million questions hovered in his mind, but he knew he wouldn't have the answers to any of them until he confronted her.

A few minutes later he pulled up and parked at the small corner coffee shop that sported a lopsided doughnut sign. He stared at the place in astonishment, trying to imagine Kelly working *here* of all places.

With a shake of his head, he ducked out of the BMW and dashed toward the entrance, shaking the rain from his collar as he stepped under the small awning over the door.

Once inside, he looked around before taking a seat in a booth on the far side of the café. A waitress who was not Kelly came over with a menu and slapped it down on the table in front of him.

"Just coffee," he murmured.

"Suit yourself," she said as she sashayed off to the bar to pour the coffee.

She returned a moment later and put the cup down with enough of a jolt to slosh the dark brew over the rim. With an apologetic smile, she tossed down a napkin.

"If there's anything I can get you, just let me know."

It was on the tip of his tongue to ask her about Kelly when he looked beyond her and saw a waitress with her back to him standing across the room at another table.

He waved his waitress off and honed in on the table across the café. It was her. He knew it was her.

The honey-blond hair was longer and pulled into a ponytail, but it was her. He felt, more than visualized her, and his body quickened in response even after all these months.

Then she turned and presented her profile, and he felt every ounce of blood drain from his face.

What the everloving hell?

There was no mistaking the full curve of her belly.

She was pregnant. *Very* pregnant. Even more pregnant than Bryony by the looks of her.

His gaze lifted just as she turned fully and their eyes met. Shock widened her blue eyes as she stared across the room at him. Recognition was instant, but then why would she have forgotten him any more than he could have forgotten her?

Before he could react, stand, say anything, fury turned those blue orbs ice-cold. Her delicate features tightened and he could see her jaw clench from where he sat.

What the hell did she have to be so angry about?

Her fingers curled into tight balls at her sides, almost as if she'd love nothing better than to deck him. Then, without a word, she turned and stalked toward the kitchen, disappearing behind the swinging door.

His eyes narrowed. Okay, that hadn't gone as he'd imagined. He wasn't sure what he'd expected. A weeping apology? A plea to take her back? He damn sure hadn't expected to find her heavily pregnant, waiting tables in a dive more suited to a high school dropout than someone who was well on her way to graduating with honors from university as Kelly had been.

Pregnant. He took a deep, steadying breath. Just how pregnant was she? She had to be at least seven months. Maybe more.

Dread took hold of his throat and squeezed until his nostrils twitched with the effort of drawing air.

If she was pregnant, seven *months'* pregnant, there was a possibility it was his child.

Or his brother's.

Kelly Christian burst into the kitchen, struggling to untie her apron. She swore under her breath when she fumbled uselessly at the strings. Her hands shook so bad she couldn't even manage this simple of a task.

Finally she yanked hard enough that the material ripped. She all but threw it on the hook where the other waitresses hung their aprons.

Why was he here? She hadn't done a whole lot to cover her tracks. Yes, she'd left New York, and at the time she hadn't known where she'd end up. She hadn't cared. But neither had she done anything to hide. That meant he could have found her at anytime. Why now? After six months, what possible reason could he have for looking for her?

She refused to believe in coincidences. This wasn't a place Ryan Beardsley would ever just happen to be. Not his speed. His precious family would die before sullying their palates in anything less than a five-star restaurant.

Wow, Kelly, bitter much?

She shook her head, furious with herself for reacting this strongly to the man's presence.

"Hey, Kelly, what's going on?" Nina asked.

Kelly turned to see the other waitress standing in the doorway to the kitchen, her brow creased with concern.

"Close the door," Kelly hissed as she motioned Nina inside.

Nina quickly complied and the door swung shut. "Is everything all right? You don't look good, Kelly. Is it the baby?"

Oh, God, the baby. Ryan would have been blind not to have seen her protruding belly. She had to get out of here.

"No, I'm not well at all," she said, grasping for an explanation. "Tell Ralph I had to leave."

Nina frowned. "He's not going to like it. You know how he is about us missing work. Unless we're missing a limb or vomiting blood, he's not going to be forgiving."

"Then tell him I quit," Kelly muttered as she hurried toward the alley exit. She paused at the rickety door and turned anxiously back to Nina. "Do me a favor, Nina. This is important, okay? If anyone in the diner asks about me—anyone at all—you don't know anything."

Nina's eyes widened. "Kelly, are in you in some kind of trouble?"

Kelly shook her head impatiently. "I'm not in trouble. I swear it. It's…it's my ex. He's a real bastard. I saw him in the diner a minute ago."

Nina's lips tightened and her eyes blazed with indignation. "You go on ahead, hon. I'll take care of things here."

"Bless you," Kelly murmured.

She ducked out the back door of the diner and headed down the alley. Her apartment was only two blocks away. She could go there and figure out what the heck to do next.

She almost stopped halfway there. Why was she running? She had nothing to hide. She'd done nothing wrong. What she *should* have done was march across that diner and bloodied his nose. Instead she was running.

She took the flimsy stairs to her second-story apartment

two at a time. When she was inside, she closed the door and leaned heavily against it.

Tears pricked her eyelids and it only made her more furious that she was actually upset over seeing Ryan Beardsley again. No, she didn't want to face him. She never wanted to see him again. *Never* did she want anyone to have the kind of power he had to hurt her. Never again.

Her hands automatically went to her belly, and she rubbed soothingly, not sure who she was trying to comfort more, her baby or herself.

"I was a fool to love him," she whispered. "I was a fool to think I could ever fit in and that his family would accept me."

She jumped when the door behind her vibrated with a knock. Her heart leaped into her throat, and she put a shaky hand to her chest. She stared at the door as if she could see through it.

"Kelly, open the damn door. I know you're in there."

Ryan. God. The very last person she wanted to open the door to.

She put a hand to the wood and leaned forward, unsure of whether she should ignore him or respond.

The force of his second knock bumped her hand, and she snatched it away.

"Go away," she finally shouted. "I have nothing to say to you."

Suddenly the door shuddered and flew open. She took several hasty steps backward, her arms curling protectively over her belly.

He filled the doorway, looking as big and formidable as ever. Nothing had changed except for new lines around his mouth and eyes. His gaze stroked over her, piercing through any protective barriers she thought to construct.

He'd always had a way of seeing right to the heart of her. Except when it mattered the most.

Fresh grief flooded through her chest. Damn him. What else could he possibly want to do to hurt her? He'd already destroyed her.

"Get out," she said, proud of how steady her voice sounded. "Get out or I'll call the police. I have nothing to talk to you about. Not now. Not ever."

"That's too bad," Ryan said as he stalked forward, "because I have plenty to talk to *you* about. Starting with whose baby you're pregnant with."

Two

Kelly willed herself not to rage at him. Instead, she looked calmly at him, coolly, while emotions boiled beneath the surface like molten lava ready to erupt. "It's none of your business."

His nostrils flared. "It is if you're carrying my baby."

She crossed her arms over her chest and stared him down. "Now *why* would you think that?"

For a man only too willing to believe she'd slept around, it seemed pretty damn ridiculous that he'd barge into her apartment demanding to know whether or not her baby was his.

"Damn it, Kelly, we were engaged. We lived together and were intimate often. I have a right to know if this is my child."

She raised an eyebrow and studied him for a moment. "There is no way to know. After all I was with so *many* other men, your brother included." She shrugged nonchalantly and turned away from him, going into the kitchen.

He was close on her heels and she could feel the anger emanating from him. "You're a bitch, Kelly. A cold, calculating bitch. I gave you everything and you threw it away for a little gratuitous sex on the side."

She whipped around, the urge to hit him so strong that she had to curl her fingers into a fist to keep from doing just that. "Get out. Get out and don't ever come back."

His eyes glittered with anger and frustration. "I'm not going anywhere, Kelly, not until you tell me what I want to know."

She bared her teeth. "It's not your baby. Happy? Now go."

"Is it Jarrod's then?"

"Why don't you ask him?"

"We don't talk about you," he bit out.

"Well, I don't want to talk about *either* of you. I want you out of my apartment. It isn't your baby. Get out of my life. I did as you asked. I got out of yours."

"You didn't give me a choice."

She looked scornfully at him. "Choice? I don't remember having a choice either. You made that choice for both of us."

He stared at her in disbelief. "You're a piece of work, Kelly. Still the innocent martyr, I see."

She walked over to the door and opened it, looking expectantly at him.

He didn't move. "Why are you living this way, Kelly? I can't wrap my head around why you did what you did. I would have given you everything. Hell, I still gave you a hefty amount of money when we broke up because I didn't like to think of you being without. But now I find you living in squalor working a job that is far beneath your abilities."

A wave of hatred hit her hard. In this moment she

realized that she truly loved and hated him in equal measure. Her chest hurt so bad that she couldn't breathe. Her mind went back to the day when she'd stood in front of him, devastated, completely and utterly broken, while he scribbled his signature on a bank draft and disdainfully shoved it toward her.

The look in his eyes had told her that he didn't love her, had never loved her. He didn't trust her. He didn't have faith in her.

When she'd needed him the absolute most, he'd let her down and treated her like a paid whore.

She would *never* forgive him for that.

She slowly turned and dragged herself over to the kitchen drawer where she kept the crumpled envelope containing the check. A reminder of broken dreams and ultimate betrayal. She'd looked at it often but had sworn she would never walk into a bank and cash it.

She picked it up and walked back over to where he stood, his expression inscrutable. She crumpled the envelope into a ball and hurled it at him, hitting him in the cheek.

"There's your check," she hissed. "Take it and get the hell out of my life."

He bent slowly and retrieved the balled-up envelope. He unfolded it and then opened it, taking out the worn check. He frowned and then stared back at her. "I don't understand."

"You've never understood," she whispered. "Since you won't leave, I'm out of here."

Before he could stop her, she walked past him and slammed the door behind her.

Ryan stared at the check in his hand in stunned disbelief, unable to formulate his thoughts. Why? She acted as though he was a piece of scum. What the hell had he ever done to her but make sure she was taken care of?

He glanced around at the efficiency apartment, noting the disrepair and the cheapness of the furnishings. Two cabinet doors were barely hanging on their hinges and there was nothing inside. No food.

With a frown he stalked to the refrigerator and threw open the door. He cursed when he saw only a carton of milk, half a package of cheese and a jar of peanut butter.

He hastily rummaged through the rest of the kitchen, growing more furious when he found nothing more. How was she surviving? Furthermore, why was she living like this?

He glanced back down at the check and shook his head. There were enough zeros in the amount for her to live a good, modest life for years to come.

The ink had run in several places and it was smudged with fingerprints. But she'd never tried to cash it. Why? There were so many questions running around in his head that he couldn't process them all.

Did she feel guilty over what she'd done? Had she been ashamed to take money from him after betraying him?

Not the best time to develop a conscience.

One thing was for certain. He wasn't leaving. There were too many unanswered questions and he wanted answers. Why was she here in this run-down place with a job that obviously didn't net her enough money to feed herself, much less live a comfortable life? What in the world was she going to do when the baby came? Whether it was his baby or not, he couldn't allow himself to walk away. Not when she had meant so much to him.

She wasn't taking care of herself. He had always taken care of her in the past and he would do it again. Whether she liked it or not.

* * *

Kelly cut behind her apartment complex using the side street. She didn't go back to work, although it was what she should do. A day's lost wages wasn't the end of the world, but the tips she missed would be a blow to her meager savings.

She needed time to think. To compose herself. And Ryan would only go back to the diner to force another confrontation.

The rain had stopped but the skies were still cast in gloomy shades of gray with more black clouds in the distance, a sure signal that the rain wasn't over for the day.

Tears threatened, much like those ominous storm clouds, but she sucked in her breath—determined not to allow her unexpected face-to-face with Ryan to break her.

The small playground just three blocks from her apartment was abandoned. No children playing. The swings were empty, swaying in the breeze and the merry-go-round creaked as it rotated slowly.

She slid onto one of the benches, her mind in chaos from the bombardment of anger, grief and shock.

Why had he come?

Her pregnancy was obviously a huge surprise to him. There was no faking the what-the-hell expression on his face in the diner. Nor was their meeting some bizarre coincidence.

She'd given their relationship a lot of thought over the past months, when she wasn't doing everything possible to make herself forget him. Like that was going to happen.

She knew several things. One, they'd moved way too fast. From their meeting in the café where she'd served him coffee to their rush engagement, she hadn't taken the time to be sure of him. Oh, she'd been plenty sure of herself. She'd fallen head over heels from the first look.

She'd allowed herself to be swept into a relationship with him, never questioning his commitment to her. Or his love.

The obstacles then had seemed insignificant. He was out of her league, but she'd naively assumed that love would conquer all and that it didn't matter if his family or friends disapproved. She would prove herself worthy. She'd fit in with his lifestyle.

No, she didn't have his money, his connections, his breeding or heritage. But who even cared about that stuff in this day and age?

She'd been stupid. She'd put off school, at least temporarily, because she'd been consumed with being the perfect girlfriend, fiancée and eventually wife to Ryan Beardsley. She'd allowed him to outfit her in the finest clothing. She'd moved into his apartment with him. She'd agonized over saying the right thing and being the ideal complement to his life.

And she'd never had a chance.

Anyone who thought love was a cure for all things was a misguided fool. Maybe if he'd loved her enough—or at all. How could he ever have loved her when he turned on her at the first opportunity?

She closed her eyes against the unwanted sting of tears. She'd fled New York and ended up here in Houston. She'd forged a new life for herself. It wasn't the best life, but it was hers.

She'd known that she couldn't go back to school until after her baby was born and so she'd worked and saved every penny for that eventuality. She lived in the cheapest apartment she could find and earmarked all her earnings for when her child arrived. Then she would move into a better place, somewhere safe to raise a child and complete the two semesters she had left of school so she could make a better life for both herself and her precious baby. Without

Ryan Beardsley and his filthy money and his horrid family and all the mistrust and betrayal she'd been subjected to.

Now… Now what? Why was Ryan here? And what would his discovery of her pregnancy mean for her future? Her plans? Her determination never to allow herself back into a situation where she risked so much hurt and devastation?

She rubbed her forehead tiredly, willing the ache to go away. She was tired, worn thin and in no position to defend herself from whatever onslaught Ryan was preparing.

Her fingers tightened and anger penetrated the haze. Why the hell was she sitting on a park bench hiding? She wasn't in the wrong. Ryan couldn't make her do anything he wanted; and, furthermore, he would leave her apartment or she'd get a restraining order against him.

He had no power over her anymore.

She breathed in deeply, steadying her shot nerves. Yeah, he'd caught her off guard. She hadn't been prepared to see him again. But that didn't mean she was going to let him mow over her.

Even as she made that resolution, nervous fear fluttered in her chest and tightened her throat. The future that she'd planned suddenly seemed in peril with Ryan's reappearance in her life.

If he got it in his head that it was his child she carried, he wouldn't go away. The problem was, even if she managed to convince him that it wasn't his child, he'd only assume it was Jarrod's. That still made the Beardsley family a serious impediment to her future.

"One thing at a time, Kelly," she murmured.

The very first thing she had to do was get Ryan out of her apartment so she could weigh her options. She may not have his money or connections but that didn't mean she was going to fold at the first sign of adversity.

A raindrop hit her forehead and she sighed. It had begun sprinkling again, and if she didn't get back, she'd be caught out in the downpour that was surely coming.

As she trudged in the direction of her building she cheered herself up by imagining that he wouldn't be there. That he'd given up and left, deciding she wasn't worth the effort. She snorted as that thought crossed her mind. He'd already done that once. It wasn't a stretch that he'd simply dismiss her from his life again.

By the time she climbed the stairs to her apartment, she was soaked through and her hair clung limply to her head. She shivered as she fumbled with the lock to let herself in.

It didn't surprise her to see Ryan pacing the floor of her living room. She stiffened her shoulders just as he whirled around.

"Where the hell have you been?" he demanded.

"None of your business."

"The hell it's not. You didn't go back to work. It's raining and you're soaked to the skin. Are you crazy?"

She laughed and shook her head. "Clearly I am. Or I was. But not anymore. Get out, Ryan. This is my apartment. You have no rights here. You can't bully your way in here. I'll swear out a restraining order if I have to."

His forehead wrinkled and he stared at her in surprise. "You think I'd hurt you?"

She lifted a shoulder in a shrug. "Physically? No."

He swore under his breath. Then he ran his hand through his hair in agitation. "You need to eat. There's no food in this apartment. How the hell are you taking care of yourself and a baby when you're on your feet all day? You're clearly not eating here. There's nothing to eat!"

"My, my, one would think you cared," she mocked. "But we both know that isn't true. Don't worry about me, Ryan. I'm taking care of myself and my baby just fine."

He stalked toward her, his eyes blazing. "Oh, I care, Kelly. You can't accuse me of not caring. I wasn't the one who threw away what we had. That's on you. Not me."

She held up a hand and hastily backed away. Her fingers trembled and she felt precariously light-headed. "Get. Out."

His nostrils flared and his lip curled up as if he was about to launch another offensive. Then he took a step back and blew out his breath.

"I'll leave, but I'll be back at nine tomorrow morning."

She lifted one eyebrow.

"You have an appointment to see a doctor. I'm taking you."

He'd been busy while she was gone, and he worked fast. But then for a man like Ryan, all he had to do was pick up a phone. He had countless people to do his bidding. She shook her head in disgust. "Maybe you don't get it, Ryan. I'm not going anywhere with you. We are nothing to each other. You aren't responsible for me. I have my own doctor. You aren't hauling me to another one."

"And when was the last time you saw this doctor?" he demanded. "You look like hell, Kelly. You aren't taking care of yourself. That can't be good for either you or your child."

"Don't pretend that you care," she said softly. "Just do us both a favor and leave."

He looked like he was going to argue, but again, he bit back the words. He walked toward the door and then turned around to her again. "Nine o'clock tomorrow. You're going if I have to carry you there myself."

"Yeah, and maybe hell will freeze over," she muttered as he slammed out of her apartment.

She woke up early as a matter of habit. A quick check of her watch, however, told her she had overslept by fifteen minutes. She would have to hurry to get to the diner by six. After a brief shower, she pulled on her loose-fitting jumper over a shirt and headed for the door.

She held her breath, almost expecting Ryan to be outside. She shook her head and walked down the stairs. He was messing with her head and making her paranoid. Any thought that she was over him and moving on had been shot to hell the moment he showed up in her diner.

A few minutes later, she hustled into the diner to see that Nina was already at work serving their early-morning breakfast customers. Kelly donned her apron, picked up her order tablet and headed toward her section of tables.

For the first hour, she forced thoughts of Ryan and the dread that he'd make another appearance to the back of her mind. Unfortunately, it was obvious that she failed miserably after she messed up three orders, spilled coffee on a customer and retreated to the kitchen to get herself together.

She'd just given herself a stern lecture, calmed her shaking hands and was preparing to return out front when Ralph burst through the doors, a scowl on his face.

"What the hell are you doing here?"

Kelly frowned. "I work here, remember?"

"Not anymore you don't. You're out of here."

Kelly paled and stared at him as panic rolled through her chest. "You're firing me?"

"You walked out yesterday during our busiest time. No word, no nothing. You didn't come back. What the hell did you expect? And now you're back here this morning and I have a diner full of pissed-off customers because you don't have your head on right."

She took a deep breath and tried to steady her nerves. "Ralph, I need this job. Yesterday… Yesterday I got sick, okay? It won't happen again."

"Damn right it won't. I never should have hired you in the first place." He curled his lip in disgust. "If I hadn't needed a waitress so desperately, I would have never hired a pregnant woman to begin with."

Oh God, she didn't want to beg, but what choice did she have? The chances of her finding another job at this advanced stage of pregnancy were nil. All she needed was a few more months, just until the baby was born. By then she'd have enough money to stop working and take care of her baby. She'd have enough money to finish the rest of her classes.

"Please," she choked out. "Give me another chance. You've never heard a single complaint from me. I've never missed work for any reason. I have to have this job."

He pulled out an envelope from his shirt pocket and thrust it toward her. "Here's your final check, minus the hours for yesterday's disappearing act."

She took it with a shaking hand and he turned and walked out of the kitchen, the door swinging wildly behind him.

Anger and frustration overwhelmed her. Ryan was still ruining her life, months later. She yanked off her apron, tossed it in the direction of the hook and then left through the back entrance, squinting when she was nearly blinded by sunlight.

As she walked back toward her apartment, she stared at the envelope in her hand. Despair weighed her down until each step felt unbearable. Her damn pride. She should have taken the check Ryan had given her. To hell with him and his nasty accusations. That check represented a way for her to finish school and provide for her child.

She had every reason to refuse it. To tear it up into little pieces and shove it under his nose. Maybe that's why she'd held on to it for so long because a part of her wanted the satisfaction of throwing it back at him.

It had been important to her that he know she wasn't some whore to be bought, but what had that got her? A dead-end job that sucked the life out of her on a daily basis and a shabby apartment that she never wanted to bring her child home to.

Enough with her pride. Ryan Beardsley could go to hell. She was going to cash that check.

Three

Ryan mounted the steps to Kelly's apartment, grimacing as he took in the missing handrail and the shaky stairs. It was a wonder she hadn't already fallen down them. He wasn't entirely expecting to find her home, but he'd stopped in at the diner in case she'd gone to work, only to be told by a surly man named Ralph that she wasn't there.

It annoyed him that her door wasn't locked. He pushed it open to find her on her hands and knees, peering under the rickety recliner. She made a sound of frustration and then pushed herself upward.

"What the hell are you doing?"

She shrieked and whirled around. "Get out!"

He held out a placating hand. "I'm sorry I frightened you. Your door was unlocked."

"And so you thought you'd just come on in? Did the art of knocking escape you? Get a clue, Ryan. I don't want you here." She went into the kitchen, opening and shutting cabinets, obviously looking for something.

He sighed. It wasn't that he'd expected her to be any more compliant today, but he'd hoped after the initial shock, she'd be a little less…angry.

When she got back down on the floor again, a surge of irritation hit him once more.

He crossed the room and leaned down to help her to her feet. "What are you looking for?"

She shrugged off his hand and wiped her hair from her eyes. "The check. I'm looking for the check!"

"What check?"

"The check you wrote me."

He frowned and reached into his pocket for the folded, worn piece of paper. "This check?"

She lunged for it but he held it higher out of her reach.

"Yes! I've changed my mind. I'm cashing it."

He put his hand out to ward her off and shook his head in confusion. "Sit down, Kelly, before you fall. And then tell me what on earth is going on here. You wait this long, throw the check in my face and tell me to take my money to hell with me and now you've changed your mind? Are you crazy?"

To his utter surprise, she slumped down onto one of the small chairs that accompanied the two person table in the kitchen and buried her face in her hands. To his further dismay, her shoulders shook and quiet sobs erupted from her bowed head.

For a moment he stood there, unsure what to do. He'd never been able to stand it when she cried. An uncomfortable feeling settled in his stomach and he dropped down to one knee to gently pry her hands from her face.

She looked away, seemingly discomfited by the fact he was witnessing her breakdown.

"What's wrong, Kelly?" he asked gently.

"I lost my job," she choked out. "Because of you."

He reared back. "Because of me? What the hell did I do?"

She whipped her head up, her eyes flashing. "Your standard line. What did I do? Of course you did nothing wrong. I'm sure this was all my fault, like everything else that went wrong in our relationship. Just give me the check and get out. You won't ever have to be bothered with me again."

He stared incredulously at her. "Do you honestly expect me to just walk away *now?*" He shoved the check back into his pocket, his lips thin as he controlled the urge to lash out at her as she had done to him. "We have a hell of a lot to work out, Kelly. I'm not going anywhere and neither are you. The very first thing we're going to do is go to the doctor so you can get a decent checkup. You don't look well. I can't be any more blunt than that."

She slowly stood and stared him in the eye. "I'm not going anywhere with you. If you won't give me the check, then get out. We have nothing more to discuss. Ever."

He fingered the paper in his pocket and then lifted his gaze to meet hers once more. "We'll discuss the check after we go to the doctor."

Disgust flared in her eyes. "Resorting to blackmail now, Ryan?"

"If that's what you want to call it. I really don't care. You're going to the doctor with me. If he gives you a clean bill of health, then I'll hand over the check and walk out of here."

Her eyes narrowed suspiciously. "Just like that."

He nodded, not bothering to tell her that there wasn't a doctor in this world who could possibly give her a clean bill of health. She was dead on her feet. She was pale and very likely significantly underweight.

She nibbled at her lip for a long while as if deciding

whether or not to acquiesce. Then finally she closed her eyes and let out her breath in a long exhale.

"All right, Ryan. I'll go to the doctor with you. After he verifies that I'm perfectly fine, I don't want to see you again."

"*If* he says you're okay, then you'll get your wish."

She lowered herself back into the chair, clearly exhausted. He bit back a curse. Was she blind or just that heavily into denial? She needed someone to take care of her. Make sure she ate three good meals a day. Someone to make her put her feet up and rest.

He checked his watch. "We should be going. Your appointment is in half an hour and I don't know how bad traffic will be."

Defeat crept over her face, but then she hardened her expression and rose once more. She retrieved her purse from the recliner and started for the door, leaving him to follow.

Kelly stared sightlessly out the window as Ryan maneuvered through traffic. She was mentally exhausted from her confrontation with Ryan. She just wanted him gone. She couldn't even look at him without all the hurt from the past crashing through her and turning her inside out.

He parked in the garage of a downtown medical clinic and ushered her inside the modern building. They rode the elevator to the fourth floor and Kelly stood numbly as Ryan checked in with the receptionist.

After filling out her medical history, she was ushered back for the prerequisite pee in a cup. When she exited the bathroom, a nurse directed her into one of the exam rooms where she found Ryan waiting for her.

She bared her teeth in a snarl, prepared to order him out when he held up a hand, his expression as fierce as her own had to be.

"I will hear firsthand everything the doctor has to say."

His eyes dared her to argue. She swallowed nervously, knowing he'd make a scene if she pushed the issue. She turned her back on him and leaned on the exam table.

She just had to get past the exam, have the doctor tell Ryan that everything was fine, and then she'd be rid of him.

A few minutes later, a young doctor came in and smiled at her. He gestured for her to get onto the table and recline. After measuring her and listening to the baby's heartbeat, he wheeled in a small machine and then applied cool gel to her stomach.

She lifted her head. "What are you doing?"

"Thought you might like to get a look at the little guy or girl. I'll do a quick sonogram for dates and measurement, make sure everything is okay. Is that all right with you?"

She nodded and the doctor began moving the wand over her stomach. Then he stopped and gestured toward the small screen. "There's the head."

Ryan crowded in so he could see the monitor. She craned her neck to see around him. Ryan looked back at her then hastily slipped a hand underneath her neck to lift her so she could see. Tears filled her eyes and her lips widened into a smile. "She's beautiful!"

"Yes, she is," Ryan said huskily in her ear.

"Or he," she said quickly.

"Would you like to find out what you're having?" the doctor offered. "We can take a look."

"No…no, I don't think so," she said. "I want it to be a surprise."

The doctor took a few more minutes and then stood up, wiping her belly clean. He handed her a picture he printed out of the baby's profile and returned to his clipboard.

After a few scribbled notes, he looked back up at her. "I'm concerned about you."

She frowned and struggled to sit up. Ryan eased her into a sitting position, and she looked questioningly at the doctor.

"Your blood pressure is elevated and there are traces of protein in your urine. There is significant edema to your hands and feet and I'd bet, judging by your weight, that you aren't getting enough nutrition. You're exhibiting signs of preeclampsia and it could lead to serious repercussions."

Kelly regarded him in stunned silence.

Ryan turned to the doctor with a frown. "What is pre-eclampsia?"

"It's related to an increase in blood pressure and an increase in protein in urine output. Typically it affects women after their twentieth week of pregnancy. It can progress to seizures, at that point it becomes eclampsia."

The doctor turned his stern gaze on Kelly before continuing.

"You are only a hairbreadth from going into the hospital and staying there until you deliver, and unless I exact a promise from you and your husband that you'll remain off your feet and take better care of yourself, I'll forgo the warning and straight into the hospital you'll go."

"He's not my—" she began.

"Consider it done," Ryan smoothly interjected. "She won't so much as lift a finger. You have my word."

"But—"

"No buts," the doctor said. "I don't think you fully under-stand the direness of your situation. If your condition progresses, it can mean your death. Eclampsia is the second leading cause of maternal death in the U.S. and the leading cause of fetal complications. This is serious and you need to take all the necessary precautions to prevent an escalation in your condition."

Ryan blanched, and she felt the blood drain from her own face as well.

"I can assure you, Doctor, Kelly won't be doing anything but resting and eating from now on," Ryan said grimly.

The doctor nodded approvingly and shook both their hands. "I'd like to see her back in a week. And if the swelling gets worse or she develops a severe headache she's to go directly to the hospital."

After the doctor left, Kelly sat on the exam table, stunned by the doctor's pronouncement. Ryan slid his hand over hers and squeezed.

"I don't want you to worry, Kelly."

Worry? She nearly let out a hysterical laugh. Her life was a total and complete mess and she wasn't supposed to worry. She was ready to run screaming from the building.

"Come on," he said quietly. "Let's go."

She let him lead her out of the doctor's office and to the car without protest. This couldn't be happening to her. She sat mutely in the car as they drove away, refusing to even look at Ryan. She had no job, and now if the doctor was to be believed, she couldn't have worked even if she hadn't been fired. How was she going to support herself, let alone her baby? She had some savings but it was all earmarked for the baby and school.

Helplessness gripped her and she didn't like it one bit. The shrill ring of a cell phone startled her and she looked over to see Ryan put it to his ear as he expertly weaved through traffic. Her ears perked up when she heard her name.

"We're going by Kelly's apartment to get her things. Book us a flight from Houston and call me back with the flight number and time. Then call over to Dr. Whitcomb's office on Hillcrest and get Kelly's medical report faxed to Dr. Bryant in New York. Cover for me and have Linda go over any contracts needing my signatures. I'll be in the office in a few days."

He ended the conversation abruptly and set the phone aside.

"What were you talking about?" Kelly said in bewilderment.

He glanced over at her, a grim expression tightening his face. "I'm taking you home."

"Over my dead body," she snarled. She crossed her arms over her belly and pressed her lips firmly together.

"You're going," he said in a tone that brooked no argument. "You need someone to take care of you since you refuse to do it yourself. Do you want to risk the baby's health? Or yours? Give me a solution, Kelly. Prove to me that I can leave here knowing you'll be okay."

She stared woodenly at him. "Don't you understand that I want nothing to do with you?"

"Oh yes, you made that clear to me when you slept with my brother. But the fact is you're likely carrying my child—or my niece or nephew, and either way I'm not going to disappear until I know you're both safe. You're coming to New York with me if I have to carry you on the plane."

"It's not your child," she said fiercely.

His gaze raked over her. "Whose is it then?"

"None of your business."

There was a long silence before he finally said, "You're going with me. I'm not just doing this for a child that may or may not be mine."

"Why are you doing it then?" she shot back.

He ignored her and stared out the windshield, his fingers curled tight around the steering wheel.

When they arrived at her apartment, she got out of the car before he could come around for her and she hurried up the stairs. She could hear him behind her and when she tried to shut the door, he put up his hand and pushed his way inside.

"We have to talk, Kelly."

She whirled around. "Yes, we do. You said we'd talk about the check. You were certainly willing to throw it at me when you called me a whore. I want it now and I don't give a damn what you think about the fact I'm taking it."

"I'm no longer offering it."

"Oh, nice," she said sarcastically.

"I want you to come back to New York with me."

Her mouth fell open. "You're insane. Why would I go anywhere with you?"

"Because you need me."

Pain speared through her chest, robbing her of breath. "I needed you before."

She turned away before he could respond. She framed her belly with her palms and tried not to panic.

Behind her Ryan was silent. Disturbingly so. Then when he spoke there was an odd, strained tone to his voice.

"I'm going out to have your prescriptions filled. I'll pick us up something to eat. When I get back, I want you to be packed."

His footsteps were heavy on the floor and then the door shut quietly behind him.

She sank onto the tattered recliner and massaged her forehead. Two days ago she had a plan. A good plan. She had everything mapped out. Today she had no job, her health was suspect and her ex-fiancé was pressuring her to go back to New York with him.

It made her cringe, but she realized she was going to have to call her mother. She'd once sworn she'd have to be dying to ever ask her mom for anything, but right now that seemed the lesser of two evils.

"What doesn't kill me will make me stronger, right?" she muttered.

Lame. So lame.

Still, she picked up the phone, drew in a deep breath and called the last number she had for her mother. It was entirely possible Deidre no longer lived in Florida. Who really knew with her?

She'd washed her hands of Kelly the minute Kelly graduated high school and all but shoved her out of the house so she could move in her latest boyfriend. She'd informed Kelly that she'd done her duty and devoted eighteen of the best years of her life—years she'd never get back—to raising a child she'd never intended to have.

Good luck, see you later, don't ask me for anything else.

Yeah.

Kelly was about to hang up when her mother's voice came over the line.

"Mom?" Kelly said hesitantly.

There was a long pause. "Kelly? Is that you?"

"Yeah, Mom it's me. Look, I need your help. I need a place to stay. I'm…pregnant."

There was an even longer pause this time. "Where's that rich boyfriend of yours?"

"I'm not with him any longer," Kelly said in a quiet voice. "I'm in Houston. I lost my job and I'm not well. The doctor is worried about the baby. I just need a place to stay for a little while. Until I get back on my feet."

Her mother sighed. "I can't help you, Kelly. Richard and I are busy and we just don't have the space."

Hurt crowded into her heart. She'd known this was

pointless, but somehow she'd hoped… Quietly, she turned the phone off without saying anything else. What was there to say anyway?

Her mother had never been more than a resigned babysitter.

Kelly smoothed a hand over her belly. "I love you," she whispered. "I'll never begrudge a single moment I have with you."

She leaned back in the recliner and stared up at the ceiling, hating the helplessness that gripped her. She closed her eyes in weary resignation. She was exhausted.

The next thing she knew she was being shaken awake. She yanked her eyes open to see Ryan standing over her, a plate and glass of water in his hands.

"I brought you Thai," he said gruffly.

Her favorite. She was surprised he remembered. She struggled to sit upright and then took the plate and glass from him.

He pulled a chair from the kitchen and sat across from her as she ate. His scrutiny made her uncomfortable and so she focused on her food, not looking up.

"Ignoring me isn't going to help."

She paused, set her fork down and then leveled a stare at him. "What do you want, Ryan? I still don't understand why you're here. Or why you want me to go back to New York with you. Or why you care, period. You let me know in no uncertain terms that you wanted me as far out of your life as possible."

"You're pregnant. You need help. Isn't that enough?"

"No, it's not!"

His jaw tightened. "Let's put it this way. You and I have a lot to work out, including whether or not you're pregnant with my child. You need help that I can provide. You need someone to take care of you. You need top-notch medical care. I can give you all of those things."

She thrust a hand into her hair and leaned back against the recliner. He immediately leaned forward, slipping from his chair and going to his knees in front of her. He touched her arm, tentatively, as if afraid she'd recoil.

"Come with me, Kelly. You know this has to be worked out between us. You have to think about the baby."

She held up a hand, furious that he'd try to manipulate her with guilt. But he caught her hand and lowered it, and then ruthlessly pressed his advantage.

"You can't work. The doctor said you have to rest or you risk the health of your child as well as your own. If you can't accept my help for yourself, at least do it for your baby. Or is your pride more important than his or her welfare?"

"And what are we supposed to do when we get to New York, Ryan?"

"You're going to rest and we're going to figure out our future."

Her stomach lurched. It sounded so ominous. Their future.

She was a fool to agree. She'd be a fool not to agree.

She was willing to swallow her pride and take the check. Shouldn't she be willing to accept his help for her baby's sake? For their baby's sake?

"Kelly?"

"I'll go," she said in a low voice.

Triumph flashed in his eyes. "Then let's get you packed and get the hell out of here."

Four

When Kelly woke the next morning, she struggled to make sense of her surroundings. Then she remembered. She was in New York—with Ryan.

In a matter of hours, Ryan had had her packed and hustled to the airport. They'd landed at LaGuardia close to midnight and he'd ushered her into a waiting car.

By the time they'd arrived at his apartment, she was dead on her feet. Once inside, she took her one bag and headed toward the guest room. The aching familiarity of the apartment—an apartment that used to be hers—threatened to unhinge her. It even smelled the same—a mixture of leather and raw masculinity. She'd never tried to change that. It had reminded her too much of Ryan, and she hadn't wanted to remove it.

Down the hall was the bedroom where she and Ryan had made love countless times. It was where their child was conceived and where her life had been irrevocably altered.

Once again, she'd been reminded of how much of an idiot she was to come back here.

But this morning she felt resigned to her fate. After a quick shower, she dressed and padded into the living room where Ryan was already sitting typing on a laptop. He looked up when he heard her come in.

"Breakfast is ready. I was waiting on you to eat."

Wordlessly, she followed him into the kitchen where she saw a table set for two. Taking a platter off the warmer, he carried it over to the table and began spooning healthy portions of eggs, toast and ham onto their plates.

As she sat down, she was forced to admit that she felt better than she had in weeks. She had certainly gotten more rest in the past twenty-four hours than she had in a long time.

"How are you feeling this morning?" he asked as he took a seat across from her.

"Fine," she mumbled around a mouthful of egg. Her appetite was coming back and she concentrated on the delicious food in front of her.

This whole thing was weird. The ultrapoliteness. The cozy breakfast for two. It was so awkward that she wanted to go back to the bedroom and crawl back into bed.

After a long silence, Ryan spoke up. "I've made arrangements to work out of the apartment for the time being."

She stopped chewing then swallowed the food in her mouth. "Why?" she asked flatly.

"I would think the answer is obvious."

"This isn't going to work, Ryan. I can't stay here with you hanging over my shoulder all the time. Go to work. Do whatever it is you normally do, and just leave me alone."

His lips thinned and then he got up and walked away without another word.

She stared down at her plate, furious that he acted like the victim. As if she was some horrible, ungrateful bitch.

Fury and aching sadness knotted her throat. How could she ever get past what he'd done to her? Maybe he was just as determined not to forgive her for her supposed transgressions, but Kelly was the innocent one in this whole sordid mess. Ryan had turned his back on her. He didn't seem to want to acknowledge that little fact.

She fiddled with her remaining food, pushing it around her plate until restlessness forced her to her feet.

Wandering aimlessly back into the living room, she stopped in front of the large window offering a view of the Manhattan skyline.

"You shouldn't be on your feet," Ryan said from behind her.

She sighed and turned around, shocked to see him in just a towel. She swiveled back to the window, but the image burned in her eyes. His broad chest rippled with well-defined muscles and his lean abdomen was sculpted like a fine work of art. She used to spend hours exploring the dips and curves of his body.

"I'm sorry if I embarrassed you," he said in a low voice. "I guess I didn't give it a thought considering our past relationship."

She had the ridiculous urge to laugh. Embarrass her? The only embarrassing thing was how her mind was currently wandering way below the makeshift waistline of his towel.

And of course, in his arrogance, he would assume—considering the "nature of their relationship"—that he could cavort about in the nude.

Drawing up her shoulders, she turned around again and stared coolly at him. "If you think because we were once lovers that you can take up where we left off, you're sadly mistaken."

He blinked in surprise and then anger replaced the surprise. "God, Kelly. Do you think so little of me that I would try to force you into a sexual relationship when you're pregnant and unwell?"

"You don't want to know the answer to that."

He swore long and hard. "What makes you think I would ever want to sample my brother's secondhand goods anyway?"

She balled her hands into fists and forced a careless reply. "Well, since your brother didn't mind, I assumed it was a family trait."

His blue eyes became ice chips and his jaw twitched spasmodically. Then he spun around and disappeared into his bedroom, the sound of the door slamming reverberating throughout the apartment.

Kelly sighed and sank into a nearby armchair. What demon had forced her to throw more fuel on the flames she would never know. The need to defend herself had long since fled. He should have believed in her *then*. She didn't really care what he chose to do now. The desire for him to stand behind her and protect her had fizzled when she realized that she'd *never* had his love or his faith.

God, what was she doing here? Just being in New York again brought back too many memories she would be better off forgetting.

Restless and sick at heart, she made her way back into the kitchen and took stock of the contents of the refrigerator and cabinets. Deciding that she had all the necessary ingredients for one of her favorite dishes, she began laying them out on the countertop. At least it would give her something to do and lunch would be taken care of. She'd always loved to cook for Ryan when they lived together.

"What the hell do you think you're doing?" Ryan

demanded, materializing out of nowhere and taking the pan she was holding from her. He steered her firmly away from the counter and back into the living room. "Sit," he ordered once they reached the couch. He propped her feet up on the coffee table, placing a pillow under them. He stood back, his expression lacking the anger of just a few minutes ago.

"Maybe you didn't understand the doctor's orders. You're to rest. Stay off your feet." He enunciated each word in clipped tones as if he were speaking to a dolt. Well, that wasn't entirely untrue. She was the biggest dolt in the world for getting caught up in this mess.

He seemed calm. And she was calm, too—at least for now. It was time to get things out in the open. "Ryan, we need to talk."

He looked surprised and a little wary over her change in tone, but he sat down across from her and regarded her with open curiosity. "Okay, talk."

"I want to know why you came to Houston." She was careful to keep her emotions in check as she waited for his response.

He didn't look pleased with her question. He looked away, at the wall, his jaw tight.

"And how did you know where to find me?" she continued when he remained silent.

"I hired an investigator," he said after a moment's pause.

Her mouth fell open. So much for being calm. "Why? So you could accuse me of being a whore all over again? So you could sweep in and upend my life? I don't get it, Ryan. You hate me. I know what you think of me. You made it very clear when you threw me out of your life. Why the hell would you come looking to dig up the past again?"

"Damn it, Kelly!" he exploded. "You disappeared

without a word to anyone. You didn't cash the check. I thought you were out there hurt and scared—or dead."

"Too bad for you I wasn't."

"Don't you make this about me," he growled. It was obvious he had only a tenuous grip on his control. "You took what we had and threw it in my face. *You* decided I wasn't enough for you. I looked for you because no matter what you had done or how badly I wanted to forget you, I couldn't stand the thought of you being out there somewhere scared and alone."

He broke off and looked away. When he looked back at her, his eyes were shuttered. "I've answered your questions, now I want mine answered."

They both glanced up at the sound of the front door opening and, to Kelly's horror, Ryan's brother, Jarrod, stood in the entryway. "Hey Ryan, the doorman told me you were back…." His voice died when he saw her. "Uh… hi, Kelly."

Ryan watched as Kelly's expression became glacial. Damn it, she was going to think he planned this. And while yes, the three of them certainly needed to hash out a few things, now wasn't the time. He rose from his seat and headed in his brother's direction.

It had taken Ryan months to see beyond his rage and jealousy to be able to entertain resuming a normal relationship with his younger brother. Before Ryan hadn't given a second thought to Jarrod coming and going at will. He had a key. Ryan had always encouraged him to drop in and had looked forward to his visits.

But that was before Jarrod had slept with Kelly. Before the two most important people in his life had betrayed him. When he finally talked himself around to forgiving Jarrod and allowing him back into his life, he'd also considered that if he was willing to forgive his brother then perhaps he should also find Kelly and at least listen to her reasons why.

Things weren't perfect between him and his brother now. Maybe they never would be. But they were better and Jarrod had started coming around more, even if he was more cautious than he'd ever been in the past.

Now Ryan had brought Kelly back and they'd all be forced to face the inevitable confrontation. A part of him dreaded it, but the other part of him knew he'd never be able to move forward unless this was fully resolved. But it would be done when he decided and not before. He and Kelly had too much to work out between them before they tackled the issue of Jarrod and her infidelity.

"This isn't a good time, man," he said in a low voice when he reached his brother.

Unease flickered across Jarrod's face, and he glanced nervously over Ryan's shoulder toward Kelly. "I can see that. I'll come back another time."

Ryan turned and saw Kelly tremble and then her fingers flexed and curled into fists. She was as pale as death, her eyes large and haunted."What did you want?" he prompted when Jarrod made no move to leave.

"Nothing important. Just came over to say hi and to tell you Mom wanted us over for dinner Saturday night. I hadn't seen you in a while. I know you've been busy with your resort deal. I'd hoped we could get together like old times."

Ryan sighed. He and Jarrod had always been close. Until Kelly. He hated this. Hated it all. Hated that a woman had come between him and the brother he'd all but raised after their father died.

"I'll call Mom later, okay? And we'll get together. Just not right now."

"Yeah, I understand. I'll see you later." He backed

toward the door, and Ryan followed. As Ryan gripped the doorknob to close it after Jarrod, his brother whispered, "Are you taking her back after what happened?"

Ryan drew his brows together. "Aren't you concerned that she could be carrying your child?"

Jarrod flinched and his cheeks lost color. "Is that what she told you?"

Ryan studied him for a moment, his brows drawing together as he observed Jarrod's reaction to the suggestion. "No, she didn't tell me that, but surely you know it's possible."

"Uh-uh, can't be mine," Jarrod said, shaking his head emphatically.

"So you say."

Jarrod stepped into the hall and then shoved his hands into his pockets as he stared back at Ryan. But he didn't quite meet Ryan's gaze. "I wore protection. Look, I'm sorry. I know this is a bad situation. But the baby can't be mine."

Ryan watched him walk toward the elevator, the same frustrated helplessness clutching his throat. He stepped back and shut the door, angry. Angry at Kelly, angry at Jarrod and angry with himself all over again. So the baby was his unless…surely she hadn't had other partners besides him and Jarrod. He wouldn't even give that consideration.

When he returned to the couch he wasn't prepared for the absolute hatred and revulsion in Kelly's expression. Before he could say anything she fixed him with a look that froze him to the bone.

"If he ever comes over here again, I'm out of here. I won't be in the same room with him."

Ryan was taken aback. "You know he's here all the time."

Her teeth were clenched and her knuckles white. "I won't stay here."

Why the hell was she so angry with Jarrod? If anyone deserved to be angry it was Jarrod, after Kelly had accused him of trying to rape her. Nothing about this entire situation made sense. And he was tired of trying to figure it out.

"Jarrod said he wore protection," he said, gauging her reaction.

Pain rippled across her face. Not the reaction he'd imagined. "And of course you believed him," she said in a voice that sounded like she was dangerously close to tears.

"Are you saying he didn't? Are you maintaining the baby is mine?" He'd had no idea how badly he wanted the baby to be his until now. His eyes pleaded with her to confirm it. To say that *he* was the father.

The indecipherable mask was back on her face again. "I don't maintain anything," she said, frost dripping from her voice.

Frustration hit him like a ton of bricks. She had shut herself off again and nothing was going to open her to him. He wanted to put his fist through the wall.

"I'm going out for a while," he finally ground out. "I'll bring back lunch."

He turned and stalked out before he said things he'd only regret.

As he made his way to the underground garage where his BMW was parked, his cell phone rang, rudely intruding on his thoughts. "What?" he barked into the receiver.

"Ryan?" His mom's voice bled through his dour mood.

"Sorry, Mom, didn't mean to snap." He opened the door and slid into the seat, settling back, not bothering to start the engine yet.

"Ryan, what's wrong?"

"Nothing, Mom, just a busy day. What's up?"

"I was hoping you and Jarrod would have dinner with me tomorrow night."

Ryan closed his eyes, pinching the bridge of his nose between two fingers. There was no easy way to say this and his mom would know soon enough now that Jarrod had been over. Best she know now so she could get used to it. "Mom, you should know…Kelly is with me…and she's pregnant."

There was a sharp intake of breath on the other end followed by thick silence. "I see," she finally said. "I guess inviting Roberta is out of the question."

Ryan blew out his breath at his mother's snippy tone. Roberta Maxwell was a woman his mom had been shoving at him ever since Kelly had disappeared.

Though his mother had never come out and said I told you so, she didn't have to. It was there as plain as if she'd hung a banner.

She'd never approved of Kelly. Never liked that Ryan was marrying her. She'd been polite, though. Ryan had demanded it of her. He wouldn't allow any of his family to disrespect the woman he'd chosen to be his wife.

After what had happened with Jarrod and Kelly, he'd expected his mother to be more smug; but she'd been oddly sympathetic. The last thing he wanted at the moment, though, was to bring Kelly to an awkward dinner where his mom would sit with that pinched look on her face and Jarrod would say God knows what.

He'd wondered what would happen when the inevitable confrontation with Jarrod occurred. Now he knew, and it hadn't gone at all as he'd imagined.

"I think we'll do dinner another time. Kelly and I aren't up to it at the moment."

He said his goodbyes and hung up, starting the car and

slamming it into Reverse. He needed some distance before he went off the deep end.

He drove aimlessly and ended up at his office building before he even realized that he was heading in that direction. He didn't often drive, and usually only when he was leaving the city. He kept his car parked and used his car service. But today he hadn't been in any mood to wait for pickup.

He parked and went up to his office, acknowledging Jansen's look of surprise since he'd just told his assistant that morning that he wouldn't be in for several days.

He waved off Jansen's question of whether or not he needed anything and shut the door to his office. Then he flopped into his chair and swiveled around to stare out the window.

The weather had turned cold and gray, much more suited to his mood. After spending several days in Texas, where it was a good deal warmer, even in winter, coming back to the cold of the Northeast was a bit of an adjustment.

His cell phone rang, and he almost didn't answer. It was Cam, and Cam would want to know what had prompted his departure from Moon Island. Ryan was supposed to fly back to New York with Cam and Devon but he'd left in a hurry with a flimsily uttered excuse.

Deciding not to delay the inevitable, he put the phone to his ear.

"You and Dev make it back?"

"There you are. Been trying to call you for the past twenty-four hours. Where the hell did you go in such a hurry?" Cam demanded.

Ryan sighed. "My investigator called. He found Kelly." There was dead silence and then he heard Cam murmuring to someone else. Probably Dev.

"And?" Cam finally said.

"She was in Houston. I left the island to go and see if it was her."

"And?" Cam asked again.

"It was. I brought her back to New York with me."

"You did *what?* Why the hell did you do that?"

Ryan sighed at the incredulity in Cam's voice. And then because he needed to unload on someone, he said, "She's pregnant, Cam."

"Oh, Christ. What is with all the pregnant women showing up? I'll ask you the same question I asked Rafael when Bryony appeared out of nowhere. How do you know it's yours?"

"I don't believe I said it was mine," Ryan said mildly. "What I said was that she's pregnant."

"Uh-huh, and you'd just bring your ex-fiancée back to New York with you because she's pregnant with someone else's baby?"

"Don't be a smart-ass. The thing is, it *could* be my baby. Or it could be my brother's. Are you seeing my problem now?"

"Man, I'd say you have a whole hell of a lot of problems that I'm glad I don't have. What does she say about all of this?"

"That's just it. She's pissed. At me. She acts like I've wronged her. I don't get it. She hasn't said whose baby it is. She hasn't denied that it's my child but neither has she confirmed that it's mine."

"Has it ever occurred to you that she doesn't know?" Cam asked dryly.

Ryan scowled and then pinched the bridge of his nose between his fingers.

"Sorry, man, it had to be said. If she was sleeping with you and your brother plus God knows who else, she probably doesn't have a clue who the baby daddy is."

"God, stop with the snark. You're giving me a headache. Kelly isn't some whore."

"I never said she was."

"You implied it."

"Look, you're getting pissed at the wrong person here. I'm just asking—as a friend—whether you've lost your everloving mind. But then again, I thought you were insane for hiring an investigator to find her. Well, you found her and now you have to deal with the fallout. I'll tell you just what I told Rafael when he was faced with similar issues. Call your lawyer. Get paternity testing done."

"I don't want it to come to that," Ryan said quietly. "Damn it, I just want to know what went wrong." He broke off and shook his head. This was a pointless conversation to be having. Cam was an unforgiving bastard on his best day. As soon as he heard what Kelly had done, he'd basically written her off. Cam might be a hard-ass but he was a loyal hard-ass.

Cam was silent for a moment. "Look man, I'm sorry. I get that this has you tied in knots. Personally, I think you ought to go out, have a few drinks and get laid. Come off that self-imposed celibacy stint you've been on since you threw her out. But I know you won't so I won't go there."

Ryan laughed and shook his head.

"Dev wants to talk to you a minute so hang on."

"See ya," Ryan muttered to empty air.

A second later, Dev came on the phone.

"I won't repeat all Cam has said other than to ditto everything. What I wanted to tell you is that I'll be out of pocket for a while."

"Oh? Eloping with Ashley?"

Dev muttered a not-so-nice directive and Ryan chuckled.

"No, there's an issue with the construction and we've already suffered so many delays on this project that I don't want to risk any more. I'm going down there myself. It'll be quicker than conference calls and playing phone tag."

Ryan frowned and then leaned back in his chair. "How soon were you planning to leave?"

"Day after tomorrow. I'd go sooner, but I can't. And Cam is going to be out of the country starting tomorrow and I can't very well ask Rafe to leave his honeymoon."

"Ah. So really you and Cam were calling to see if I'd do it."

"Well, yeah, but after hearing what's on your plate, I'll go. I can break away after tomorrow."

Ryan thought a moment and then made a split-second decision. "No, I'll go."

"Whoa. Wait a minute. I thought you had Kelly with you. A pregnant Kelly."

"Yeah, I do. I'll take her with me. It'll be perfect. It'll give us time away from… It'll give us some time alone to sort things out."

Ryan could hear Dev sigh all the way through the phone.

"You honestly want her back? After everything that's happened?"

Ryan gripped the phone and stared out his window. "I don't know yet. I need some answers before I make that kind of decision. But if she's pregnant with my baby, I'm not letting her go again."

"Okay, you go. I'll email you all the issues. Just keep me posted and let me know if you have problems. I can be there at a moment's notice."

"Will do. Look, I know you and Cam think I'm nuts, but I appreciate you having my back."

Dev's dry response was immediate. "Yeah, you're nuts. But whatever makes you happy, man."

Ryan hung up and stared at the phone for a long

moment before summoning Jansen. He gave him a list of instructions, starting with the need for Kelly to see an obstetrician immediately. She'd need a doctor's clearance to travel, but if the doctor gave the okay, he planned for them to spend a few days alone. And maybe they could start putting the pieces back together.

Then he started a shopping list, ignoring Jansen's grimace. Kelly needed outfitting from head to toe.

Five

Kelly sat cross-legged on her bed, staring into empty space. She couldn't stay here. She'd been stupid to think that she could exist in an environment where she was exposed to Jarrod.

It had been all she could do to keep it together. She was furious that she'd sat there while that bastard stood in the doorway with his bewildered look of innocence, but she'd been paralyzed the moment he'd walked into Ryan's apartment.

She hated the feeling of helplessness and she'd never, *never* allow herself to be such a passive respondent again. Going forward, if she saw the bastard, she'd kick his ass, pregnant or not. And then she'd tell Ryan precisely what he could do with his precious brother.

She hated Jarrod with a passion she reserved for few things in her life. And she *hated* Ryan for turning his back on her when she absolutely needed him the most.

No, she couldn't stay here. Not a minute longer.

She forced herself to consider her alternatives. This time she wasn't fleeing on ragged impulse without caring which way the wind blew her. No, she would come up with a solid plan of action. She'd go someplace quiet and safe—a good place to raise her son or daughter.

"You're leaving, aren't you?"

Ryan's voice came from the door. She started guiltily and finally raised her eyes to his. Angry because she allowed herself to feel guilt even for a second, she hardened her gaze as she stared back at him.

"There's no reason for me to stay."

"Come with me into the living room," he said, holding his hand out to her. For a long moment she simply stared at his outstretched hand. She should refuse, but something in his voice made her comply and she slipped her hand into his much larger one. He pulled her up from the bed and led her into the living room.

Sitting on the couch, he pulled her down beside him. He ran an agitated hand through his hair. "I've been an ass and I'm sorry. You're in no condition to bear this stress and pressure and I've only added to your burden."

She opened her mouth to speak and he placed a finger over her lips. "Let me finish. I've been in the office all morning and I've got some problems arising with an extremely important project that my partners are unable to attend to. Problems that require my immediate attention and presence. I want you to come with me."

She stared blankly at him. Why? She didn't get it. Why torture themselves? Why was he so persistent in flogging the dead horse that was their relationship? He'd been the one to end it. He had rendered judgment and tossed her aside like she'd never meant anything to him.

She opened her mouth to ask him just that, but again, he silenced her with his finger.

"Let me take care of you, Kelly. Let's forget for the time being all the problems in the past and just concentrate on the present."

"You can't be serious."

"I'm very serious. I've never been more serious in my life. We have a lot to work out. We can't do that if we aren't willing to spend the time together and talk."

She'd never wanted to break down and cry more in her entire life. If only he'd been willing to listen *before*. If only he'd been willing to talk, to understand *then*. The one person she should have been able to count on above all others had coldly looked through her and called her a liar. And now he wanted to kiss and make up?

He touched her face with his fingers, and she was surprised that they trembled against her skin. His eyes were imploring her and she wavered on the edge of indecision. God, was she actually contemplating this farce? Even as she posed the question to herself she was shaking her head in automatic refusal.

He stopped the negative sway of her head by cupping her cheek and stroking his thumb lightly over her lips.

"No pressure, no promises, no obligations. Just you and me and a restful week on the beach. It's a start. It's all I'm asking for. I'll only ask for what you're willing to give."

"But the baby—"

"I would never do anything to endanger the baby," he said quietly. "Or you. You'll have to see the doctor here and get his okay to travel. It's the only way I would consider taking you on this trip."

Her eyes dropped to her hands knotted in her lap. It was tempting, so very tempting. He was asking, not demanding, and for a moment she was transported back to their time together—to the wonderfully tender and caring Ryan she had been engaged to. Could she leave him again after spending a week with him? Because she had no future with a man who could so coldly discard their relationship over the word of another.

The silence stretched out between them as she grappled with the decision. Yes, she would do it. She wasn't sure why. Nothing could come of it, but she wanted this time with him before she left to get on with her life. She nodded her assent and relief was stark in Ryan's eyes. It was so easy to pretend he cared when he put on such a good act. But clearly he didn't. If he had, they would still be together, married, awaiting the birth of their first child.

"We have to get you to the doctor this afternoon for a checkup. If he gives the thumbs-up we'll fly out tomorrow, so it's important you get plenty of rest today and tonight. Once we get there, the most strenuous thing you'll have to do is walk from the hotel room to the beach."

"I want separate rooms," she said.

"I've reserved us a suite."

She frowned but didn't argue.

"You won't regret this, Kell," he said, reverting to his pet name for her. She had the strangest urge to weep. How had they gotten so far away from the plans they had made just months earlier?

"We can do this. We can work it out."

She closed her eyes. The thing was, it was easy to be seduced by the intensity in those words. But going forward would be impossible until they'd addressed their past. And she never ever wanted to go back to that horrible day when her world had been so brutally upended.

The doctor was very approving of a week of rest and relaxation for Kelly and cautioned her to seek medical attention if the swelling got worse or she developed other symptoms.

Ryan had hung on to every word the doctor said and had acted just like a concerned husband and father. Instead of making her feel good, it depressed the hell out of her because it drew attention to the fact that their situation was hopeless.

When they arrived back at the apartment there were several department store bags stacked just inside the door. She eyed them curiously because they were decidedly feminine-looking, and if she wasn't mistaken, there was even a bag from a well-known lingerie store.

She glanced at Ryan, one eyebrow arched in question.

"Oh good, Jansen's been by," Ryan said as he walked over to the assortment of bags. "They're for you. For our trip." He gathered the handles and brought everything over to the couch, gesturing for her to have a look.

A little befuddled, she opened the packages, finding several maternity sundresses and sleek designer outfits, as well as beach attire all the way to a pair of sandals. As suspected, there were even all the girlie accoutrements in the lingerie bag.

"You shouldn't have done this," she murmured. How quickly they had fallen back into their old routine, and her discomfort level was off the charts.

"*I* didn't," he replied. "Jansen went shopping for me."

Despite herself, she smiled at the image of Ryan's hunky assistant traipsing through the maternity department in search of clothes and—even more hilarious—going into the lingerie store to buy panties and bras.

"How is Jansen?"

"Fine," Ryan replied. "Same as ever."

"Thank you for this," she added, swallowing her all-important pride for the moment.

His smile was genuine. "You're quite welcome. Why don't you go lie down for a while and I'll pack our suitcases. Then we can have dinner. We'll call it an early night since we're leaving tomorrow morning."

She left the clothes on the couch and slowly rose. It was stupid of her to soften toward him. It was stupid to wish even for a moment that things were back to the way they'd been before.

But being stupid didn't stop the yearning deep inside her aching heart. Sadness overwhelmed her, and she hurriedly left the living room so he wouldn't see her tears.

The next morning Ryan gently shook her awake and she stretched languidly before getting up. After her shower, he fixed them breakfast. When they were done eating, he gathered their luggage to take down to the car.

On the drive to the airport Kelly was quiet. A part of her felt a tingle of excitement at the prospect of a week in paradise with Ryan, while the other part dreaded the forced intimacy. She had focused so much on her anger and hatred that it had come as a shock to her that she was still deeply in love with Ryan. And that frustrated her more than anything. Was she a masochist?

First of all to love a man who quite obviously did not love her in return, but to love him even after his most cutting betrayal? Pathetic.

To her surprise, they weren't taking a commercial flight. Ryan had chartered a private jet to take them nonstop to the island.

The flight was just a few hours, but halfway through she began fidgeting in her seat. She was nervous, edgy, and she was suffering a major case of cold feet.

"Why don't you recline your seat," he said, reaching over to help her.

When she was tilted back he nudged her over. "Turn on your side and I'll rub your back."

Too uncomfortable to turn down his touch, she faced the window and settled on her side.

Strong, tender fingers began a slow exploration of her back, rubbing and kneading. She sighed in contentment and relief as the tension faded in her muscles. Yawning widely, she snuggled deeper into the seat, enjoying the delicious sensations his touch was bringing.

For just a little while, she forced the past from her mind. She forced thoughts of the future away as well. All she focused on was the fact that she was with Ryan and he was acting as tender and loving as he had when they'd been together.

She went to sleep with a smile on her face.

As they prepared to land, Ryan shook her awake and raised her seat back up. She was so relaxed and lethargic that she sat there quietly while the plane touched down.

Fifteen minutes later, Ryan wrapped a protective arm around her as they exited the plane. He seated her in the waiting car while he saw that the luggage was loaded and then they drove away.

They checked into the lavish hotel that was situated directly on the beach, and Ryan jokingly informed her that when his partnership's resort was built, it would make the one they were staying in look like a two-star hotel instead of the five stars it boasted.

Kelly found that hard to believe when they were ushered into a sprawling suite that was many times bigger than her apartment in Houston.

She sank into the couch, that looked out the sliding patio doors to the private expanse of beach beyond. Ryan put away their luggage and then knelt in front of her, slipping her shoes off to inspect her feet for swelling. He began massaging the souls, moving up to the instep and arch. A moan of absolute pleasure escaped her lips.

"Feel good?"

"Oh my God, does it."

He continued his ministrations, watching her silently. Her hand crept to her rounded belly and she smiled as the baby rolled beneath her fingers.

"Is the baby moving?" Ryan asked.

She nodded and he stopped rubbing her feet.

"Can I feel?"

She brought his hand to her stomach and placed it over the spot where her hand had been. He jerked in surprise as her stomach bumped beneath his palm, and his expression was akin to awe.

"That's incredible. Doesn't it hurt?"

Chuckling, she said, "No. It isn't always comfortable, but it's certainly not painful."

He kept his hand there a few more moments and then rose, a regretful glint in his eyes. "Would you like to have dinner on the patio or do you want to go eat in the restaurant?"

"Here, please," she replied. "I like our view and it's private."

He nodded his agreement and went to phone in their room service order.

Thirty minutes later the meal was wheeled in on a serving cart and the attendant set the table out on the patio. The two ate in silence, enjoying the setting sun and the sound of the waves crashing in the distance.

As they finished, Ryan suggested she go to bed; but she wasn't tired. She was quite rested actually and felt an eagerness to explore their secluded cove. When she expressed the desire to take a walk along the beach, Ryan hesitated at first, but agreed to accompany her when she was adamant about going.

Kelly breathed deeply of the salty air as the ocean breeze whipped at her long hair, lifting it from her waist. She slipped her sandals off and bent awkwardly to pick them up. Ryan quickly gathered them for her and tucked them under his arm. Digging her toes into the damp sand, she ventured into the bubbling surf, letting the foam wash over her feet.

Ryan removed his shoes and joined her after he rolled up the cuffs of his jeans. He slipped an arm around her as they made their way down the beach, but she resisted the urge to move closer to his side.

"We shouldn't go far," he cautioned. "You aren't supposed to be on your feet for this long. I promised the doctor this would be a restful trip for you."

"This is a lot more restful than being on my feet twelve hours a day," she said lightly.

He frowned and his hand tightened around her waist. "That won't happen again."

She didn't respond, but turned back toward their suite. Ryan's hand slipped from her waist as she walked ahead of him. When they walked back inside the patio doors, Kelly sank onto the plush couch.

"Would you like something to drink?" he asked.

"Juice, if you have it."

He rummaged in the well-stocked fridge and came back with a glass of orange juice a moment later.

"You should go on to bed," he said gently. "There'll be plenty of time to explore the beach after you've had a good night's rest."

Even though she was tired, the day had been so...perfect... that she hated to bring it to an end. Spending the time with

Ryan had been bittersweet, a throwback to happier times when things had been…

She sighed. She had to stop with the endless string of memories. She had a week with Ryan. One week when the past wasn't supposed to matter. If he could forget then she would try to as well. And when it came to an end, maybe her memories of him wouldn't be quite so bitter.

She struggled to get out of the ultrasoft couch and laughed when she realized she was well and truly stuck. Ryan reached down to help her to her feet and she finally managed to stand.

For a long moment she stood in front of him, her gaze stroking softly over the chiseled lines of his face. It was the first time she'd allowed herself to stare unguardedly at him.

"Good night, Ryan," she whispered softly.

He looked as though he wanted to kiss her and for a moment she wondered how she would react if he did. But finally he said, "Good night, Kelly. Sleep well."

She turned to go into her bedroom, little twinges of regret nagging her the entire way.

Six

Kelly didn't sleep that night. Not that it should have come as any surprise to her. She lay awake in her bed, reliving the past. The first time she met Ryan. How he'd swept her off her feet and into a passionate and all-consuming relationship.

From the day he first asked her out, they hadn't spent a single day apart for several weeks. By the end of the first month, she'd moved into his apartment, and by the end of the second month of their whirlwind courtship, his ring was on her finger.

She had never been quite sure why he'd chosen her. It wasn't as if she thought she was inferior, but Ryan Beardsley was an extremely wealthy man. He could have his pick of women. Why Kelly?

She didn't have family connections. She didn't have money or prestige. She was a simple college student eking out a living on a waitress's salary.

Until Ryan.

Everything had changed for her, and maybe she'd been too caught up in the fairy tale that was her relationship with Ryan to ever question the important things. Like whether he loved and trusted her.

How would he react now if once again she tried to tell him what had really happened the day he'd tossed her out of his life? He hadn't believed her then. Why would now be any different?

Tears blurred her vision as her thoughts drifted back to that day.

Kelly stared at the pregnancy test, a mixture of joy and worry bubbling through her chest. She quickly hid the stick and then smiled as she imagined telling Ryan the news. She didn't think he'd be upset. They were planning to marry soon and they'd often talked of their desire to start a family.

She couldn't wait to tell him. She searched her memory for what he had going on at the office today. He didn't have any important meetings and he was supposed to be in his office for the entirety of the afternoon. That meant she could pop in and surprise him.

She hugged herself in excitement, nearly dancing across the floor of their bedroom as she imagined his reaction.

A noise from the living room halted her. Then she smiled. Oh, this would be perfect. Ryan was home. He sometimes surprised her by dropping in for lunch. Today his timing was impeccable.

She started to call out to him when Jarrod, appeared in the doorway to the bedroom.

She was momentarily speechless. While Jarrod popped in frequently, he always did so when Ryan was at home. He had to know Ryan was working today.

"Jarrod, what are you doing here? Ryan's at work. I don't expect him home until later."

"I came to talk to you," Jarrod said.

She cocked her head to the side. "Okay. What's up? Let's go into the living room."

He ignored her and took another step into the bedroom. Unease prickled down her spine. Something was definitely off with him.

"How much would it take for you to walk away from Ryan?"

Her eyes widened in shock. She couldn't have heard him correctly. "Excuse me?"

"Don't play dumb. You're a smart girl. How much would it take for you to dump Ryan and take off?"

"You're offering me money? Did your mother put you up to this? You're both out of your minds. I love Ryan. He loves me. We're getting married."

Something that looked like genuine regret flickered across Jarrod's face. He fidgeted nervously and then pinned her with his stare. "I'd hoped you'd make this easy. It's not a small amount of money we're offering."

The "we" in that statement confirmed Kelly's suspicions that Ryan's mother was indeed the mastermind of this operation. She was about to tell Jarrod exactly where he and his mother could get off when he took another step toward her. The look in his eyes had her hastily backing away.

"I think you should go now," she said even as she reached for the phone.

Jarrod lunged across the bed, knocking the phone from her hand. She was so stunned by the sudden attack that for a moment she didn't—couldn't—defend herself.

He shoved her down on the bed, his hands moving roughly over her body, pushing at her shirt, pulling at her pants. She drew her knee up, trying to catch him in the groin, but he dodged and then rolled her underneath him.

She cried out in pain at the rough mauling. She was furious and terrified. He fully intended to rape her in Ryan's bed. Had he lost his mind? Ryan would kill him for this.

His hands moved over her skin with bruising force. Knowing if she wasn't able to fight him off that he'd assault her in her own home, she began struggling with renewed force.

She finally managed to land a blow between his legs, which had him doubling over, clutching at himself. She rolled, falling to the floor, her hands desperately grabbing at her clothing.

She got to her feet, her hand clutching her bruised throat. "He'll kill you for this," she gasped. "How did you think you'd get away with it? My God, you're his brother! You bastard."

She started for the door, her only thought to get to Ryan, but Jarrod's words gave her pause.

"He'll never believe you."

"You're insane," she choked out even as she ran for the door.

But Jarrod had been right. Ryan hadn't believed her. Jarrod had called his brother from Ryan's own apartment before she could arrive at Ryan's office. He'd given Ryan his own accounting of what happened, and the genius of his story was that he told Ryan exactly what Kelly would tell him. Only Jarrod told Ryan that Kelly had been the instigator and that when Jarrod told her he was going to tell Ryan that Kelly had cheated on him, Kelly concocted a smug story that Jarrod had assaulted her.

Jarrod played his part to the hilt. That he was *the*

victim of Kelly's lies and manipulations. So when Kelly ran to Ryan's office and related the exact story that Jarrod warned Ryan she would tell, Ryan had been coldly furious.

He'd written her that damn check and he'd thrown her out of his life.

Kelly lay in her bed, numbed by the painful memories. And now, here on this island, she was supposed to forget the past. Put it behind her. Move forward and pick up where she and Ryan had left off.

Forgetting that she'd been horribly betrayed by people she trusted.

When Ryan knocked softly at her door, she roused herself from the weight of her thoughts, cursing that it was already morning and she'd done little better than catnap.

She struggled out of bed and hauled her robe around her body then staggered to the door to open it.

Ryan stood outside, dressed in slacks and a dress shirt. He had impending business written all over him.

"I've left breakfast on the bar for you. I have to run out to the construction site for a few hours. Will you be all right alone?"

She nodded, relieved that she wouldn't immediately have to face him. She needed time to regain her composure. Time to mentally reconstruct her defenses.

"Yes, of course. When will you be back?"

He checked his watch. "It's eight now. I shouldn't be later than noon. We can have lunch in the hotel restaurant and then go for a walk on the beach if you like. Take it easy while I'm gone. I'll worry if I know you're on the beach by yourself."

She rolled her eyes. "I think I'm capable of leaving the hotel room alone."

"I know you are," he said quietly. "I just worry and I'd prefer to be with you."

There wasn't much she could say to that, so she nodded. "I'll see you at lunch."

He lifted his hand in a wave and then walked away. For a moment she stared after him and then she closed the door, leaning against it.

Day one of attempting to forget the past and forge ahead.

"How's that working out for you?" she muttered as she traipsed into the bathroom.

Though she had every intention of at least taking in the portion of the beach right outside the patio of her suite, she still wanted a long, hot bath. Even if it meant she'd still have to shower when she came in with sand in all her nooks and crannies.

After drawing a tub full of steaming water, she sank up to her ears and sighed in complete bliss. She hadn't made the water too hot, and she wouldn't stay long. Then she'd go bake in the sun for a bit.

After twenty minutes, regretfully, she toed the lever for the drain and then hauled herself out of the tub. Her stomach growled and she hurriedly went through the motions of dressing and putting on enough makeup to look presentable in public.

She devoured the bagel, the cinnamon roll and the fruit Ryan had left for her. She ate every crumb and licked her fingers, feeling like a pig, but a very satisfied pig. It had been a while since she'd had a hearty appetite and it had been weeks since anything had actually tasted good to her.

After downing an entire glass of juice, she smacked her lips in pleasure and went in search of a beach towel she could spread out on the sand.

She'd seen umbrellas dotting the private section of the

beach reserved for the hotel guests and she planned to make good use of one while she waited for Ryan to return.

After months of being on her feet for hours on end, working a thankless job for paltry wages, a day lounging on the beach sounded about as decadent as it got. She was going to enjoy every minute.

She didn't bother with sandals since she wasn't going far. The sand felt luxurious beneath her feet. So warm and soft. She sighed in contentment as she headed for one of the nearby umbrellas.

The sound of the ocean filled her ears, beautiful and so peaceful. Here was a place where she could forget the pain of her past. It was a place made for being soothed. A vacation for the soul.

It sounded ridiculous and a little corny but she liked it and quickly adopted it as her motto for this trip.

She spread the towel out over the sand, positioned the umbrella just so and then sank down, drawing her knees up as she stared over the rolling waves.

Closing her eyes, she inhaled deeply and enjoyed the breeze dancing across her face. Her sleepless night quickly caught up to her as tight muscles relaxed and the tension she'd held for so long gradually fell away.

Soon it was hard to keep her eyes open, so she stretched out on the towel and turned on her side to face the ocean. The umbrella provided plenty of shade. A nap was too tempting to pass up. She'd simply wait for Ryan here.

Shortly after noon, Ryan let himself into the room and looked around for Kelly. He called out to her but got no answer. He checked the bedroom in case she was napping, but found that the maid service had already come through to make the beds.

He sighed, knowing she hadn't paid the least bit of

attention to his concern over her going onto the beach without him. It wasn't as if he thought anything would happen to her or that she was incapable of being alone, but her medical condition concerned him. And yeah, he was probably being a little overprotective, but he found with Kelly—just as he always had—he tended to overreact.

He stepped out onto the patio and scanned the beach, looking for any sign of her. When he didn't immediately spot her, he began walking toward the umbrellas that dotted the sand.

When he got to the third, he saw her lying on her side, eyes closed and looking so damn beautiful—and vulnerable—that it made his chest ache.

He watched the soft rise and fall of her chest. The mound of her belly moved in a ripple across the floral sarong she wore. Her feet were bare and he could still detect signs of swelling around her ankles.

It wasn't as bad as it had been, but it still concerned him a great deal.

He eased down onto the towel beside her and stroked his hand through her silky blond hair. He slid his fingers down her arm, over the curve of her hip and then down to the tight ball of her belly.

She sighed in her sleep and shifted closer to his hand. The urge to pull her into his arms was so strong that he jerked his hand away so he wouldn't do just that.

If only he could erase the past six months and have things back the way they were. But now he had to deal with not only Kelly's betrayal, but the fact that she carried his child. Whether she admitted it or not he felt strongly that she carried *his* baby. He wouldn't allow himself to think otherwise.

Reaching out, he shook her, not wanting her to be exposed to the midday rays of sun, umbrella or not. She came awake slowly and blinked sleepily at him. Her soft smile of pleasure warmed him to his toes.

"When did you get back?" she asked in a groggy, sleep filled voice.

"A few minutes ago," he said, smiling at her. "Are you ready to go eat?"

She nodded and pushed herself up. He reached down to help her up, and she slid her fingers into his, allowing him to pull her to her feet. Wrapping his arm around her shoulders, he guided her back to the suite, enjoying the few moments of intimacy afforded him.

While she showered and changed, he called Devon to give him an update on the construction schedule. The two men talked for a few minutes and Dev didn't mention Kelly once. Something Ryan was glad for.

No matter that his friends and his family thought he was crazy, this was something he simply had to do. He hadn't been able to stop thinking about Kelly in the months since their relationship had ended. He might be the biggest fool in the world, but he was determined to figure this out between them. Even if it meant eventually going their separate ways.

When Kelly reemerged from her room, there was a lightness to her eyes that had been absent ever since he'd found her in the café in Houston. She looked a lot like the old Kelly. The Kelly he'd been crazy about. The one who always had a ready smile, was quick to laugh and who offered her affection freely.

The reserved, angry Kelly was someone he didn't know.

She seemed a little nervous and unsure as she came to stand by the bar, and he hated that there was a tangible barrier between them. Before she wouldn't have hesitated to launch herself into his arms and give him one of her big, squeezing hugs.

Now? He ached to get close enough to her that she didn't withdraw.

"You ready?" he asked, forcing a casual note into his voice.

She nodded. He put his hand to her back, noting the expanse of flesh bared by the sundress. Jansen had done well. The dress fit her like a dream, molding in all the right places. The bodice was held up by ends tied at the nape of her neck; but her flesh was bare all the way down to the small of her back.

Where his palm rested, he itched to caress and stroke until she responded to him, until he proved that the attraction between them hadn't died.

They walked down to the restaurant that overlooked the ocean and were seated in a private alcove that had a huge glass window, giving them an unobstructed view of the beach.

As they looked over their menus, Ryan stole a glance at Kelly. Seeming to sense his perusal, she looked up and offered a tentative smile. He smiled back, captivated by the sparkle in her blue eyes.

She was…beautiful. And this time when she looked at him, he didn't see the dark anger that had sparked so often since their reunion.

The moment came to a shrieking halt a second later.

"Ryan! What are you doing here?"

The feminine voice rang out over the secluded area, making him wince and Kelly jump in surprise. He glanced up to see Roberta Maxwell bearing down on their table and he muttered an appropriate expletive under his breath.

As she approached the table, he rose to return her greeting. He brushed a polite kiss over her cheek when she presented it to him and tried to extricate his hand from hers when she grabbed on to it.

"I'm here on business. The question is, what are *you* doing here?"

Her laughter tinkled out like fine china. "Oh, this is one of my favorite places to visit. The food is just divine, and the accommodations can't be beat." She turned to Kelly who was eyeing Roberta warily. "Who is this, Ryan?"

Like hell she didn't know who Kelly was and like hell she just happened to be here. He'd lay odds that Roberta Maxwell had never been to St. Angelo in her life. She was shockingly transparent and didn't seem to give a damn. That could only mean she was here to cause trouble. His mother's name was written all over this and he was so furious he wanted to strangle Roberta's skinny neck. And then move on to his mother. He never should have informed his mother that he'd be out of town and he damn sure shouldn't have told her *where* he was going. He'd hoped… Well, it didn't really matter what he'd hoped. Roberta was here and it was apparent it wasn't some damn coincidence.

"Roberta, meet Kelly Christian. Kelly, this is an acquaintance of mine, Roberta Maxwell."

Roberta's smile was dazzling and she playfully fluttered her fingers at Ryan. "Oh la, darling. Surely I rate higher than an acquaintance."

Kelly's eyes narrowed and Ryan decided that politeness was overrated.

"We're having a private dinner, Roberta. If you'll excuse us, please?"

Undaunted, Roberta entwined her arm in his and her voice dropped to a low purr. "We must get together while you are here. Perhaps have dinner ourselves. I was so sorry to have missed you the last time I had dinner with your mother. I do love her so."

He extricated himself from her grasp and stepped

back a few paces from her. "I'm afraid my time here is spoken for," he said. "Perhaps when we return to New York, Kelly and I can have you over for dinner." He said the last pointedly, not that he really expected it to deter Roberta. It wasn't his fault she was as thick as a brick.

Roberta's eyes flashed with annoyance and her finely painted lips formed a full pout. "Really, darling, when did you decide to take back the little cheater?"

Kelly's face blanched and she threw down her napkin. Ryan's hand shot up to silence Roberta. "You know, I've had about enough. It's time you left. Give my *regards* to my mother, and while you're at it, tell her to stay the hell out of my affairs. Advice you'd be well advised to take as well."

She twisted her pouty lips and ran a well-manicured set of nails down the lapel of his suit. "No need to get huffy, darling. I know you have to be polite to her since you don't know whose baby she carries."

With a careless wave, she walked gracefully away, leaving Ryan so furious that he wanted to hurl his chair across the room. But his anger had nothing on the fury flashing in Kelly's eyes when he turned to see her standing in front of her seat, her fists clenched and pressed to the top of the table.

Seven

Ryan gripped the back of his seat with one hand and ran a hand through his hair with the other. "I'm sorry."

"I've lost my appetite," she stated flatly as she pushed away from her seat.

"Kelly, don't," he protested. "You have to eat. Don't let that cat ruin our dinner."

Her lips tightened in fury. "That *cat* seems to know an awful lot about our situation, wouldn't you agree?"

She turned from the table and stalked toward the entrance of the restaurant. As soon as she hit the lobby, she turned down the long corridor leading to their suite. Angrily, she jammed the card into the lock, swearing when the light didn't immediately flash green. She slammed the card in again and yanked at the handle when the telltale whir sounded.

Once inside, she bolted the door behind her and went into her bedroom. She perched on the edge of the bed, and in the distance she heard knocking and then Ryan's angry voice through the door.

She was too angry to give a damn that he'd have to walk all the way around to the patio glass doors to gain entrance.

She'd had enough of this farcical…hell, she didn't even know what to call it this time around. Whatever it was, she wanted out.

It was enough that she'd been humiliated by Ryan and his brother, but now she had to put up with some brainless airhead piling on as well? They could all go to hell.

Her head came up when her bedroom door flew open, revealing a livid Ryan. Yeah, well he wasn't the only one, and she wasn't backing down. She got to her feet and faced him head-on.

"What the hell is wrong with you, Kelly? It isn't like you to go to such extremes. What do you hope to accomplish by locking me out? Ignoring our problems isn't going to make them go away."

"How would you know what isn't like me?" she retorted. "It would seem you never knew me at all."

His eyes flashed and he nodded. "That much is certainly true."

Pissed at the innuendo in his response, she fixed him with a cold stare. "I want out of here. I want the first flight out I can get. This is ridiculous. It's a waste of time. It's never going to work between us, Ryan."

He swore and moved to stand just in front of her, his hands gripping her shoulders. "We had an agreement. One week together and we forget the past."

She gaped at him incredulously. "Did you not witness that debacle in the restaurant? How on earth would she know so much about me and our relationship unless *you* told her? How the hell are we supposed to forget the past when your little floozy is busy throwing it in my face? I don't appreciate being made a fool of. And I certainly don't appreciate being bandied about in conversation like yesterday's garbage."

"I never discussed you with her," he said emphatically.

"Amazing then that she knew so much."

"Why is it you have so little faith in me, Kelly? *I* didn't betray *you*."

She flinched. It always came back to this. No matter what, it always came back to the fact that he believed she had betrayed him and refused to entertain any other possibility.

She turned away from him, trying to control the tide of rage boiling over her. Shaking with her attempts to tamp down her angry shouts, she clenched her hands and closed her eyes tightly.

Suddenly she was spun around to face him again and he crushed his lips to hers, cupping her face in his hands. She brought her hands up between them to push against his chest, but his arms went tightly around her back, pulling her even closer to him.

She moaned low in her throat as his kiss gentled and became exploratory. He moved her to the edge of the bed and lowered her onto the mattress, never ceasing his slow movement over her lips. "Damn it, Kelly, just don't say anything for a while. No words. We can't seem to have a conversation without hurting each other, so for just a little while let's communicate without talking."

She gazed into his eyes as he drew away from her and studied his expression. How could she want him so much after all the mistrust and hurt? His fingertips caressed her cheek and she closed her eyes, arching further into his hand.

What if she let him make love to her? Would it be so bad? Or would it just confirm his low opinion of her.

Like a bucket of ice water, that thought quashed any desire she had to surrender to his lovemaking. He must have sensed her withdrawal because he drew away, looking at her in confusion.

"I can't do this," she said, scrambling to sit up on the bed. "Not knowing what you think of me."

The words caught and raggedly slipped from her lips. Drawing protective arms around her chest, she sat on the rumpled covers watching him warily.

"Don't stare at me like you expect me to pounce," he said in disgust. "I am not into unwilling women."

He left the room, slamming the door solidly behind him.

Feeling more alone than she had when she left him the first time, she edged off the bed and walked into the bathroom to splash cool water on her flushed face.

She stared back at her reflection and saw the utter misery in her eyes. Tears welled. Her chest hurt. Her heart hurt. This was no way to live.

She wouldn't beg him to believe her. She'd already done that. On her knees no less. What was left? He didn't believe her. She wasn't going to beg him again. There was nowhere for this relationship to go but straight to hell in a handbasket.

Turning the water off, she put her elbows on the countertop and buried her face in her hands as sobs billowed from her throat.

She hadn't been happy in six long months but now her misery was even more pronounced. Her circumstances hadn't been the best in Houston, but she hadn't had to look at the man she loved and know that he thought the worst of her.

Tears still sliding down her face, she went blindly back into the bedroom and curled into a ball on the bed. Her shoulders shook and the tears that she'd held back for so long streamed down her cheeks in steady trails.

After a few minutes, the bed dipped and Ryan put a hand to her cheek. "I'm sorry, Kell," he said hoarsely. "Don't cry. Please don't cry."

Gently he lifted her into his arms and cradled her to his chest. She clung to him and buried her face in his neck as her tears soaked into his shirt.

"I'm sorry. This isn't how I wanted things to go. I never meant to upset you or make you feel worthless. I swear it."

His voice was thick with regret and it trembled with emotion as he stroked his hand over her hair.

"You have to know that Roberta was here for the sole reason of causing trouble between us."

She went still against him, knowing that what she was about to say would probably only piss him off more, but she was through pulling her punches.

"Are you ready to admit that your mother hates me and would do anything to get rid of me? If you didn't talk to Roberta about us, then who the hell do you think did?"

"I know," he said quietly. "It won't work, though. As soon as we return home, I'll put an end to this. I promise. She won't be allowed to hurt you like this."

She sagged against him. She wanted so desperately to believe him this time. His eyes were slowly being opened. Did this mean he would eventually accept her version of what happened six months ago?

He pressed his lips to the top of her head and whispered softly. "Stay with me, Kelly. We have so much to work out. God knows we've been through a lot together. But in order to do that I need you here with me. Not a thousand miles away in some godforsaken hellhole where I can't take care of you and our baby."

He pulled her carefully away and wiped at the trails of wetness on her cheeks with his thumbs. His gaze was haunted, intense and dark with emotion. Honest to God, he looked like he was hurting every bit as much as she was.

It had been on the tip of her tongue to deny that he was the father yet again, but this time she didn't. It was pointless to argue with him, and besides, he *was* the father.

He too was obviously expecting her to deny it because when she remained silent his eyes lit with hope.

"Give us a chance, Kell. Let me take care of you and the baby. Whatever is wrong between us, we can fix it."

"I wish I had your optimism," she murmured. How to explain that their problems were insurmountable in the face of his lack of trust in her?

He lowered his lips to hers, kissing her so lovingly that she felt a resurgence of tears. She broke away and then laid her cheek against his chest. It felt so good to be back in his arms, for just a moment to let go of all the pain and resentment.

He put a hand to her hair, his touch tentative.

"Kell, we need to talk about the baby. But first we have to settle this matter between us."

She closed her eyes, feeling dread settle in the pit of her stomach. "If I tell you the baby is yours, will you believe me?"

He went still against her and then he let all his breath out. He cupped his hand to the side of her face and held her against his chest.

"I'll believe you, Kell."

Slowly she pushed against his chest until she was eye level with him. How it hurt that he was willing to believe her now about their child, but he hadn't been willing to believe her then when it came to his brother.

"She's yours," she said in a quiet voice.

Satisfaction was a savage light in his eyes. He framed her face tightly in his hands and then lowered his mouth to take hers in a possessive, fierce sweep.

Her lips were swollen when she managed to tear her mouth away. Her pulse raced and they stared at each other in silence. She was afraid to believe in him. So afraid she was nearly paralyzed with it.

"Do you believe me? I have to know, Ryan. We can't go forward unless you believe me."

His hand drifted down to the bulge of her belly and he slid his palm over the curve, splaying his fingers out until he covered a wide area.

"I believe you."

She bit her lip to keep from asking him if he'd believe her about everything else. She knew he didn't, he hadn't. And maybe it was too late. Wasn't it?

"Kelly?" His soft entreaty broke through her musings. He stroked her cheek with the tip of one finger. "I believe you. Okay? Jarrod said he wore a condom and the timing was right for us. I won't believe you slept with anyone else. It was just that one time with Jarrod, wasn't it?"

The soft plea froze her to the bone. Hurt crashed through her heart—a heart she thought was already irreparably shattered. She was wrong. She hadn't thought there was anything Ryan could do to hurt her further. She'd been wrong about that too.

"Why does that make you cry?"

Ryan wiped at the tear that trailed down her cheek, his expression one of complete bewilderment. Then he leaned in and kissed the moisture away.

She braced her hands on his arms, her mind a chaotic

twist of anger and wretched grief. It took every bit of her strength to gather her shattered composure and speak to him when what she wanted to do was flee.

"If this has any hope of working, you'll never breathe his name to me again. You were the one who wanted this. One week. No past. Forget the past. It's what you said. I'm holding you to it. You bring him up ever again, and I walk—no, I run. Are we clear?"

He looked shocked by her vehemence. He opened his mouth as if he wanted to push further, but she shook her head and started to slide from his lap.

He made a grab for her, pulling her close to him again. "All right. No past. I won't bring it up again. I promise. Will you stay, Kelly? Will you work with me?"

She closed her eyes again and the fight left her. Her head dropped down and exhaustion crept in, gripping the back of her neck, squeezing until her entire head ached vilely.

His fingers slid around her neck, rubbing and caressing with gentle pressure. Had she been that obvious?

"I still care about you, Kelly."

She leaned her forehead against his. His onslaught was relentless and he didn't play fair.

"I'm afraid," she whispered.

"So am I."

Surprised by his admission, she retreated a few inches and flicked her gaze up and down, searching for the truth in his eyes.

"Don't look at me like that. You aren't the only one hurting. I... Damn it, I promised we wouldn't bring the past up. I'm not going to. But you aren't the only one who got hurt in all this. I cared about you. I wanted to marry you. I..."

He dragged a hand through his hair. He suddenly looked

haggard and tired, worn down by the dark emotion that flowed between the two of them.

"I still want to marry you," he quietly admitted.

Eight

The admission was stark, so plainly and painfully laid out. Almost as if he wasn't happy with the truth of the words but said them all the same. He stared at her, his discomfort growing by the second.

She stared back, baffled and unable to form a single-word response to his declaration.

He didn't love her. Didn't trust her. He believed the absolute worse about her. All he seemed willing to accept was that her child was his—and only because his brother had claimed to have worn a condom.

But he wanted to marry her.

She laughed.

It was a hysterical, shrill, unpleasant sound.

His eyes narrowed. "That wasn't exactly the reaction I'd hoped for."

Her own eyes widened. "Was that a proposal?"

She swallowed the laughter this time because he was wearing an extremely dark, agitated look.

He gripped the back of his neck. "No, yes, maybe. I'd like that to be where we end up. But we've got a long way to go before we get there. I just want you to say that you still care. Enough to want to stay and work things out. We'll take it slow. One day at a time. I won't let anything happen again like what happened at lunch."

"And how are you going to do that?" she asked softly. "How can you make your family or your acquaintances accept me? And they don't, Ryan. You always told me I imagined it, but let's be honest here. Your mother couldn't stand me. Your friends couldn't understand what you saw in me. And it's obvious your brother thought I was unfaithful. An opinion you adopted."

He rose abruptly. She slid off his lap and onto the mattress as he stood by the bed, his hand still at his nape.

"You said you didn't want to talk about the past. Either we're going to or we aren't, but none of this pick and choose your shots."

He dropped his hand and then leaned over her, planting his hands on either side of her legs. "Just answer the question, Kelly. Are you going to stay? Do you even want to try? Are you willing to work this out so that maybe we can be happy together again?"

He asked it as though it was something she could answer immediately. It wasn't a simple matter. No matter which way she answered, she would be hurt.

She licked her lips. Her heart screamed at her that she was an idiot to get involved with him again. Her head told her that without trust their relationship was doomed from the start, and he'd already proved he had absolutely no faith in her.

Was she willing to put herself in a position where everyone else's word would be taken above her own?

But something deeper, beneath the pain and the anger

and the betrayal, stirred and twisted within her at the thought of being together with Ryan again.

She told herself that there was nothing wrong with staying with him until her child was born so she'd have a safe haven and a place to live. Food to eat. She'd have comfort. All the things she'd been denied for the past six months.

But she also knew she couldn't stay with him without involving her heart again. So the decision was whether she wanted to forgive and forget and move on or whether she wanted to make a clean, permanent break and move on, whatever that entailed.

Or maybe she should settle for a few stolen moments with a man she loved and hated with equal fervor.

The longer she was silent, the more the hope faded in Ryan's eyes. He seemed resigned to her inevitable rejection, and she couldn't help but draw the parallel between now and the time she'd stood so vulnerable in front of him, begging for his trust, his love, his support.

The idea of revenge didn't appeal. It left a heavy feeling of sadness and brought her no happiness and certainly no peace.

She was a fool. And that too brought her no peace.

"I'll stay," she said in a voice devoid of the joy the decision should have brought.

Though it was lacking in her own tone and expression, hope flared back to life in Ryan's eyes. He gripped her arms and then slid his hands up over her shoulders and neck to gently hold her in place as he pressed a tender kiss to her lips.

There was a wealth of emotion conveyed in the simplest touch of his mouth. His breath came in ragged spurts from his chest and for the first time she realized how much he'd feared her rejection.

She wasn't a huge believer in karma but now she wondered if this was his penance. To feel as she had felt so many months before.

But that thought brought her no satisfaction either. She wouldn't wish that feeling on anyone.

He drew away and brushed the hair from her cheek and continued to stroke the contours of her face.

"Spend the afternoon with me, Kell. You need to eat. I'll order us food and we can go eat on the beach. Watch the sun go down. I had Jansen pack a bathing suit for you if you'd like to go in the water."

She reached for the hand that rested against her cheek and curled her fingers around it, holding it there for a long moment.

"I'd like that," she finally said.

She and Ryan strolled to the same umbrella she'd used for her nap earlier that morning and he spread out a blanket on the sand. After he was satisfied she would have a comfortable seat, he helped her down and then began unpacking the picnic basket prepared by the restaurant.

He settled beside her and they began to eat.

Kelly stared out over the water as she munched on one of the tasty little confections whose name escaped her. It had cheese and shrimp. She wasn't sure of the other ingredients, but it was good and she was starving.

The sky had started to soften. Wispy pastel tendrils flirted across the horizon as the sun sank lower. She closed her eyes and allowed the breeze to soothe her fried nerves.

She'd expended more emotional energy over the past months than she had in a lifetime. She wanted to exist free of distress. Just for a little while. She wanted to forget the nights she'd been unable to sleep for crying or the nights she'd lain awake hurting so much that she'd wondered if it would ever stop.

Here she just wanted to be. Here she could at least pretend that the past six months hadn't happened. This could very well have been her honeymoon. A romantic island getaway.

Ryan had certainly played the part of the solicitous husband.

"Penny for your thoughts?"

Slowly she dropped her gaze from the vivid splash of blue and turned her head to Ryan.

"I was thinking that it's easy to pretend here."

The blue in his eyes deepened until it ran darker than the water rolling onto shore.

"We could pretend," he acknowledged. "But we don't have to."

"So did you get things straightened out at the building site?" she asked, not wanting to delve into pretend versus real. They were supposed to forget the past. At least for this week. That didn't leave a whole lot to talk about.

"Just a misunderstanding. I should have it cleared up by tomorrow. I have a joint meeting in the morning with the local contractors and the man we hired to oversee the project. If all goes well, I'll be finished and we'll have a few days to do what we want."

"When do you have to be back in New York?" she asked carefully. Because she knew the whole fantasy would come to a screeching halt once that happened.

"I don't know yet. I'm not in a hurry," he said as he studied her. "Right now I prefer to concentrate on the time we have here together."

She nodded, her acceptance coming a little easier now that she'd had more time to grasp the idea.

"Will you sleep with me tonight, Kelly?"

Her eyes widened.

He cursed. "That came out completely wrong. I'd like for us to sleep together. Actually sleep. In the same bed. I'd like to hold you again. Nothing more. Just let me hold you."

The idea of lying in his arms, of snuggling into his body and tangling her legs with his… It was so compelling that she suddenly wanted it more than her next breath.

Taking a deep breath, she nodded.

He reached over, took her hand and simply held it, their fingers wound tightly. He leaned back and positioned himself up on his elbow at an angle and then pulled her so she could rest against his chest.

They remained that way until hotel workers came out to light the torches along the beach as dusk deepened and the stars began to pop in the sky.

Soft music floated from down the beach where an outdoor lounge area was located. The notes with the waves made for incomparable music.

She leaned her head back in the crook of his neck and gazed dreamily up at the sky now that the umbrella had been folded down. He turned his face so that his lips brushed across her cheek in a kiss and then he too glanced skyward.

"Make a wish," she murmured.

"I have my wish. Now make yours."

She took a deep breath and held it for a long second. Then she closed her eyes and made her wish. Sadness crept in and took hold because she knew that some wishes couldn't come true.

After a moment, Ryan stirred under her and then carefully pushed her upward so he could move from behind her. He got to his feet, dusted sand from his jeans and reached down for her hand.

Thinking he was ready to head back to their suite, she let him pull her up. But instead of walking toward the hotel, he took her closer to the water's edge.

Moonlight splashed like silver across the surface of the water. The sky was filling rapidly with stars, scattered like fairy dust across the horizon.

How fanciful she was tonight. Wishes and fairy dust. It seemed appropriate for such a magical setting, though. Maybe she'd wake up in the morning and this would have all been a dream.

If that was the case, she was determined to exist in her dream world for as long as possible.

Without a word, Ryan took her in his arms and began to move to the distant strains of music. He gathered her close and she tucked her head beneath his chin, leaning into him as they swayed in time with the ocean and the soft melody lilting through the air.

Closer and closer they melted together until they were barely moving at all. She was tucked securely against his body, a perfect fit.

He laid his cheek atop her head and turned slowly, his feet guiding their rhythm.

Finally they stopped moving at all and stood locked together as night fell around them. He ran his fingers through her hair and kissed the top of her head.

She tilted back so that she looked into his eyes and she saw need and desire, but she also saw hope.

Her eyelids grew heavy as he slowly, ever so slowly, lowered his head until their mouths were so close but not yet touching. The moment stretched on, their breaths mingling, their gazes never breaking apart.

As the music drifted quietly away, he kissed her.

It was the most romantic, exquisite kiss she'd ever been given. It was a kiss that told her more than words ever could that this man cherished her. He wanted her. He would have her.

And when he finally pulled his mouth away, he tugged her into his arms and stood holding her tight as the moon bathed them in pale light.

Nine

Kelly pulled the nightgown over her head and warily glanced down her body. There was no doubt the garment was beautiful. A concoction of lace and satin that floated over her skin and molded to all the contours.

But she felt far too exposed. Her breasts looked too... big. Her belly looked enormous. Thank God she couldn't see her feet.

She eyed her door, knowing she was supposed to go to Ryan's room after she'd undressed for bed, but she couldn't seem to make herself take those few steps.

It wasn't that she didn't trust Ryan. No, it was herself she didn't trust. She'd already made a big enough fool of herself when it came to this man. Once back in his arms, snuggled up close to him, she'd probably lose what little common sense she had left.

She sighed and sank onto the edge of her bed. Her hesitation was just another sad indication of the rift in their relationship. She'd never been inhibited around Ryan before.

He'd often be propped up in bed with his laptop, his brow creased in concentration as he worked on who knew what. She'd crawl into bed with exactly nothing on and tease and taunt him until his laptop and work were forgotten.

He used to laughingly say that he knew better than to bring work home because she never let him get away with it.

And now she couldn't even bring herself to walk into his bedroom.

A knock sounded at her door and then it opened a crack. Ryan stuck his head in. He stopped when he saw her sitting on the bed.

"Everything okay?"

She nodded.

He eased the door all the way open and walked in. He stood in front of her for a moment and then sat down on the bed next to her. He didn't say anything. He simply laid his hand on her lap, palm up, and waited for her to take it.

After a moment, she slid her hand over his. He twined his fingers through hers and squeezed gently. Then he stood and pulled her to her feet.

"We're both tired," he said. "Let's turn in and we'll worry about tomorrow when it gets here."

That didn't sound like the Ryan she knew. He was a man who planned everything to the nth degree. He had schedules, lists, planners, calendars. He not only worried about tomorrow, but the next year as well.

He led her into his bedroom and motioned for her to get into bed. He hung back, maybe out of deference to her obvious unease. Taking a deep breath, she crawled beneath the covers and turned so she'd face away from him when he got in.

The bed dipped behind her, and she felt his warmth as soon as he slid beneath the covers. He moved about for a few seconds and then the next thing she knew, he was flush against her back.

He wrapped one arm over her and pulled her in close. He nuzzled her hair before resting his cheek over her ear.

It was all she could do not to break down. It had been so long and it felt so right. Just like so many other nights in his arms. She'd missed him. Unbelievably, she'd missed him.

"No past," he murmured in her ear. "Just us. Right now."

She closed her eyes. It had been stupid to agree not to bring up the past. They might not talk about it but it loomed over them like a cloak of doom. It lay between them, awkward and unwieldy. There was no forgetting the past.

What they were doing was called denial. And it wasn't particularly effective.

He kissed her neck and snuggled a little closer. He cupped his hand over her belly affectionately. But the moment was bittersweet. This was how it should have been between them all along.

"Relax and go to sleep, Kell. I just want to hold you."

And oddly enough it was what she wanted too.

When Kelly opened her eyes, the first thing that registered was how comfortable she was. And warm. The second thing she realized was that she was on top of Ryan.

Not just on top of him, but sprawled across him as if she owned him. Her cheek was plastered to his shoulder and her forehead pressed against the side of his neck.

It was the way she'd woken every morning when they'd lived together.

Appalled that she could betray herself like this, she started to ease away but Ryan tightened his arm around her.

"Don't go. This is nice."

She raised her head and stared into eyes that were unclouded with sleep. Evidently he'd been awake for a while and content to lie there with her draped over him like a blanket.

"One thing hasn't changed," he said as he touched her cheek. "You're still beautiful when you wake up."

She soaked in the words, her heart tugging at the sincerity in his voice. Before she could question her sanity, she slowly lowered her mouth and touched it tentatively to his.

He seemed surprised and pleased by her taking the initiative. He lay still while she carefully explored his firm mouth.

She licked over the closed seam, and when his lips parted, she slid her tongue lightly over his bottom lip before moving inward to rasp over the end of his tongue.

Strong hands gripped her upper arms, holding her in place as he began to kiss her back. Softly at first, as if he was wooing her, and then harder. His breath sped up and came in little bursts through her mouth.

He sucked at the tip of her tongue and then she nipped at his when he let her go.

Before she realized it, she was on her back and he was over her, his knee between her legs as he devoured her mouth.

Hot. Breathless. Fast and hard and then slow and gentle.

With one hand he popped the two tiny buttons that held the bodice together. The material separated and her breasts strained precariously out of the gown. The satin caught on her hard, erect nipples and he tugged insistently until one breast came completely free.

He cupped the plump mound and then lowered his head, sucking the nipple into his mouth.

A shot of adrenaline slivered through her veins, edgy and sharp. She twisted restlessly beneath him as he sucked harder. She plunged her fingers through his short, cropped hair and then gripped the back of his head, holding him in place as she silently begged for more.

He pulled at her nipple, drawing his head back until the taut nub came free of his mouth. Then he lifted his gaze to meet hers and butterflies scuttled around her belly when she saw the look in his eyes.

"I want to make love to you, Kell. I need you so much. But I won't do this if it's only going to make things worse. You have to want this as much as I do."

"I want it more," she said hoarsely. And that was the truth. She'd always wanted him more. Craved him. Missed him when he wasn't with her.

Seeing him now, having him over her, his mouth on her, brought back those memories—happier memories—when things were perfect between them.

But had they been? Ever? Really?

She shook off the dark shadow that plagued her and reached up to caress his cheek.

"I need you, too."

Fire exploded in his eyes. Satisfaction and triumph glittered brightly as he swept down to claim her mouth again.

When he finally pulled back, he eased to the side and gathered her in his arms, holding her as if she was a precious piece of glass he was afraid might break.

For the longest time, his gaze stroked over her while

he reacquainted himself with her all over again. Then he slid his hand over her shoulder and eased the strap of her gown down her arm.

He moved to the other side and hooked one finger in the strap, pulling it down until the gown bunched over the ball of her belly.

Levering up on one elbow, he coaxed her to lift her hips so he could pull the gown completely free. He worked it down her legs and then tossed it over the edge of the bed.

Now she was only clad in her underwear and it didn't feel like any sort of barrier to his gaze or his touch.

He cupped his hand just above her pelvis and caressed the round, firm bulge of her abdomen.

"Our baby," he said hoarsely.

Then he hovered over her and lowered his head so that his mouth pressed to the center of her belly in a tender kiss.

The gesture brought tears to her eyes, stinging the lids, and she swallowed against the quick knot that formed in her throat.

"Beautiful," he murmured. "I regret that I've missed watching her grow, watching you expand and watching your shape change. You're so unbelievably sexy."

"Her? You think it's a girl, too?"

Ryan smiled down at her. "You always say her. I guess I've just gotten used to it. I really don't care if it's a girl or boy. I just want you both to be okay."

She felt a little light-headed, as if she had an alcohol buzz without the alcohol.

He trailed his fingers lower, to her pelvis and through her damp, slick folds. She jumped in reaction when he brushed over her clitoris and then she moaned when he delved lower and carefully dipped the tip of his index finger inside her warmth.

"I love how you respond to me. I've always loved it."

She shifted restlessly as he continued his gentle exploration of her sensitive, quivering flesh. Already she was on edge, so close, and he'd only begun touching her.

She was impatient, wanting him now, but she also didn't want the sensation to end too quickly. After months without him, she wanted to savor every single moment with him.

"Spread your legs for me," he murmured.

Helpless to deny him, she relaxed her thighs and let them fall open as he moved down the bed. For a moment he got up and then he put his knee on the mattress, crawling between her thighs.

His eyes smoldered with heat and desire as he stared hungrily at her. Then he lowered himself, inserting one hand between her thighs to push them further apart.

She inhaled sharply and held her breath in anticipation as his head went down. He kissed her folds, right over her clitoris. Just a gentle, featherlike touch that had her spasming in need.

With careful fingers, he parted her flesh, exposing her to his mouth. He kissed her again, this time directly on the puckered, taut nub. Even as she arched, his tongue swept out and he licked from her opening to the top of the delicate hood that encased her most sensitive flesh.

She closed her eyes. Her fingers curled into tight balls, gathering the sheets and then releasing them once more as her body flew in about a dozen directions.

It was intense. It was wonderful. It was beautiful.

Something inside her shattered—or it felt like it. Wave after wave of sharp pleasure rolled over her with rigid intensity.

She panted softly, her breath squeezing from lungs

that felt robbed of air. Her hips lifted rhythmically off the mattress as he nuzzled her down from her orgasm.

When she gathered her senses and looked down, he was staring at her, satisfaction burning brightly in his blue eyes. There was a fierceness there that made her shiver, as if he was sending a silent message. *You're mine.*

With his hands cupped underneath her legs, he raised himself up. He pushed back enough that she was completely exposed to him and then reached between them to position himself at her opening.

She gasped at the hot, hard feel of him barely breaching her. And then he slid all the way in with one push.

It was enough to send her spiraling into another fast, reckless orgasm. She was still coming when he pulled back and pushed in again. Her body clutched desperately at him, hugging him tightly.

They both let out harsh sounds as he cupped her buttocks and lifted her so his angle put him even deeper.

"I can't hold on," he said. "It's too good. It's been too long. I'm sorry, baby."

She reached for him, clutching at his shoulders and pulling him to her. Still, he braced his hands on either side of her, holding his weight off her belly so that he didn't crush her.

He thrust, harder this time and she felt the shudder roll through his body as he held himself deep inside her.

He kissed her. Hungry. Passionate. With more desperation than she'd ever experienced from him. Their love-making had always been good, but he'd never lost control so quickly.

She kissed him with just as much hunger, her hands sliding down his back and then up again to hold his head to hers.

His hips trembled against her. They lay locked together,

with him barely holding himself off her. Wanting that closeness to him—especially now—she urged him over to his side, rolling with him so they stayed together.

Their limbs were tangled, their arms wrapped tightly around each other, and he was still pulsing deep inside her body.

She tucked her head underneath his chin and breathed deeply of his scent, felt the erratic thump of his heart against her cheek.

It was easy to forget all that had happened between them. It was easy to forget the months of pain and loneliness. It was easy to imagine that they'd never been apart and that they were home in bed, just waking in Ryan's apartment—their apartment.

And just for a moment, she refused to allow the hazy euphoria to evaporate under the weight of reality.

Ten

Ryan lay there, Kelly in his arms, trying to sort out what had just happened. On the surface it had been a very quick, very hot sexual interlude. One of the best he'd ever had.

But it went deeper. It wasn't just sex. If it was just sex, his heart wouldn't feel as though it was going to burst out of his chest. He wouldn't be so overwhelmed that he had no idea how to process what he felt.

It was… It was more intense than sex had ever been between them. They had been a study in hot, flirty, fun in bed. He teased. She teased.

But this had been almost…heartbreaking, and he couldn't shake the heaviness that pervaded his chest even now.

He rubbed his hand up and down her back and pressed a kiss to her hair in an effort to soothe some of the tightness in his throat.

He put a hand between them to touch her cheek and

then he carefully pulled her away until he looked down into her eyes.

The stark emotion there. The devastation. It was like a knife to the gut. She looked so very vulnerable. Fragile. And scared. She looked scared to death.

Was she afraid of him? Of what had happened? He couldn't bear it if she hated herself for giving in to the overwhelming tension that had been building ever since he'd taken her back to New York.

"What are you thinking?" he asked hoarsely. "Tell me you don't regret this, Kell. Anything but regret."

Slowly she shook her head and he felt something loosen inside him. Relief. But it was only the first step.

He caressed her cheek, enjoying the feel of her satiny skin. No matter how much he'd told himself that he was better off without her, that he was well rid of her, he could no longer lie to himself.

He wanted her. He wanted her back, no matter what she'd done in the past. He'd been forced to examine their relationship after he'd broken their engagement and ordered her out of his apartment—and his life. Maybe he'd been partially to blame. Maybe he'd worked too many hours. Maybe he'd neglected her.

Whatever the case, something had gone horribly wrong and he was determined to find the cause so that it didn't happen again.

Unable to resist, he kissed her forehead and then each eyelid. He gently kissed each cheekbone and then her mouth before nibbling a path to her ear.

Amazingly, his groin tightened and he swelled inside the clasp of her satiny flesh. He flexed his hips against her eliciting a low whimper as her fingers curled into his shoulder.

He slid easily in and out and he nudged her leg up with his own so that he had easier access.

"Do you like it here on your side?" he murmured. "Are you comfortable? Or would you prefer to be on top?"

She flushed and he smiled, delighted by this suddenly shy side of her. She'd never been bashful about taking the initiative in the past and suddenly he wanted to coax that out of her again.

Without waiting for her to respond, he gathered her in his arms and rolled so she was astride him, her hands planted on his chest for balance.

She was hot and tight around him and he clenched his teeth, closing his eyes as he sucked in steadying breaths. He'd already lost every ounce of control the first time. He wanted to make it last this time.

Her knees locked at his sides and she lifted her hips the tiniest bit before lowering her weight once more to surround him with silky, heated sweetness that had sweat beading his forehead.

She seemed inhibited and a little unsure and this new shyness from her continued to be endearing as hell. He reached for her, wanting to offer reassurance, but as his hands stroked up her lush body, over her swollen belly to her gorgeous breasts, he forgot all about offering her anything except the pleasure of his touch.

He stroked the swell of her breasts, enjoying the new fullness. Her nipples were darker, more pronounced, and his mouth watered with wanting to taste them again.

He pulled ever so gently at the tips, just enough to make them harden and pucker. She sucked in her breath and fluttered around his erection until he groaned and gritted his teeth to keep from orgasming.

"I love your body. You're beautiful pregnant, Kelly.

I can't keep my hands or mouth off you. You make me crazy."

She smiled then, a brilliant smile that he felt all the way to his soul. Her eyes lit up and sparkled and he felt as if he'd been handed the world in the palm of her hand.

Hell, if that was all it took to make her smile like that, he'd gladly tell her every single day how gorgeous she was.

She reached for his hands, laced her fingers in his and then used his hands for leverage as she raised her hips just enough so he slid through her sweetness all over again.

His breath escaped in a long hiss and then she slid down, resheathing him all over again.

"You drive me crazy," he muttered.

She smiled, clearly satisfied with his admission.

He savored the feel of her much smaller hands engulfed by his. They held on tightly as she began a slow, rhythmic ride.

Their gazes locked. They never looked away, never broke eye contact as she made love to him, driving him closer and closer to ultimate release.

Her breaths grew more rapid and erratic. Her face became flushed and she tightened around him. She was close. He was closer. But he was determined to take care of her first.

It took every ounce of his concentration. His body strained. He was rigid, painfully rigid, and then she pulsed and went wet around him. Her body shuddered.

He pulled her down, holding her as he took control of their movements. He stroked and caressed her, kissing her hair, murmuring to her how beautiful she was.

As the last of her orgasm rolled through her body, his began. Through it all, their fingers remained entwined, their hands clasped.

He brought their hands to rest between them, against

their chests, over their hearts, as he surged upward, his mind numb, his body awash with the sweetest of pleasure.

She collapsed over him, going limp as she nuzzled against his neck. She kissed him just below the ear and he smiled at the sweetness of the gesture.

He missed her affection. Missed the way she had always seemed to be touching him or kissing him or just offering him a smile.

He'd missed *her*.

And now he had to find a way to make sure she didn't leave again. He didn't think for a minute that sex was a fix-all for a relationship. It wasn't even a good bandage.

He knew it wasn't going to be easy. There was too much mistrust and hurt between them, but somehow they had to find their way back. He wouldn't allow himself to think any differently.

She was his. She carried his child. To him, that made things simple. She belonged with him. She needed him to take care of her. He wanted to take care of her.

If he was willing to forget the past, then shouldn't she be willing to try their relationship again? It wasn't as if he'd betrayed her.

But she carried so much hurt and anger. Something inside her had been broken. Had he done it when he'd tossed her out of his apartment? What had she expected?

He stroked her hair and willed himself not to become embroiled in the past. He'd promised himself—and her—that he'd put everything behind him.

And if he was willing to do that, then he saw no reason she shouldn't be willing to let the past rest as well.

"How about breakfast in bed?" he asked.

"Mmm, that sounds nice. I don't think I can move and I'm suddenly feeling lazy."

He smiled because he couldn't imagine anything better

than the two of them sharing an intimate meal in bed. Hell, if he had his way they wouldn't leave the bedroom for the rest of the day.

"Let me go order room service. You stay here and get comfortable. I'll be right back."

He kissed her nose and then carefully disentangled himself from the warm clasp of her body. He eased her onto her side, pulled the rumpled sheet over her and rolled toward the nightstand, sitting up and putting his legs over the edge of the bed.

He glanced back to see that she'd immediately commandeered his pillow, which made him chuckle, because it was exactly what she'd done in the past.

He picked up the phone, ordered breakfast for them both and then rolled back over to face her.

"You can't have your pillow back," she mumbled.

He smiled and propped his head in his palm. "Never let it be said I interfered with the comfort of my woman."

One eyebrow went up and she studied him for a long moment. He could see her mind swirling with something and so he simply waited to see if she'd say what was on her mind.

"Am I?" she finally asked.

His brow furrowed. "Are you what?"

"Yours," she said simply. "I need to know what this was, Ryan. Are we back together? I don't know what I'm supposed to do here and I'm not about to assume anything."

He took a deep breath because it was important to handle this just right. The last thing he wanted to do was screw everything up when he felt as if he was this close to having her where he wanted her.

"I think that's up to you," he said carefully. "I think I've been up front about what I want, about where I'd like to see our relationship. It's time for you to decide if this is where you want to be. With me. I'm not saying we have to take a huge leap, but we can at least decide to be together so we can work things out."

She visibly swallowed and he could see fear in her gaze again. It ate at his gut because he honestly didn't know what scared her so bad. Was he such an ogre? Could she really blame him or hold against him the reaction he'd had to her being unfaithful?

"My mind tells me I'm an idiot for even considering this," she muttered.

"What does your heart tell you?" he asked softly.

She sighed and stared helplessly back at him, her blue eyes churning with emotion.

"My heart tells me that I want this. No matter how much I think I *shouldn't* want it, I do. Maybe this is a bad time to have a discussion about our relationship when our minds are mush after sex."

He touched his finger to her lips. "I think it's the perfect time to have it because our guards are down. It's just us. No barriers. No walls. Just us and how we feel."

"How *do* you feel, Ryan? Do you really want this?"

"Yeah, I do, Kell. I want it so damn much that the thought of you walking away has my gut in knots."

Her eyes widened. "But I never walked away from you."

He blew out his breath. "Let's not talk about that, okay? Whatever happened in the past, the point is, I don't want you to walk away *now*. I can't stand the thought of it."

"Okay," she said so quietly he almost didn't hear.

He reached out and nudged her chin up. "Okay?"

"I want to stay. I have no idea how we'll work all this out, but I want to try."

Satisfaction ripped through him, so savage that for a moment he couldn't breathe. He had to temper his reaction because he wanted nothing more than to grab her, haul her into his arms and hold her so damn tight that she could never escape.

"We'll do more than try," he vowed. "We're going to fix this, Kell. We're going to make it work this time."

Eleven

"She doesn't give up, does she?" Kelly murmured as she watched Roberta approach their table, a determined expression on her face.

Ryan looked up and to his credit heaved a sigh and appeared to be extremely irritated with the impending interruption. After a morning and most of the afternoon in bed, they'd ventured out for dinner and now here was Roberta, circling like a hawk.

And it wasn't that Kelly was jealous. Honestly, Roberta wasn't Ryan's type, though she supposed his type could have changed after he'd broken their engagement.

What bothered her was the seemingly public knowledge of their relationship. It just proved Kelly's assertion that his family and friends alike loathed her. Something Ryan was finally coming to accept. But acceptance didn't make anything easier.

While love was supposed to be "everything," she wasn't naive enough to think that relatives hating you didn't put an unbearable strain on a relationship. Who could be happy when, at every turn, your lover's family did everything they could to make their disapproval known?

Maybe they'd both been too naive the first time. Maybe now they could be stronger together. But then what would happen if and when Ryan finally knew the truth about Jarrod? And his mother's part in the whole affair?

Once again, Kelly would be the wedge between him and his family. Their relationship might not survive a second time.

Roberta stopped at the table and bent to kiss Ryan on either cheek, but when he turned away, she caught him full on the lips, leaving a smear of lipstick.

Kelly sighed and sat back, resigned to another uncomfortable scene.

Ryan looked…pissed.

"Roberta, what the hell?"

He didn't even try to be polite this time.

"Oh, I just came around to say goodbye. My flight leaves in the morning and I hoped we could set up a time to get together when you return to New York. Your mother would like us all to have dinner."

She flicked a sideways look of disdain—and challenge—in Kelly's direction, but Kelly purposely yawned and sent a bored look in return.

Roberta frowned but turned eagerly back to Ryan. "Shall we say this weekend perhaps? I'm sure Kelly wouldn't mind. After all, you and I are old friends."

"I mind," Ryan said in a clipped voice. "Now if that's all, we'd appreciate being left to our meal."

"I'll call you," Roberta murmured. "We'll talk…later." The inference being they'd talk when Kelly wasn't around. Was the woman stupid?

It was tempting to put her firmly in her place, but

frankly it would take too much effort and Kelly was quite content to remain in her seat and watch Roberta stew in her own ignorance.

Roberta touched Ryan's face in a gesture that repulsed Kelly then slid one long nail down his jaw before fluttering her fingers at him as she walked away.

Ryan turned, his lips tight. "God, I'm sorry, Kell. You have to know I haven't encouraged her."

Kelly smiled and handed him a napkin to wipe the lipstick off his mouth. "Yeah, I figured that much out. She's…she's interesting. And awfully dense. You were pretty blatant with the brush-off. It makes me wonder what your mother promised her."

Ryan frowned as he swiped at his lips. He pulled the napkin away, frowning even harder at the red smear on the material. Then he reached across the table and took her hand. "Let's not let her ruin what has otherwise been a spectacular day."

Kelly rolled her eyes. "You're just saying that because of the sex. Give a man sex and it's the most amazing day ever."

He grinned. "Well, there is that, but it's not just sex with you, Kell. It's…more."

She flushed in pleasure at the sincerity in his voice. He made her believe all sorts of crazy things, like they could actually work through the serious issues facing them.

"So what do you want to do after dinner?" she asked lightly.

"How about another walk on the beach? Maybe we'll stop in the cabana down the way for some dancing."

"I liked how we danced last night," she said in a dreamy voice. "Just you and me. No one else around. It was an amazing night."

He studied her for a long moment, his fingers idly

caressing hers. "Yeah, it was." He lifted her hand and brought it to his mouth where he proceeded to kiss each fingertip before turning her hand over and nuzzling into her palm. "I thought maybe tomorrow we could get out and see some of the sights as long as you're feeling up to it. I don't want you walking, but I've arranged for a convertible so we can drive where we like. Top down, wind-in-our-hair sort of thing."

"It sounds fun." And it had been a long time since she'd simply had fun. She smiled, feeling her chest grow lighter with each passing second.

Impulsively she squeezed his hand.

"I love that you're smiling again," he said. "You're beautiful when you smile. I want you to be happy, Kell. I'll do whatever it takes to make you happy."

With that statement, she felt some of her hurt and anger recede. For the first time she began to believe that maybe they could get beyond the past and forge ahead.

He seemed so sincere. Whatever he thought of her in the past, he seemed willing to push aside those feelings and start over. Why would he go to such lengths if he didn't care about her?

"I want this to work," she said earnestly. And for the first time she really believed wholeheartedly that she did. That they could find their way back to each other seemed an impossible dream. It would take forgiveness and sacrifice, but she wanted it more than anything.

"Let me see your feet," Ryan said as he lowered himself onto the couch next to her.

He reached down, took her feet and maneuvered them until they rested on his lap. He examined them with the precision of a physician, testing for swelling. Then he settled into a gentle massage until she all but wilted in pleasure.

"They're looking better. The swelling's down quite a bit." He paused for a moment, his hands still moving over her arches, and stared at her. "You look better, Kell."

"Thanks. I think," she said in amusement.

His expression grew serious. "You looked tired and worn down when I found you in Houston."

"I was," she admitted. "But I'd rather not talk about it."

"Yet another thing that's off-limits?"

She shrugged. "Nothing good can come of it."

"I worried I kept you on your feet too much this evening," he said as he continued to rub. "But I enjoyed dancing with you on the beach. It was an excuse to hold you."

She smiled and leaned back, allowing the pleasure of his touch to wash through her body. "I feel fine. Really. Not so tired anymore. I have more energy now than I've had since early in my pregnancy. Being on my feet all the time eventually wore me down."

He went silent and he looked brooding, his expression intense. He massaged her soles and then worked up to her toes.

He seemed to battle whether or not he wanted to speak, but finally he locked his gaze with hers and said, "Why didn't you cash the check, Kelly? I gave it to you so you'd be provided for. No matter what you did, how angry I was or how things were between us, I intended you to be cared for. Do you have any idea what it did to me to find you working in that god-awful place and living in a dive, barely making it? Hell, you didn't even have food in your apartment."

"I ate at the diner," she said.

He made a sound of exasperation. "Like that's supposed

to make me feel any better? Why didn't you use the money? You could have finished college. You could have lived for a long time to come without ever having to work."

"I have pride. It took a beating but it's still intact. I guess if I hadn't been able to find a job and the choice was between starving or taking money that made me feel dirty, I would have sucked it up and done it anyway."

"Did you hate me so much?" he asked hoarsely. "That you would rather work in such deplorable conditions than accept anything from me?"

She leveled a stare at him. "Don't ask questions you aren't prepared to hear the answers to."

He closed his eyes. "That's answer enough, I suppose."

She shrugged. "You hated me, too."

He shook his head and her eyes widened. "No? Ryan, you said and did some terrible things. Not the least of which was tossing that check at me with so much disdain that I can still remember the way I felt."

"What did you expect?" he asked. "For God's sake, Kelly, I'd just found out you slept with my brother. You had my ring on your finger, we were planning our wedding and you slept with my *brother*."

"And of course he's blameless in the whole thing," she said scornfully. "Tell me, Ryan, how long did it take you to forgive him? How long before he was coming back over and you were having family dinners at your mother's?"

His face flushed a dull red and then he dragged a hand raggedly through his hair. "It took a while, all right? I was furious with him—and you. I had to decide whether to allow what happened to ruin our relationship. He's family. He's my brother."

She leaned forward, forgetting their vow not to dredge up the past. "And I was the woman you were supposed to marry, Ryan. Didn't I deserve anything from you? Besides a payoff and a get-the-hell-out-of-my-life?"

"I'm here now," he said quietly. "I was angry. I had a right to be. I won't apologize for that. But I'm here now and I want us to try again. We both made mistakes."

She had to let go of the resentment and anger that still bubbled up every time they spoke of the past. She had to put it away because there was no way for her to win.

She leaned back again and wiggled her foot in his hand to hint for him to continue his massage.

"So where are we going to drive tomorrow? Should I wear one of those scarves and huge sunglasses so I look chic?"

He relaxed, relief stark in his eyes that she was letting the matter drop.

"Wear that very sexy sundress that Jansen bought you."

She arched an eyebrow. "Which one? He bought several."

"Clearly you haven't seen the one then. Or you'd know what I was talking about. It's red. Perfect with your coloring. Strapless, clingy in all the right places. Just make sure to bring something to protect your head from the sun."

"It sounds fun. Carefree," she said wistfully. It had been far too long since she'd done anything remotely resembling carefree.

"I intend for us to have a lot of fun together again, Kell. We used to. We were happy."

She had to acknowledge that they had been. Once. So she nodded and he smiled.

"Are you ready for bed yet?" he asked.

"Depends on what you have in mind," she murmured.

A gleam entered his eyes and he slid his hands up her legs, stroking and caressing.

"Well, I sure wasn't planning to go to sleep. Not for a good long while."

"In that case, definitely take me to bed."

He rose and then unexpectedly he reached down, slid his arms beneath her and lifted her up, cradling her against his chest.

"Ryan, put me down. I'm too heavy!"

He silenced her with a kiss. "A—you're still a little bit of a thing. And B—are you suggesting I'm not manly enough to carry my woman around?"

She laughed. "Forget I said anything. Carry on then."

Twelve

There weren't enough words to explain how much she dreaded getting on that plane and flying back to New York. The past two days had had a dreamlike quality. They were like the best fantasy imaginable, unmarred by a single incident.

And now they were going back to reality.

Cold, gloomy New York City.

She hadn't always felt that way about the city but now it only held bad memories for her. She wasn't as optimistic as Ryan that they could somehow pull the pieces of their relationship back together and sustain it with so many factors against them.

As if sensing her reluctance, Ryan slid an arm around her waist and urged her onto the plane.

A few moments later, they were seated and Ryan reached over to buckle her seat belt for her.

"It's going to be all right, Kell. Trust me."

She wished it was that easy.

Still, she offered him a reassuring smile and settled back for the flight.

But it was Ryan who seemed to grow more tense as the flight neared its end. He touched her frequently, and at first she thought it was to ease her nerves, but she wondered now if it was to reassure himself.

Did he think she'd bolt and run as soon as they landed? She might be tempted but she'd given him her promise and she intended to keep it. Even if it killed her.

They hadn't really talked about what would happen when they got back to New York. Maybe they'd both been too determined not to ruin their time on the island.

Once again when they landed, there was a car waiting for them, and Ryan hurried her out of the cold and into the warm confines of the vehicle.

A mixture of snow and sleet fell from gray skies and she shivered even though the heat was on full blast in the back of the car. It was a shock to leave sunshine and sandy beaches for the bitter chill of New York in the throes of a cold front.

The euphoria that had enveloped much of their stay on the island evaporated and depression settled over her until her mood matched the weather.

Ryan pulled her into his side and kissed her temple. "I have a distinct urge to order in tonight, eat in front of the fire and then make love to you for the rest of the night."

She sighed and snuggled into his side. Somehow he'd known just what to say to make some of the oppressive worry melt away.

"I had fun with you the last few days," she said, wanting him to have that admission at least.

"I'm glad. I had fun with you too. It felt like old times, only…better."

She nodded because it had been better. More honest. Or maybe they hadn't taken a single moment for granted as they'd done in the past. They'd enjoyed every single minute together, making the most of each one.

They'd laughed and loved and they'd made love. The very last day they hadn't left their hotel room. Their meals had been delivered and they'd stayed in bed, only leaving it to take a leisurely shower together.

She wished it could have lasted.

But they had to face the music sooner or later.

"I had Jansen make you an appointment to see the doctor tomorrow. I want to be sure everything is okay with you and the baby."

She smiled, loving the concern in his voice. "Spending the time away with you did more for me than any doctor ever could."

He looked pleased with her response, pleased that she'd admitted it. He bent to kiss her again as they pulled up outside Ryan's apartment building.

Ryan hastily got out, helped Kelly from the car and rushed her out of the cold and into the building. As they rode up in the elevator, Kelly realized just how much she dreaded being back here, in this apartment. In this city.

"My driver will bring the luggage up soon. Why don't you go get comfortable on the couch? I'll turn the fire on and fix us something to drink. Are you hungry?"

"Hmm, no, but I'd love Thai takeout later. For now I'll have some juice."

"Thai sounds good. Get comfortable. Take your shoes off and prop your feet up. I bet your ankles are swelling from sitting with your feet down for that long."

Kelly chuckled at the mother hen sound to his voice but did as he said and settled on the sumptuous leather couch.

She kicked off her shoes and winced at the puffy look of her ankles as she propped them on the ottoman.

She'd have the doctor and Ryan both griping at her, but heck, she'd done nothing except eat good food, rest and relax for the past several days. What more could she do?

Ryan had just set their drinks on the coffee table and settled next to her when his phone started ringing. She supposed it was to be expected since he'd been out of the country. It wasn't as if his being tied up with work was anything new. In the past, though, she'd never hesitated to needle him or distract him. Something that had both exasperated and thrilled him in equal parts.

But now she sat quietly as he fished his BlackBerry out of his pocket.

His lips thinned a bit before he put the phone to his ear. "Hello, Mom."

Kelly sighed. That hadn't taken long.

Ryan wasn't one of those guys who was tied to the apron strings, but he respected his mother, as any son should, and like most children, she supposed, had a bit of a blind spot when it came to her.

Or maybe he just didn't want to see her as the conniving vindictive witch that Kelly knew her to be. Kelly was sure his mother had her good points. She obviously loved her sons. But she'd never be someone Kelly would warm to. Ever.

"Yes, we're back. Listen, Mom, why did you send Roberta there? I don't appreciate you interfering. I won't tolerate any disrespect toward Kelly. You need to accept that she's with me. If you can't do that, then you and I are going to have a serious problem."

Kelly's eyes rounded. There was anger in Ryan's voice and his eyes were hard.

"We'll see," he continued. "Right now Kelly and I need

some time together without interference, no matter how well meaning. I'll call you when we're ready to have dinner together."

Ugh. It took all of Kelly's control not to make a face. But this was Ryan's mother. This was her child's grandmother, no matter how much Kelly wished it to be different.

"I love you too, Mom. Let me go. We just got in and we're both tired."

He tossed the BlackBerry on the couch. Kelly looked inquisitively at him.

"Mom wants to express her apologies for Roberta's actions. And her own. She wants to have dinner with us one night. I told her I'd be in touch when we were ready for that."

There wasn't anything she could say so she remained silent. She leaned forward to pick up her glass of orange juice to mask the awkwardness of the moment and leaned back, sipping at the sweet and tart drink.

He glanced at her propped-up feet and then frowned. "Your feet are pretty swollen."

She lifted one and sighed. "Yeah. Apparently I'm a water-retaining cow."

"Are they hurting? Want me to rub them?"

"No, I'm fine. They ache a little but right now I don't want anyone touching them. I'll just sit like this for the rest of the evening and drink lots of water. The potassium in the OJ will help."

He leaned over and kissed her forehead just as the buzzer sounded.

"That'll be our luggage. Be right back."

She adjusted her position so that some of the tension was relieved in her back. The truth was she was tired of sitting after being on the airplane for so many hours, but neither did she want to be on her feet with swollen and aching ankles.

Deciding to dispense with sitting at all, she turned on her side, stuck a cushion between her legs and let out a sigh at the bliss of being off her behind and her feet.

She stared across the room out the panels of glass that led onto the balcony and watched as a few snowflakes spiraled downward. The weather didn't seem to be able to make up its mind whether it wanted to rain, sleet or snow; but, at least for now, a few fat flakes were falling.

The flames from the gas fireplace gave the living room a warm, homey feel and as she adjusted her gaze to the fireplace, lethargy stole over her.

She reached for the throw draped on the back of the couch and pulled it over her body, sighing that she finally felt comfortable after traveling for so long.

Her eyelids were drooping and she didn't fight the urge to sleep. Ryan would wake her in time for dinner.

When Ryan returned to the living room, he found Kelly fast asleep on the couch, her hand tucked under her cheek. He was struck by how young and innocent she looked. Not at all like someone who played brother against brother.

He supposed it was unfair to think such thoughts when they'd both made an effort to get beyond the past, but the dark thoughts always crept in.

What fault did he have that would cause Kelly to seek comfort with his brother? And why had she been vengeful enough to want to ruin his relationship with his only sibling when Jarrod had told her that he was going to confess to Ryan that they'd had sex?

Ryan felt more like a father to Jarrod than a brother. Eight years separated them in age and their father had died when Ryan was barely a teenager. He'd stepped in, assuming the paternal role with Jarrod, who was still a boy.

He'd attended all his baseball games, taken him to

sporting events. Taken him to movies. He'd been there for his graduation from high school. Had helped him move when he went off to college and supported his decision to return home and pursue a career in finance.

Nothing should come between brothers. Certainly not a woman. But one had. Kelly had. Not only had it struck a blow to his relationship with Jarrod that he still hadn't recovered from but it had destroyed his relationship with Kelly as well.

A relationship he was determined to rebuild.

But to go forward, he had to determine what had gone wrong in the past.

No matter what they'd vowed, at some point the past had to be addressed. It couldn't be ignored forever.

He picked up his phone and quietly walked into the next room to call Devon and Cam.

Thirteen

Ryan took Kelly to the doctor the next day. She'd assumed that *she* would go to the doctor. As in alone. And that Ryan would go back to work since he'd been out of the office for nearly a week.

But he'd ridden with her, gone into the exam room with her and stuck to her side throughout the entire appointment.

The doctor made noises about the swelling and noted that there was still protein in her urine. He asked her endless questions about how she felt and then issued a stern lecture about taking it easy.

Ryan latched on to every word and by the time they left, Kelly was sure that he'd lock her in her bedroom and not allow her out until the baby was born.

She was prepared to be stir-crazy in advance, but he said nothing. When they arrived back at the apartment, he didn't make her prop her feet up even though that was precisely what she did as soon as they walked through the door.

"I think as long as you don't overdue it that there's no reason you can't get around in moderation," Ryan said. "The doctor was in agreement that we just need to watch you closely for any change and be sensitive to when you're not feeling well to make sure it doesn't develop into something more serious."

Thank God he was prepared to be reasonable.

"I thought we could eat out tonight if you feel up to it. It's cold but it's not supposed to snow or sleet. I know you like going out."

Touched that he'd remembered—although she wasn't sure why he wouldn't—she smiled and nodded in excitement. She did love the city at night. Loved the lights, the cozy restaurants and little hole-in-the-wall cafés and local eateries.

"I sent Jansen out for warmer clothing and a coat for you. Just until you feel up to shopping for yourself," he said. "I'll go with you when you want to. Just say the word."

Knowing how much Ryan hated shopping, she was touched and idiotically emotional over the fact that he'd offered to go with her.

"We should also think about going shopping for the baby very soon," Ryan said in a husky voice.

She blinked in surprise. But then she stared down at her belly and realized that he was right. She only had a short time—weeks—until the baby would arrive. Six weeks? But babies often came early. And she was horribly unprepared.

In Houston she'd lived from paycheck to paycheck, just praying to be able to make rent and save money for when she had to take time off when the baby was born. There hadn't been money for all the things people bought in preparation for a baby, so she'd never even thought about it.

Panicked now that she realized how unprepared she was, she stared in dismay at Ryan.

"Hey," he said as he scooted over next to her. "I didn't mean to stress you out. I thought you'd be excited to shop for the baby."

"I don't have anything," she confessed. "No baby clothing. No crib. Diapers. Oh God, I don't even know what-all I need. I was always happy to just make it through another day in Houston. I never looked ahead. It was too overwhelming."

He gathered her in his arms and held her as he ran his hand soothingly over her hair. "There's no hurry, okay? I'll send out for some parenting books and magazines and for the next few days, I want you to rest, put your feet up and do as much reading as you like. Make a list. We'll look at stuff together. It'll be fun. We still have plenty of time before she gets here."

She squeezed him in a tight hug. "Thank you. I think you just prevented a meltdown. I feel so awful. I don't even have any cute baby booties. What kind of mother am I going to be?" she asked mournfully.

He squeezed her back. "You'll be a wonderful mom. You've had a lot to deal with. Cut yourself some slack, okay? Now why don't you go take a long soaking bath and get ready for dinner?"

She reached up and pulled him down to kiss him. It was on the tip of her tongue to say she loved him, but she swallowed the words and kissed him again instead.

He kissed her back, lingering over her lips, savoring the taste and feel of her.

It shouldn't make her feel so sad that she still loved him. But she couldn't shake the heaviness from her chest as she pulled away and then got up and headed for the bathroom.

* * *

"I got a call from Rafael today," Ryan said over dinner.

Kelly frowned. "How is he doing? I still can't believe he got into a plane crash, lost his memory and then fell in love with a woman he completely screwed over for land."

Ryan winced. "You make it sound so…"

She lifted an eyebrow. "Awful? I know he's your friend, but he's always been arrogant and a bit of a jerk. Especially toward women. He never liked me."

"Rafe has changed. I know it sounds weird, but after his accident he did a one-eighty. Anyway, he and Bryony are back from their honeymoon and they're coming into town in a few days to put his apartment on the market."

"He's moving?"

That shocked Kelly. Rafael was an urbanite through and through. He loved the city. Loved to travel. She couldn't imagine him anywhere else.

"Yeah, he and Bryony are going to maintain a residence on Moon Island."

"Wow. Rafael must really be in love."

"Amazing what men in love will do for the women they love," Ryan said softly.

Kelly didn't meet his gaze and concentrated instead on her soup. Lobster bisque. After six months of bland diner food, she savored every bite. Her taste buds were all simultaneously orgasming.

She'd eaten more in the past week than she had in all those months in Houston, and she was going to balloon like a blowfish if she kept this up. She'd even closed her eyes when they'd weighed her at her doctor's appointment the previous day, not wanting to know how much weight she'd gained.

"He wants us all to get together."

Her eyes narrowed. "Define us."

"Me, you, Dev and Cam and, of course, Rafael and Bryony. I also thought it would be good to invite Mom so you'd have the buffer of other people. We can get it over with in one clean sweep."

It sounded like an evening from hell, not that she'd admit that to him. She couldn't imagine anything worse than being surrounded by Ryan's closest friends, who of course all had been told that she'd cheated on Ryan with Jarrod. She nearly bared her teeth in response to that thought. And then there was his darling mother. All the evening lacked was…Jarrod.

"And Jarrod?" she asked icily.

"He won't be invited. I wouldn't do that to you, Kell," Ryan said quietly.

"When is this supposed to take place?"

"Next week. Probably at the end of the week. They'll be busy organizing his apartment. We'll eat at Tony's. You like it there. It's nice and casual. We can leave at any time and there won't be any obligation to stay and visit."

She sighed. She had to hand it to him. He was working hard to make things as easy for her as possible. The least she could do is be accommodating. His friends were important to him. His mother was important to him.

"All right," she said in a low voice. "Of course we can go." She forced a smile. "It'll be nice to see everyone again." She nearly choked on the lie, but the relief in Ryan's eyes made it worth it.

He reached for her hands. "We're going to make it this time, Kell."

She caught his fingers and returned his squeeze. "It makes me feel better to know you think so."

"Do you have doubts?"

"I'd be lying if I said I didn't. I'm scared witless. I'm scared to go out of your apartment," she said honestly. "I don't like the person I've become, but it doesn't change the fact that I'm a very different person than the Kelly you knew. I'm more cautious now. I'm…harder. I don't like it about myself, but I've learned to be that way out of necessity."

He took her hand in both of his and propped his elbows on the table as he stared over at her.

"Marry me."

She jerked her hand back in shock and stared at him. *"What?"* Where the hell had that come from?

"Marry me."

He withdrew one hand and then reached into his pocket to pull out a small ring box. With his thumb, he flipped it open and she saw a stunning diamond ring nestled in velvet.

He held it out to her and she lifted her gaze to stare at him as if he'd lost his mind.

"I couldn't decide whether or not to give you back your old one or buy you a new one. I kept the old ring. I kept it with me the entire time you were gone. But then I decided that we deserve a fresh start. So I bought a new one for a new beginning."

Her hand trembled in his and she stared speechlessly at him.

He ruefully shook his head. "I know it's not the most romantic proposal. It's not even under the best circumstances. I'd intended to wait. Until it was the right time. Until we'd sorted out things between us. But I couldn't wait any longer. And when my friends and family see you again, I want them to know that we're together, that you're the woman I'm going to marry and that you have my support."

Tears filled her eyes and her chest ached with emotion. He made no move to take the ring out of the box and put it on her finger for her. He simply held it in the palm of his hand, waiting for her to make the decision.

"But Ryan," she began helplessly. "There's so much… The past…"

"Shh," he murmured. "I know what you're saying. We have a lot to talk about. We have a lot to work out. But I wanted to do this first so that you know that no matter what comes out when we eventually revisit the past that I still want to marry you. I need you to know that. Maybe it'll help. Maybe it'll make it easier knowing that it won't change things between us *now*."

She wiped furiously at the moisture on her cheeks, determined not to ruin the moment by breaking down. "In that case, yes. I'll marry you."

He looked thunderstruck, like maybe he really hadn't expected her to agree. And then he smiled and such joy flashed across his face that it left her breathless. His eyes lit up and his grip on her hand tightened until her fingertips were bloodless.

He fumbled with the box, took the ring out. The hand he held hers with shook as he positioned her finger so he could slide the ring on.

Then he leaned across the table and kissed her. When he pulled away, he still held her hand and he suddenly stood, pulling her to her feet.

"Let's go," he said hoarsely. "Let's go home where we can be alone. I just want to hold you away from everyone else."

She went willingly into his arms and they walked past the other diners, uncaring of the stares they received. She never felt the cold, brisk air as they exited the restaurant and walked to the curb where Ryan's car waited.

For once she felt warm on the inside. After feeling cold and alone for so long, sunshine rushed through her veins.

Fourteen

Kelly woke to find Ryan gone from bed. She rolled to check the clock on the nightstand and realized why she was alone. It was after nine and Ryan would have long since gone into the office.

When they'd returned from St. Angelo, Kelly had moved into Ryan's room. It wasn't as though a big production had been made. He'd simply carried her luggage into his room. And when it was time for bed, he'd carried her to his bed.

And she'd stayed.

How easily they'd fallen back into a comfortable routine. Just like before.

Before, it had been easy to take for granted the rapport between them. The comfort and trust. She hadn't known then as she knew now how quickly things could be broken.

Even now she questioned how it could have happened.

There was always an excuse, a reason. He hadn't loved her enough. He hadn't trusted her. Their relationship was too new to weather something so difficult.

But no matter the reason, the end result had been the same. When things had gotten difficult, their relationship had crumbled like stale bread.

It didn't speak well for their future.

But she wouldn't think of that right now. Sure, it was stupid of her to allow herself to have such faith in him. But hope was a powerful thing. It made a person willingly blind to the truth.

She kept telling herself maybe this time…

Maybe this time they would truly get things right. Even if it meant forever bearing the burden of having the man she loved think she'd betrayed him with another man. His brother.

So many times she wanted to confront him. She wanted to try again to make him listen to her. Make him hear the truth. But each time she bit her lip because what purpose would it serve?

He might not believe her. He might. But would it change anything in the past? Would it change their future?

It wouldn't even make her feel any better because she knew the truth. Ryan believed she'd lied to him but he wanted to forget and move on. Was she an idiot to want more than that? Was she stupid to want him to know how wrong he'd been?

It was a dilemma that plagued her every single day that she and Ryan were back together. Part of her wanted to make him listen and to demand that he accept that he'd been wrong if he expected her to give this whole thing another shot.

Another part of her told her that her pride and her anger were barriers to her own happiness.

Wasn't a life with Ryan what she ultimately wanted? Did it matter how she achieved that goal?

She stared up at the ceiling as she lay in bed.

Yeah, it did. It really did. She couldn't go through their life together knowing it was in the back of Ryan's mind that she'd slept with someone else when she'd promised to be faithful to him.

She had to accept that what she really feared was that when she did confront Ryan, he'd reject her all over again, and if that happened, she knew she couldn't spend her life with someone who didn't trust her.

She was a coward, but it was the cold, hard truth that fear was what held her back. Not pride. Not anything else. She knew that if he didn't believe her this time they could never be together.

Not wanting the weight of anxiety to bear down on her today, she shook the bleak thoughts from her mind and crawled out of bed. She padded into the living room to see that Ryan had turned the fire on for her.

To her further surprise, she found a breakfast tray waiting for her on the table with bagels, cheese and an assortment of fruit.

But what caught her eye was the tiny pair of yellow baby booties.

She picked up the soft, fuzzy little booties, her throat knotting as she read the accompanying card.

Because you said you didn't have a pair yet. Love, Ryan.

She sank into the seat, her eyes stinging with tears. She held the booties to her cheek and then touched the card, tracing the scrawl of his signature.

"I shouldn't love you this much," she whispered. God, but she couldn't help herself. She craved him. He was her other half. She didn't feel whole without him.

And so began a courting ritual that tugged on her heartstrings.

Every morning when she crawled out of bed, there was a new present waiting for her from Ryan.

There was a baby book that outlined everything she could expect from birth through the first year of life. One morning he left her two outfits. One for a boy and one for a girl. *Just in case,* he had written.

On the fifth morning, he simply left her a note that told her a gift was waiting in the extra bedroom.

Excited, she hurried toward the bedroom she'd once occupied and threw open the door to see not one present but a room full of baby things.

A stroller. A crib that was already put together. A little bouncy thing. An assortment of toys. A changing table. She couldn't take in all the stuff that was there. She didn't even know what all of it was for.

How on earth had he managed to sneak this in without her hearing?

And there by the window was a rocking chair with a yellow afghan lying over the arm. She walked over and reverently touched the wood, giving the chair an experimental push.

It creaked once and then swayed gently back and forth.

Already her feet protested her being up, so she moved the blanket and sat, staring around at the room full of treasures for their child.

She had been more tired in the past couple of days, but she'd been careful not to worry Ryan. He'd worked so hard to make each day special for her.

If possible, she had fallen more deeply in love with him than ever before.

Tonight was the dinner with his friends and his mother, but even that couldn't dim her excitement or her happiness. And maybe that had been his plan all along. To take extra measures to make sure she knew that he supported her against any possible animosity or disdain.

It had certainly worked, because she couldn't imagine

anything they could do or say that would make the cloud she walked on evaporate.

Ryan cared about her. He wanted to marry her. What else mattered?

She hugged that thought to her later as she picked through her clothing, trying to find the perfect outfit to wear to the dinner.

Before, it wouldn't even occur to her that an outfit was too sexy or revealing. If it looked good on her, and if she knew Ryan would like it, that was her only criteria.

But now she worried that with the sentiment already being that she was a…slut…she would merely perpetuate that belief if she wore anything that wasn't ultraconservative. And that pissed her off. She shouldn't care what these people thought of her. But it wasn't that easy. They were important to Ryan and Ryan was important to her.

Warm hands suddenly stole over her body, sliding around to her belly. She was drawn into a hard chest and sensual lips nibbled at her neck.

She sighed and relaxed into Ryan, her pulse speeding up.

"Is there a particular reason you're standing in your closet staring at your clothes?" he murmured against her ear.

She turned and laced her arms around his neck as she rose up on tiptoe to kiss him. "You're home early."

"Couldn't wait to see you. So what's with the closet?"

Her lips twisted into a frown and she let out a disgruntled sigh. "Just trying to find something to wear tonight. Something that doesn't make me look like the tramp they think I am."

Ryan's expression gentled and he trailed a finger over her cheekbone. Taking her arms, he backed out of her closet and toward the bed until the back of his legs bumped against the mattress.

He sat down and pulled her down with him.

"You'll look beautiful no matter what you wear. Stop worrying so much."

"I know. It's silly. I can't help it. I'm nervous."

"I don't want you to worry, Kell. The past is in the past. I don't know that I've ever said the words, but I forgive you. And if I can forgive you then they should be able to do the same."

She went completely still. Pain jolted through her chest as if someone had stabbed her. Not that she knew what it felt like but it couldn't be worse than this.

He forgave her.

For something she'd never done. For something he refused to believe she hadn't done.

It took all the strength she possessed not to react, not to lash out. He hadn't said it to hurt her. but he couldn't possibly imagine how much she was bleeding inside right now.

He was trying to do the generous thing. He was trying to make her feel at ease.

He kissed her gently on the brow. "We both made mistakes. I'm not blameless. The important thing is that we never let what happened in the past happen again."

Numbly she nodded. She didn't trust herself to speak. What could she say?

She closed her eyes and leaned into him. He hugged her to him and rubbed his hand up and down her back. He offered comfort. He thought she was worked up about tonight. How could he possibly know that his "forgiveness" made her want to die?

He eased her to the side until she was perched on the edge of the bed and then he stood and walked into the closet. After a moment, he returned with a gorgeous, midnight-blue dress. He held it up and smiled.

"This one would look fantastic on you."

She struggled to collect her shattered senses and pretend that nothing was wrong.

"It's awfully…clingy," she said. "I'd look eleven months' pregnant in it."

"I love your belly," he said in an ultrasexy voice that sent shivers down her spine. "I love that this shows the world you're pregnant with my baby. You'll look gorgeous. Wear it for me."

There wasn't a woman alive who could refuse a request like that. She nodded silently, her heart aching all the while.

He laid the dress carefully on the bed and then bent down to kiss her once more.

"I'll leave you to get ready. The driver will be here for us in an hour."

She clung to him a little longer than was necessary but he didn't seem to mind. He touched her cheek as he pulled away and then walked toward the bathroom, loosening his tie as he went.

She stared at the dress. It was a fabulous creation. And it would definitely highlight her pregnancy, something Ryan seemed very keen on.

She closed her eyes. He forgave her. She wanted to weep.

It should be her who had to offer forgiveness. Not him.

Fifteen

Kelly swallowed her mounting dread as she and Ryan entered the restaurant. Ryan spoke in low tones to the maître d' and then they were ushered to a table in the back.

Ryan broke into a broad smile when he saw Rafael already seated next to a woman Kelly assumed was his wife, Bryony. Ryan's mother was also seated, as were Devon and Cameron. Just great. They were last to arrive, and so they made an "entrance."

Kelly stood by Ryan's side as he greeted everyone, then said, "Of course, you all remember Kelly. Except for you, Bryony."

He turned to Kelly. "Kelly, this is Bryony de Luca, Rafael's wife. Bryony, this is my fiancée, Kelly Christian."

The room went absolutely silent at his declaration. The expressions ranged from his mother's ill-disguised horror to outright disbelief on his friends' faces.

Even Bryony looked skeptical as she rose to extend her hand to Kelly. It was then that Kelly noticed that Bryony appeared every bit as pregnant as Kelly was.

"It's nice to meet you," Bryony said with what looked to be a forced smile.

Hell, how much could Bryony possibly know about Kelly anyway? It wasn't as if she'd been around for that long. But she, like the others, didn't appear to roll out the welcome mat.

Kelly offered a nervous smile and allowed Ryan to seat her. This was going to be a long night.

"How are you, Kelly?" Devon asked politely.

He was seated next to her and she supposed common courtesy dictated his question.

"I'm good," she replied in a low voice. "Nervous."

He seemed surprised by her honesty.

Ryan conversed with his friends and his mother. Kelly sat quietly beside him and watched the goings-on around her. No one tried to include her in conversation and the one time she offered a comment, the awkward silence that ensued told her all she needed to know.

They were tolerating her for Ryan's sake, but she didn't miss the looks they cast in his direction when they thought she wasn't watching. Looks that plainly said, *Are you crazy?*

By the time the food was served, she was extremely grateful to have something to focus on. She felt out of place. She felt conspicuous. This was going down as one of the worst nights of her life and she was counting the minutes until she and Ryan could make their escape.

The food felt dry in her mouth. Her stomach churned and after only a few bites, she gave up trying to force herself to eat. Instead, she sipped at her water and pretended she was back on the beach with Ryan, about to dance underneath the moonlight.

That was her problem. She was living in a fantasy world, avoiding reality. And reality sucked. Her reality was sitting here at a dinner table while five other people judged her. Her reality was living with a man—a man she intended to marry—who felt he needed to forgive her for sins she hadn't committed.

At what point in her life had she decided she didn't deserve better than this?

It was a startling discovery. The blinders had come off.

Why was she putting up with this?

She was prepared to end the entire thing when she looked up and saw Jarrod walk to the table. He leaned over and kissed his mom then held up a hand in greeting to the others before turning his gaze on her and Ryan.

She broke into a cold sweat. Ryan stiffened beside her and the others fell silent.

It was as if everyone in the room waited for the inevitable fireworks. Her head pounded viciously. Her stomach cramped and she wanted to die from the humiliation. More than that, she was so furious she couldn't see straight.

"Sorry, I'm late," he said. "I got caught in traffic."

As he took the empty chair beside his mother, bile rose in Kelly's throat. Her heart was shredded. She was bleeding on the inside, so hurt, so devastated she wanted to die. She refused to look at Ryan. How could he have done it? She didn't believe for a moment that Ryan had actually invited his brother…had he? But why hadn't he made it clear that he wasn't welcome?

Everyone stared at her. They likely thought she deserved whatever humiliation was heaped upon her tonight. But she refused to look back at them. She wouldn't give them the satisfaction of seeing her so shattered.

Instead her gaze locked onto Jarrod Beardsley and his mother.

How they must hate her. The coldness in Ramona Beardsley's eyes reached out to Kelly. They said, *You'll never win. I'll never let you.*

What had she ever done besides love Ryan? Enough was enough.

Kelly deserved better.

She was through paying penance.

She was done with being looked down on, condemned and *forgiven*.

Forcing a smile in Ryan's direction, she pushed back her chair and slowly rose as if she hadn't a care in the world. She stared across the table at Jarrod and his mother and let the full force of her hatred shine. She didn't care if they ever accepted her. She didn't accept them. They could both go to hell. She'd buy them a first-class ticket.

Then she turned to face the entire table. "I'm done here. You've all sat and stared your disapproval. You've sent pitying glances Ryan's way. You've judged me and found me not good enough. To hell with all of you."

Then she turned back to Jarrod, her voice coming out in a low hiss. "You son of a bitch. You stay away from me and my child. I'll see you in hell before I ever let you near me again."

Ryan started to rise, but she shoved him back into his seat. "By all means, you stay. You wouldn't want to disappoint your family and friends."

Before he could react, she stalked away.

She bypassed the doorway leading to the bathrooms and kept on walking. She burst into the cold, shivering because she hadn't bothered to collect her coat. She embraced the chill, welcomed the cold slap in the face.

Her head had ached all afternoon, but after spending the past hour with her teeth gritted and her jaw tight, the headache had exploded into vicious pain.

She walked a block before the cold penetrated the thin layers of her dress. She stopped and waved at a passing cab but it didn't stop. It took two more attempts before she managed to get one to pull over for her.

She was barely able to get out Ryan's address before the tears started to fall.

Ryan's first thought was to go after Kelly, but he was furious, and this had to be ended now. Like hell he'd ever allow anyone to make Kelly feel the way she'd obviously felt tonight. He bolted to his feet, palms smacking the table as he lunged toward his brother.

"What the hell was that?"

He included his mother in his furious gaze, not backing down when she recoiled from his anger.

Jarrod looked taken aback, his face pale. He looked sick, but at this point Ryan didn't care. He'd had enough. This was a huge mistake and he wasn't going to let it go this time. He never should have let it go. Never should have played down the obvious discord between Kelly and his family.

Their mother leaned forward, her expression tight. "Don't be angry with him, Ryan. I invited him. If you insist on a relationship with this woman we're going to have to sit down together at some point. Or do you plan never to see your family? Hasn't she caused us enough pain?"

Ryan let out a curse that made his mother flinch. "Haven't you hurt her enough? It ends tonight. I'm done with this. I'm done subjecting Kelly to your insensitivity and your blatant attempts to drive us apart."

Then he turned in his friends' direction. "Rafael, it was good to see you and Bryony again. I hope to see you before you leave the city."

He nodded at Devon and Cam, who looked as if they'd rather be anyplace but where they were. That made three of them.

"Sorry, man," Devon murmured.

Not sparing his mother or brother a second glance, Ryan left the table and went in search of Kelly, hoping she hadn't made it past the door yet. He'd take her home, apologize profusely and then he'd promise that he wouldn't subject her to another gathering of his friends and family.

He shouldn't have this time but he'd hoped… He wasn't sure what he'd hoped but he'd been a damn fool and he'd hurt Kelly in the process.

He stalked toward the coatroom, but found Kelly's coat still hanging. Then he hurried toward the entrance, but found no sign of her there either. Dread tightened his gut.

"Did you see a pregnant woman leave? Short, blond, wearing a blue dress?" he demanded of the maître d'.

"Yes, sir. She walked out just a few seconds ago."

Ryan swore. "Did you see which way she went?"

"No, I'm sorry, but you might ask outside to see if anyone got her a cab."

Ryan hurried into the night, praying she'd gone home. But what if she hadn't? What if she'd finally had enough and said to hell with him and everyone else?

After being told that Kelly was seen walking down the street, Ryan panicked and took off at a run. Fear lanced through him at the idea of her being out alone, upset, on her feet when she had no business walking such a distance.

He brushed by countless people and then he saw her just ahead, getting into a cab at the next block. He yelled her name, but the door shut and the cab drove off—leaving him standing on the sidewalk, his heart about to explode out of his chest.

He waved at a passing cab, frustrated when it didn't slow. The next one stopped and he climbed in, directing the driver to his address. The entire way back to his apartment he prayed that she'd be there.

When the cab pulled up to his apartment building, he got out and hurried toward the door. When he reached the doorman, he stopped.

"Did you see Miss Christian come in a few minutes ago?"

The doorman nodded. "Yes, sir. She got here just before you arrived."

Relief staggered him. He bolted for the elevator. A few moments later, he strode into the apartment.

"Kelly? Kelly, honey, where are you?"

Not waiting for an answer, he hurried into the bedroom to see her sitting on the edge of the bed, her face pale and drawn in pain. When she heard him, she looked up and he winced at the dullness in her eyes.

She'd been crying.

"I thought I could do it," she said in a raw voice, before he could beg her forgiveness. "I thought I could just go on and forget and that I could accept others thinking the worst of me as long as you and I were okay again. I did myself a huge disservice."

"Kelly…"

Something in her look silenced him and he stood several feet away, a feeling of helplessness gripping him as he watched her try to compose herself.

"I sat there tonight while your friends and your mother looked at me in disgust, while they looked at you with a mixture of pity and disbelief in their eyes. All because you took me back. The tramp who betrayed you in the worst possible manner. And I thought to myself I don't deserve this. I've *never* deserved it. I deserve better."

She raised her eyes to his and he flinched at the horrible pain he saw reflected there. Then she laughed. A raw, terrible sound that grated across his ears.

"And earlier tonight you forgave me. You stood there

and told me it no longer mattered what happened in the past because you *forgave* me and you wanted to move forward."

She curled her fingers into tight balls and rage flared in her eyes. She stood and stared him down even as tears ran in endless streams down her cheeks.

"Well, I don't forgive *you*. Nor can I forget that you betrayed me in the worst way a man can betray the woman he's supposed to love and be sworn to protect."

He took a step back, reeling from the fury in her voice. His eyes narrowed. "You don't forgive *me?*"

"I told you the truth that day," she said hoarsely, her voice cracking under the weight of her tears. "I begged you to believe me. I got down on my knees and *begged* you. And what did you do? You wrote me a damn check and told me to get out."

He took another step back, his hand going to his hair. Something was wrong, terribly wrong. So much of that day was a blur. He remembered her on her knees, her tear-stained face, how she put her hand on his leg and whispered, "Please don't do this."

It made him sick. He never wanted to go back to the way he felt that day, but somehow this was worse because there was something terribly wrong in her eyes and in her voice.

"Your brother *assaulted* me. He *forced* himself on me. I didn't invite his attentions. I wore the bruises from his attack for two weeks. *Two weeks.* I was so stunned by what he'd done that all I could think about was getting to you. I knew you'd fix it. You'd protect me. You'd take care of me. I knew you'd make it right. All I could think about was running to you. And, oh God, I did and you looked right through me."

The sick knot in his stomach grew and his chest tightened so much he couldn't breathe.

"You wouldn't listen," she said tearfully. "You wouldn't listen to anything I had to say. You'd already made your mind up."

He swallowed and closed the distance between them, worried that she'd fall if he didn't make her sit. But she shook him off and turned her back, her shoulders heaving as her quiet sobs fell over the room.

"I'm listening now, Kelly," he forced out. "Tell me what happened. I'll believe you. I swear."

But he knew. He already knew. So much of that day was replaying over and over in his head and suddenly he was able to see so clearly what he'd refused to see before.

And it was killing him.

His brother had lied to him after all. Not just lied but he'd carefully orchestrated the truth and twisted it so cleverly that Ryan had been completely deceived.

Then she turned, her beautiful eyes haunted, defeated. "It doesn't matter if you believe me anymore," she whispered. "You wouldn't believe me when it *mattered*. He tried to rape me. He assaulted me. He touched me. He hurt me. And when I fought him off and told him that I would tell you what he'd done, he told me he'd make sure you never believed a word of any of it.

"And you know what the funny thing is? I told him he was wrong. I told him that you l-loved me and that you would make him pay for hurting me."

She broke off as another sob racked her.

Oh God. Oh God. What had he done? He remembered the phone call from his brother as though it was yesterday. He hadn't believed him. At first. Not until Kelly had arrived in an agitated state telling him the exact same story that Jarrod had just told him over the phone.

"He told you the truth," Kelly said scornfully as if she'd plucked the thoughts right out of his head. "He told you *exactly* what happened, only he said that it was all a *lie,* that I made it up because I didn't want you to know what really supposedly happened. He wanted to make sure that when I ran to you and told you what happened that you wouldn't believe a word. And how better to do that than to tell you that I would *claim* to be attacked, that I'd *claim* he tried to rape me."

Ryan stared at her in horror as the realization of what had really happened that day hit him.

"And sure enough. I run straight to you and tell you that your precious brother just tried to rape me and you look at me with those cold eyes and call me a liar. All because he told you that's what I'd say."

"Did he?" Ryan asked in a near whisper. "Did he rape you, Kelly?"

"He *touched* me. He touched me in a way that only you were allowed to touch me. He hit me. He bruised me. Isn't that enough?" she asked in a hysterical voice. "The irony in all of this is that you were so worried I was pregnant with his baby. We never had sex though God knows he tried."

She broke off again and buried her face in her hands. He wanted to go to her, take her in his arms, but he was afraid that just as he'd rejected her before, so would she reject him now.

She yanked her hands down, her face ragged and ravaged by grief, the same grief that was tearing through him.

"I should have been able to come to you," she whispered. "Of all the people in the world, you should have been the one to believe in me. And I just can't get past that. You should have been the one to hold me and tell me it would be all right. I was so excited that day. I took a pregnancy test that morning and found out I was pregnant. I was so excited and nervous. So worried about how you'd react. But so thrilled that I was pregnant with your child."

She broke off again, sobs tearing from her throat. She buried her face in her hands as her shoulders shook violently.

"Kelly, I'm so sorry. I thought… He was my *brother*. I never considered he would do something like that. He'd never shown any animosity toward you. He'd never been anything but accepting of you. The two of you seemed to get along well. I never dreamed he'd do something that despicable."

She raised her head and stared at him with dull eyes. "But you thought I would."

The sudden silence was damning. He stared at her, completely frozen. He had no defense because at the time he'd believed *Jarrod*. He'd made his choice and it hadn't been Kelly. Even when she'd begged him. She'd told him the truth. She'd come to him for protection. She'd come to him hurt and afraid. And he'd thrown her out after making her feel like a whore. All because he couldn't imagine his own flesh and blood committing such an atrocity. It had appeared to him that it was everything Jarrod said it was, a ridiculous accusation to hide the sin of her infidelity.

His eyes burned. His throat swelled and knotted. For the first time in his life he was faced with a situation where he had no idea what to do. She had every right to hate him.

She put a hand to her head and rubbed. She swayed and then bent over as if she was about to fall.

"Kelly!"

He went forward, but she jerked upright again and thrust out a hand to ward him off.

"Just stay away," she said in a low, desperate voice.

"Kelly, please."

It was his turn to beg. And God, he would. He'd do anything to make her stay long enough that he could make it up to her.

"I love you. I never stopped loving you."

She lifted her gaze again, her eyes drenched with tears—and pain. "*Love* isn't supposed to hurt this much. Love isn't this. Love is trust."

He moved forward again, so desperate to hold her, to offer the comfort he had denied her when she'd needed him most. Anger and sorrow vied for control. Grief welled in his chest until he thought he might explode. Rage surged through his veins like acid.

She put her hand to her head again and started to walk past him. He caught at her elbow, anything to stop her, because he knew in his heart she was going to walk away. He didn't deserve a second chance. He didn't deserve for her to stay. He didn't deserve her love. But he wanted it. He wanted it more than he wanted to live.

"Please don't go."

She turned back to him, sadness so deep in her gaze that it hurt him to look at her. "Don't you see, Ryan? It can never work for us. You don't trust me. Your family and friends hate me. What kind of life will that be for me? I deserve more than that. It's taken me long enough to figure that out. I settled again, when I swore I'd never do it. I agreed to marry you. Again. Because I was so in love with you and I believed that we could move forward. But I was a fool. Some obstacles are insurmountable."

She closed her eyes as another spasm of pain crossed her face. And she swayed, her hand flying out to brace herself against the dresser.

"Kelly, what's wrong?" he demanded.

She rubbed her hand across her brow and opened her

eyes, but her stare was unfocused. "My head." A sound like a whimper escaped her and he knew that something was wrong. Something beyond the emotional distress she was experiencing.

Her face took on a gray pallor that alarmed him. Panic flared in her eyes and just for a moment she looked to him for help.

Before he could react, her knees buckled and she slid soundlessly to the floor.

Sixteen

"Kelly!"

Ryan dropped to the floor. His immediate reaction was to gather her in his arms, but she was rigid and her body convulsed. Light foam gathered at her lips and her jaw was tight. Frantically he reached for his phone and clumsily punched 911.

"I need an ambulance," he said tersely. "My fiancée. She's pregnant. I think she's having a seizure." He knew he didn't make sense. His heart and mind were screaming even as he tried to stay calm. The 911 operator asked questions and he answered them mechanically as he leaned over Kelly, desperate to help her.

After a moment her body went slack and her head lolled to the side. He put his fingers to her neck, praying that he'd find a pulse. He laid his head over her chest, listening and feeling for air exchange.

"Don't leave me, Kelly," he whispered desperately. "Please hang on. I love you so damn much."

He lifted her limp hand, the one that bore his ring and pressed her palm to his cheek. He kissed the skin, his breaths coming in ragged, silent sobs. He'd never been more scared in his life.

The minutes dragged to eternity. The operator continued to ask him questions and offered him encouragement. But Kelly remained unconscious and the longer she lay there, still, on the floor, the more his panic and sense of helplessness grew.

After what seemed an interminable wait, he heard the EMS crew call out from the door.

"In here!" he called hoarsely.

They hurried in, motioning him away from Kelly as they began to administer care. Through it all, Ryan stood there numbly, watching as they lifted her onto a stretcher and hurried toward the elevator.

He followed behind, whispered prayers falling from his lips. They loaded her onto the waiting ambulance and he climbed in behind her.

Halfway to the hospital, he pulled out his phone but then stared blankly down at it. Who would he call? There was no one. Cold fury iced his veins. The very people he'd trusted—especially his brother—had acted unforgivably. Until now he'd never really experienced true hatred.

He buried his face in his hands and willed himself not to lose his composure. Not now. Kelly needed him. He hadn't been there for her before. He'd already made the mistake of abandoning her when she'd needed him the absolute most.

Now he'd die before he ever allowed her to think she wasn't the most important thing in the world to him.

Ryan stood listening to the doctor tell him that Kelly's condition was indeed serious. She was on a magnesium sulfate drip to lower her blood pressure and prevent future seizures, but if she didn't respond in the next few hours an emergency C-section would have to be performed.

"And the risks to the child?" Ryan croaked. "It's too soon, isn't it?"

The doctor gave him a look of sympathy. "We won't have a choice. If left untreated, both mother and child could die. The only cure for eclampsia is delivery of the baby. We're doing tests to determine the lung maturity of the baby. At thirty-four weeks' gestation, the child has a very good chance of survival without complications."

Ryan dug a hand into his hair and closed his eyes. He'd done this to her. She should have been cherished and pampered during her entire pregnancy. She should have been waited on hand and foot. Instead she'd been forced to work a physically demanding job under unimaginable stress. And once he'd brought her back, she'd been subjected to scorn and hostility and endless emotional distress.

Was it any wonder she wanted to wash her hands of him and his family?

"Will…will Kelly be all right? Will she recover from this?"

He didn't realize he held his breath until his chest began to burn. He let it out slowly and forced himself to relax his hands.

"She's gravely ill. Her blood pressure is extremely high. She could seize again or suffer a stroke. Neither is good for her or the baby. We're doing everything we can to bring her blood pressure down and we're monitoring the baby for signs of stress. We're prepared to take the baby if the condition of either mother or child deteriorates. It's important she remain calm and not be stressed in any way. Even if we're able to bring down her blood pressure and put off the delivery until closer to her due date, she'll be on strict bed rest for the remainder of her pregnancy."

"I understand," Ryan said quietly. "Can I see her now?"

"You can go in but she must remain calm. Don't do or say anything to upset her."

Ryan nodded and turned to walk the few steps to Kelly's room. He paused at the door, afraid to go in. What if his mere presence upset her?

His hand rested on the handle and he leaned forward, pressing his forehead to the surface. He closed his eyes as grief and regret—so much regret—swamped him.

Finally he opened the door and eased inside. It was dark with only a light from the bathroom to illuminate the room. Kelly lay on the bed, a vast array of medical equipment on either side of her.

He approached cautiously, not wanting to disturb or upset her. He hovered by her side, staring down at her pale face. Her eyes were closed, but her brow was creased, whether in worry or pain he wasn't sure. Maybe both.

Her chest barely rose with the shallow breaths. Suddenly, everything that had happened tonight caught up to him in one painful rush.

Never. *Never* would he forget her grief-ravaged face as she bitterly told him what his brother had done to her, what she'd tried to tell him months before. But he hadn't listened then. He'd been convinced she was lying.

He pulled up a chair so he could sit as close to her as possible while she slept. Tentatively, he slid his fingers underneath the hand that didn't have an IV attached and he brought it to his lips, holding it against his mouth.

"I'm sorry, Kell," he said brokenly. "I'm so damn sorry."

"Ryan. Ryan, man, wake up."

The whisper stirred Ryan and he opened his eyes

and groaned at the monster crick in his neck. Daylight streamed through the blinds on the window and he winced.

His gaze first found Kelly, who was still sleeping, her cheek resting on the mound of pillows. Her bed was elevated slightly so she wasn't lying flat and some time recently her IV bag had been replaced because it was now full.

Then he turned, his hand going to rub the kinks in his neck. Devon was standing next to the chair Ryan had slept in, his eyes dark with concern.

"What the hell happened?" Devon said in a low voice.

Carefully, Ryan stood, not wanting to risk waking Kelly up. He motioned for Dev to follow him outside the hospital room. When they walked out, Ryan saw Cam shove off the wall, his eyebrow arched in question.

"What are you two doing here?" Ryan asked with a frown.

"Last night was tense," Devon said. "We tried to call you but couldn't get you so we went by your apartment. Your doorman told us that Kelly had been taken to the hospital by ambulance so we came over to see if she's okay."

Ryan closed his eyes as his throat knotted all over again.

"Whoa, man, you need to sit down," Cam said. "Have you eaten?"

Ryan shook his head.

"Want to tell us about it?" Dev prompted.

Ryan stared at his two friends and emitted a harsh laugh. "How do you explain that you've made the worst mistake of your entire life and you're not sure you can ever make amends?"

"That bad, huh," Cam said.

"Worse."

"Is Kelly going to be all right?" Dev asked. "And the baby?"

"I wish I knew. They might have to deliver the baby early if her blood pressure doesn't go down. I did this to her. She's lying in a hospital bed because I wasn't there for her or my child. What kind of a bastard does that make me?"

Cam and Devon exchanged glances.

"Look, granted I don't know the whole story, but I'd say that you aren't solely to blame for the problem," Devon said carefully.

"My brother *assaulted* her," Ryan said as rage flooded him all over again. "He tried to rape her and when she fought him off, he called me with an ingenious story. He claimed they slept together but when he told her it was a mistake, she threatened to tell me he tried to rape her so I wouldn't break up with her for cheating on me. So of course not half an hour later when she shows up at my office telling me *exactly* what my brother said she would, I didn't believe her. Because I couldn't imagine my brother, the brother I all but raised, doing something so despicable. And when she begged me, when she got on her knees and *pleaded* with me to believe her, I wrote her a check and told her to get the hell out of my life."

Devon and Cam both looked at him stunned, speechless.

"How am I ever supposed to get past something like that," Ryan snarled. "Tell me how *she's* supposed to get past that. Do you know that just last night before dinner I magnanimously told her that I forgave her? That I wanted us to forget the past and move forward and that I *forgave* her for cheating on me."

He broke off and laughed a dry, harsh laugh.

"Yeah, from the start I've been all about being the bigger person and wanting to start over when all along I treated her so unforgivably. She came to me for help, for protection, because I was the one person she counted on, and I turned my back on her."

Ryan turned away as his composure slipped. Tears burned his eyes. Angry, furious tears. He wanted to ram his fist into the wall. He wanted to roar with rage.

His friends flanked him, each slipping a hand over his shoulder.

"I don't know what to say," Devon said quietly. "I know you love her."

"Yeah, I did, do, always have. I loved her and yet I did this to her. How is she ever going to be able to trust me again?"

"Someone needs to beat the hell out of that little bastard," Cam growled.

Ryan slowly raised his head, his face set in stone. "He'll never ever come close to her again. I'm going to kill him."

"Damn," Devon muttered. "Look, I know you're pissed and you have every right to be, but don't do anything stupid. He deserves to have his ass kicked, but don't do anything to land yourself in jail. Kelly needs you. You can't help her if you're behind bars."

"I can't let him get away with it," Ryan said. "He touched her. He violated her. He *hurt* her."

"I'm going with you," Cam said tersely.

Ryan shook his head.

"You don't get a choice. It's either I go with you or I'm calling the police. The difference is, I'll let you beat the crap out of him. But I won't let you kill him. The police aren't going to let you touch him. So what'll it be?"

Ryan's lip curled into a snarl.

Devon sighed. "You should see yourself, man. It's a good thing Kelly is sleeping. Whatever it is you need to do, you need to get it done so that when she wakes up you can be the support she needs. You'll just scare her to death if she sees you like this."

"Devon can stay with Kelly," Cam volunteered. "I'll go with you to confront Jarrod. Then you can get your ass back here where you belong and put this whole thing behind you."

Cam made it sound easy, but Ryan knew better. Kelly might not ever forgive him and he wouldn't blame her if she didn't. But if she did and if she and Ryan were going to be together, he was going to make damn sure his family was never an issue for her again.

"Will you do it?" Ryan asked. "Will you stay with her for a while? If she wakes let her know…"

"I'll handle it," Devon said. "You just go so you can get your head on straight again. And rip his nuts off for me. The bastard deserves it."

Seventeen

Jarrod's expression was one of resignation when he opened the door to Ryan's insistent knock. Ryan didn't give him time to do or say anything. He grabbed his brother by the shirt and propelled him backward into the small studio apartment Jarrod lived in.

"What the—?"

Ryan silenced him with a fist. Jarrod went sprawling and Ryan and Cam both stood a few feet back waiting for him to pick himself up off the floor.

Jarrod wiped at the blood on his mouth as he stumbled to his feet. "What the hell, Ryan?"

"Why did you do it?" Ryan asked in a deadly quiet voice. *"Why?"*

An uneasy expression crawled across Jarrod's face. His lips drooped and his eyes went dull. At least he wasn't going to pretend he didn't know what Ryan was talking about.

Jarrod dragged a hand across his mouth again, his hand coming away smeared with blood. "I know it won't mean much, but I'm sorry."

Ryan exploded at him. Jarrod didn't even try to defend himself. He went down on the floor and this time he didn't get up.

"Sorry? You're *sorry?* You tried to rape her. You lied to me about her. What the hell is wrong with you? She was the woman I was going to marry. Why would you do something like that?"

"Mom," Jarrod said in a weary voice.

Ryan took a step back, stunned. "Mom? *Mom* put you up to this?"

Jarrod dragged himself only up enough to lean against the living room wall and he put a hand through his hair, his expression weary and defeated.

"Yeah. She went ballistic when she found out you proposed to Kelly. She was determined you weren't going to marry some penniless upstart. Her words not mine. I thought she was crazy at first. I mean I figured she'd throw a fit and then get over it, but then she wanted me to go buy her off. She said that if Kelly refused the offer, I should frame her with the fake rape story. I swear to you I wouldn't have raped her, Ryan. I just wanted to set it up so you'd think we slept together."

"Jesus," Cam muttered. "This is crazy."

Ryan was numb from head to toe. His own mother had done something that sick? It didn't seem possible. How could anyone hate someone else so much that they'd go to such lengths to get rid of them?

"She invited me to dinner last night. But I swear, Ryan, she told me that *you* wanted me there, that you and Kelly wanted to let the past go and start over. I wasn't going to go, because I didn't want to upset Kelly or make you angry, but Mom told me you specifically asked for me to come. And I hoped… I hoped that maybe you and Kelly could forgive the past and that we could be a family again. Like old times."

Ryan dropped his hands to his sides, suddenly so sick at heart that he just wanted to walk away. "You're no longer my family. Kelly and our child are my family. I don't *ever* want to see you again. If I ever catch you near Kelly I swear to you that you'll regret it."

"Ryan, don't. Please," Jarrod called hoarsely.

Ryan stopped at the door and slowly turned around. "Did she beg you like you're begging me, Jarrod? Did she ask you to stop?"

Jarrod's face flushed a dull red and then he looked away, no longer able to meet his brother's gaze.

"Come on," Cam said quietly. "Let's go, man."

As they walked back out, Ryan nudged Cam toward the waiting car. "You go. I'll take a cab. I'm going to see my mother."

Cam hesitated. "Sure you don't want me to go with you?"

"Yeah. This is something I have to do by myself."

Ryan knocked tersely on the door to his mother's home and issued a clipped demand to see her when one of the maids answered the door.

A moment later, as he paced the floor of the receiving room, his mother hurried in, her brow wrinkled in concern.

"Ryan? Is something wrong? You didn't call to tell me you were coming."

He stared at her, wondering how he could be so blind about the woman who'd given birth to him. There was no doubt she'd always been self-centered, but he'd never considered her malicious enough to harm an innocent woman.

Even now, after everything that had happened, he was at a loss for words. How could he possibly convey the depth of his hatred? It boiled in his veins like acid. His family. The people he should be able to count on. They were… evil.

The irony struck him hard. Kelly should have been able to count on him. But just as his family had betrayed him, he had betrayed Kelly. Maybe he was more like his mother and brother than he wanted to admit. The thought sickened him.

"Ryan?" she asked again.

She stopped in front of him and put her hand on his arm, her eyes worried.

He wiped her hand away and took a step back, choking on his disgust.

"Don't touch me," he said in a low voice. "I know what you did. I know what you and Jarrod did. I'll never forgive you for it."

Her face creased with consternation. She threw up her hand and turned away, her arms crossing over her chest.

"She's not who you should be with, Ryan. If you weren't so infatuated with her, so blinded by…lust, you'd see it too."

"You're not even going to deny it. My God. What did Kelly ever do to deserve what you did to her? She's lying in a hospital right now. She carries my child, *your* grandchild. She was pregnant when you sent Jarrod to attack her. What kind of a psychopath does that kind of thing?"

"I don't regret protecting my sons," she said stiffly. "I'd do it again. You'll understand when your son or daughter is born. You'll understand why I did what I did. With parenthood comes the knowledge that you'll do anything at all for your child. You'll protect them with everything you have. You can't just stand by and let your child make the worst mistake of their life and do nothing. Come talk to me in a few years. Then ask yourself if you still hate me so much."

He was dumbfounded by the lengths she went to justify her actions. They weren't simply morally reprehensible. They were criminal!

"I would hope that I never act as you have, that I'd never hurt an innocent woman just because I didn't think she was good enough. Here's what you don't understand, Mother. She's a better person than you'll ever be. Not good enough? We aren't good enough for her. We'll never be. I just have to hope to hell she'll accept and forgive me despite the worthless excuse for a family that I have."

His mother's eyes burned with outrage. "You're a typical man. Thinking with the lower portion of your anatomy. You're completely blinded by lust, but in a few years you won't look at her with the same lovesick puppy eyes. Then you'll thank me for trying to protect you. You can do better than her, Ryan. Why can't I make you see that?"

Ryan shook his head, sadness and grief so thick in his chest he could barely breathe. "I'll never thank you for this. You're nothing to me anymore. I'll never subject my wife or children to your poison."

Her face whitened with shock. "You don't mean that!"

"I mean it. You aren't my mother. I have no mother. I have no family save Kelly and our child. I'll never forgive you for this. Stay away from me. Stay away from Kelly. If you ever come within a hundred yards of my family, I'll forget that you gave birth to me and I'll have you hauled away in handcuffs. Are we understood?"

She stared wordlessly at him, suddenly looking every

one of her sixty years. If she hadn't so callously tried to destroy the woman he loved, he would have felt sorry for her. But she showed no remorse. No regret.

"I have nothing more to say to you," he bit out.

He turned and walked away, his mother's cries for him to stop ringing in his ears.

He walked out of her house, never looking back. He got into the waiting cab and directed the driver back to the hospital. Kelly needed him. Their child needed him.

Chances were she'd never forgive him, but he'd make sure she never wanted for another thing in her life. He'd provide for her and their child. He'd spend the rest of his life making it up to her if only she'd let him.

Kelly awoke to silence. She was so relieved to no longer hear the horrible ringing in her ears that she could weep. The vile headache was gone. It no longer felt like the top of her head was going to explode.

She was oddly free of pain.

It took her several moments of staring at her surroundings to discover that she was in a hospital room.

Then the events leading up to her collapse came back to her in a flash. Her hands flew automatically to her belly and she was only partially reassured to feel the tight ball there. Was her baby okay? Was she herself okay?

She blinked harder to bring the room more into focus. There was light shining through a crack in the bathroom door. A glance at the blinds told her that it was dark outside.

Then her gaze fell on the chair beside her bed and she found Ryan staring at her, his gaze intense. She flinched away from the raw emotion shining in his blue eyes.

"Hey," he said quietly. "How are you feeling?"

"Numb," she answered before she could think better

of it. "Kind of blank. My head doesn't hurt anymore. Are my feet still swollen?"

He carefully picked up the sheet and pushed it over her feet. "Maybe a little. Not as bad as they were. They've been giving you meds and they're monitoring the baby."

"How is she?" Kelly asked, a knot of fear in her throat.

"For now, she's doing fine. Your blood pressure stabilized, but they might have to do a C-section if it goes back up or if the baby starts showing signs of distress."

Kelly closed her eyes and then suddenly Ryan was close to her, holding her, his lips pressed against her temple.

"Don't worry, love," he murmured. "You're supposed to stay calm. You're getting the best possible care. I've made sure of it. They're monitoring you round-the-clock. And the doctor said the baby has an excellent prognosis at thirty-four weeks' gestation."

She sagged against the pillow and closed her eyes. Relief pulsed through her but she was so tired she couldn't muster the energy to do anything more than lie there thanking God that her baby was okay.

"I'm going to take care of you, Kell," Ryan said softly against her temple. "You and our baby. Nothing will ever hurt you again. I swear it."

Tears burned her eyelids. She was emotionally and physically exhausted and didn't have the strength to argue. Something inside her was broken and she had no idea how to fix it. She felt so…disconnected.

Ryan drew away, but his eyes were bright with concern… and love. But was it enough? What was love without trust? He wanted her. He felt guilty. He wasn't a jerk. He had feelings and it would destroy him now that he knew the truth. But he hadn't trusted her, and Kelly wasn't sure if they could even forge a relationship when this much hurt and betrayal was involved. Maybe they'd been stupid to even attempt it.

"What's going to happen?" she whispered. "Do I have to stay here? Do I go home?" She bit her lip because she wasn't sure where she'd go. Her relationship with Ryan was a big question mark, but she had no place to go except home with him. And her baby's health came first.

He took her hand—the one that she wore his ring on—and thumbed it absently.

"You'll stay here until a decision is made about your health. But the doctor said that if you go home, you'll be on strict bed rest for the rest of your pregnancy."

Her expression must have reflected her horror and her fear, because Ryan leaned over to kiss her forehead again. He held her hand and rubbed his thumb over her knuckles.

"I don't want you to worry, honey, okay? I'll handle everything. We'll go someplace warm and beautiful and all you'll have to do is lie on the beach or in a comfortable chair and watch the sun set. I'll hire a personal physician to oversee every part of your care."

Her brow furrowed and she could feel the pain creep back into her head.

"Ryan, we can't just go off to some island paradise somewhere. Ignoring our problems won't fix them."

He stroked a hand over her forehead, smoothing her hair back. "Right now, all you need to concentrate on is feeling better and carrying our child for as long as you can. And what I need to concentrate on is removing as much stress from your life as possible."

She opened her mouth to respond, but he kissed her lightly, silencing her.

"I know we have a lot to work out, Kell. I had no idea how much when I said this before. But right now let's put our differences aside and concentrate on our baby and your health. Can we do that?"

Her resistance slid away. She nodded slowly, not withdrawing her hand from his.

Despite what had happened in the past, she didn't doubt for a moment that he cared deeply about her and their baby. And he was right. No matter what had to be worked out between them, their child came first.

Eighteen

"I'm reluctant to release Miss Christian from the hospital," Kelly's doctor said grimly as he stood outside her hospital room. "She's shown marked improvement. Her blood pressure is normal. The baby is showing no signs of fetal distress. I'd say she has a good chance of carrying the child the full forty weeks. But I'm not comfortable releasing her yet."

Ryan rubbed the back of his neck. "What can I do to make it possible? She's unhappy here. She's not herself."

The doctor nodded. "That's precisely why I'm concerned about releasing her. At least here I can be assured she's getting the care she needs. She's not in good spirits and I'm deeply concerned about her stress level. It's imperative that she not be placed in any situation that causes her undue distress."

"If you give her the okay to travel I plan to take her away. Someplace warm where she'll never have to lift a finger. I can have a medical team fly us to the island and once there, I'll have a private physician to monitor her care as well as have the local hospital completely apprised of her condition and needs."

The doctor went silent as he seemed to mull over Ryan's suggestion. "Perhaps that's the best idea. It's cold and a bit gloomy right now. Maybe the better weather will lift her spirits and she'll regain her strength. It's not good for her or the baby if she gives birth now when she's verging on depression."

It made Ryan's heart ache to think of Kelly being sad and depressed. He'd do anything at all to make her smile again.

"Give me your okay and I'll make immediate arrangements for us to leave the city," Ryan said quietly. "I want only the best for her and I'll do whatever it takes to make her well again."

The doctor stared hard at him and then lowered his clipboard to his waist. "I believe you, Mr. Beardsley. Tell you what. You give me the name of the physician you hire as well as the name of the hospital that will be overseeing her care and I'll have her medical records transferred. I'll want to talk to her physician personally and make sure he's aware of the severity and the complexity of the situation. I'll also want to make sure the hospital is prepared to take the baby at the first sign of distress. And that they have adequately trained personnel for this situation."

"Thank you," Ryan said sincerely. "Kelly and I both appreciate your attention in this matter."

"Just take good care of her. I hate to see the young lady so sad."

Ryan nodded, his chest tight. He'd take good care of her, no doubt, but it remained to be seen if he could make her happy again. Still, he wasn't about to give up. He'd turned his back on her once. Never again would she have any cause to doubt him. If it took him forever, he'd make damn sure she knew she could count on him.

Kelly sat in the armchair by the window in her hospital room and stared out as snowflakes drifted down in crazy little spirals. Though it was plenty warm in her room, a chill crept over her shoulders and she shivered.

"Do you want a blanket?" Ryan asked.

She turned her head in surprise. She hadn't expected him back, though she should have known he wouldn't be gone for long. He'd been a constant presence over the past few days, always there, anticipating her every need.

"Sorry if I startled you," he said in a low voice.

"You didn't. I just didn't hear you come in."

He moved in front of her and perched on the windowsill. He shoved his hands in his pockets and then leveled a stare at her.

"I just finished talking to your doctor. He's willing to release you."

Her eyes widened in surprise.

"There are conditions, of course. He's very concerned over your health."

She frowned. "What conditions?"

"I've already made all the arrangements. I've taken care of everything. There's nothing you need to worry about. Just concentrate on getting well and regaining your strength."

She shook her head, trying to clear some of the constant fuzz that seemed to permeate her brain lately. She'd existed in a fog ever since her collapse, and worse, her fatigue had grown worse. Something inside stirred, though, as though she ought to protest, but she couldn't summon the mental energy to do it.

When she remained silent, Ryan continued on.

"We're leaving the city. An ambulance is going to transport you to the airport where a medical team is going to fly us to St. Angelo."

Again she shook her head in silent denial. And she finally found her objection.

"Ryan, you can't just leave here. It could be weeks before I have the baby. You can't hover over me for so long. Neither can you leave your work. Your life is *here*."

He slid to his knees in front of her and gathered her hands in his. "My life is with *you*. You and our baby are my absolute priority. I have people who are more than capable of running things in my absence. I have business partners who are more than willing to step in and take over any matters needing my attention. We'll be minutes from the resort construction site, so I can easily oversee any issues that arise there."

Nothing had been said of the night she'd collapsed after her emotional breakdown. It had been a carefully avoided issue, as was the matter of their future…and his brother. She could see the torment and the terrible guilt in Ryan's eyes, but he didn't broach the subject and neither did she. She couldn't do it without upsetting herself and, above all else, the doctor had warned her against becoming distressed. She couldn't afford another complete loss of control like the night she'd ended up in the hospital.

So she'd locked everything behind an impenetrable wall of ice and indifference. Any time she felt her emotions rising, she turned them off and didn't offer objection or resistance.

And she'd do the same now. Her heart told her to object, to not allow him to take over and whisk her away. She was tired of being hurt. But it simply took too much effort and she'd expended all of her strength.

"Kelly?" he asked softly. "What are you thinking, honey?"

She moved her gaze until it rested on him. His brow was creased in concern and he was staring hard at her as if he was trying to reach in and pluck out her thoughts.

"I'm tired," she said honestly. And weak. Heartsick. Unsure of what she wanted. Battling over what was best for her baby.

So many things that she wouldn't admit because it simply took too much effort to explain.

He touched her cheek, caressing gently. "I know you are, baby. I have no right to ask this of you, but I'm asking anyway. Trust me. Let me take care of you. Let me take you away. You loved it on the island."

How easy he made it for her to cede control. He was offering her everything she'd ever wanted. His love. His care. Fantasy. He was offering her a fantasy. But fantasies never lasted. They'd already done this once. Escaped from reality for a few idyllic days on the island, but when it was all over they'd had to return to the cold reality of their lives.

"I want to stay there until I have the baby," she said quietly. She didn't want her baby born here. She didn't want to be surrounded by people who despised her. She didn't want her child exposed to the animosity she herself had been a victim of.

"Already arranged."

Her eyes widened in surprise.

"Come with me, Kell. Trust me. At least for now."

Maybe she could stay on the island after the baby was born. Surely Ryan saw the impossibility of them having a relationship by now. But she and the baby could live there. They wouldn't need much. A small cottage or even an apartment. As soon as she was back on her feet, she could find work. She'd waitressed. She wasn't afraid of hard work.

And when Ryan wanted to see their child he could come to the island. For a man with his own jet and a resort that would be completed within a year, it wouldn't be a hardship to visit his child often.

Encouraged by having a goal, a plan, she nodded.

Ryan's relief was palpable. He leaned forward to kiss her, but she turned her head so that his mouth glanced off her cheek instead.

"I have to leave for just a little while," he said when he pulled back. "I need to finalize all the arrangements for our departure and make sure your needs will be met for the entire trip. I'll be back as soon as I can. Is there anything I can bring you?"

She shook her head and he rose but before he walked away, he stroked a hand over her hair. "I'll do anything to make you smile again, Kell."

Before she could respond, he turned and walked quietly from the room, leaving her to stare out the window as it snowed.

The flight and subsequent transportation to the villa on the beach was seamless. Ryan had ensured that she was given every consideration. She was endlessly pampered and waited on and when they arrived on the island, they were greeted not only by the physician who would be monitoring her care, but a personal nurse who would reside at the villa with her and Ryan.

When Kelly got her first look at the sprawling villa, it took her breath away. They drove through a gate and down a winding driveway that was lined with lush, gorgeous flowers. Just for a moment the driveway paralleled the beach before it ended in front of the main house.

The house couldn't be more than a few steps from the

beach. The idea that she could walk out the back door and be on the sand sent excitement coursing through her veins.

Ryan insisted on carrying her inside. He cradled her close as he walked through the front door and she craned her neck to take in the interior.

Instead of showing her around, he took her to the glass doors that led to the wraparound porch in the back. As she had suspected, there were only three stones marking the very short pathway from the porch to the sand.

As soon as she stepped onto the porch, the breeze from the water ruffled her hair. She closed her eyes and inhaled deeply, savoring the tang of the salt and the lush, warm air that surrounded them.

"It's beautiful," she breathed.

He smiled. "I'm glad you approve—because it's yours."

She went still in his arms and locked her gaze with his. For a long moment she was too stunned to find her voice. When she finally did, it came out as a croak. "I don't understand."

He eased her down onto the steps leading to the sand. Then he sat beside her as they stared over the shimmering blue of the water.

"I bought it for you. For us. This is your house."

She was at a complete loss for words. The numbness that she'd worn for so long was melting away. It was as if the warmth of the sun was thawing the ice and with it, brought new awareness. She saw things more clearly. She saw Ryan. She saw him making a huge effort to make her happy. To take care of her. Hope began to beat inside her chest, but she pushed it back, afraid to give it free rein. She didn't dare make assumptions.

"But Ryan, you live in New York. Your life is there. Your family is there. Your job, your business, your friends. You can't just move here because we had a few days of happiness."

"Can't I?" he challenged.

He picked up her hand and laced his fingers through hers. "There's a lot you don't know, Kelly. I didn't want you to know at the time. You were dealing with enough stress in the hospital. I've cut my brother and my mother out of my life. Out of *our* lives."

"Oh, Ryan." Tears swam in her eyes. No matter how much she despised them, she had never wanted this for him.

He wiped a tear away with his thumb. "Don't you dare shed a tear for them or for me. They aren't worth your tears. I don't regret what I've done. I only regret that I allowed them to hurt you and that I never saw what they were doing to you."

"But you wouldn't have done it if it weren't for me," she said painfully. "They're your family, Ryan. Maybe you're angry with them now, but what about a year from now? Or five years from now? At what point will you resent me for being the wedge between you?"

"You aren't responsible for their actions," he said fiercely. "You didn't do this. They did. No one else. I hate them for what they did. They are beyond despicable. They don't deserve your consideration. They don't deserve mine. I never want our child exposed to that kind of poison. It was my decision, Kelly. Do you honestly think I would allow them in any part of our lives after what they did to you?"

Tears slid down her cheeks. This hadn't been her goal. No matter how much she wanted to never be around them again, the last thing she wanted was to cause Ryan pain.

"Let's not talk about them," he said quietly. "They're no longer an issue. What I want to talk about is us. Can you ever forgive me, Kell? Can you possibly love me again?"

He rose from his perch beside her and went down the

two steps to the beach below her. Then he slowly slid to his knees in front of her and reached for her hands.

"You once got on your knees and begged me to believe you. You begged me not to turn my back on you. It's my turn to beg, Kelly. I don't deserve your forgiveness. I wouldn't blame you if you *never* forgave me. But I'm begging all the same. I love you. I want us to have a life together. Here. On the island. Away from all the unhappiness of the past."

"You want us to stay here?" she whispered.

He nodded even as his hands trembled around hers. "I bought the house. I have the hospital on standby. I've made sure that our child will have the best possible care. I want us to start over, *really* start over this time. I'm begging you for that chance. Give me the chance to make you love me again."

Her heart twisted and the mind-numbing grief that had sweltered so long in her soul silently slipped away, leaving renewed hope—and love—shining in its stead. This time she didn't try to squash the hope. She let it fly.

She reached for him, framing his face, stunned to feel the shock of tears on his cheeks. His eyes were tormented and there was desperation—fear—in his gaze, but there was also answering hope.

"I love you so very much," she said brokenly. "I've spent so long being angry, telling myself I hate you. The anger took over until I was miserable with it. It's been a constant weight pressing down on me. It's poison and I can't live this way anymore. I don't *want* to live this way anymore."

He closed his eyes and when he reopened them there was such relief and such vulnerability that she knew without a doubt that she'd made the right choice.

"If you can forgive all the hurtful, hateful things I've said to you then I can forgive you for not trusting me."

"Oh, God, Kell," he said in a wretched, pained voice. "I deserved everything you've said and more. What I did to you was unforgivable. How can you forgive me when I can't forgive myself?"

She leaned forward and kissed him, still holding his face in her hands. She stroked her hands through his hair and then over his cheeks again, smiling a tender smile all the while.

"We make quite a pair, don't we? We've made mistakes. But I like to think that we haven't given up. And that maybe we're stronger for it all. It makes me hurt that you've given up so much for me. Your family. Your friends. The city you grew up in. And you gave it up, bought a beautiful house you knew I'd love all because you loved *me*. If I don't forgive you then I'm denying myself that love and I don't want to live without you, Ryan. Or your love. Not anymore. The last months have been the worst of my life. I don't ever want to relive that kind of agony again."

He pulled her into his arms, leaning forward so they didn't tumble into the sand. He held her so tightly she couldn't breathe, but she didn't care. They were together. Finally. Without all the hurt and pain of the past. Without reservations or barriers.

As soon as she'd told him she loved him and that she forgave him it was like the weight of the world had been lifted. She felt lighter and freer than she'd ever felt. She felt…happy. Joyously, giddily happy.

"I love you so damn much, Kell," he said hoarsely. "I've always loved you. I never stopped loving you. I went to bed at night thinking about you, worrying and wondering where you were, if you were happy, if you were all right. I made all sorts of excuses for hiring someone to find you but the truth was that I couldn't live without you."

She smiled and leaned her forehead against his. "Do you think maybe we can stop beating ourselves up over things we can't change and make a pact to love each other for the rest of our lives and be happy for every day of them?"

He slid his hands over her arms, up to her neck to cup her face again. "Yeah," he breathed. "I can do that."

He pulled away, smiling, his eyes raw with emotion. "Marry me, Kell. Right away. I don't want to wait even a day. Marry me here on our beach. Just you and me and our baby."

"Our beach," she said softly. "I love the sound of that. And yes, I'll marry you. Today, tomorrow, forever."

For the longest time they sat there on the steps leading to their beach. A beach where they'd raise their children. Where they'd laugh and love and remember how they'd pledged their love and made vows to stay together through all the trials that life threw at them.

They sat until the sun sank below the horizon and the soft colors of dusk settled over the ocean. And then when the moon rose and spilled silver over the water, Ryan carried Kelly down to the beach and they danced to the soft melody of the rolling waves.

* * * * *

TEMPTED BY HER INNOCENT KISS

BY
MAYA BANKS

One

There came a time in a man's life when he knew he was well and truly caught. Devon Carter stared down at the brilliant diamond solitaire ring nestled in velvet and acknowledged that this was one such time. He snapped the lid closed and shoved the box into the breast pocket of his suit.

He had two choices. He could marry Ashley Copeland and fulfill his goal of merging his company with Copeland Hotels, thus creating the largest, most exclusive line of resorts in the world, or he could refuse and lose it all.

Put in that light, there wasn't much he could do except pop the question.

The doorman to his Manhattan high-rise hurried to open the door as Devon strode toward the street, where his driver waited. He took a deep breath before ducking into the car, and the driver pulled into traffic.

Tonight was the night. All of his careful wooing—the countless dinners, kisses that started brief and casual and became more breathless—was a lead-up to tonight. Tonight his seduction of Ashley Copeland would be complete, and then he'd ask her to marry him.

He shook his head as the absurdity of the situation hit him for the hundredth time. Personally he thought William Copeland was crazy for forcing his daughter down Devon's throat. He'd tried everything to sway the older man from his aim to see his daughter married off…to Devon.

Ashley was a sweet enough girl, but Devon had no desire to marry anyone. Not yet. Maybe in five years. Then he'd select a wife, have two-point-five children and have it all.

William had other plans. From the moment Devon had approached him, William held a calculated gleam in his eye. He'd told Devon that Ashley had no head for business. She was too soft-hearted, too naive, too…everything to ever take an active role in the family business. He was convinced that any man who showed interest in her would only be seeking to ingratiate himself into the Copeland fold—and the fortune that went with her. William wanted her taken care of and for whatever reason, he thought Devon was the best choice.

And so he'd made Ashley part and parcel of the deal. The catch? Ashley wasn't to learn of it. The old man might be willing to barter his daughter, but he damn sure didn't want her to know about it. Which meant that Devon was stuck playing stupid games. He winced at the things he'd said, the patience he'd exerted in his courting of Ashley. He was a blunt, straight-forward person, and this whole mess made him grit his teeth.

If she was part of the deal, he'd rather all parties know that from the outset so there would be no misunderstandings, no hurt feelings and no misconceptions.

Ashley was going to think this was a grand love match. She was a starry-eyed, soft-hearted woman who preferred to spend time with her animal rescue foundation over board meetings, charts and financials for Copeland Hotels.

If she ever found out the truth, she wasn't going to take it well. And hell, he couldn't blame her. Devon hated manipulation, and he'd be pissed if someone was doing to him what he was doing to her.

"Stupid old fool," Devon muttered.

His driver pulled up to the apartment building that was home to the entire Copeland clan. William and his wife occupied a penthouse on the top floor, but Ashley had moved to a smaller apartment on a lower floor. Various other family members, from cousins to aunts and uncles, lived in all places in between.

The Copeland family was an anomaly to Devon. He'd been on his own since he was eighteen, and the only thing he remembered of his parents was the occasional reminder not to "screw up."

All this devotion William showered on his children was alien and it made Devon uncomfortable. Especially since William seemed determined to treat Devon like a son now that he was marrying Ashley.

Devon started to get out when he saw Ashley fly through the door, a wide smile on her face, her eyes sparkling as she saw him.

What the hell?

He hurried toward her, a frown on his face.

"Ashley, you should have stayed inside. I would have come for you."

In response, she laughed, the sound vibrant and fresh among the sounds of traffic. Her long blond hair hung free tonight instead of being pulled up by a clip in her usual careless manner. She reached for his hands and squeezed as she smiled up at him.

"Really, Devon, what could happen to me? Alex is right here, and he watches over me worse than my father does."

Alex, the doorman, smiled indulgently in Ashley's direction. It was a smile most people wore around her. Patient, somewhat bemused, but nearly everyone who met her was enchanted by her effervescence.

Devon sighed and pulled Ashley's hands up to his waist. "You should wait inside where it's safe and let me come in for you. Alex can't protect you. He has other duties to attend to."

Her eyes sparkled merrily, and she flung her arms around his neck, startling him with the unexpected show of affection.

"That's what you're for, silly. I can't imagine anyone ever hurting me when you're around."

Before he could respond, she fused her lips hungrily to his. For God's sake the woman had no sense of self-control. She was making a spectacle here in the doorway to her apartment building.

Still, his body reacted to the hunger in her kiss. She tasted sweet and so damn innocent. He felt like an ogre for the deception he was carrying out.

But then he remembered that Copeland Hotels would finally be his—or at least under his control. He would be a force to be reckoned with worldwide. Not bad for a man who had been told that his sole ambition should be not to "screw up."

Carefully, he pulled her away and gently offered a reprimand.

"This isn't the place, Ashley. We should be going. Carl is waiting for us."

Her lips turned down into a momentary frown before she looked beyond him to Carl, and once again she rushed forward, a bright smile on her face.

He shook his head as she greeted his chauffeur, her hands flying everywhere as she spoke in rapid tones. Carl grinned. The man actually *grinned* as he handed Ashley into the car. By the time Devon made it over, Carl had already reverted back to his somber countenance.

Devon slid into the backseat with Ashley, and she immediately moved over to nestle into his side.

"Where are we eating tonight?" she asked.

"I planned something special."

As expected she all but pounced on him, her eyes shining with excitement.

"What?" she demanded.

He smiled. "You'll see."

He felt more than heard her faint huff of exasperation and his smile broadened. One thing in Ashley's favor was that she was extraordinarily easy to please. He was unused to women who didn't wheedle, pout or complain when their expectations weren't met. And unfortunately, the women he usually spent time with had high expectations. *Expensive* expectations. Ashley seemed happy no matter what he presented her with. He had every confidence that the ring he'd chosen would meet with her approval.

She nestled closer to him and laid her head on his shoulder. Her spontaneous demonstrations of affection still unbalanced him. He wasn't used to people who were so…unreserved.

William Copeland felt that Ashley needed someone who understood and accepted her nature. Why he thought Devon fit the bill Devon would never know.

When they married, he would work on getting her to restrain some of her enthusiasm. She couldn't go through her entire life with her emotions on her sleeve. It would only get her hurt.

A few minutes later, Carl pulled up to Devon's building and got out to open the door. Devon stepped out and then extended his hand to help Ashley from the car.

Her brow was creased in a thoughtful expression as she stared up at the building.

"This is your place."

He chuckled at her statement of the obvious. "So it is. Come, our dinner awaits."

He ushered her through the open door and into a waiting elevator. It soared to the top and opened into the foyer of his apartment. To his satisfaction, everything was just as he'd arranged.

The lighting was low and romantic. Soft jazz played in the background and the table by the window overlooking the city had been set for two.

"Oh, Devon, this is perfect!"

Once again she threw herself into his arms and gave him a squeeze worthy of someone much larger than herself. It did funny things to his chest every time she hugged him.

Extricating himself from her hold, he guided her toward the table. He pulled her chair out for her and then reached for a bottle of wine to pour them both a glass.

"The food is still hot!" she exclaimed as she touched the plate in front of her. "How did you manage it?"

He chuckled. "My super powers?"

"Mmm, I like the idea of a man with super cooking powers."

"I had someone in while I was gone to collect you."

She wrinkled her nose. "You're horribly old-fashioned, Dev. There was no reason to collect me if we were spending the evening at your apartment. I could have gotten a cab or had my father's driver run me over."

He blinked in surprise. Old-fashioned? He'd been accused of a lot of things, but never of being old-fashioned. Then he scowled.

"A man should see to his woman's needs. All of them. It was my pleasure to pick you up."

Her cheeks pinkened in the candlelight, and her eyes shone like he'd just handed her the keys to a brand-new car.

"Am I?" she asked huskily.

He cocked his head to the side as he set his wineglass down. "Are you what?"

"Your woman."

Something unfurled inside him. He wouldn't have considered himself a possessive man, but now that he'd decided that she would be his wife, he discovered he felt very possessive where she was concerned.

"Yes," he said softly. "And before the night is over, you'll have no doubts that you belong to me."

A full body shiver took over Ashley. How was she supposed to concentrate on dinner after a statement like that? Devon stared at her across the table like he was going to pounce at any moment.

He had the most arresting eyes. Not really brown, but a warm shade of amber. In the sunlight they looked golden and in the candlelight they looked like a mountain lion's. She felt like prey, but it was a delicious feeling, not at all threatening. She'd been waiting for the moment when Devon would take their relationship a step further.

She'd longed for it and dreaded it with equal intensity. How could she possibly keep pace with a man who could seduce a woman with nothing more than a touch and a glance?

He'd been a consummate gentleman during the time they'd been dating. At first he'd only given her gentle, nonthreatening kisses, but over time they'd become more passionate and she'd gotten a glimpse of the powerfully sensual man under the protective armor.

She had a feeling that once those layers were peeled back, the man behind them was ferocious, possessive and…savage.

Another shiver overtook her at the direction of her thoughts. They were fanciful, yes, but she truly believed her assessment. Would she find out tonight? Did he plan to make her his?

"Aren't you going to eat?" Devon prompted.

She stared down at her plate again. What was it anyway? She wasn't sure she could eat a bite. Her mouth felt as if it was full of sawdust, and her entire body trembled with anticipation.

She moved the shrimp with her fork so that it gathered some of the sauce and slowly raised it to her lips.

"You aren't a vegetarian, are you?"

She laughed at the look on his face, as if the idea had just occurred to him.

"Tell me I haven't been serving you food you won't eat all

this time," Devon said with a grimace. "You would have said something, wouldn't you have?"

She put the shrimp into her mouth and chewed as she put the fork down. When she'd swallowed she reached over to touch his hand.

"You worry too much. I would have told you if I was a vegetarian. A lot of people assume since I'm so active in my animal rescue organization that I refuse to eat meat of any kind."

The relief on his face made her laugh again.

"I'll eat chicken and most seafood. I'm not crazy about pork or the more uppity stuff like veal, foie gras and stuff like that."

A shudder worked over her shoulders.

"There's something about eating duck liver that just turns my stomach."

Devon chuckled. "It's actually quite good. Have you tried it?"

She wrinkled her nose in distaste. "Sorry. I have a thing about eating any sort of innard."

"Ah, so no cow's tongue for you then."

She held up her hands and shook her head back and forth. "Don't say it. Just don't say it. That's beyond disgusting."

"I'll make a note of your food preferences so that I never serve you animal guts," he said solemnly.

She grinned over at him. "You know, Devon, you're not as stiff as everyone thinks you are. You actually have quite a sense of humor."

One finely arched eyebrow shot upward. "Stiff? Who thinks I'm stiff?"

Realizing she'd put her foot solidly in her mouth, she stuffed another shrimp in to keep the foot company.

"Nobody," she mumbled around her food. "Forget I said anything."

"Has someone been warning you off of me?"

The sudden tension in his voice sent a prickle of unease over her.

"My family worries for me," she said simply. "They're very protective. Too protective," she finished with a mutter.

"Your *family* is warning you about me?"

He acted as though it was the very last thing he expected. Was he so sure that her entire family was pushing for a match between them?

"Well no, not exactly. Definitely not Daddy. He thinks you hung the moon. Mama approves but I'm sure it's because Daddy does. She thinks he can do nothing wrong so if you have his stamp of approval you have hers."

He seemed to relax in his chair. "Who then?"

She shrugged. "My brother wants me to be careful, but you have to understand he's been saying the same thing about all the guys I've ever dated."

Again that eyebrow went up as he raised the glass of wine to his lips. "Oh?"

"Yeah, you know, you're a philanderer, a player. Different woman on your arm every week. You aren't serious. You just want to get me into bed."

A blast of heat surged into her cheeks and she ducked her head. Stupid thing to blurt out. Stupid!

"Sounds like a typical older brother," Devon said blandly. "But he's right about one thing. I do want you in my bed. The difference is, once you're there, you're going to stay."

Her lips popped into an *O*.

He smiled, a lazy, self-assured smile that oozed male confidence.

"Finish eating, Ashley. I want you to enjoy your meal. We'll enjoy…each other…later."

She ate mechanically. She didn't register the taste. For all she knew she *was* eating cow's tongue.

What did women do in situations like these? Here was a man obviously determined to take her to bed. Did she play it cool? Did she go on the offensive? Did she offer to undress for him?

A bubble of laughter bounced into her throat. Oh, Lord, but she was in way over her head.

Firm hands rested on her shoulders and squeezed reassuringly. She yanked her head up to see Devon behind her. How had he gotten there?

"Relax, Ash," he said gently. "You're wound tighter than a spring. Come here."

On shaking legs, she rose to stand in front of him. He touched her cheek with one finger then raised it to her temple to push at a tendril of her hair. He traced a line over her face and down to her lips before finally moving in, his body crowding hers.

He wrapped one arm around her waist, and cupped her nape with his other hand. This time when he kissed her there was none of the restraint she'd seen in the past. It was like kissing an inferno.

Hot, breathless, so overwhelming that her senses shattered. How could one kiss do this to her?

His tongue brushed over her lips, softly at first and then more firmly as he forced her mouth to open under his gentle pressure.

She relaxed and melted into his embrace. Her body hummed. Her pulse thudded against her temples, at her neck and deep in her body at her very core. She wanted this man. Sometimes she felt like she'd been waiting for him forever. He was so…right.

"Devon," she whispered.

He pushed far enough away that he could see her, but he still held her firm in his embrace.

"Yes, sweetheart?"

Her heart fluttered at the endearment.

"There's something I need to tell you. Something you should know."

His brow furrowed, and he searched her eyes as if gauging her mood.

"Go ahead. You can tell me anything."

She swallowed but felt the knot grow bigger in her throat. She hadn't imagined it being this difficult to say, but she felt suddenly silly. Maybe she shouldn't say anything at all. Maybe she should just let things happen. But no, this was a special night. It needed to be special. He deserved to know.

"I—I've never done this." She gripped his upper arm with nervous fingers. "What I mean is that I've never made love with a man before. You…you'd be the first."

Something dark and primitive sparked in his eyes. His grip tightened around her waist. At first he didn't say anything. He kissed her hungrily, his lips devouring hers.

Then he pulled away, savage satisfaction written on every facet of his face.

"I'm glad. After tonight you'll be mine, Ashley. I'm glad I'm the first."

"Me, too," she whispered.

Some of the fierceness in his expression eased. He leaned forward and kissed her on the brow and held his lips there for a long moment.

His hands ran soothingly up and down her arms, stopping to squeeze her shoulders. "I don't want you to be afraid. I'll be very gentle with you, sweetheart. I'll make sure you enjoy every moment of it."

She reached up on tiptoe to wrap both arms around his neck. "Then make love to me, Devon. I've waited so long for you."

Two

Ashley stared up at Devon, unsure of what to do now. He didn't suffer any such problem. Dropping another kiss on her brow, he bent and lifted her into his arms and carried her to the large master bedroom in the corner of the apartment.

She sighed as she laid her head on his chest. "I've always dreamed of being carried to bed when the big moment came. I probably sound silly."

Soft laughter rumbled from his chest. "Glad I could fulfill one of your fantasies before I even get you naked."

She blushed but felt a giddy thrill at the idea of him undressing her. That was number two on her fantasy list for when she lost her virginity.

After listening to so many girls in high school and college talk about how utterly unremarkable their first times were, Ashley had vowed that her experience would be different. Perhaps she'd been too picky as a result, but she'd been determined to choose the right man and the right moment. So she was feeling pretty damn smug because it didn't get any more perfect than Devon Carter right here, right now.

He set her down just inside the doorway and she glanced nervously around his enormous bedroom. A person could get swallowed up in here. And the bed was equally huge. It looked custom-made. Who needed a bed that big anyway? Unless he regularly hosted orgies and slept with ten women.

"I'm going to undress you, sweetheart," he said in a husky voice. "I'll go slow and you stop me if you feel uncomfortable at any time. We have all night. There's no rush."

Her heart melted at the tenderness in his voice. He seemed so patient, and she warred with appreciating this unerringly patient side of him and being frustrated because she wanted to be ravished.

It's your first time only once.

She could hear herself issue the reprimand. And she was right. She had plenty of time for down-and-dirty, hot monkey sex. But she would only have this night once and she wanted it to be a night she'd always remember.

"Turn around so I can unzip your dress."

Slowly she turned and closed her eyes when he gently moved her hair over one shoulder so he could reach the zip. A moment later, the light rasp of the zipper filled the room and the dress loosened precariously around her bust.

She slapped her hands over the strapless neckline just before it took the plunge down her body.

Devon's hands closed around her bare shoulders and he kissed the curve of her neck. "Relax."

Easy for him to say. He'd probably done this a hundred times. That thought depressed her and she made herself swear not to dwell on how many bed partners he may have had.

He turned her back around, his smile tender enough to melt her insides. Carefully he pried her fingers away from their death grip on her dress until it fell down her body, leaving her in only her panties.

She flushed scarlet. Why, oh, why hadn't she just worn the strapless bra? She felt like a hussy for not wearing anything but it wasn't as if she had a huge amount of cleavage and the dress fit tightly over her chest so she hadn't been in danger of flopping out of it.

And it wasn't as if she knew she was going to be seduced tonight.

She'd hoped. But then she'd hoped every time Devon took her out. She'd given up on trying to predict when or if the day might come.

"Very sexy," Devon breathed out as his gaze raked up and down her body.

Thank goodness she'd worn the lacy, sexy panties and not the plain white cotton ones she sometimes wore when she was feeling particularly uninspired or just didn't give a damn whether she felt girly and pretty or not.

"You're beautiful, Ash. So damn beautiful."

Some of her trembling stopped as she absorbed the look in his eyes. The eyes didn't lie and she could read arousal and appreciation in those golden depths.

He took her shoulders, gently pulled her to him and kissed her again. Hot. Forceful. In turns fierce and then gentler as though he had to remind himself not to overwhelm her.

She wanted to be overwhelmed.

She may be a virgin but she was no stranger to lust, desire and extreme arousal. She wanted Devon with a force that bordered on obsession. He'd fired many a fantasy that had kept her up at night.

And it wasn't as if she hadn't been tempted in the past. She'd been courted by other men. Some she felt absolutely no desire for but with others she'd experienced a kernel of interest and had wondered if she should pursue a sexual relationship. In the end, she hadn't been sure and if she wasn't absolutely sure, she'd promised herself she wouldn't take the plunge.

Not so with Devon. She'd known from the moment he introduced himself to her in that husky, sexy-as-hell voice that she was a goner. She'd spent the last weeks breathless in anticipation of this night. Now that it was here, her entire body ached for him to take her.

He pulled away for a moment and she stared at him with glazed eyes. He touched her cheek, tracing a path down her face with his fingertip. Then he kissed her again. And again.

Hot. Breathless. His tongue slid between her lips and feathered over her own. Warm and decadent, his taste seeped over her tongue and she drank him in hungrily, wanting more.

His harsh groan exploded into her mouth and the rush of his exhalation blew over her face. "You make me crazy."

She smiled, some of her nervousness abating. That she had this effect on this gorgeous, perfect man infused her with a sudden rush of feminine confidence.

He fastened his mouth to her jaw and kissed a line down to her neck. He pressed his lips just over her pulse point and then lightly grazed his teeth over the sensitive flesh.

Shivers of delight danced over her shoulders. His hands glided up her arms and then gripped her just above the elbows. He held her in place as his mouth continued its downward trek. Over the curve of her shoulder and then down the front.

He went to his knees in front of her so that his mouth was barely an inch from her nipple. She sucked in her breath, afraid to move, wanting so badly for him to touch her there. His mouth, lips, tongue… She didn't care. She just knew she'd die if he didn't touch her.

He lowered his head and kissed her belly instead. Just above her navel. She sucked in her breath, causing her stomach to cave in. He moved up an inch and kissed her again, tracing a path between her breasts until finally he pressed a kiss directly over where her heart beat.

A slow smile turned his lips upward, the movement light against her skin.

"Your heart's racing," he murmured.

She remained silent. It didn't require acknowledgement from her—her heart *was* beyond racing. It was damn near about to explode out of her chest.

But her hands wouldn't remain still. Drawn to the light brown wash of his hair, she threaded her fingers through the short strands. In a certain light, she could see the shades of his eyes. Amber. Golden. That warm, liquid brown.

Her fingers moved easily through his hair. No styling products stiffened the strands. A little mussed. Never quite the same from day to day. He paid as little attention to his hair as he did to the other things he deemed inconsequential.

He glanced up, her fingers still thrust into his hair. "Are you afraid?"

"Terrified," she admitted.

His gaze softened and he wrapped his arms around her body, pulling her into his embrace. The shock of her naked body against his still fully clothed one sent shivers up her spine.

"I'd feel less afraid if you were naked, though."

He blinked in surprise and then he threw back his head and laughed. "You little tease." He pushed upward to his feet until he towered over her. "I'm happy to accommodate you. *More* than happy to accommodate you."

She licked over suddenly dry lips as he pulled away and began unbuttoning his shirt. He tugged the ends from his slacks and unfastened his cuffs before shrugging out of the sleeves.

She swayed precariously because oh, Lord, was the man mouthwateringly gorgeous. He was lean in an "I work out" way but he wasn't so muscled that he looked like he got carried away with the fitness regimen. He was hard in all the right places without being a neckless, snarling, swollen, knuckles-dragging-the-ground caveman type.

A smattering of light brown hair collected in a whorl in the center of his chest and then tapered to a fine line that drifted down his abdomen and disappeared into the waist of his pants.

She wanted to touch him. Had to touch him. She curled her fingers until they dug into her palms and then she frowned. There weren't rules to seduction, right? She could touch. No reason for her to stand here like a statue or an automaton while he did all the work. While taking things slow did have its good points, there was simply too much she wanted to experience to stand idly by while seduction *happened*. She wanted to take an active part.

He'd only began to undo his pants, when she slid her hands over his chest and up to his shoulders. He went still and for a moment closed his eyes.

His response fascinated her. Did her touch bring him as much pleasure as his touch brought her? A sudden rush of power bolted through her veins, awakening the feminine roar inside her.

She moved in closer, wanting to feel his naked flesh against hers. Hot. She gasped when her breasts pressed against his chest. It was an electric sensation that was wildly intoxicating. She wanted more. So much more.

"What are you doing?" he asked hoarsely.

"Enjoying myself."

He smiled at that and remained still, his hands still gripping the fly of his pants. She ran her palms openly over his chest, exploring each muscled ridge, enjoying the rugged contrast between his hardness and the softness of her own body.

"Take them off," she whispered when her hands drifted perilously close to where his hands were positioned.

"Has the blushing virgin turned temptress?"

On cue, she flushed but he smiled and then let go of his pants to frame her face in his palms. He kissed her, nearly scorching her lips off with the sudden heat. "You take them off me," he murmured into her mouth.

Sudden nerves made her fingers clumsy as she fumbled

with his pants, but he stood there patiently, his hands caressing her face, gaze locked with hers as she pushed his pants down his legs.

Swallowing, she chanced a look down to see his erection straining hard against the cotton of his briefs. Plain, boxer briefs. Somehow she'd imagined something a little more... She wasn't sure. She just knew she hadn't imagined plain boxer briefs but then he was a no-fuss kind of guy. Yes, he wore expensive clothing, but it was comfortable expensive clothing. The kind you only knew was expensive because you recognized the label. Not because it looked terribly pricey.

Simply put, Devon Carter looked like a man who'd made money but wasn't overly concerned with appearing as though he was wealthy. It wasn't as if he couldn't look the part. She'd seen him in full business attire with the sleek designer labels and the polished, arrogant look to match. But she'd spent much more time with him privately. When he was relaxed. Less guarded. That was the word. In public situations, he was intensely guarded at all times. Almost as if he was determined to let no one in. It thrilled her that he trusted her enough to see his more casual side.

"Put your hand around me," he coaxed in that low husky tone that had her melting.

Tentatively she slid her fingers beyond the waistband of his underwear and delved lower until she encountered the velvety hardness of his erection. Emboldened by the immediate darkening of his eyes, she curled her fingers around the base and slowly slid upward, lightly skimming along his length.

His hands left her face and he impatiently pushed his underwear down until he was completely nude, cupped in her hands as she gently caressed him.

Having nothing but stolen glimpses of elicit photos to compare him to, he seemed to measure up adequately in the size department. At least he didn't look so huge that she feared compatibility issues.

He gently took her wrists and pulled her hands away from his erection. Then he pulled her hands up until they were trapped between them against his chest. His thumb lightly caressed the inside of her palm as he stared into her eyes.

"You, my love, are driving me slowly insane. It was me who was supposed to do the seducing and yet you utterly enslave me with every touch."

She flushed with pleasure, her skin growing warm under the intense desire blazing in his eyes.

He kissed her again, and he pressed in close until he walked her backward toward the bed. He stopped when the backs of her legs brushed against the sumptuous comforter.

He wrapped his arm around her waist and lowered her back until she was lying on the mattress, him hovering above her.

His expression grew serious and he brushed her hair from her forehead in a tender gesture. "If at any time I do something that frightens you, tell me and I'll stop. If at any time you simply want to slow down, just let me know."

"Oh," she breathed out. Because it was impossible to say anything else around the tightness in her throat.

She reached for him, pulled him down to meet her kiss. She felt clumsy and inept but it didn't seem to matter to him. She wished she was more artful. More practiced. But she couldn't wish for experience because more than anything she was glad she'd waited for this moment. For him.

"I love you," she whispered, unable to hold back the words that swelled and finally broke free.

He went still and for a moment she was terrified that she'd effectively thrown a wet blanket over a fire. She drew away, eyes wide as she searched his face for something. Some reaction. Some indication that she'd breached some forbidden barrier.

Trust her to ruin what would have been the most exciting, wonderful, splendiferous moment of her life by opening her big mouth. She'd never been able to restrain herself. She tried. Most of the time.

"Devon?"

His name came out in a near croak. Her lips shook and she started to withdraw, already feeling the heat of embarrassment lick over her with painful precision.

Instead of answering her, he moved over her in a power-ful rush. He took her mouth roughly, devouring her lips as his tongue plunged inside, tangling with hers.

Her body surged to life, arching up into his. She wrapped her arms around his neck as he gathered her tightly against him. Their bodies were as fused as their mouths. Between her legs, she could feel him so hard. Hot.

His hips jerked, almost as if he could barely contain the urge to push inside her. She gasped for air, partly out of excitement, partly out of sudden, delicious fear and anticipation.

His hands and mouth were everywhere. A sensual assault on her senses. Magic. Gentle caresses mixed with firmer, rougher touches. He slid down her body until his mouth hovered over one taut nipple. And then he flicked his tongue out and licked the tip.

She cried out, nearly undone by the shock of such a simple touch. Pleasure rocked over her and she shuddered violently, her fingers suddenly digging into his flesh, marking him.

Not satisfied with the intensity of her reaction, he closed his mouth over the rigid peak and sucked strongly.

Her vision blurred. She gasped but couldn't seem to draw air into her lungs. Oh, but it was heaven. So edgy. She couldn't even find the words to describe such a decadent sensation as his mouth sucking at her breast.

But then his hand slid between them, over the softness of her belly and lower.

She held her breath as his fingers tentatively brushed through her sensitive folds and then he found her heat, teas-ing, touching. He knew better than she knew herself exactly how to pleasure her. Where to touch her. *How* to touch her. Each stroke brought her to greater heights.

It was as though she was being wound tighter and tighter. Tension coiled in her belly. Low. Humming through her pelvis. She wasn't ignorant of orgasms, but this was nothing like she'd ever experienced before. It was powerful. Relentless. Nearly frightening in its intensity.

His fingers left her and he carefully parted her legs. His hand glided soothingly up the inside of her thigh and then he stroked her intimately again as he positioned himself above her.

His mouth left her breasts and she moaned her protest. He covered her lips once more with his own and then whispered softly to her.

"Hold on to me, love. Touch me. I'm going to go inside you now. I'll be gentle. There's nothing to be afraid of."

She trembled from head to toe. Not in fear or trepidation. She was so close to release that she feared the moment he pushed inside her the barest inch that she'd go over the edge, and she wanted it to last. She wanted to enjoy every single moment of what was to come.

"Wait," she choked out.

He went still, the tip of his erection just touching the mouth of her opening. Strain was evident in his face as he stared down at her, but he held himself in check.

"Are you all right? Did I frighten you?" he asked urgently.

She shook her head. "No. No, I'm fine. I just needed a second. I'm so close. Just need to catch up."

He smiled then, his eyes gleaming with a predatory light. "Tell me when."

She reached up once more, feathering her hands over his shoulders and to the bunched muscles of his back. Her gaze met his and she drowned in those beautiful amber eyes. "When."

He swallowed hard and his lips tightened into a harsh line.

Then he closed his eyes and flexed his hips, pushing into her inch by delicious inch.

At one point he stopped and she stirred restlessly, a protest forming.

"Shh," he murmured as he kissed the corner of her mouth. "Give me just a moment. I don't want to hurt you. Better to have done with it quickly."

She nodded her agreement just as he surged forward, burying himself to the hilt.

Her eyes widened and a strangled sound escaped her throat as she sought to process the sudden wash of conflicting sensations that bombarded her from every angle.

He was deep. Impossibly deep. She surrounded him. He surrounded her. Their hips were flush against each other. His body covered hers possessively. There was a burning ache deep inside her, and she couldn't discern whether it was pleasure or pain.

She just knew she wanted—needed—more.

She whimpered lightly and struggled, not against him, not in protest. She wanted something she couldn't name. She wanted…him. All of him.

"Easy," he soothed.

He kissed her, stroked his tongue over hers and then deepened the kiss just as he began to move inside her. Gently. He was so gentle and reverent. He lifted his body off of her and arched his hips, pushing deep then retreating.

Then he levered himself down, resting on his forearms, never breaking away from her eyes.

"Okay?"

She smiled. "Very okay."

"You're beautiful, Ash. So very beautiful. So innocent and perfect and mine."

His. The possessive growl in his voice thrilled her and sent another cascade of pleasure through her body.

"Yes, yours," she whispered.

"Tell me how close you are. I want to make sure you're with me. I can't hold off much longer."

"Then don't." Her voice shook. She was nearly beyond the ability to think much less speak. Her body was taut. Her senses were shattered and she was so very close to losing all control. Just one touch. One more touch…

He gathered her close and thrust again. And then again. He forced her thighs farther apart, plunged deeper and she lost all sense of herself.

She cried out his name. Heard him murmur close to her ear. Soothing. Comforting. Telling her beautiful things she could barely make sense of. She was spiraling at a dizzying speed, faster and faster until she closed her eyes.

It was the single most beautiful, spectacular sensation she could imagine. She'd wanted wonderful, but this far surpassed even her most erotic fantasies.

When she regained at least a modicum of sanity, she was firmly wrapped in Devon's embrace and his mouth was moving lightly over her neck. For that matter she was on top of him. Her hair was flung to one side while he nuzzled at the curve of her shoulder, moving up and down to just below her ear and back to her shoulder.

She raised her head to stare down at him, still feeling a little fuzzy around the edges. "How did I get here?"

He smiled and slid his hands over her naked body. They stopped at her behind and he squeezed affectionately. "I put you here. I like you covering me. I could get used to it."

"Oh."

He raised one eyebrow. "Speechless? You?"

She sent him a disgruntled look but was too wasted to follow up with any sort of admonishment. Okay, so obviously she was speechless.

He chuckled and pulled her down against him. She settled over him with a sigh and he rubbed his palm over her back, stroking and caressing as she lay draped over him like a wet noodle.

"Did I hurt you?"

She smiled at the concern in his voice. "No. It was perfect, Dev. So perfect I can't even find the words to describe it. Thank you."

He lifted a strand of hair and lazily twined his fingers around it. "Thank you? I don't think I've ever been thanked by a woman after sex."

"You made my first time special," she said quietly. "It was perfect. You were perfect."

He kissed the top of her head. "I'm glad."

She yawned against his chest and cuddled deeper into his hold.

"Go to sleep," he murmured. "I want you to sleep here tonight."

Her eyes were incredibly heavy, and she was already drifting off when his directive registered in her consciousness.

"Want to sleep here, too," she mumbled.

His fingers stilled in her hair and then his hands wandered down her body, bold and possessive. "That's good, Ash, because from now on, you'll sleep every night in my bed."

Three

Devon woke to the odd sensation of a female body wrapped around him. Not just wrapped but completely and utterly surrounding him.

Ashley was draped across him, her legs tangled with his, her breasts flattened against his chest, her arm thrown across his body and her face burrowed into his neck.

He…liked it.

He lay there a long while watching the soft rise and fall of her body as she slept soundly across him. She was really quite beautiful in an unsophisticated, effervescent way. She lit up a room when she walked in. You could always pick her out of a crowd. She was extremely…natural. Perhaps a bit too exuberant and unrestrained but in time with the proper guidance, she'd be an excellent wife and mother.

He ran the tips of his finger lightly up her arm. She was pale. Not so pale she looked unhealthy, but it was obvious she wasn't a sun bunny, nor did she indulge in salon tanning. Perhaps what he liked most about her was that she looked the same no matter when he saw her. Though she wore makeup, she didn't wear so much that she was transformed into someone completely different when they went out.

Glossy lips and a touch of coal to already long, lush lashes seemed to be all she did, but then he was hardly an expert on women's gunk.

But she didn't seem fake. At least not that he could tell. Yet. Who knew what the future would bring. He liked to think she wasn't an accomplice in this ridiculous plan of her father's even when he knew it was best for all parties involved to know the entire story from the start.

The selfish bastard in him liked the idea that she felt affection for him, free of machinations. If her words from the night before weren't merely a result of being overwhelmed in the moment, *affection* was perhaps the wrong term. She'd said she loved him.

It both complicated the matter and gave him a certain amount of satisfaction.

While he may approach the marriage as a matter of necessity, convenience and a chance at a successful business venture, the idea that she would be coming into the marriage for the same reasons bothered him immensely.

It made him a flaming hypocrite but he was happy for her to want him because she desired him and yes, even loved him.

First, however, he had to get the preliminaries out of the way. One of which was making their upcoming nuptials official. She didn't know it yet, but she would become Mrs. Devon Carter.

He carefully extricated himself from the tangle of arms and legs, but he needn't have worried because she slept soundly, only wrinkling her nose and mumbling something in her sleep when he slipped away completely.

He pulled on his robe and glanced back at the bed. For a moment he was transfixed by the image she presented. The sun streamed through the window across the room and bathed her in its warm glow.

Her blond hair was tousled and spread out over his pillow. One arm shielded most of her breasts from view, but there, just below her elbow, one nipple peeked out. The sheet slid to just over her buttocks but bared the dimple just below the small of her back.

She was indeed beautiful. And now she was his.

He dug into the pocket of the jacket he'd discarded the night before to retrieve the box with the ring in it and then quietly left the room. When she awoke, he'd put into place the next part of his carefully orchestrated plan.

Ashley stirred and stretched lazily, blinking when the sun momentarily blinded her. She kept her eyes shut for a moment, simply enjoying the warmth and comfort of the sumptuous bed. Devon's bed.

She sighed in contentment. As virginal deflowering went, that had to top the list of all-time most awesome. How could it possibly have been any better? A wonderful night. Romantic dinner for two. Devon staring at her with those gorgeous eyes and murmuring that she would now be his. Oh, yeah, perfect.

Then she realized that he was no longer in bed with her and she opened her eyes with a frown. Only to see him standing just across the room. Staring at her.

He was clad in a robe, though it dangled loosely, open just enough that she could see his bare chest. He was leaning against the doorway to the bathroom and he was simply watching her. For some reason that sent a giddy thrill up her spine.

Then a flash of color caught her eye and she glanced downward to see a lush red rose lying on the sheet next to her. But it was the tiny card propped next to a dazzling, truly spectacular diamond ring that took her breath away.

Blood rushed to her head and she stared openmouthed at the items before her. She pushed to her elbow and reached for the ring, hands shaking so badly that she was clumsy, nearly dropping the small velvet box where the ring rested.

Then she glanced at the note again, sure she'd misunderstood. But no, there it was. In his neat, distinctive scrawl.

Will you marry me?

"Oh, God," she croaked out.

She looked at the ring, looked at the note and then back up to him, almost afraid that he'd be gone and that she'd imagined this whole thing.

But he was still there, an indulgent smile carving those handsome features.

"Really?" she whispered.

He nodded and smiled more broadly. "Really."

She dropped the rose, the ring, the note—everything—and flew out of bed, across the room, and launched herself into his arms.

He stepped back and laughed as she kissed his face, his brow, his cheek and then his lips. "Yes, oh, yes! Oh, my God, Devon, yes!"

He made a grab for her behind before she could slide down him and land on the floor. Then he hoisted her up so they were eye level. "You know it's customary to actually put the ring on."

She glanced down at her hand and then over her shoulder to the bed. "Oh, my God! Where is it?"

Shaking his head, he carried her over to the bed then set her on the edge while he reached behind her.

A moment later, he took her hand and slid the diamond onto her ring finger. She sucked in her breath as the sun caught the stone and it sparkled brilliantly in the light.

"Oh, Dev, it's beautiful," she breathed.

She threw her arms around his neck and hugged him tightly. "I love you so much. I can't believe you planned all this."

He gently pulled her arms down and then collected her

hands in her lap as he stared into her eyes. "I don't want a long engagement."

Was this supposed to worry her? She beamed back at him. "Neither do I."

"In fact, I'd prefer to get married right away," he added, watching her all the while.

She frowned and chewed at her bottom lip. "I wouldn't mind. I mean if it was just me, but I don't know how my family would take that. Mama will want to plan a big wedding. I'm her only daughter. It's not that I care about a big fuss—I don't. But it would hurt her if she wasn't able to give us a big wedding."

He touched her cheek. "Leave your family to me. I assure you, they'll be on board with my plans. You and I will have the best wedding—one that your mother will be more than satisfied with. I think you'll find they won't object to our plans at all."

Excitement hurtled through her veins until it was nearly impossible to sit still. "I can't wait to tell everyone! Won't this just be amazing? Everyone will be so thrilled for me. I know Daddy despaired of me ever finding a suitable man and settling down. He always says I'm too unsettled, but really, I'm still young."

He gave her an amused smile. "Are you saying you don't want to get married?"

She stared at him in shock. "No! That's not at all what I was saying. I was merely going to say that I was waiting for the right man. In this case, you."

"That's what I like to hear," he murmured.

He leaned forward to kiss her brow. "How about you take a long bubble bath to recover from last night's activities and then we'll have breakfast together."

She flushed red. She had to be flaming. But she nodded, eager to discuss their future.

Mrs. Devon Carter. It had such a nice ring to it. And speaking of rings… She glanced down, transfixed by the radiance of the diamond that adorned her finger.

"Like it?" he asked in a teasing voice.

She looked back up at him, suddenly serious. "I love it, Dev. It's absolutely gorgeous. But you didn't need to get me something so expensive. I would have loved anything you gave me."

He smiled. "I know you would. But I wanted something special."

Her heart did a little dance in her chest. "Thank you. It's just perfect. Everything is perfect."

He kissed her again, long and leisurely. When he pulled away, his eyes were half-lidded and they were glowing with desire.

"Go draw your bath before I forget all about breakfast and make love to you again."

"Breakfast?" she whispered. "Were we planning to eat?"

He made a sound in his throat that was part growl, part resignation.

"I don't want to hurt you, Ash. As much as you tempt me, I'd rather wait until you're fully healed from last night."

She pushed out her bottom lip.

"As adorable as you are when you pout, it won't move me this time. Now get your pretty behind out of bed and hit the bathroom. Breakfast will be served in forty-five minutes. Plenty of time for you to soak."

She sighed. "Okay, okay. I'm going."

She got up and walked toward the bathroom but just as she got to the doorway, something he'd said the night before came back to her. She paused and turned around, her head cocked to the side.

"Dev, what did you mean last night when you said I'd be sleeping here with you every night from now on?"

He rose and pulled his robe tighter around his waist. He stared back at her, his gaze intense and serious.

"Exactly what I said. I'll want you to move in as soon as

possible. I'll arrange to have what you need transferred from your apartment. You're mine, Ash. From now on, you'll spend every night in my bed."

Four

"Well, you finally took the leap," Cameron Hollingsworth said as he stared across the room to where Ashley stood with a group of women.

Devon took a sip of the wine, though the taste went unappreciated. He was too distracted. Still, he forced some of it down, hoping it would at least take the edge off.

The official announcement would be made in a few moments. By Devon himself. Ashley's father had wanted to do the honors, but Devon had preferred to do it himself. William Copeland had already orchestrated entirely too much of Devon's relationship with Ashley. From now on, things would be done his way.

Though everyone in attendance was well aware it was an engagement party they had been invited to, Ashley had insisted on waiting until all the guests had arrived before their engagement was announced.

"Cold feet already?" Cam asked dryly. "You haven't said two words since I got here."

Devon grimaced. "No. It's done. No backing out now. Copeland has all but signed off on the deal. After the ceremony he'll fax the final documents and we'll move forward with the merger. I'll want to meet with you, Ryan and Rafe as soon as I return from the honeymoon."

Cam arched an eyebrow. "Honeymoon? You're actually going on one?"

"Just because this marriage is part and parcel of a business deal doesn't mean Ashley has to have any less of a marriage or honeymoon," Devon murmured.

Cam shrugged. "Good idea. Keep her happy. If she's happy, Daddy's happy. You know what they say about Daddy's girls."

Devon frowned. "Don't be an ass. She's…"

"She's what?" Cam prompted.

"Look, she has no idea what her father's done. She thinks this is a wildly romantic courtship that culminated in an equally romantic marriage proposal. If I don't take her on a honeymoon, it's going to look strange."

Cam groaned. "This can't end well. Mark my words. You're screwed, my friend."

"Anyone ever tell you what a ball of joy you are?"

Cam held his hands up in surrender. "Look, I'm just trying to warn you here. You should tell her the truth. No woman likes being made a fool of."

"And have her tell me to go to hell and take my proposal with me?" Devon demanded.

He sighed and shook his head. Yeah, he knew Cam had been through the wringer in the past. He couldn't blame his friend for his cynicism. But he wasn't in the mood to hear it right now.

"This deal is important to all of us. Not just me," he continued when Cam remained silent. "Marriage isn't my first choice, but Ash is a sweet girl. She'll make a good wife and a good mother. Everyone gets what they want. You, me, Ryan and Rafe. Ashley, her father. Everyone's happy."

"Whatever floats your boat, man. You know I'm behind you all the way. But remember this. You don't have to marry her to make this work. We'll find another company. We've suffered setbacks before. Not one of us expects you to martyr yourself for the cause. Rafe and Ryan are deliriously happy. There's no reason you shouldn't hold out for the same."

Devon snorted. "Turning into quite the rah-rah man. I'm fine, Cam. There is no love of my life. No other woman in the picture. No one I'd rather marry. I'll be content with Ashley. Stop worrying."

Cam checked his watch. "Your intended bride is looking this way. I think you're on."

Devon glanced over to where Ashley stood surrounded by friends and relatives. He could never sort out who was who because there were so many. She smiled and waved and then motioned him over.

He handed Cam his wineglass and made his way through the throng of people until he reached Ashley.

She sparkled tonight. She wore a radiant smile that seemed to captivate the room. But then she always drew people. She'd talk to anyone at all about anything at all.

As soon as he approached, she all but pounced on him, took his hand and dragged him into her circle. He smiled at each of the women in turn, but their names and faces kind of blended. After a moment he bent to murmur in Ashley's ear. "It's time, don't you think?"

She all but quivered in excitement. Her eyes lit up and she smiled as she squeezed his hand.

"Excuse us, ladies," he said smoothly as he drew Ashley away and back in Cam's direction. There wasn't anyone standing around Cam. Cam had that effect on people. It was the perfect place to call for attention and announce their engagement.

"Hi, Cam," Ashley sang out as they walked up to his friend. She let go of Devon's hand and threw her arms around

Cam's neck. Cam grinned and shook his head as he attempted to extricate himself from her embrace.

"Hello, Ash," he said before dropping an affectionate kiss on her cheek. "Come stand by me while Devon makes a fool of himself."

Devon sent a glare Cam's way before taking Ashley's hand and pulling her to his side. Laughing, Cam handed him a fresh wineglass and a spoon.

"What, are you kidding me?" Devon asked. "You want me to bang on a wineglass to get attention?"

Cam shrugged then tossed the spoon aside. Then he put his fingers to his lips and emitted a shrill whistle. "Everyone, I'd like your attention please. Devon here has an announcement for us."

"Thanks, Cam," Devon said dryly. Then he turned to face the room filled with Ashley's friends and relatives. And they were all staring at him expectantly. All wanting him to make this moment perfect for Ashley. Hell. No pressure or anything.

He cleared his throat and hoped like hell that he'd manage to get through it without sticking his foot in his mouth.

"Ashley and I invited you all here tonight to join us in celebrating a very special occasion." He glanced fondly down at Ashley and squeezed her hand. "Ashley has made me the happiest of men by consenting to marry me."

The room erupted in cheers and applause. To the right, Ashley's mom and dad stood beaming at their youngest child. William nodded approvingly at Devon while Ashley's mother wiped at her eyes as she smiled at her daughter.

"It's our wish that you'll all attend our wedding to take place four weeks from today and help us celebrate as we embark on our journey together as man and wife."

He held up his wineglass and turned again to Ashley whose entire face was lit up with a breathtaking smile. "To Ashley, who's made me the luckiest man alive."

Everyone raised their glasses and noisy cheers rang out again as everyone toasted Devon and Ashley.

"Quite an eloquent speech there," Cam murmured in Devon's ear. "One would almost think you meant every word."

Devon ignored Cam and slid an arm around Ashley as they braced for the onslaught of well-wishers pushing forward.

His head was spinning as he processed face after face. Bright smiles. Slaps on the back. Admonishments to take care of "their girl" as everyone in the family seemed to have a claim on Ashley.

She was everyone's younger sister, daughter, best friend or person in need of protection. It bewildered him and annoyed him in equal parts that everyone in Ashley's family seemed to think she was incapable of taking care of herself. Nothing in his relationship with Ashley had led him to believe this was an accurate assessment.

Yes, she was flighty. She was too trusting, definitely. She was a bit naive. He grimaced. He supposed he could understand that in a family of business sharks she was an anomaly, and perhaps they were right to worry that she'd be swallowed up.

But it didn't mean she was totally incapable of taking care of herself. It just meant she needed someone who'd look out for her best interests and occasionally protect her from herself. Someone like him.

Her hand feathered over his arm and she leaned up on tiptoe. He immediately lowered his head, realizing she wanted to tell him something.

"We can leave anytime," she whispered. "I know my family is a lot to take."

He almost laughed. Here he'd been thinking of how she needed his protection and she was busy protecting him from her overwhelming family.

"I'm fine. I want you to enjoy yourself. This is your night."

Her brow furrowed and her eyebrows pushed together as she stared up at him. "And not yours?"

"Of course it is. I only meant that you're surrounded by your family and friends and I want you to enjoy yourself."

She smiled, kissed him on the cheek and then settled back at his side as they were besieged my more congratulations.

"Ashley! Ashley!"

Devon turned to see a young woman barreling through the crowd practically dragging a man in her wake. He looked a bit harried but wore an indulgent smile. Devon stared a moment and then realized that whomever the woman was, she bore a striking resemblance to Ashley and she had every appearance of sharing many of the same personality traits. Probably one of her many cousins.

"Brooke!" Ashley cried. She put out her hands just as Brooke careened to a halt and Brooke grabbed hold, beaming from ear to ear.

"Guess what, guess what?" Brooke said breathlessly.

"Oh, don't make me guess. You know I'm horrible at it!" Ashley exclaimed.

"I'm pregnant! Paul and I are going to have a baby!"

Ashley's shriek of excitement could be heard over the entire room. Devon winced then quickly glanced around as everyone stared their way.

"Oh, my God, Brooke! I'm so excited for you! When? How far along are you?"

"Just ten weeks. I had to tell you as soon as I found out, but then you've been so busy with Devon and then I heard you guys were getting married and I didn't want to intrude—"

"You should have texted me at least," Ashley said. "Oh, Brooke, I'm so thrilled for you. I can only imagine how excited I'll be when I become pregnant. I hope our babies are close together and can be playmates!"

Ashley had grown louder and louder, her exuberance drawing the attention of the others, who cast indulgent smiles in Ashley's direction.

She was animated and talking a mile a minute, throwing her hands this way and that, and nearly crashed into a passing waiter. Only Devon's and Cam's quick lunge for the tray of drinks prevented complete disaster. Ashley continued, oblivious to the chaos around her.

Then she impulsively hugged Brooke again. For the third time. Then she hugged Paul. Then she hugged Brooke again, the entire time wringing her hands in excitement.

Cam chuckled and shook his head. "You've got quite the chore on your hands, Dev. Keeping up with her is going to wear your stick-in-the-mud ass out."

"Don't you have somewhere else to be and someone else to torture?" Devon muttered.

Cam glanced Ashley's way once more and Devon swore he saw genuine affection in his friend's eyes.

"She's cute," Cam said as he put his wineglass aside.

"Cute?"

Cam shifted uncomfortably. "She's sweet, okay? She seems... genuine and you can't ask for more than that."

Devon stared agape at his friend. "You like her."

Cam scowled darkly.

Devon laughed. "You like her. You, who doesn't like anyone, actually like her."

"She's nice," Cam muttered.

"But you don't think I should marry her," Devon prompted.

"Shh, she's going to hear you," Cam hissed.

But Ashley had already drifted away from Devon and was solidly ensconced in a squeal-fest with Brooke as others had heard the news and had descended. She wasn't going to hear an earthquake if a fault suddenly opened up under the building and sucked everyone in.

"If you think she's so cute and nice, why the big speech

about not being a martyr and getting married, et cetera?" Devon persisted.

Cam sighed. "Look, I just hate to see her get hurt and that's what's going to happen if you aren't straight with her. Women have a way of knowing when men aren't that into them."

"Who the hell says I'm not into her?"

Cam arched an eyebrow. "Are you saying you are? Because you don't act like a man who's into his future bride."

Devon frowned and looked around, making sure they weren't overheard. By anyone. Least of all Ashley's overprotective family. "What do you mean by that? You, Rafe and Ryan know the real circumstances of my relationship with Ashley but no one else does. I've given no one reason to suspect that I'm marrying her for any other reason than I want to."

Once again Cam shrugged. "Maybe you're right. Maybe because I know the real story it's easier for me to see that you aren't as excited as your lovely bride to be is over your impending nuptials."

"Damn it," Devon swore. "Now you're going to have me paranoid that I'm broadcasting disinterest."

"Look, forget I said anything. I'm sure it'll be fine. It's none of my business anyway. She just seems like a sweet girl and I hate to see her get hurt."

"I'm not going to hurt her," Devon gritted out. "I'm going to marry her and I'm damn sure going to take care of her."

"And you're being summoned again," Cam said, nodding in Ashley's direction. "I'm going to take off. I'll walk with you over to Ashley so I can offer my congratulations again and say good night."

Devon started in Ashley's direction then listened attentively while she introduced him to one of her cousins—one of the many in attendance—and then waited while Cam said his goodbyes and kissed her on both cheeks.

But the entire time, his mind was racing as he processed

his conversation with Cam. Was he coming across as someone who was less than enthused about his upcoming marriage? The very last thing he needed to do was drop the ball when everything was so close to being in his grasp. Finally.

He'd worked too damn hard and long to allow any slips now. If he had to wed Satan himself to seal this deal, he'd don the fire retardant suit and pucker up.

Five

No matter how many nights she'd already spent in Devon's apartment, she still got butterflies when she entered his bedroom to get ready for bed. Granted she'd only been here a week and it was still a little uncomfortable and awkward because she still didn't feel any sense of ownership when it came to his home.

She was pulling on her satin nightgown when Devon's chuckle broke the silence in the room. She turned quickly, her brow furrowed as he regarded her in amusement.

"What's so funny?"

"You. Every night you spend so much time putting on that lovely nightgown only for me to promptly take it off you when you come to bed. By now one would think you wouldn't bother."

She flushed. "It seems…presumptuous…to think you want…I mean to assume you'd want…"

"Sex?" he finished for her.

She nodded, her cheeks flaming.

He grinned and pulled her toward the bed. "I think it's a safe presumption that I'll always want sex with you. Feel free to assume all you want. I assure you…" He bent and kissed her lingeringly. "That I'll never ever…" He slid his mouth down her jaw to her neck and nibbled at her ear. "*Not* want…" He licked the pulse point at her neck, and her knees buckled. "To have sex with you. Unless I'm in a body cast and even then I'll be thinking about it."

Her nose crinkled and she shook with silent laughter. "It's true then. That sex is all a man ever thinks about?"

"We occasionally think about food."

She laughed aloud this time. "My mother is scandalized that I've practically moved in with you."

"Not practically," he said as he slid one strap over her shoulder. "You *have* moved in with me."

She shrugged. "Well she was aghast. My father told her to stop being such a worrywart, that you and I were getting married and it was only natural that we'd want time together before the big day to see if we were compatible. Eric, on the other hand, seemed pretty ticked. He thinks Daddy's nuts to *allow* me to move in with a man who's boned half the city— his words, not mine."

Devon straightened his stance and stared at her with an open mouth. "Do you *always* do that?"

She sent him a perplexed frown. "Do what?"

He shook his head. "Blurt out whatever comes to mind."

Her frown grew deeper. "Well, I guess. I mean I haven't really thought about it. It *is* what he said. I mean I didn't really pay any attention to him. He's just really protective of me and he always gets snarly when a guy starts paying attention to me."

"I hardly think me asking you to marry me can be compared to some random guy paying attention to you," he drawled.

"Well, but I'm living with you now so he obviously knows

we're having sex and he doesn't like to imagine his little sister having sex. With anyone."

Devon shuddered. "Who would?"

She grinned. "My point is, he's just being Eric and he had to get his two cents in."

"For the record, I have not *boned* half the city."

She wrapped her arms around his neck and pulled him down to kiss her. "As long as I'm the only one you'll...well, you know, in the future? I don't really care about the past."

"The future? Oh, yeah. And the present. Like right now."

She shivered as he lowered her to the bed. For having been a virgin a mere week ago, her education was no longer sorely lacking. Every night he'd taken her to places she'd only halfway imagined, and others she hadn't even known existed.

If this was a precursor to how life with him was going to be, she was going to be one very happy woman.

"Joining our meeting via video conference call this morning are Ryan Beardsley and Rafael de Luca," Devon said as his two friends' faces flashed up on the monitor on the wall. "Ryan is on location at our site build on St. Angelo Island, where our flagship resort is in its first stage of development. When completed, this resort will be the standard for every new Copeland property. Good morning, Ryan. Perhaps you could give us a progress report on the construction."

Devon tuned out Ryan and glanced over at Cam, who was slouched in a chair. Devon knew well the progress on construction. He got daily and sometimes hourly reports. Though Ryan was on site, his focus was on his very pregnant wife, who could deliver at any moment. To that end, Devon kept in contact with the foreman so that any issues that arose could be swiftly dealt with.

Cam hadn't dressed for the occasion. He'd never quite bought in to the idea that image is everything in the business world. But then he didn't really care what others thought or didn't think. It was easier for Cam, though. He'd been born to this world, while Devon had to claw and dig his way in, one torn fingernail at a time.

Cam looked like a man who could be heading to the beach for the day or at the very least planning to spend the day kicked back with a beer in one hand and a cigar in the other. But then Cam didn't drink or smoke. The man had no vices. He was disgustingly perfect in his imperfection.

Members of Tricorp's staff listened attentively to Ryan's report. Jotted down appropriate notes. The secretary took detailed minutes. There was an air of expectancy in the room. Everyone knew it was a matter of time before the big merger was announced.

Devon thought it kinder to wait. Maybe he was getting old and soft. Maybe he didn't even deserve to be on the verge of the biggest coup of his career. Because at the very moment when he stood to gain everything he'd ever wanted, he'd actually gone to William Copeland and suggested that they postpone the announcement for six months. He thought it would be kinder to Ashley if she were to think that business had nothing to do with their marriage and that the merger came after. William wouldn't have it, however. He insisted that things proceed as planned.

He thought Devon worried too much about Ashley's potential reaction. She loved him, wasn't that enough? It had made Devon cringe that apparently the whole world knew she was madly in love with her husband to be.

Besides, William pointed out that as disinterested in the family business as Ashley was, the chances of her actually putting it all together were slim. William's advice to Devon? Keep her busy and happy.

Suddenly in the midst of Ryan's report, a sound jangled over the room. There was a series of starts as his employees looked down and then around. Devon frowned. What the hell was it? It sounded like a ring tone, but it wasn't one he'd ever heard before.

Then slowly everyone's gaze turned to him and it was then he realized it was his phone going off in his pocket.

"What the hell?" he muttered.

Cam snickered.

Devon yanked his phone out of his pocket to see Ashley's name on the LCD. He nearly groaned aloud.

"Excuse me a moment," he said as he rose. "I'll take this outside."

He hurried out the door, irritated by Cam's look of amusement. He knew damn well who was calling Devon.

As soon as he was outside the conference room he punched the answer button and brought the phone to his ear. "Carter," he said tersely.

Ashley wasn't even remotely put off by his greeting. Or lack of one.

"Oh, hi, Dev! How's your day going?"

"Uh, it's good. Look, was there something you needed? I'm kind of in the middle of something here."

"Oh, nothing important," she said cheerfully. "I just wanted to call and tell you I love you."

An uncomfortable knot formed in his stomach. What was he supposed to say to that? He cleared his throat. "Ash, did you change the ring tone on my phone?"

"Oh, yeah. I did. I downloaded one so you'd know when I'm calling. Neat, huh?"

Devon closed his eyes. The cheerful cascade of noise that sounded like a cross between Tinker Bell sneezing fairy dust and a waltz at some damn princess ball would make him the laughingstock of the office in short order. Not to mention that Cam would never, ever let him live this down.

"Neat," he lamely agreed. "Look, I'll see you tonight, okay? We still on for dinner at nine?"

"Yes, that's perfect. I'm at the shelter until eight so if it's okay I'll just meet you at the restaurant."

He frowned. "Do you have a ride?"

"I'll get a cab."

He shook his head. "I'll send a car for you. Stay put at the shelter until it arrives. I'll arrange it for eight."

She sighed but didn't argue further. "Have a good day, Dev. Can't wait until tonight!"

"Thanks. You, too," Devon said but she'd already hung up.

He stared at his phone for a long moment and then punched a series of buttons. How did you even change the ring tone? He'd never designated a special ring tone for a person. His phone rang, the contact showed up, and if he wanted to answer he did. If he didn't, he let it go to voice mail. No way he wanted sparkly Tinker Bell music to play every time Ashley called him. What if she made a regular habit of it?

To his never-ending grief, she called him every single day. It baffled him that her timing was utterly impeccable. She always managed to catch him right in the middle of a meeting or when he was with a group of people.

After the second instance, he began silencing his phone and putting it on vibrate, but on two occasions, he simply forgot and his entire meeting was treated to Tinker Bell on crack.

After two weeks, he began to get amused, indulgent looks from some. Sympathy from others. Delighted grins from the women personnel. And Cam laughed his fool head off.

Ashley simply called whenever the mood struck, and unfortunately for him, he could never be sure when she would be moved to call him. Sometimes she wanted advice on wedding details. Like flowers. How the hell did he know what the difference between a tulip and a gardenia was? And invitations. Elopement to Vegas had never looked so enticing as it did right now.

Rafael and Ryan hadn't gone through all of this for their

weddings. They'd both had exceedingly simple affairs. Devon was in hell. A wedding that was being planned by the entire Copeland clan.

He was ready to throw his cell in the Hudson.

Six

"Dev?"

Devon stuck his head out of the bathroom then proceeded toward the bed, rubbing his hair with a towel. She was laying stomach down on the bed, feet dangling in the air as her jaw rested in her palm.

There was a slight frown marring her delicate features, which told him she was thinking about something. He almost didn't want to ask because he'd quickly learned that Ashley's thoughts ran the gamut.

He sat on the edge of the bed and rubbed his hand over her back. "What's up?"

She turned slightly so she could stare up at him. "Where are we going to live? I mean after we get married. We haven't really talked about it."

"I assumed we'd live here."

Her lips turned down just a bit and her brow wrinkled. "Oh."

"That doesn't sound like a good 'oh.' Do you not like the

apartment? It's bigger than yours so I naturally thought it would accommodate us better."

She scrambled up and sat cross-legged beside him. "I do like it. This is a great apartment. It's a little manly-looking. More like a bachelor pad. It's not really appropriate for children or pets."

"Pets?" he croaked out. "Uh, Ash, I don't know about pets."

Her frown deepened, which he found distressing. Ashley rarely pouted about anything, which was good, because it was damn hard to resist her when she looked unhappy. Maybe it was because she was rarely ever anything but happy.

"I've always wanted a house in the country. A place for kids and pets to run and play. The city isn't a good place to raise a family."

"Lots of people raise families here," Devon pointed out. "You were raised here."

She shook her head. "Not always, no. We didn't move to the city until I was ten. Before that we lived on this really great farm. Or at least it was a farm before my father bought it. It was such a beautiful place to live."

The wistful note in her voice was a shot to the gut.

"It's something we can discuss when the time comes," Devon said by way of appeasement. "Right now, my focus is on making you my wife, having a week of uninterrupted time with you on our honeymoon and getting you permanently moved into my apartment."

She smiled and leaned up to brush her lips across his jaw. "I love it when you talk like that."

He raised a brow as she drew back. "Like what?"

"Like you can't wait for us to be together."

She snuggled against him and wrapped her arms around his waist. And again he was assailed by an unfamiliar nagging sensation in his chest. It wasn't comfortable. He wasn't sure he liked it even as he didn't want it to go away.

"It won't be long now," he said. And then some strange urge

to continue on and at least make a token effort to lift her spirits pushed stubbornly at him. He stroked a hand over her silky hair and pressed a kiss to the top of her head. "We can always revisit the issue of where to live later. Right now, though, I want our concentration to be on each other."

She squeezed him tighter and then pulled away as she'd done before to stare up at him, her blue eyes shining. "Can we talk about one other thing?"

"Of course."

"When you say you want our concentration to be on each other, does that mean you'd prefer to wait to start a family? We've talked casually about children. I've made it no secret that I'd love to become pregnant right away but you haven't said what you want in that regard."

A sudden picture of her swollen with his child and her radiant, beautiful smile flashed through his mind. It shocked him just how gratifying the image was. He was assailed by a surge of longing and possessiveness that baffled him.

He'd always viewed marriage, a wife and eventual children with clinical detachment. Almost as if they were components of a to do list. And maybe they had been. Right underneath his goals of business success.

Now that he was suddenly faced with all of the above, he had a hard time thinking rationally about what he wanted. It was a very damn good question.

At some point he'd stopped looking at marriage to Ashley as the chore it had begun as. He'd resigned himself to the inevitability and honestly, he could do so much worse. She was intelligent, good to her core, sweet, affectionate and tenderhearted. She'd make a perfect mother. Much better than his own had ever been. But would he make a good father?

"Dev?"

He glanced down to see her staring at him with worry in her eyes. It was instinctual to want to immediately soothe the concern away. He kissed her brow. "I was just thinking."

"If it's too soon to be having this conversation, I'm sorry. Daddy always says I get too far ahead of myself. I just can't help it. I get excited about something and I just want to reach out and grab it."

He couldn't help but smile. It was such an apt description of her. She embraced life wholeheartedly. And she didn't seem to much care if she stumbled along the way. He wondered if anything ever got her down at all. People like her were a puzzle to him. He didn't understand them. Couldn't relate to them.

He pulled her onto his lap until she was astride him. "What I think is that you'll be a perfect mother. I was just imagining you pregnant with my child and decided I quite liked the image. I also had the thought that I've never used protection, which is hugely irresponsible of me even given the fact that we both have clean histories and are safe, which makes me wonder if subconsciously I was hoping to get you pregnant all along."

She sighed and went soft, melting into his chest as she leaned toward him. "I was hoping you'd say that. I mean about wanting children. It's not that I *have* to have them right away. A small part of me realizes it would probably be better to wait but I've always wanted a large family and I don't want to be old when they're graduating high school."

"You realize we've done nothing to prevent pregnancy so far," he said in a low voice.

"Do you mind?" she asked anxiously. "I mean would you be upset if I was actually pregnant before we got married?"

He chuckled. "It would be the height of hypocrisy for me to be upset over something I could have very well prevented."

"I just want to be sure. I don't want us to have a bad start. I want everything to be…perfect."

He touched her nose and then traced a path underneath her eye and down the side of her face. "Do you suspect that you're already pregnant, Ash? Is that why you're bringing this up tonight? I don't want you to be afraid to tell me anything. I'd never be angry with you for something that is equally my responsibility, if not more so. You were an innocent when I made love to you. Birth control absolutely should have been my responsibility."

She shook her head. "No. I mean I don't know. I don't think so anyway."

He rested his forehead on hers and thought for a moment that they already acted like a married couple who were at ease in their relationship. Strangely, he trusted Ashley and felt comfortable with her. There was a sense of rightness that he couldn't deny. Maybe William Copeland had known what he was doing after all.

"Well, if you are, then fantastic. Really. I want you to tell me if you even suspect you could be. And if you aren't? We'll work on remedying that. Deal?"

She grinned and a delicate blush stained her soft cheeks. "Deal."

"Now what do you say we go to bed so you can have your evil way with me?"

Her cheeks grew even redder and he smiled at the shy way she ducked her head.

He leaned in to nibble at her ear and then he whispered so the words blew gently over her skin. "I'll do my very best to make you pregnant."

To his surprise, she shoved him forward. He landed on his back on the mattress with her looming over him, a mischievous grin dimpling her cheeks. Then her expression grew more serious and her eyes darkened. "I love you so much, Devon. I'm the luckiest woman on earth. I can't wait until we're married and I'm officially yours."

As she lowered her mouth to his, he was gripped by the feeling that she was completely and utterly wrong. It wasn't she who was the lucky one.

Seven

"Ashley, if you don't sit still we're never going to get your hair and makeup right," Pippa said in exasperation.

"I still think she should have just called in a stylist," Sylvia said as she eyed the progress Tabitha was making on Ashley's hair.

"Tabitha *is* a stylist, silly," Ashley said. "She's the best and who doesn't want the best on their wedding day? And who knows more about makeup than Carly?"

Pippa snorted. "That's so true. I'm convinced cosmetic companies should just pay her to endorse their products."

"Close your eyes, Ash," Carly said. "Time for mascara. Just a bit, though. Don't want you looking clumpy on the big day."

Ashley frowned. "Definitely not clumpy."

"Darling, are you almost done?" Ashley's mother sang out from the doorway. "You're on in ten minutes."

"Ten minutes?" Tabitha shrieked. "No way. Can you stall them, Mrs. C.?"

"I'm not going to be late to my own wedding," Ashley said

firmly. "Just hurry faster, Tab. My hair will be fine. Just put the veil over the knot."

"Just put the veil over the knot," Tabitha grumbled. "As if it's that easy."

Sylvia rolled her eyes, pushed between Tabitha and Ashley and quickly affixed the veil to the elegant chignon. "There, Ashley. You look beautiful."

"Lip gloss and we're done," Carly announced. "Make a kissy face."

Ashley smacked her lips and a moment later, Carly pulled away to allow Ashley to see herself in the mirror.

"Oh, you guys," she whispered.

Her best friends beamed back at her in the mirror.

"You look beautiful," Pippa said, her eyes bright with tears. "The most beautiful bride I've ever seen."

"Absolutely you do," Tabitha said.

The four women crowded in to hug her.

"Girls, time for you to go. Your escorts are waiting. We don't want to make the bride late," Ashley's mother called.

Her friends scrambled toward the door, bouquets in hand.

"Your father is coming to get you now," her mother said as she walked over. She paused when she got to Ashley and then smiled, tears glittering in her eyes. "My baby, all grown up. You look so beautiful. I'm so proud of you."

"Don't make me cry, Mom. You know I have no willpower."

Her mom laughed and reached for her hands. She squeezed them and then helped her to her feet.

"Let me fix your gown. Your father will be pacing outside the door. You know how he hates to be late for anything."

She fussed with Ashley's dress and then there was a knock on the dressing room door.

"That will be him now. Are you ready, darling?"

Sudden nerves gripped Ashley and her palms went sweaty. But she nodded. Oh, God, this was really it. She was about to walk down the aisle and become Mrs. Devon Carter.

She threw her arms around her mom and hugged her tight. "Love you, Mom."

Her mother squeezed her back. "Love you, too, baby. Now let's go before your father wears a hole in the floor."

She went ahead of Ashley to open the door and sure enough, her father was outside checking his watch. He looked up when he heard them and his expression softened. A glimmer of emotion welled in his eyes and he held out his hand to take hers.

"I can't believe you're getting married," he said in a tight voice. "It seems like only yesterday you were learning to walk and talk. You look beautiful, Ash. Devon is a lucky man."

She leaned up to kiss his wrinkled cheek. "Thank you, Daddy. You look pretty spiffy yourself."

The wedding coordinator hurried up to them and motioned with rapid flying hands. She shooed them toward the entrance to the aisle and then spent a few seconds arranging the train of her dress.

Ashley's mom was escorted down the aisle and seated, which only left Ashley to be walked down the aisle with her father.

The music began, the doors swung open and every eye in the church turned to watch as Ashley took her first step.

Her bouquet shook in her hands and she prayed her knees would hold up. The dress suddenly seemed to weigh a ton and despite the cold outside, the church felt like a sauna.

But then she caught sight of Tabitha, Carly, Sylvia and Pippa all standing at the front of the church, their smiles wide and encouraging. Pippa winked and held a thumbs-up then pointed toward Devon and made a motion like she was fanning herself.

And finally her gaze locked on to Devon and she forgot about everyone else. Forgot about her nervousness, her sudden doubt. Nothing but the fact that he awaited her at the front of the church and that from now on, she'd belong to him.

It gave her a warm, mushy feeling from head to toe.

And then her dad was handing her over to Devon. Devon

smiled reassuringly down at her as they took the step toward the priest and the ceremony began.

It pained her to later admit that she didn't remember most of the ceremony. What she did remember was Devon's eyes and the warmth that enveloped her standing next to him as she pledged her love, loyalty and devotion. And the kiss he gave her after they were pronounced husband and wife scorched her to her toes.

Suddenly they were walking back down the aisle, this time together, as a married couple. They ducked into an alcove to await the others and Devon pulled her close into his side.

"You look absolutely stunning."

He kissed her again. This time slower. More intense. Long and lingering. He took his time exploring her mouth, and when he pulled away, she swayed and caught his arm to steady herself.

Around her, the noise of well-wishers grew and she realized that guests were coming out of the church.

"Darling, they need you back inside the church for pictures," her mother called as she hurried towards Ashley and Devon. "All your attendants are already gathered. The others are going ahead to the reception. The car is waiting to take you and Devon after you're finished with all the photos."

Devon looked less than happy at the idea of posing for so many photographs but he gave a resigned sigh and took Ashley's hand to lead her back into the sanctuary.

"It'll be over soon," she whispered. "Then we can be off on our honeymoon."

He smiled down at her and squeezed her hand. "It's the only thing making the next few hours bearable for me. The idea of you and me locked in a hotel suite for days."

She flushed but shivered in delight at the images his words invoked. She too couldn't wait for them to be alone.

But at the same time, this was her day and she was going to enjoy every single moment of it. She smiled as she was swarmed by her friends. She was surrounded by countless cousins, her uncles and aunts, her parents, her brother, distant relatives, friends.

It was truly the happiest day of her life.

Devon collected a glass of wine while Ashley's brother took his turn on the dance floor with her. Devon should probably be dancing with one of her family members but she had so many female relatives that he couldn't keep track.

Cam immediately found him and Devon whistled appreciatively to mock the formal tuxedo his friend wore.

"Only for you would I wear this getup," Cam said darkly. "I didn't wear this for Rafe's wedding and Ryan married Kelly so fast we were lucky to get a phone call saying the deed was done."

"You weren't *required* to wear one for Rafe's wedding," Devon pointed out.

Cam shrugged. "True, but then I wasn't required to wear one for yours, either. I didn't want to disappoint Ash. She thinks I look hot."

Devon shook his head. "I can't believe you've stuck around this long. Not like you to be out of your cave for such an extended period of time."

Cam made a rude noise. "I'm supposed to convey my congratulations or commiserations, whichever you need or prefer, from Rafe and Ryan. They were both sorry they couldn't make it but with wives about to drop the package at any moment, they understandably remained at home by their sides."

"You have to cut it out," Devon said. "My getting married isn't the end of the world. You didn't give Rafe and Ryan this much grief."

"Oh I did," Cam said with a grin. "I totally did. But they deserved it. They were both total douche bags."

"Like you're a shining example of chivalry, Mr. I-hate-everyone-and-women-in-particular."

Cam sobered. "Don't hate women at all. I like them too much if anything. Kind of sucks if you ask me. Besides, it's fun to give you hell. I think Ashley is perfect for a stuffy stick-in-the-mud like yourself."

"I didn't mean that, man," Devon said wearily. "I'm just on edge. I'll be glad when this is all over with. Too much stress. I've worried on a daily basis that she'd find out the truth and tell me to go to hell. The sooner we can get the hell out of here and on the plane to St. Angelo, the better I'll feel."

"For what it's worth, I wish you well," Cam said. "I think you made a huge mistake marrying someone over a business deal, but she's a sweet girl and you could certainly do worse. It's not you I worry about anyway. It's her."

"Gee, thanks," Devon said dryly. "Glad you've got my back on this one."

Cam's gaze found Ashley on the dance floor as her brother spun her around. She laughed and her smile lit up the entire room. It was clear she was having the time of her life.

"At least you won't suffer a broken heart," Cam said in a low voice. "Can you say the same for Ashley?"

"I'm not going to break her heart, damn it. Can we drop this? The last thing I need is for someone to overhear us."

"Yeah, sure. Think I'll go cut in on Ashley's brother, pay my respects to the bride before I head back to the cave you accuse me of crawling out of."

Devon watched as Cam sauntered onto the dance floor. A moment later, Eric relinquished Ashley into Cam's arms.

"You've made my little girl very happy," William Copeland said.

Devon turned around to see his father-in-law come up behind him. William smiled broadly and clapped Devon affectionately on the back. "Welcome to the family, son."

"Thank you, sir. It's an honor."

"You take Ashley and you two have a good time. Don't

worry a thing about the business. We'll have plenty of time to focus on what needs to be done when you get back."

Devon nodded. "Of course."

"Ashley's mother wanted me to tell you that the car taking you and Ashley to the airport is waiting outside. Now tradition is that you stick around, do silly stuff like cut the cake and stuff it into each other's faces, but if it were me and I'd just married one of the sweetest girls in New York City, I'd duck and make a run for it. You could be to the airport before anyone notices you're gone."

Devon smiled. "That sounds like the best plan I've heard all night. You'll cover my exit?"

William smiled back conspiratorially. "That I will, son. Go on now. Go collect your bride. Everyone here will be more than happy to eat the cake for you. No groom I ever knew gave a damn about cake anyway."

Devon laughed and then waded into the crowd to go retrieve Ashley from Cam.

Eight

The sun was sinking over the horizon when Devon carried Ashley through the doorway of their suite. As soon as he put her down, she ran to the terrace doors, flung them wide and gasped in pleasure at the burst of color splashed across the sky.

"Oh Devon, it's beautiful!"

He came up behind her, slipped his arms around her body and pulled her into his chest. He nibbled at her ear and she sighed in pleasure.

"I can't believe this is our view for the next week. Do you know how long it's been since I've been to the beach? I was a little girl."

"What?" he asked in mock horror. "You don't go to the beach?"

"I know. Terrible, isn't it? I don't know why. It's just not where our family ever went on vacation and my friends aren't really beachgoers. I just haven't made it a point to go and yet here we are and it's so fabulously gorgeous that I don't even have the words to describe it," she said breathlessly.

He chuckled. "Sounds to me like you have plenty of words. But I'm glad you like it."

She turned in his arms, allowing his hands to drop to her waist as he held her there. "How on earth did you find this place? I'd never heard of St. Angelo."

"We're constructing a resort here. We broke ground several weeks ago. Ryan and Kelly live here, remember?"

Her nose wrinkled. "Oh yes, you told me about them. I remember now. I've never met them. I've only met Cam."

"A situation I'll remedy soon. Bryony and Kelly are both very near to their due dates and so they aren't able to travel. We'll have dinner with Ryan and Kelly while we're here and I'm sure we'll have the occasion to meet Rafe and Bryony before long."

"I can't wait."

"I couldn't care less about them at the moment," Devon murmured. "I'm more interested in our wedding night."

Heat exploded in her cheeks at the same time a delicious shiver wracked her spine. "I have to get ready," she said in a low voice. "I have something special. It's a surprise."

"Mmm, what kind of surprise?"

"Umm, well, it was a gift from my girlfriends. They assured me no man alive would be able to resist me in it."

"Oh hell, remind me to thank them."

She raised an eyebrow. "You haven't seen me in it yet."

"I'll like it. I'm sure I'll like it. I'd like you in sackcloth. Whatever it is they bought you, I'm sure I'll appreciate it. Right before I peel it off your delectable body."

She all but wiggled in excitement. She was barely able to contain herself. "Okay, you wait here. Give me fifteen minutes at least. I want to look perfect. And no peeking!"

He held up his hands. "Would I do such a thing?"

Her eyes narrowed. "Promise me."

He sighed. "Okay, okay. But get moving. I'm going to go down and arrange for a very good bottle of wine and also give them our breakfast order for the morning. You have until I get back to do your thing."

She went up on tiptoe, kissed him and brushed past him into the suite. She waited just until he walked by and out of the bedroom before she hurriedly retrieved the bright pink, totally girly gift box from her suitcase.

At her lingerie shower, her girlfriends had delighted in making her eyes grow wide at all the things they'd bought her. The gifts had ranged from totally classy and elegant to absolutely outrageous and daring.

For her wedding night, she'd chosen a gown that was the perfect blend of elegant and sensual. It was sexy without being over-the-top siren material, although Ashley had no objection over the siren part. Being a seductive temptress for an evening had its merits and she was determined that she'd eventually work up the nerve to pull that one off.

She hurriedly changed and then went to survey herself in the mirror in the corner. The gown was beautiful. She felt like a princess and she liked that feeling very much. A pampered, cherished princess.

She reached for the clip holding her hair up and let the strands tumble down onto her shoulders. She fluffed it a bit, ran her fingers through the ends to straighten it and then took another step back to survey her reflection.

The bodice plunged deep between her breasts and offered just a hint of a view of the swells. If she turned just right, her nipple was almost bared. Almost, but not quite.

The skirt of the gown was sheer and it shimmered over her legs like a dream. Maybe she'd underestimated the siren quality of the lingerie. It seemed innocent enough in the box, but on her…? It took on a more seductive air and made her look less innocent and more brazen.

Not a bad look to achieve on one's wedding night.

She flashed herself an impish grin and turned away from

the mirror. Impulsively, she swirled around, outstretching her arms as she pretended to dance with an imaginary partner.

Humming lightly she twirled again, sighing dreamily as she performed the steps to the waltz she and Devon had danced at her reception. He was a good dancer. He didn't seem entirely comfortable with dancing as a rule, but he'd been more than adept at it. He moved like a dream. Commanding. Graceful with a hint of arrogance that made her all giddy inside.

She closed her eyes and whirled again. Her outstretched hand smacked against something hard and pain flashed over her knuckles at the same time a crash jolted her out of her fantasy.

Devon's laptop that had been resting on the mantel of the fireplace along with his wallet, keys and the contents of his pockets, was now lying on the floor in pieces.

She dropped to the floor, groaning her dismay. It looked as if the battery had just popped out but how could she be sure? What if she'd broken it? Who knew what all-important, irreplaceable things he had on his laptop. If he was anything like her father and brother and countless other family members, his entire life was in the damn thing.

Okay, she knew her way around computers. She may not spend her life on one, but she was capable of working one. Or determining whether or not she'd just broken her husband's.

She put the battery back in, checked for further damage and then pressed the power button, praying that it would come on. After a moment, the black screen of death remained and she let out another groan.

In frustration, she punched several buttons on the keyboard, willing something—anything—to come to life. The problem was, as soon as she began pressing the keys, the monitor blinked and she was treated to a dozen programs opening and flashing in rapid succession.

At least the damn thing worked.

She bit her lip in consternation and began closing the programs down. There were lots of Excel spreadsheets, countless charts and graphs that made her head swim. Halfway through she was struck by the fear that none of these were saved or that she was losing valuable information.

As much as she didn't want to ruin the moment, she'd be better off telling Devon what happened and let him sort out his laptop. That way tomorrow when he opened it up, there would be no nasty surprises.

She downsized the pdf that looked to be more a mammoth-sized report when her name caught her eye. She slowed down to read, her fingers pausing on the keyboard. It was an email from her father and she smiled as she saw the reference to her as his baby. But what she read next halted her in her tracks.

I've had time to consider your reservations in regard to Ashley and perhaps you were right to be concerned. I don't want you to think I discounted your intuition, but rather I want you to understand that I want her protected at all costs. Her knowing the truth of our arrangement isn't necessary even as I understand why perhaps you're uncomfortable with it. She's my only daughter and I love her dearly. The truth is, I'd rather she never know that the marriage is a condition of the merger. You are a welcome addition to this family and I trust that you'll always act in her best interests, which is why I implore you to remain silent as to our agreement.

Stunned, Ashley stared at the screen, sure that she couldn't have understood this correctly. She was jumping to conclusions, something her mother had always accused her of.

She admonished herself to remain calm even though her pulse was racing so hard that she could literally feel it jumping in her neck and in her temples.

She returned to the email, forcing the blurry words to focus.

"Ashley?"

She yanked her head up, startled as Devon suddenly loomed over her.

"It fell," she croaked out. "Off the mantel. I was afraid it was broken. The battery fell out of it. When I put it back together and started it back up, all these programs opened and I was trying to shut them all down."

He reached down to take the laptop, but she held onto it, with bloodless fingers.

He swore when he caught sight of what she was reading and he wrested the computer from her grip.

"Give it back, Devon. I want to know what it says."

He closed it with a sharp snap and tucked it underneath his arm. "There's nothing you need to see."

"Don't lie to me," she grit out. "I read most of it. Or at least the important parts. I want to know what the hell it means."

Devon stared back at her, his lips drawn in a thin line. He looked as though he'd rather be anywhere but here, doing anything but having this conversation with her. Too bad. She wasn't about to back down.

"Nothing good can come of it, Ash. Just forget it, okay?"

She gaped at him. "Forget it? You want me to just forget I saw an email from my father basically admitting he bought me a husband? Or at least manipulated you somehow into marrying me? This is my wedding night, Devon. Am I supposed to pretend I didn't see that email?"

Devon cursed and ran his hand through his hair. "Damn it, Ashley, why the hell did you open the laptop?"

"I didn't mean to! Believe me I'd give anything not to have knocked the damn thing down. But the fact is I did and now I want to know what's going on. What kind of a deal did you strike with my father? Tell me the truth or I swear I'm walking out of here right now."

"This is precisely why you're your own worst enemy at times, Ash. You're too impulsive. You don't think before you act. You just go around wading into situations and you end up getting hurt. If it enters your mind, you simply do it. That quickly. At some point you have to learn some control."

She gaped at him, openmouthed, as his frustrated, angry words bit into her. How was she the bad guy here? What the hell had she done? This wasn't her fault. She hadn't entered this marriage under false pretenses. Devon knew precisely where she stood. God knew she'd told him enough times.

His eyes flashed and he turned his back. He walked across the room to the dresser and slapped the laptop down on it. For a long moment, he stood there, not facing her, silent. Tension rose sharp and so thick it was uncomfortable. Fear struck a deep chord within her because she realized that she was about to learn something truly terrible about her life. Her fate. Her marriage.

"Devon?" she whispered.

She thought back on their relationship. The whirlwind courtship. Suddenly the blinders were off and she began to analyze every date. Everything he'd said to her. How much of it had been a lie? Was any of it true?

She didn't want to ask. She wasn't sure she could bear to know the answer to her most burning question, but she also realized she had no choice.

He turned around and his eyes were shuttered. His expression was impassive almost as if he hoped to quell any further discussion.

Suddenly the circumstances of her marriage didn't matter to her. There was only one thing she absolutely had to know. The most important thing. The one thing that would determine her future. And whether she had one with him.

"Just answer me one question," she said faintly. "Do you love me?"

Nine

Dread had a two-fisted grip around Devon's throat. He stared at Ashley's pale, stricken face and he knew his time had come. Maybe he'd always known that this moment would come. He'd never really believed that it was possible to prevent Ashley from finding out the truth and furthermore it was stupid to try to keep it from her.

Damn fool of an old man. William Copeland didn't want his precious daughter hurt and yet he'd set her up for the biggest fall of her life. Nice. And now Devon was going to look like the biggest bastard of all time.

"I care for you a great deal," he said evenly.

Anger and fear warred with one another in her eyes. His answer sounded lame even to his own ears but he couldn't bring himself to destroy her even further. Hadn't she endured enough already?

"Let's have the truth," she demanded. "Don't patronize me or pat me on the head while whispering pretty words to pacify me. It's a very simple question, Devon. Do you love me?"

His nostrils flared. "The truth isn't always a pretty thing, Ash. The truth isn't always pleasant to hear. Be careful when you ask for the truth because it can hurt far more than not knowing."

If possible she went even paler. Her eyes were stricken and all the light vanished from their depths as if someone had extinguished a flame. For a moment he thought she'd let it go, but then she squared her shoulders and said in a low, dead voice, "The truth, Dev. I want the truth. I need to hear it."

He bit out another curse and thrust his hand into his hair. "All right, Ashley, no, I don't love you. I care about you a great deal. I like and respect you. But if you want to know if I love you, then no."

She made a broken sound of pain that was like a knife right through his chest. Why couldn't he have just lied to her? Because she would have known the truth whether he admitted it or not and she'd already been deceived enough.

And maybe now they could finally go forward with complete and utter honesty and he could stop feeling like the worst sort of bastard at every turn.

She started to step backward, but she swayed precariously and flailed out one arm to catch herself on the mantel. He bolted forward, caught her shoulders and then guided her to the bed, forcing her down into a sitting position.

He took one step back and then heaved out a breath. Before he could launch into what he wanted to say, she found his gaze and he flinched at the raw vulnerability reflected in those eyes.

"What a fool I've made of myself," she whispered. "How stupid and naive. How you must have laughed."

"Damn it, Ash, I've never laughed at you. Never!"

"I loved you," she said painfully. "Thought you loved me. Thought we were getting married because you wanted me, not my father's business or whatever it was he offered you. How much did I cost you, Dev? Or should I ask how much my father offered you to marry me?"

Furious at the senseless direction this was heading, he yanked the chair out from the desk, turned it around and sat so he faced her.

"Listen to me. There's no reason we can't have an enjoyable marriage. We're compatible. We get along well together. We're good in bed. Those are three things many married couples don't have going for them."

She closed her eyes.

"Look at me, Ash. This may be painful to hear but maybe it's for the best if we get it all out in the open. You're far too emotional. You wear your feelings and your heart on your sleeve and it's only going to get you hurt. Maybe it's time for you to grow up and face the fact that life isn't a fairy tale. You're too impulsive. You dash about with no caution and no sense of self-preservation. That's only going to cause you further pain down the road."

She shook her head in utter confusion. Her eyes were cloudy and it was clear she was battling tears. "How could I possibly ever hurt as much as I do now? How can you be so…so… *cold* and calm and so matter-of-fact as if this is nothing more than a business meeting where you're discussing figures and projections and sales and a whole host of other things I don't understand?"

His gut twisted into a knot. He'd never felt so damn helpless in his life. He wished to hell it was as simple as telling her to be harder and for her not to let this destroy her, but he knew it was pointless because Ashley was one of the most tender-hearted people he knew and he was an ass to sit here and tell her to get over it.

She covered her face in her hands and he could see her throat working convulsively as she tried to keep her sobs silent. But they spilled out, harsh and brittle in the quiet.

He lifted his hand to touch her hair but left it in the air before finally pulling it back. She wouldn't welcome comfort from him, of all people. If it were any other woman, she'd have already come after his nuts and he'd deserve everything she dished out and more.

"Ash, please don't cry."

She lifted her ravaged face and pushed angrily at her hair. "Don't cry? What the hell else do you suggest I do? How could you do this? How could my father? Tell me, Devon, what was the price put on my future? What do you get out of the bargain?"

He stared at her in silence.

"Tell me, damn it! I think I deserve to know what my happiness was traded for."

"Your father wanted me to marry you as part of the merger between Tricorp Investments and Copeland Hotels," he bit out. "Happy now? Can you tell me what possible good it does for you to know that?"

"It doesn't make me happy but I damn well want to know what I've gotten myself into, or rather what my father got me into. Did I ever even have a chance? Did you study up on all the ways to worm your way into my heart?"

"Christ, no. Look, it was all real. It's not like I faked an attraction to you. It wasn't exactly a hardship to pursue you. If I hadn't wanted to marry you, no merger or deal would have persuaded me differently. I thought and still think that we'd make a solid marriage. I don't see why love has to be the be-all and end-all in this equation. Mutual respect and friendship are far more important aspects of a relationship."

"Maybe you can tell me how the hell I'm supposed to respect a man who doesn't love me and who manipulated me into a marriage based on deception. Does everyone think I'm a brainless twit who should be pathetically grateful that a man sweeps into my life and offers to take care of me? I've got news for you and my family. I hadn't married yet because it was my choice. I hadn't had sex with a man yet because I had enough respect for myself that I wasn't going to be pressured into something I wasn't ready for. It's not like I haven't had men interested in me. I'm not pathetically needy nor was I going to waste away if I wasn't married by the ripe old age of twenty-three. I was happy. I had a good life."

"Ashley, listen to me."

He leaned forward, caught her hands and stared until she quieted and returned his gaze.

"Right now you're upset and you're hurting. But don't discount the possibility that we could enjoy a comfortable, lasting marriage. Don't make a snap decision you may regret later. Take some time to think about it when you've calmed down. When you're not so volatile, you'll be able to look at the situation more objectively."

"Oh screw off," she snapped. "Could you be any more patronizing? 'Don't be so high-strung, Ashley. Don't be so stupid and naive. Don't expect ridiculous things like love and affection in a marriage. How perfectly absurd would that be?'"

"I don't think we should have this conversation any longer," he said tightly. "Not until you've had time to calm down and think about what you're saying." He stood abruptly and she looked hastily away but not before he saw the silver trail of her tears streaking down her cheeks.

He wanted more than anything to pull her into his arms and let her cry on his shoulder. He wanted to comfort her, hold her, soothe her fears and tell her it would be all right. But how could he when he was the sole reason she was devastated?

"I'm sorry, Ash," he said hoarsely. "I know you don't believe that, but I'm more sorry than you'll ever know. I would have done anything at all to spare you this pain."

"Please, just go away and leave me alone," she choked out. "I can't even look at you right now."

He hesitated a moment and then sighed in resignation. "I'll take the couch in the living area. We'll talk more in the morning."

It took every ounce of his willpower to turn around and walk out of the bedroom. His instincts screamed at him not to leave her alone. To take her in his arms and force the issue. Make her listen to him. To not relent until she agreed that their marriage could and would work if only they could set aside the emotional volatility that always seemed to accompany declarations of love.

He had only to point at his friends to know this was an inevitable truth. Their lives were emotional messes brought on by the letter *L*.

All that angst and suffering in the name of love. Rafe and Ryan had spent more time in abject misery and all because they'd been ripped to shreds by…love.

Devon grimaced and sank onto the couch in the dark living room. What a wedding night this had turned out to be. Maybe he'd always known that it was inevitable that she learn the truth. How could she not? But he'd hoped they'd have a lot more mileage behind them. Then she could see that their marriage wasn't defined by love or emotion, volatility or vulnerability.

Friendship, companionship, trust, respect.

Those were all things he was on board with.

Love? Not so much. It was a messy, raw emotion he had no desire to embroil himself with.

Ten

Ashley sat on the private veranda and stared over the ocean as the sun began its hesitant rise. She felt empty. Rung out. She felt stupid and so horribly naive that she cringed. It still baffled her that a life she'd thought was so perfect just hours before was a complete facade.

All night she'd sat huddled in an uncomfortable chair trying to come to grips with the fact that she'd been lied to at every turn. She'd been used and manipulated, not just by Devon, but by her own father. And all over a business deal.

She couldn't wrap her head around it.

Why? Why had it been so important for Devon to marry her? Was her father so unconvinced of Ashley's ability to manage her own life that he'd all but hired a man to be her husband? She winced at the thought, but it was appropriate. At the very least, she'd been used as a bargaining chip.

She rubbed at eyes that felt full of sand. She'd cried all that she was to allow herself to cry. She be damned if she shed another single tear over her husband.

A dry laugh escaped her. Her husband. What was she going to do about her marriage? Her complete and utter farce of a marriage.

She closed her eyes against the humiliation of it all. What a fool she'd made of herself over the last month. She wanted to die from it.

Had he laughed at her the entire time? Had he joked with his friends about what a gullible idiot she was? She didn't like to imagine he could be so cruel, but the man she'd faced down the night before and demanded the truth from had been brutally honest. At her insistence, but crushingly forthright all the same.

"It's time you had the cold hard truth, Ashley," she whispered. She'd been living a fantasy.

She rubbed at her temples, willing the vicious ache to go away. But the pain in her head was nothing compared to the unbearable ache in her heart.

Should she leave him? Should she ask for a divorce? They could have the shortest marriage on record. She could go back home. Chalk it up to a lesson learned the hard way. It was doubtful at this point that her father would pull the plug on the deal because Devon had lived up to his end of the bargain. It wasn't Devon who was unhappy with the result. It was her. Everyone had evidently thought she was the very last person who should be consulted about her life.

But the idea of divorcing Devon held as little appeal as living in the cold, sterile state her marriage now existed in. She deeply loved him and love wasn't something you could switch off at will. She was hurt beyond belief. She was angry and she felt horribly betrayed. But she still loved him and she still wished that they could go back to the way things had been before she'd found out the damnable truth.

It was true what they said about ignorance being bliss. She'd give anything at all to go back to being that innocent little girl who still believed in happily ever after with Prince Charming.

For just a little while Devon had been that prince. He'd been perfect. She'd built him into something he wasn't, and that wasn't entirely his fault. He couldn't be blamed for her utter stupidity.

No, she didn't want a divorce. But neither did she want to live a life with a man who didn't love her.

She thought back to all the things he'd said to her the night before. His criticisms had stung. They'd stunned her. She'd never imagined that he'd thought of her in such a negative way. But maybe he was right.

Maybe she was too impulsive, too flighty, too exuberant. Perhaps she should be more controlled, more guarded, show more of a knack for self-preservation.

It was evident that he didn't want the person she was. It was evident he didn't love flighty, impulsive, tender-hearted, animal-loving Ashley Copeland, who called him at work just to say she loved him.

If he didn't want or love that person, then the only two options left to her were to walk away and get a divorce or to *become* someone he could love.

Could she make him fall in love with her? Her family always worried that she was too trusting. Too naive. Too everything. Apparently they were right.

The only person who didn't seem to think anything was wrong with who Ashley Copeland was, was Ashley herself. And it was becoming increasingly clearer that her judgment stank.

It was time for one hell of a makeover.

But the idea didn't excite her. It didn't infuse enthusiasm into her flagging spirits. It was a bleak thought and she dimly wondered if Devon was worth such an effort.

Would his love be enough, provided she could even make him fall in love with her?

A voice in the back of her mind whispered that it was time for her to grow up. It was a voice that sounded precariously close to Devon's. He thought she should grow up. Her father evidently thought the same. Maybe they were both right.

She stiffened when she heard a sound on the terrace. She knew it was Devon but she wasn't ready to face him yet.

"Have you been out here all night?" he asked quietly.

She nodded wordlessly and continued to stare over the water.

He walked to the thick stone railing that enclosed the private viewing area, shoved his hands in his pockets and for a moment stared over the water as she was doing. Then he turned to face her and leaned back against the stone.

He looked as bad as she felt, though she had no sympathy. His hair was rumpled. He was still in the same clothes as the night before.

"Ash, don't torture yourself over this. There's no reason we can't have a perfectly good marriage, no matter the circumstances of *how* we came to be married."

He was starting to repeat his arguments from the previous night and the truth was, she couldn't stomach hearing again how she was naive and impulsive and whatever else it was he'd said when he outlined all her faults.

She bit her lip to keep the angry flood from rushing out because at this point it did her no good and she didn't have the emotional energy to spare.

She held up a hand to stop him and cursed at how it trembled. She put it back down and tucked it into her gown, blinking as she realized she was still in her sexy, lacy lingerie that she'd so painstakingly picked out for her wedding night.

Unbidden tears welled again in her eyes as she realized just what a disaster her wedding night had been. What should have been the most special night of her entire life would forever be a black hole in her past no matter what happened in the future.

"I agree," she said before he could launch into another list of her shortcomings.

He promptly shut his mouth and then stared at her, his brows drawn together in confusion. "You do?"

She nodded again because the words seemed to stick in her throat. Almost as if they were rebelling. It took her a few moments to force out what she wanted to say.

"You're absolutely right. I was being silly. I had unrealistic expectations and I shouldn't allow them to get in the way of marriage."

He winced but remained quiet.

"I am agreeable to at least a period of time in which we see how things progress."

He frowned at that but she looked up with dead eyes. "Be glad I'm not on a plane home with an appointment to see a divorce lawyer."

He pushed out a breath and then slowly nodded. "All right. How long do you think this test period will last?"

She shrugged. "How would I know? I can't exactly put a time frame on when I can give up all hope of having a happy marriage."

"Ash."

The low growl in which he said her name only served to make her angrier. She curled her fingers into tight balls, determined not to give in to the urge to scream at him. She was determined to get through this, no matter how excruciating it was.

"I'm not trying to punish you, Devon. I'm trying to get through this without losing what little pride I have left."

He went pale and pain flickered in his eyes. And shame. Though that hadn't been her intention, either. She wasn't trying to make digs at him because that wouldn't make this go away. It wouldn't give her back her happiness. It would only make her more miserable than she already was.

"You seem to think we can have an enjoyable marriage. I personally find no joy in being married to a man who doesn't love me, but I'm willing to try. You're probably right in that I shouldn't allow something so silly as love to enter the equation."

"Damn it, I care a lot for you—"

"Please," she bit out, halting his words in midsentence. "Just don't. Don't try to make it better by offering me platitudes. It was hard to hear your assessment of my faults. Does anyone ever like to hear that about themselves? But I'm willing to work on not being so impulsive and exuberant or whatever else it was that you mentioned. I'll try to be the best wife I can be and not disappoint you."

He bit out a sharp curse but she ignored him and plunged ahead before she lost all her courage and fled.

"I just have one thing to ask in return," she whispered.

She was trying valiantly not to break down again. She'd already made such an idiot of herself in front of him. She was forever making a total cake of herself with him.

His lips were thin. His eyes were dark with raw emotion. At least he wasn't totally unaffected by her distress.

"I find the situation I'm in immensely humiliating. I'll make every effort to be a wife you'll be proud of. All I ask is that you please not embarrass me in front of my family by making our issues known to anyone. What I'm asking you to do is pretend. At least with them."

"God, Ash. You act as though I despise you. I'd never embarrass you."

"I just don't want them to know you don't love me," she choked out. "If you could just act like—like a real husband in front of them. You don't have to go overboard. Just don't treat me with indifference now that you don't have to pretend in order to get me to marry you anymore."

And then another thought occurred to her that very nearly had her leaning over to empty the contents of her stomach.

"Are you all right?" Devon asked sharply. Then he swore. "Of course you aren't all right. You look as if you're going to be ill."

"Is there someone else?" she croaked out. "I mean did you ever plan to be faithful? I won't stay married to you if you're going to sleep around or if you have a mistress on tap somewhere."

This time the curses were more colorful and they didn't stop for several long seconds. He closed the distance between them, knelt down in front of the lounger she was curled up in and grasped her shoulders.

"Stop it, Ashley. You're torturing yourself needlessly. There is no other woman. There won't be another woman. I take my marriage vows very seriously. I don't have a mistress. There's been no other woman since well before you entered the picture. I have no desire to sleep around. I want *you*."

Her shoulders sagged in relief and she leaned away from him so that his hands slipped from her arms.

"Damn it, I wanted to tell you the truth from the very beginning but your father wouldn't hear of it. My mistake. I should have told you anyway. But it doesn't change anything. I still want to be married to you. If I found the idea so abhorrent, I'd simply wait until the deal was done and begin divorce proceedings. There wouldn't be a damn thing your father could do at that point."

She closed her eyes wearily and rubbed at her head. The sun's steady creep over the horizon was casting more light onto the terrace and each ray speared her eyeballs like a flaming pitchfork.

"Do you have one of your headaches?" he asked, his voice full of concern. "Did you bring your medicine?"

She opened her eyes again, wincing as she tried to refocus. "I want to go home."

Devon's expression darkened. "Don't be unreasonable. What you need is to take your medicine and get some sleep. You'll feel better once you rest and eat something."

"I won't stay here and pretend. It's pointless. You even brought me to the island where you're building a resort, I'm sure so you could keep up with the progress. So don't tell me I'm being unreasonable for wanting to dispense with the fairy-tale honeymoon. You and I both know at this point it's a joke and we'll just spend all week staring awkwardly at each other or you'll just spend most of the time at the job site."

His jaw ticked and he stood again, turning briefly away. Then he turned back, irritation evident in his gaze. "You wanted me to pretend in front of your family. Why can't you pretend now?"

"Because I'm miserable and it's going to take me a little time to get over this," she snapped. "Look, we can say I wasn't feeling well. Or you can make up some business emergency. It's not as if anyone in my capitalistic family would even lift an eyebrow at the idea of business coming first. Right now my head hurts so damn bad, we wouldn't even be lying."

Some of the anger left Devon's gaze. "Let me get you some medication for your headache. Then I want you to get some rest. If…" He sighed. "If you still want to leave when you wake up, I'll arrange our flight back to New York."

Eleven

She slept because the pill Devon gave her would allow her to do no less. She rarely resorted to taking the medication prescribed for her migraines for the reason that it made her insensible.

When she awoke, she was in bed by herself and it was nearly dusk. Her headache still hung on with tenacious claws and when she moved too suddenly to try to sit up, nausea welled in her stomach. Her head pounded and she put a hand to her forehead, sucking air through her nostrils to control the sudden wash of weakness.

The room was blanketed in darkness, the drapes drawn and no lights had been left on. Devon had made sure she had been left in comfort, only a sheet covering her and the air-conditioning turned down so it was nearly frigid in the room.

Before, his consideration would have been endearing. Now, she could only assume he was operating out of guilt.

She pushed herself from the bed and sat on the edge for a moment, holding her head while she got her bearings. After a moment, she got to her feet and wobbled unsteadily toward the luggage stand, where her still-packed suitcase lay open.

She ripped off the silky gown she'd so excitedly donned the night before and tossed it in the nearby garbage can. If she never saw it again, it would be too soon.

She dug through the suitcase, bypassing the chic outfits, the swimwear and the other sexy nightwear she'd purchased, and pulled out a faded pair of jeans and a T-shirt. She briefly contemplated shoes, but the idea had formed in her head to take a long walk on the beach. Maybe it would clear her head or at least stop the vile aching. For that, she wouldn't need shoes.

Having no idea where Devon was, or if he was even still in the suite, she opted to leave through the sliding glass doors to the veranda. The breeze lifted her hair as soon as she walked outside the room and she inhaled deeply as she took the steps leading down to the beach.

The night was warm and the wind coming off the water was comfortable, but she was cold to her bones and she shivered as her feet dug into the sand.

It was a perfect, glorious night. The sky was lit up like a million fireflies had taken wing and danced over the inky black canvas. In the distance the moon was just rising over the water and it shimmered like a splash of silver.

Drawn to the mesmerizing sight, she ventured closer to the water, hugging her arms around her waist as the incoming waves lapped precariously close to her toes.

At one point, she stopped and allowed the water to caress her feet and surround her ankles. There she stood, staring over the expanse of the ocean, stargazing like a dreamer. It would take a million wishes to fix the mess she was currently in. And maybe that was what had gotten her into this situation in the first place.

Stupid dreams. Stupid idealism. She'd been a fool to wait for the perfect guy to give her virginity to. She'd always been somewhat smug and a little holier-than-thou with her friends who'd given it up long ago. But they at least had gone into the situation with their eyes wide open. They hadn't confused sex for love. They weren't the ones on their honeymoon with the migraine from hell and a husband who didn't love them.

They were looking pretty damn smart for shopping around and Ashley was looking like a moron.

She pulled out her cell phone and stared down at her contacts list. She could use the comfort of a good friend right now but she wavered on whether to send a text. She was already humiliated enough. Could she bear to tell her friends or even one friend the truth about her marriage? Or would she go back home, live a lie and hope that Devon would pretend as agreed.

Could she ever make him love her?

She lowered the hand holding the phone and then she shoved it back into her pocket. What could she say anyway in the limited number of characters allowed by a text message? Or maybe she should just tweet everyone.

Marriage fail. Honeymoon fail.

That would get the message across with plenty of characters left over.

She shoved her hands into her pockets, closed her eyes and wished for just one minute that she could go back. That she would have asked more questions. That she would have picked up on the fact he'd never said he loved her even when Ashley made it a practice to tell him every day.

She'd just assumed he was a typical guy. Devon was reserved. He was somewhat forbidding. But she'd been wildly attracted to those qualities. Thought they were sexy. She'd been convinced that he quietly adored her and that his actions spoke louder than words.

She'd never considered even once that his actions were practiced, fake and manipulative.

Another shiver overtook her and she clamped her teeth together until pain shot through her head.

"Enough," she said.

She had beat herself up for the last twenty-four hours, but it was Devon who was the jackass here. Not her. She'd done nothing wrong. Naiveté wasn't a crime. Loving someone wasn't a crime. She wouldn't apologize for offering her love, trust and commitment to a man who didn't deserve any of it.

He was wrong. She wasn't.

The only thing she could control from here on out was what she did with the truth. It was no longer about what Devon wanted. If he could be a selfish jerk-wad, she could at least focus on what she wanted from this fiasco.

Then she laughed because what she wanted was the jerk-wad to love her. That might make her pathetic.

No, she couldn't text Sylvia or Carly or Tabitha. Definitely not Pippa. Pippa would have her in front of a lawyer in a matter of hours and then she'd likely take out a hit on Devon.

Plus her friends would tell her she was being stupid for wanting to stay in the marriage. And she may well be an idiot, but she didn't want people telling her that. She'd already made one mistake. It wouldn't be the first or last and well, if it didn't work out, at least then she could cite incompatibility and she wouldn't have to tell everyone that the marriage had fallen apart before it had ever gotten off the ground.

She had just enough of an ego to want to save face. Who could blame her?

Feeling only marginally better about taking control over a perfectly out-of-control situation, she turned to retrace her steps. She was hungry but the thought of food made her faintly nauseous and her head was hurting so badly she wasn't sure she could keep anything down anyway.

She was still a good distance from the steps leading to her and Devon's suite when she saw him striding toward her on the sand.

Even now after so much time to think and decide how she wanted to proceed, she wasn't prepared to face him. How could she just go on after finding out he was nothing like the man she'd thought she'd married? It was as if they were strangers. Intimate strangers who would now live together and pretend a loving existence to outsiders.

There weren't manuals for this. Certainly no one had ever given her advice on such a matter. She wasn't good at artifice. She hated lying. But it was what she'd asked him to do. It was what she herself had just decided to do with her friends and family. To the world.

"Where the hell have you been?" Devon demanded as he approached. "I was worried sick. I went in to check on you and you were gone."

Before she could answer, he put his hand around her elbow and pulled her toward the glow cast from the torches that lined the beach.

She flinched away from the burst of light and he muttered something under his breath.

"Your headache isn't any better, is it?"

She slowly shook her head.

"Damn it, Ash, why didn't you come to me? Or take another pill. You should be in bed. For that matter you've eaten nothing in twenty-four hours. You're as pale as death and your eyes are glazed with pain."

She braced herself as he reached for her again, but his touch was in direct contrast to the tone of his voice. He was infinitely gentle as he pulled her against his side and began leading her back to the suite.

Unable to resist the urge, she laid her head on his shoulder and closed her eyes, trusting him to at least get her safely up the steps. His hold tightened around her and then to her shock, he simply swung her into his arms and began carrying her back.

"Put your head on my shoulder," he said gruffly.

Relaxing against him, she did as he directed and for a few moments, basked in the tenderness of his hold.

Pretending was nice.

He carried her back into the suite, into the still-darkened bedroom, and carefully laid her on the bed.

"Would you be more comfortable out of your jeans?" he asked. But even as he asked, he was unfastening her fly and pulling the zipper down.

He efficiently pulled her pants down her legs, leaving her in her panties and T-shirt. She lay there, cheek resting on the firm, cool pillow, and willed the pain to go away. All of it.

He sat on the edge of the bed and then turned, sliding his leg over the mattress and bending it so he was perched next to her.

"I'll get you another pill, but I don't think you should take it on an empty stomach. It might make you ill. But neither do you look as though you could keep down much so I'll call down for some soup. Would you like something to drink? Could you handle some juice?"

As he spoke, he smoothed his hand over her hair, stroking gently, and she had to bite her lip to keep the hot tears from slipping down her cheeks again. This wasn't going to work if she broke down every time he was nice to her or took care of her.

And it wasn't as if he was doing anything different than he'd done all along. It was one of the things that had made her think he loved her to begin with, even absent of the actual words. He'd been so…good…to her. So caring. Protective. Possessive. A guy couldn't fake all of that, could he?

"Soup sounds good," she said faintly.

He continued to stroke her hair and then his hand went still and he frowned. "Is that bothering you? I wasn't thinking. I'm sure you must be supersensitive to any touch or sound."

"It was…nice."

"I'll be right back. Let me order your soup. You need to get something in your stomach. It might help with the headache, too."

She closed her eyes as he stood and walked across the room.

He stepped outside but she could just make out the low murmur of his voice as he ordered room service. A moment later, he returned and gently laid his hand over her forehead.

"It'll be here in a few minutes. I told them to put a rush on it."

"Thank you."

He was silent for a few seconds and then he said in a voice full of resignation, "I'll make arrangements for us to fly home in the morning. Perhaps it's best if you're back in familiar surroundings. I don't want you to suffer with a headache the entire week we were supposed to be here. At least at home, you'll have your family and your friends to surround you and…make you feel better."

She nodded, her chest heavy and aching with regret. It should have been different. They should have spent the week making love. Laughing. Spending every waking moment immersed in each other.

Instead they'd go back home to a very uncertain future in a world that was suddenly unfamiliar to Ashley. Where she'd have to guard every word, every action.

It frightened her. What if she failed? What if even after she removed the annoyances he still felt nothing more for her than he did now?

Then he doesn't deserve you, the voice inside her aching head whispered in her ear.

He didn't deserve her now. The intelligent side of her knew and accepted this. But she wanted him. Wanted his love, his approval. She wanted him to be proud of her.

If that made her an even bigger moron than she'd already been, she could live with that. What she couldn't live with was just walking away without seeing if their marriage could be salvaged.

"It will be better when we get home," she whispered.

His hand stilled on her hair but he remained silent as he

seemed to contemplate her words. His expression was grim and tension radiated from his body in waves.

Then there was a distant knock and he rose once more. "That'll be the food. Just stay here. I'll wheel the cart in and we'll get you a comfortable spot made up so you can eat in bed."

He strode out of the room and Ashley lay there a moment mentally recovering from what felt like a barrage of emotional turmoil. Finally she pushed herself upward and sat cross-legged on the bed, with pillows pushed behind her back to keep her propped up.

Devon returned with the rolling table and parked it at the end of the bed. As soon as he uncovered the bowl of soup, the aroma wafted through the air and her mouth watered. On cue, her stomach protested sharply and sweat broke out on her forehead.

"You okay?" Devon asked as he positioned the tray in front of her.

His gaze was focused sharply on her face, his forehead creased with concern. She nodded and reached for the napkin and utensils with shaking hands.

When she would have slid the bowl closer, Devon gently took her hand away.

"Perhaps it would be better if I ladled the soup into a mug so you could sip at it. Less chance of spilling it that way."

She nodded her agreement and watched as he filled one of the cups on the table with the delicious-smelling broth.

"Here. Careful now, it's hot."

She brought the steaming mug to her lips and inhaled, closing her eyes as she tentatively took the first sip.

It was heaven in a coffee cup. The warmth from the soup traveled all the way down to her stomach and settled there comfortably.

"Good?" he asked as he edged his way onto the bed beside her.

"Wonderful."

He watched as she downed a significant amount of the soup and then he took her medicine bottle from the nightstand and shook out another pill.

"Here. Take this. Once you're finished you can lie down and hopefully sleep until morning. I'll wake you up in time to catch the flight. Don't worry about your things. I'll lay out something for you to wear on the plane and I'll pack everything else and have it all ready to go. All you'll have to do is get dressed and head out to the car when it's time."

Even though she was still devastated and angry, she couldn't be so much of a bitch not to recognize or acknowledge that he was taking absolute care of her.

She leaned back against the pillows, cup in hand, and glanced his way.

"Thank you," she said quietly.

A flash of pain entered his eyes. "I know you don't believe this right now, but maybe in time you will, Ash. I never meant to hurt you. I never wanted this to happen. I wouldn't have hurt you for the world."

She swallowed and brought the rim of the cup back to her lips. There wasn't much she could say to that. She did believe that he wasn't malicious. If she hadn't discovered the truth on her own, maybe he would have never told her. She was quite certain he wouldn't have. Maybe he thought he was doing her a favor by keeping it from her.

He pulled the mug away and then cupped her chin and gently turned her until she looked back at him.

"You'll see, Ash. We'll make this work."

She nodded as she lowered the mug the rest of the way down to the tray in front of her.

"I'll try, Devon. I'll try."

He leaned toward her and pressed a kiss to her forehead. "Get some rest. I'll wake you in the morning."

Twelve

The next morning was a total blur for Ashley. Devon gently woke her and after ascertaining that her headache wasn't better, he arranged a light breakfast, hovered over her while she ate and then all but dressed her and whisked her into a waiting car.

They drove to the airport and once on the plane, he settled her into her seat and gave her another pill. He propped a pillow behind her head, put a blanket over her and then made sure every single window was shut around her.

She drifted into blissful unawareness as the airplane left the island and traveled back to the cold of New York City.

When they landed, once again Devon ushered her into a waiting car, taking the blanket and pillow with them so she was comfortable in the backseat. She dozed with her head on his shoulder until they reached his apartment and then he gently shook her awake.

"We're home, Ash. Wait inside the car while I get out. I'll help you inside."

Home. She blinked as the looming building floated into her vision through the fogged window of the car. A cold rush of air blew over her as Devon stepped out. He spoke a moment with the doorman and then he reached back in to help her out.

"Careful," he cautioned as she stepped onto the curb.

He wrapped an arm around her and guided her to the door the doorman held open for them. Once inside, he didn't loosen his hold. He kept her close all the way up in the elevator until they reached his apartment. Their apartment. It was hard to keep that distinction in her mind.

Their home was already cluttered with her things. She'd moved completely in before the wedding. Devon had suggested having a cleaning lady come in which said to her that he didn't appreciate the somewhat careless way she kept her stuff. She sighed. One more thing she'd have to work on.

When they entered the bedroom, Devon pulled out one of his workout T-shirts and tossed it onto the bed. "Why don't you get out of your travel clothes and into something more comfortable. I'll wake you for dinner so you eat something."

"I'd rather just lie down on the couch," she said, reaching for the T-shirt.

His expression darkened and for a moment she couldn't imagine what she'd done to draw his disapproval. Then it struck her that he assumed she wouldn't be sleeping in his— their—bed.

It wasn't something she'd given any consideration. The thought hadn't even occurred to her. In her mind, if she was staying and making an effort to make their marriage work, she just naturally assumed they'd still sleep together.

Perhaps it wasn't something she should assume at all. She sank onto the edge of the bed, still foggy and loopy from the medication. She rubbed wearily at her eyes before focusing back on him.

"I only meant that when I have a headache, sometimes I'm more comfortable propped on the couch so I'm not lying flat.

However, it does bring up a point that I hadn't considered. I assumed that we'd continue to..." She swallowed, suddenly feeling vulnerable and extremely unsure of herself. "That is, I just thought we'd continue to sleep together. I have no idea if that's something you want."

Devon stalked over, bent down and placed his hands on either sides of her legs so that he was on eye level with her.

"You'll be in my bed every night. Whether we're having sex or not, you'll be next to me, in my arms."

"Well, okay then," she murmured.

He rose and took a step back. "Now, if you're more comfortable on the couch, change into my shirt and I'll get you pillows and a blanket for the couch."

She nodded and sat there watching him as he walked away. She glanced around the room—to all her stuff placed haphazardly here and there—and sighed. When she got rid of this headache, she'd whip the apartment into shape. She'd been away from the shelter more days than she'd ever been away before but the animals were in good hands and they'd be fine while she got the rest of her life in order.

Devon would no doubt be back to work in the morning, which meant she'd have plenty of time alone to figure out things. She wrinkled her nose. Being alone sucked. She was always surrounded by people. In her family she didn't have to look far if she wanted company. There was always someone to hang out with. And aside from her family, her circle of friends was always available even if for a gab session.

But what was she supposed to talk to them about now? How wonderful her marriage was? Her husband? The aborted honeymoon?

Her head was too fuzzy to even contemplate the intricacies of her relationships right this second. She reached for the T-shirt, shed her own clothes and crawled into Devon's shirt.

She started to leave her clothes just where they'd dropped on the floor, but she stopped to pick them up and then deposited them into the laundry basket in the bathroom. It was technically Devon's basket and he might not want her mixing her clothes with his, but she didn't have a designated place of her own yet. One more thing for the to-do list.

She trudged out to the living room to see that Devon had arranged several pillows and put out a blanket for her. As she started across the floor, Devon appeared from the kitchen. She crawled onto the couch and burrowed into all of the pillows while Devon pulled the blanket up to her shoulders. Then he perched on the edge close to her head.

"Are you feeling any better yet?"

She nodded. "Head doesn't hurt as bad. A few more hours and it should be fine. Just fuzzy from all the medication. I've never had to take three in a row like that."

He frowned as if he realized the significance of her having the worst headache of her life after their confrontation.

"Rest for a few hours then. I'll check on you in a bit and see if you're up for some dinner. I thought we'd eat in, of course. I can order anything you like or if you prefer, I can make something here."

She nodded.

"I have some calls to make. I'll let your family know we're back and why. You just concentrate on feeling better."

Her eyes widened in alarm. "What are you going to tell them?"

He frowned again. "I'm only going to tell them that you came down with a severe headache and that we thought you'd feel better if you were back in your own home."

She sagged in relief and the knot in her stomach loosened. "They'll want to come right over, or at least Mom will. Tell her not to bother, please. Let her know I'll call her soon."

"Of course. Now get some rest. I'll sort out dinner later."

He kissed her forehead, pulled the covers up to her chin and then quietly walked away, flipping off all the lights. She heard the door to his office close and she lay there alone in the darkness.

It wasn't anything she hadn't experienced before. In the evenings when Dev got home from work, he often sequestered himself in his office for a time while she watched TV or ordered in their dinner. But she hadn't felt so alone then. Because she'd known he was just in the next room and that in theory she could walk in there at any time. Only now it was as if a gulf had opened between them and he may as well be on the other side of the moon. She didn't feel as though she had the right to interrupt him.

She lay there as the haze slowly began to wear off. She braced herself for the inevitable onslaught of pain, but there was only a dull ache that signaled the aftereffects of a much worse headache than she'd experienced in at least two years.

For that matter, she hadn't been forced to take the pain medication prescribed for her headaches in months. Emotional stress, the doctor had said, was a trigger for her. The last time she'd battled frequent headaches had been when her mom and dad had briefly separated and she'd feared an eventual divorce.

It was the very last thing she or any of their family had ever imagined because it was so obvious her parents loved each other. The separation hadn't lasted long. Whatever their issues had been, they'd worked through them quickly and her dad had moved back into the apartment with her mom and they'd gone back to being the loving couple that Ashley had always witnessed.

But for the entire period of their separation, Ashley had been deeply unhappy and stressed and she'd battled headaches on a weekly basis. The doctor had counseled her on coming up with more effective ways to manage stress but Ashley had laughed. Now she realized she was as guilty as Devon had accused her of being when it came to wearing her feelings on her shoulder. She absorbed too much of the world around her and it affected her. That wasn't something she could change, could she?

She sighed. If she had any hope of not spending the next year in bed knocked out on medication, she was going to have to harden herself. She couldn't go around being a veritable sponge and reacting so emotionally to everything.

Her husband didn't love her? So what. She'd have to find a way to be happy. As Grammy always said, you make your nest now lie in it. Well, Ashley had certainly made the biggest, messiest nest of a marriage and now it was hers to wallow in.

As the medication wore off, she found it impossible to sleep. Her mind was buzzing with a mental list of everything she needed to do. Or not do. The list of things not to do was every bit as long as the list of things that needed to be done.

Learn to cook. That one popped uninvited into her head. She frowned because how did one simply learn to cook? Even Devon possessed rudimentary know-how in the kitchen. He could prepare simple dishes. She wasn't even sure she could boil water if necessary.

Okay that one should be simple enough. Pippa was a first-rate cook and it wouldn't be strange that Ashley would want to learn to cook a fabulous meal for her new husband. She could say she wanted to surprise him with a romantic meal for two.

And cooking shows. There was an entire television network devoted to cooking. Surely there was something she could watch there that would help.

Cleaning. Okay, she knew how to clean. She just didn't possess the organization skills to do it well. But she could muddle her way through it. It simply required discipline and less of a scatterbrain mentality.

She had to curb her tongue and her reactions. That should be simple enough. Smile and nod instead of shriek and wave her hands. Her mother was an expert at all the social graces but then she'd had to be with all the business functions she'd arranged and managed for her husband.

Ashley could certainly draw on the resources around her. She'd never particularly had a desire to be more like her family. She hadn't really considered that she was so different. She hadn't thought much about how she compared. Why would she? But they could help her. She just had to make sure she employed their help in a way that didn't give away the true reason for her transformation.

The door to Devon's office opened and he stepped out, looked her way and then started toward her.

"Can't sleep?" he asked. "Do you need anything?"

She shook her head and pulled the blanket closer to her chin. "I'm fine. Just getting comfortable."

He took a seat in the armchair across from the couch. Their gazes connected but she didn't look away, as tempted as she was. She couldn't keep avoiding him, no matter how desirable the prospect was.

It was hard for her because humiliation crept up her spine every time she had to face him, but eventually that would go away or she'd harden enough that it would no longer affect her. Or at least she hoped so.

"I spoke to your parents. Your mother is naturally concerned for you. She'd like you to call her when you're feeling up to it. Your father wants to see me in the morning, so if you're okay by then, I'll be out for a few hours."

"I'll be fine," she said softly. "Headache's gone. No reason for you to stay home and babysit me."

"If you need anything at all or if you begin to feel bad again, call me. I'll come home."

Hell would freeze over before she'd ever call him at work again, not that she'd tell him that. She nodded instead and sighed unhappily. So this is what her marriage boiled down to. A stilted, awkward conversation between two people who were clearly uncomfortable in each other's presence.

"Do you think you could eat something now?" Devon asked, breaking the strained silence. "What would you like?"

Deciding to take the olive branch, or perhaps create an olive branch out of a dinner offer, she shifted and pushed herself up so that her back was against the arm of the couch.

"You could cook, if you don't mind. I could sit at the bar and watch."

He looked surprised by her suggestion, but his surprise was quickly replaced by relief. He looked almost hopeful.

"That would be nice. Are you sure you're up for the noise and the light?"

Again she nodded. She hadn't talked this little since she'd been a nonverbal toddler. Her parents always swore that because she was late to talk she'd spent the rest of her life making up for lost time.

He stood and held down his hand to her. "Come on then. Bring the blanket with you if you're cold. You can sit on one of the bar stools and wrap it around you."

Hesitating only a brief moment, she slid her hand over his, enjoying the warmth of his touch. He curled his fingers around her wrist and helped her from the couch.

She stood up beside him but he waited a moment for her to get her footing.

"Okay?" he asked. "Fuzziness gone yet? I don't want you falling."

"I'm fine."

He didn't relinquish her hand as he started toward the kitchen. He guided her toward one of the stools and settled her down. He wrapped the blanket around her shoulders and tucked the ends underneath her arms.

"What's your pleasure tonight?"

He walked around to open the refrigerator, surveyed the contents and then glanced back at her.

It was probably another sign of her shortcomings that she had no idea what was or wasn't in the fridge. Heat singed her cheeks and she dropped her gaze. Tomorrow she'd take inventory. After she cleaned the house.

"Ash?"

She yanked her gaze back up. "Uh, I don't care. Honestly. I'll eat whatever."

"Oh, good. I've been dying to cook this cow's tongue before it goes bad."

She blinked for a moment before she realized he was teasing her. The memory of the night he'd first made love to her came back in a flash. The dinner they'd had when he'd asked her if she was a vegetarian.

Unbidden, a smile curved her lips. He smiled back at her, relief lightening his eyes.

"No?" he asked.

She shook her head. "No cow's tongue. But I'd eat his flank. Or his tuchus even."

"So you'll eat cow's ass but not his tongue," Devon said in mock exasperation.

Her smile grew a bit bigger and she leaned forward on the counter, resting her chin in her palm. This pretending felt nice. Who said denial was a bad thing?

If she could effectively put out of her mind the whole debacle that had been her honeymoon and take some time to work on her shortcomings, maybe at some point the pretense could become real. He could love her. He was committed to their marriage. It was a step. He was attentive, caring and he obviously hated to see her hurting. Those weren't the characteristics of a man who loathed her. So if he didn't hate her, and he seemed to like her well enough even if she annoyed him, then eventually, possibly, he could love her.

It was a hope she clung to because the alternative didn't bear thinking about. He didn't want a divorce, but she couldn't remain married to a man who could never love her. If she lost hope that he'd never reciprocate her feelings, it would signal the end of their marriage whether he wished it or not.

Devon tossed a package onto the counter and then returned

to the fridge, where he pulled out an onion, what looked like bell peppers in assorted colors and a box of mushrooms.

"How about I do stir-fry? It's quick and easy and pretty damn good if I do say so myself."

"Sounds yummy."

She watched him in silence and soon the sizzle of searing meat filled the room. While the meat cooked, he sliced the vegetables. He stopped to give the meat a brisk stirring and then returned to the cutting board.

She decided he looked good in the kitchen. Sleeves rolled up, top button undone, his brow creased in concentration. He was efficient, but then he seemed efficient at everything he did. She wondered if there was anything he wasn't accomplished at. Was he one of those people who could pick up anything and do it well?

"Name one thing you suck at," she blurted out.

Then she promptly groaned inwardly because this was precisely what she wasn't supposed to be doing. She had to demonstrate more…control. More decorum. Or at least stop blurting out her first reaction to everything.

He glanced up, his brows drawn together as if he wasn't sure if he'd heard her correctly. "Say that again?"

She shook her head. No way. "It was stupid. Just forget it."

He put down the knife, glanced over at the skillet and then returned his gaze to her. "Why would you want to know something I suck at?"

She closed her eyes and wished the floor would just open up and swallow her. So much for her campaign to become less… everything on his complaint list about her.

"Ash? Come on. Don't leave me hanging here."

She sighed. "Look, it was a stupid question. It's just that you seem like one of these people who is good at everything. You know, a person who can pick up something and just do it and do it well. I just wanted to know one thing you suck at. Gives hope to us mere mortals."

He shrugged. "I suck at lots of things. I'm definitely not one of those people who is good at everything. I've had to work hard for everything I've earned."

This was going from bad to worse. "It didn't come out right, Dev, okay? Can we just forget it? I wasn't insinuating that you haven't worked hard. I think it's evident that you've worked for everything you have. That wasn't what I meant at all. Sorry."

She pushed her hand into her hair and focused her stare down at the countertop. Running out of the room seemed overly dramatic even if it was what she wanted more than anything.

"Then what did you mean?"

There wasn't any anger or irritation in his voice. Just simple, casual curiosity. She chanced a peek back up at him to gauge his expression.

"Well, like cooking. You seem good at that. I just wanted to know something you aren't good at. You seemed to me to be one of those people who have a natural ability to pick up on things. You know, like sports. You ever see kids who just pick up a ball and know how to play? I bet you were one of those."

He groaned. "Oh, man. Clearly you've never watched me try to play basketball. And I say try, but that's probably not even an accurate word to use. Rafael, Ryan and Cam like to torture me at least once a year when they drag me down to play a 'friendly' game of basketball. What it really is is an opportunity for them to pay me back for every imagined slight. And then they don't let me forget it for the next six months."

"So you aren't good at basketball? Is that what you're saying?"

"Yeah. That's exactly what I'm saying."

She smiled. "Oh. Well, that's okay because I'm terrible at it, too."

He smiled back at her and then tossed the vegetables into the pan he'd taken the meat out of. "We can be terrible together then."

"Yeah," she said quietly.

He busied himself finishing up the meal and five minutes later, he set a plate in front of her while he stood on the other side of the bar, leaning back against the sink while he held his plate.

She looked up and frowned. "Not going to sit down?"

"I like watching you," he said as his gaze slid over her face. "I'd prefer to be across from you."

Her cheeks warmed and she quickly looked back down at her plate. She had no response for that. It puzzled her that he'd say such a thing.

But maybe he was trying. Like she was trying. Just as she would be trying as she embarked on her to do list the next day.

It wouldn't happen overnight, but maybe...one day.

Thirteen

Ashley woke with a muggy hangover feeling but then who wouldn't after two days in a medication-induced coma?

Today was the first day in her bid to take over the world. Well, sort of. Or rather it was her attempt to *not* take on the world quite so much. *Reserve* and *caution* were her two new friends.

There would be no more lying around and feeling sorry for herself.

Devon had exited the apartment early. The previous night had been a study in awkwardness.

He'd crawled into bed next to her and they'd lain quietly in the dark until finally she'd drifted off to a troubled sleep. Sometime during the night, he'd drifted toward her, or maybe she'd attacked him in her sleep. Either way, she'd ended up in his arms and had awakened when he'd gotten up early to shower.

He'd kissed her on the head and murmured for her to go back to sleep before leaving her alone.

"Welcome to your new reality," she murmured as she pushed herself out of bed.

She spent her entire time in the shower lecturing herself on how her situation was what she made of it. It could be horrible or she could salvage it. It was just according to how much effort she wanted to invest in her own happiness. Put that way, she could hardly say to hell with it and stomp off.

She winced when she caught sight of herself in the mirror. She looked bad. Not in one of those ways where she really didn't look so bad but said so anyway. She honestly looked like death warmed over. There were dark circles under her eyes. There was a line around her mouth from having her jaw set so firmly. Her unhappiness was etched on her face for the world to see. She'd never been good at hiding any kind of emotion. She was as transparent as plastic wrap.

Thank goodness for Carly and her never-ending list of tips for any type of makeup emergency. This definitely called for the full treatment.

When she was finished with her hair and makeup she was satisfied to see that at least she didn't look quite so haggard. Tired, yes, but that could easily be explained away by the headache. Surely an ecstatic new bride would smile her way through even the worst of migraines.

First stop was her mother's, since if Gloria Copeland didn't soon hear from her chick, she'd move Manhattan to get there to make sure all was well. After that was tackled, she had work to do. A lot of work.

She took a cab over to her former apartment building and smiled when Alex hurried to greet her.

"How are you, Miss Ashley? How is married life treating you?"

It was a standard question that would likely be asked of her a hundred more times before the week was out. Right after the one where most people would ask her why the hell she was back home after only two nights on her honeymoon.

"I'm good, Alex. Here to see my mother. Will you ring up and let her know I'm on my way?"

A moment later, Ashley stepped off the elevator and into the spacious apartment that very nearly occupied an entire floor. It was where she had spent a large portion of her childhood and it still felt like home to her no matter that she'd moved out on her own some time ago.

"Ashley, darling!" her mother cried as she hurried to greet her daughter. "Oh, you poor, poor darling. Come here and let me see you. Is your headache better? I knew there was simply too much excitement going on with the wedding and your moving and all the other plans. I worried it would prove to be too much for you. We should have spaced out the arrangements better."

Her mom enveloped her in a hug and for a long moment, Ashley clung to the comfort that only a mother could offer when her world was otherwise crap.

"Ashley?" her mother asked in a concerned, hushed tone when they finally pulled apart. "Is everything all right? Come, sit down. You don't even look like yourself today."

Ashley allowed herself to be pulled over to the comfortable leather couch. It smelled like home. She settled back and immediately burrowed into the corner, allowing the familiarity to surround her like a blanket.

"I'm fine, Mama. Really. I think you were right. There's been so much excitement and stress that when we finally got to St. Angelo I just crashed. Poor Devon was stuck taking care of me while I was insensible from the medication."

"As he should have. I'm glad he took good care of my baby for me. Are you feeling better now? You're pale and there are dark smudges under your eyes."

So much for Carly's awesome makeup tips.

"I'm better. I just wanted to come over so you wouldn't worry. I have to go back soon. There's a lot I need to do in our apartment to get everything squared away."

Her mom patted her on the arm. "Of course. But first, let me fix you a nice cup of hot tea."

"Spiced tea?" Ashley asked hopefully.

Her mother smiled. "With a peppermint."

Ashley sighed and relaxed into the couch, more than willing to allow her mom to fuss over her and baby her before she crawled back into the real world. If only manufacturers could package a mom's TLC into a box of bandages, they'd make millions.

Think of the marketing opportunities. Life sucks? Slap a mom bandage on and everything's instantly better.

A few minutes later, Ashley's mother returned carrying a tray that she set on the coffee table in front of Ashley. She handed her a cup of steaming tea and then unwrapped a peppermint that Ashley dropped into the bottom.

Ashley studied her mom as she settled back onto the couch, her own cup of tea in hand. "Mom? What happened between you and dad?"

Her mom reacted in surprise and cast Ashley a startled glance as she set her teacup back on its saucer. "Whatever do you mean, darling?"

"When you separated that time. I never asked because honestly I wanted to forget it ever happened. But now that I'm married... I just wanted to know. You two have always seemed so in love."

Her mother's eyes softened and she leaned forward to put her cup down on the coffee table. Then she turned and gathered Ashley's free hand in hers.

"It's natural for you to worry about those things now that you're married yourself. But darling, don't dwell on them."

"I know, but it just seems like that if it could happen to you and Daddy that it could happen to anyone. Was he having an affair? Did you forgive him?"

"Oh, good Lord, no!" She sighed and shook her head. "I know it was difficult for you and Eric, but especially for you. I never imagined that you'd think something like that, though. I should have guessed. I was so determined not to drag you children into our mess and thought I was doing the best thing by protecting you from any of the details. I can see I was wrong."

"What happened then?" Ashley asked softly.

"Oh it sounds so silly now. But back then I was convinced that my marriage was over. Your father was doing what he's always done. The difference was, suddenly it wasn't good enough for me. I began to worry. Maybe it's normal to go through a stage where you question what you want out of a relationship or worry that perhaps your partner doesn't love or value you anymore. Your father was working a lot of long hours. He was traveling constantly. You and Eric were adults and were going your own way and suddenly I found myself feeling quite alone and no longer valuable."

"Oh, Mama. I wish I had known," Ashley said unhappily. "That sounds so very awful for you."

Her mom smiled. "It was at the time but it wasn't entirely your father's fault. He was caught completely off guard when he returned home only to discover that I'd moved his things out and he had to find another place to live. He begged me to tell him what was wrong, what he'd done wrong, how he could fix it. But the truth was, I didn't even know myself. I just knew I was unhappy and that I no longer knew what I wanted from my marriage or my husband. If I didn't know, how could he?"

"What did you do?"

"I refused to speak to him for a week. It wasn't that I was angry. I just didn't know what to say to him. I took that time to think about and articulate what it was I wanted to say to him. And during that time, I realized that it wasn't him that I needed to change. It was me. I needed to find what was going to make me happy and he couldn't do it for me.

"When I finally agreed to see him, the poor man looked like death warmed over. I felt so guilty for the way I'd made him suffer but I knew we'd never last if I couldn't get myself

together. I asked him for a period of separation. He was adamantly opposed. It wasn't until I gently reminded him that I
didn't need his permission and that we were already separated
that he backed off."

Ashley frowned. "I always assumed…I mean I just thought
that it was Daddy's decision to move out. I always wondered
if there was another woman."

Her mom twisted her lips in a regretful frown. "Yes, it's
what Eric thought too, unfortunately. He was furious with your
father. It wasn't until I explained things to him that he calmed
down. Then I think he was angry with me for making your
father move out. Eric is very black-and-white."

"Yes, I know," Ashley said with a grimace. She took another
sip of her tea and then looked back at her mom. "So what happened? What made you decide to let him move back in?"

Her mom sighed and a faraway look entered her eyes. "We
were separated for six months and in a way, those six months
were some of the best times of my life."

Ashley's eyes widened. "But Mama!"

"I know, I know, but listen to me. I didn't say they were
easy. They weren't. But those six months outlined to me in
clear detail what I wanted my life to be. And who I wanted to
spend it with. I had opportunities. There were plenty of men
who flirted with me and would have jumped at the opportunity to date or have an affair."

Ashley's mouth dropped open and her mother smiled at her
reaction. "Darling, you don't think the need for sex goes away
when you hit thirty, do you?"

"Oh, my God," Ashley muttered. "I'm so not hearing my
mother talk about all the hot guys she had a chance with while
she was separated from my father."

"I had opportunity, yes, but I couldn't do it," her mom said.

"Because you loved Daddy?"

"Because it would have been dishonorable. Your father
didn't deserve it. Because I honestly didn't want to be with

anyone other than him. And I realized that I'd been blaming him for my own unhappiness. It was easy to say he'd been neglecting me or that he spent too much time at work. But the truth was, after you children grew up and left the nest, I simply didn't know what it was I wanted to do next. And I took out my frustrations on the closest available target because I didn't want to take responsibility for my own failures and feelings of inadequacy."

"Wow, I never realized…"

Her mom smiled and reached up to touch her cheek. "What, that I'm human like everyone else? That your mom isn't perfect?"

"Well, yeah, I guess," Ashley said lamely. "It's a totally shocking discovery. You may not survive the fall from the mom pedestal."

Her mom laughed and tweaked Ashley's nose. "Such a smart alec like your father. I always thought you were so much like him."

"What? I'm nothing like Daddy. He'd probably be horrified to hear you say that. He despairs of me because I have no head for or interest in business."

Her mom smiled indulgently. "But you have a huge heart like your father does and when you love, you love with everything you have. Just like William. He was devastated when I asked him to leave. And even though I knew I absolutely had to do what I did, it was the most difficult decision I've ever made. Our marriage is better for it. When we got back together, I was a stronger, more confident woman. I didn't need him to make me complete. I wanted him. But I didn't need him and therein was the difference."

Ashley set aside her cup and then impulsively threw her arms around her mom in a hug. "I love you, Mama. Thank you for talking to me. It was just what I needed today."

Her mother stroked her hand over Ashley's hair and hugged

her back. "You're welcome, darling, and I love you, too. You know I'm always right here if you need me."

Devon sat across from William Copeland as William completed his order with the waitress. The two had met at William's favorite place to eat lunch, but Devon wasn't in the least bit hungry.

"You not eating, son?" William asked as the waitress looked expectantly in Devon's direction.

"I'll just have a glass of water," Devon said.

After the waitress left, William leaned back and for a moment looked visibly discomfited.

"I wanted to talk to you about some changes in the organization."

Alarm bells clanged in Devon's already aching head. Two nights without decent sleep and the image of Ashley's tearstained face were wearing on him. The very last thing he needed was the old man to renege on their agreement. Wouldn't that be the height of irony?

He must have seen the wariness on Devon's face because he quickly went on.

"It's not what you think. I want you to take over my position at Copeland. I know the merger with Tricorp wasn't supposed to be splashy, that we agreed to keep the Copeland name and that Tricorp would be more of a silent party, but I'm ready to resign and I want you to take my position."

Devon shook his head in confusion. "I don't understand."

William sighed wearily. "I'm sick, son. I've been having health issues. I've been trying to see to matters because I want my family provided for. I want Eric to have a position but he isn't ready to take over. And the thing is, I'm not sure he wants his future locked into the family business. Lately he's hinted that his interests lie in other areas. And Ashley… It's why I pushed so hard for the marriage to take place. I wanted her settled with a man I trusted and whom I knew would take good care of her. If it got out that my health was failing, the vultures would have descended and she would have been easy pickings."

"Sick?" Devon managed to get out. "How sick?"

"I don't know yet. I won't lie. I've been in denial. I haven't even discussed this with Gloria and she's going to hit the ceiling when she finds out. I'm not ready to die yet, though. I want a lot of years with my children and eventual grandchildren. I spent decades working my ass off to get where I am and now I want to retire and enjoy time with my wife and watch my grandchildren play. But in order to do all that, I have to make sure my company is in good hands. I don't want Copeland to die, which is why I wanted this merger so badly. It wasn't Tricorp I was after. To be honest I could have picked a dozen other companies who would bring as much to the table. But I went with Tricorp because of you. You're who I want for my daughter and my company."

"Jesus, I don't even know what to say," Devon muttered. "This is quite the bomb to drop the day after I return from an aborted honeymoon."

"I know you thought I was a crazy old man for making Ashley part of this deal. And that I'm a manipulative bastard. You'd be right on that count. I knew you wanted this partnership. I knew you wanted the Copeland name for the line of resorts you've envisioned. I also knew what I wanted. It just so happened that our wants aligned perfectly. And my children are provided for."

"Everyone but Ashley," Devon said quietly.

William looked up sharply. "What do you mean?"

"She wanted a husband who adores her, who loves her, who is the embodiment of all she's dreamed of."

"So? Any reason you can't be that man?"

It was a good question and one he wasn't sure how to answer. He rubbed his hand through his hair. "How soon are you wanting all of this done?"

"I want to tender my resignation as soon as everything is done. It won't be a secret that I'll want you to take over. Voting won't be an issue. You'll be the most logical person to take over when I retire. I hold a lot of sway over the board. They'll listen to me. I'm going to make a doctor's appointment and then tell my wife so she can rearrange my teeth for me and then drag me to the doctor. After that, she'll take over and I won't be able to scratch my ass without her permission."

The words were said with wry wit, but it was obvious from the warmth in William's eyes that he adored his wife beyond reason and absolutely didn't mind giving up control to her in his retirement.

The older man seemed totally at peace with his actions and decisions and Devon wondered how much he could really fault his father-in-law for taking steps to ensure that his family was provided for. Even if he didn't agree with the methods. Would he have done the same for his son or daughter?

He liked to think that he'd offer them something better than the occasional reminder not to "screw up."

The image of Ashley, round and lush with his child, conjured a powerful surge of emotion. He realized in an instant that he'd do whatever it took to protect a son or daughter.

"Take care of yourself," Devon said gruffly, suddenly unsteady at the idea of something happening to a man who'd seemed so determined to be a second father to him. "I'll expect you to spoil our children."

William's expression eased into a broad smile. "Planning to provide me with them soon?"

Devon shrugged. "Maybe. That'll be up to Ash. I just want her to be happy."

William nodded. "So do I, son. So do I."

They were interrupted by the waitress bringing William's entrée to the table. For a moment, William fussed over his food and then he looked up at Devon again. "I'd like you to plan a cocktail party. It'll give Ashley a chance to play hostess. I'm thinking a couple weeks out at most. I want to go ahead and announce that I'm planning to retire and that you're my choice to succeed me. I want this all to seem like a natural progression of the merger. A changing of the guard with my blessing."

"We can do that," Devon said. Or at least he hoped. Maybe by that time Ashley wouldn't be quite so upset. Right now, asking her to appear happy for an entire night in front of dozens of guests seemed unreasonable at best.

"Good. We'll talk more later and I'll give you a guest list and of course you'll have your own colleagues to invite. I just want to say again how happy I am to have you as my son-in-law. I knew from the moment I met you that you'd not only be the best thing for my company, but for my daughter as well."

Fourteen

When Devon walked into his apartment, he immediately noticed the change. There wasn't any clutter. No magazines strewn about. No shoes littering the floor. No purse hanging from a doorknob. And he could smell cleaning solution.

As he walked farther inside, his stomach knotted because not only was everything picked up, but he also realized that the apartment was completely and utterly devoid of Ashley's presence. All of the things she'd moved in and haphazardly decorated with had been put away. No silly knickknacks on the coffee or end tables.

The apartment looked precisely as it had before she moved in.

Has she packed up and left? Had she decided not to give their marriage a chance?

He experienced a faint sensation of illness. His stomach tightened with dread and the beginnings of panic gripped his throat.

Then he heard a distant sound that seemed to come from

the kitchen. He strode in that direction and realized that a television had been left on. But when he reached the doorway, he had to grip the frame to steady himself.

Relief blew through him with staggering ferocity.

She was still here.

She hadn't left.

She was sitting at the bar, her brow furrowed in concentration as she watched a cooking show. She had a notepad and pencil in front of her and she was furiously taking notes.

As his gaze took in the rest of the kitchen, he realized that she'd evidently spent the day cleaning. The surfaces sparkled. The floor shone. The scent of lemon was heavy in the air.

She was dressed in faded jeans and an old T-shirt. Her hair was pulled back into a ponytail and she wasn't wearing any makeup.

She looked absolutely beautiful.

But she also looked tired. The dark circles under her eyes were more pronounced and she had a delicate fragileness to her that made him instinctively protective of her. But he couldn't protect her from himself and it was he who had hurt her.

Drawn to the vulnerable image she presented, he slid his hands up her arms and then lowered his mouth to kiss her on the neck.

She froze immediately then turned swiftly around. "Hi," she offered hesitantly. "I didn't expect you back quite so soon."

"Technically I'm off this week," he said as he pulled away. "I had lunch with your father. We discussed business and now I'm done."

She made a face but didn't comment, which he was grateful for. Anytime her father and business were mentioned, it was going to be difficult, but the more he did it in passing, maybe it would lessen the sting.

"What happened to all your stuff?" he asked casually as he went around to open the fridge. He pulled out a bottle of water and pushed the door closed.

"Oh, I just organized everything," she said. "I didn't really have time before the wedding. Was too busy with other stuff."

"Mmm-hmm," he murmured. "And the cleaning? Should you have been doing all this today? You just came off a pretty bad headache. I wouldn't think all the cleaning stuff would be good for you to be inhaling."

"It was okay. Headache is gone. Just a little residual achiness."

He frowned. "Why don't you go lie on the couch. I'll figure out dinner and we'll watch some TV or just relax in the living room if you don't want the noise."

She rose from the stool. "No, no, I've got dinner planned. Are you hungry already? What time did you want to eat?"

Perplexed by her sudden agitation, he hastily backed off. It appeared she was at least trying for a semblance of normalcy and that relieved him. Maybe after the initial storm passed and she had time to think she'd see that nothing had changed between them.

In light of today's conversation with William Copeland, Devon was on the verge of accomplishing all his goals. And at a much faster rate than he'd ever planned. Five years down the road was here now. Copeland Hotels would be his. His dream of launching a new luxury chain of exclusive resorts under one of the oldest and most respected names in the business would be realized. He'd have a wife. Children. A family. He'd have it all.

The surge of triumph was so forceful he felt drunk with it.

"I'm in no hurry," he soothed. "Why don't we sit down and have a drink. What are you cooking?"

A dull flush worked over her face. "I'm not. At least not tonight I mean. I will another time. I thought I'd call for takeout. It's almost like a home-cooked meal but they bring it and set it up."

"Sounds wonderful. Thank you. I think a nice quiet dinner at home would be fantastic after the week we've had. We didn't really get to see each other much in the days leading up to the wedding. We can start making up for that now."

Pain flashed in her eyes but she remained quiet, almost as if she was dealing with the sudden reminder of their circumstances. He hated it. Wished he could wipe it from her memory. In time, it would fade. If he showed her that they could have a comfortable relationship, some of the rawness of her emotions would settle and they could go back to the easy camaraderie they'd shared before everything went to hell.

She squared her shoulders as if reaching a decision and then tilted her chin upward. "You go on out and have a seat. Would you like wine? Or do you want me to mix up something for you?"

He opened his mouth to tell her that he'd take care of it, but something in her eyes stopped him. There was a quiet desperation, almost as if she was barely clinging to her composure.

"Wine would be great," he said softly. "You choose something for both of us. I like everything I've stocked here so I'm good with whatever you pick out."

He left the kitchen, his chest tight. The next weeks were going to suck as they found their way in the new reality of their relationship. He had confidence that it would work out, though. He just had to be patient.

A few minutes later, Ashley came into the living room carrying two wineglasses and a bottle of unopened wine. She looked disgruntled as she set the glasses down on the coffee table.

"Can you open the wine?" she asked hesitantly. "I couldn't get the bottle opener to work properly. I'm sure I'm not doing it right."

He reached for the bottle and let his fingers glide over hers. "Relax, Ash. Take a seat. I'll pour."

Reluctantly she backtracked and sank down onto the couch. In truth she still didn't look well and it wouldn't surprise him if her head was still hurting her. Her brow was wrinkled and she looked tired. Maybe a glass of wine would ease some of her tension.

He opened the bottle and then poured a glass for her first. After pouring his own, he set the glass on the table and took a seat in the armchair diagonal to where she sat on the couch.

"Your father wants us to host a cocktail party in a week or two," he said.

"Us?" she squeaked. "As in you and me? Why wouldn't he want Mama to host it? She's awesome at hosting parties. Everyone always talks about how much fun they have when she throws a get-together."

"He's going to be announcing some changes at Copeland soon and this is his way of easing into that. Your father is looking at taking a less active role in the managing of things. He's ready to retire and focus on his family."

She looked despondent.

"Ash, this isn't a big deal. Most of the people who'll attend are people we already know. We'll pick a nice venue, have it catered, hire a band. It'll be great."

She held up her hand. "I'll handle it. No problem. I don't want you to worry about it. I just need to know exactly when. I'm sure you and Daddy will be busy with…whatever it is you're busy with. Mama always handled parties for Daddy. No reason I can't do it for you."

The dismay in her voice troubled him. He thought it rather sounded like she would be planning a funeral, but he wasn't about to shut her down when she was making such an effort. That she was so willing to try when it was obvious he'd crushed her endeared her to him all the more.

"I'm sure whatever you come up with, I and the others will love," he said.

She took a long drink of her wine, nearly draining the glass.

"Want to watch a movie?" he suggested.

She nodded as she put her wineglass back on the coffee table. "Sure. Whatever you want to put on is fine."

He picked up the remote but he didn't return to his own chair. He eased onto the couch next to her and put his arm along the top of the sofa behind her head.

For a long moment she sat there stiffly, almost as if she wasn't sure what she was supposed to do. He cursed the awkwardness between them. Before she wouldn't have hesitated to burrow underneath him and snuggle in tight. She'd drape herself over him when they watched movies. She would have kissed him, hugged him and generally mauled him with affection through the entire show.

Now she sat beside him like a statue, tension and fatigue radiating from her like a beacon.

"Come here," he murmured, pulling her underneath his arm. "That's better," he said when she finally relaxed against him and laid her cheek on his chest.

They were silent as the movie played and he was fine with that. There wasn't a lot he could say. There were only so many times he could apologize or tell her he hadn't meant to hurt her.

It wasn't the movie that captured his attention, though. He sat there enjoying her scent. Her hair always smelled like honeysuckle. Even in winter in the city. She had an airy, floral scent that clung to her. It suited her.

And he loved the feel of her next to him. He hadn't realized how much until he'd spent the last several days with a wall between them.

He touched her hair, idly sifting through the strands with his fingers, savoring the sensation of silk over his skin. By the time the credits rolled, he couldn't have even said what the movie was about. He hadn't cared.

"Ash, are you sure you don't want me to go out for some dinner?" He waited a moment. "Ash?"

He glanced down to see that she'd fallen sound asleep against his chest. Her lashes rested delicately on her cheeks and her lips were tight, almost as if she were deep in thought even at rest.

Gently he kissed her forehead and rested his chin there for a long moment. Somehow, someway, he would make it up to her. He was reaching the high point in his life and career where everything he'd worked so hard and so long for was his. And damn it, he wanted her to be on top of the world with him.

Fifteen

"This is hopeless," Ashley said as her shoulders sagged.

Pippa wrapped her arm around Ashley and squeezed tight. "You're not hopeless. You'll get it down. You're being way too hard on yourself."

"After three weeks, you'd think I'd be able to perform the simplest tasks in the kitchen," Ashley said forlornly. "Let's face it. I'm a culinary disaster."

"Are you all right, hon? You seem really down lately and not just about this cooking stuff. Is everything okay with you?"

Ashley smiled brightly and straightened her stance. "Oh, yeah, fine. Marriage is exhausting work. Who knew? Just trying to get my routine down. I've been spending my mornings at the shelter so I can be at home when Devon gets in from work. I keep hoping one of my meals will actually turn out but I keep having to call in backup."

Pippa laughed. "You're so silly. I don't even know why you're bothering learning to cook. Devon doesn't care if you can cook. The man's obviously crazy about you and you couldn't cook before you got married. I'm sure he's not expecting some miracle to occur."

Ashley bit her lip to keep from crying. The truth was, she was exhausted. Planning that damn cocktail party had turned out to be a giant pain in her ass. She was tempted to call her mother and beg for help but pride kept her from making that call.

The old Ashley would have laughed, thrown her hands up and admitted she was hopeless. The new Ashley was going to suck it up, be calm and get the job done.

"Are you coming to my party?" Ashley asked, suddenly worried she'd be surrounded by a sea of unfamiliar faces.

"Of course I am. I promised you I'd come. I know you're nervous, but really, this is your thing, Ash. You shine at social events. Everyone loves you and you're so sweet."

"Why don't you meet me at Tabitha's place the afternoon before. We'll get our hair done together. I'm aiming for a more sophisticated look for the party. You know, mature and married as opposed to young and flighty."

Pippa snorted. "Flighty?"

Ashley laughed it off but she knew well that Devon considered her a complete ditz.

"I need Carly's makeup skills, too."

"Honey, you aren't holding tea for the queen. You're hosting a cocktail party for friends and business associates. We already love you. And those who don't will. Stop tormenting yourself over this."

"I just don't want to look stupid," Ashley said.

Pippa shook her head. "I swear I don't know what's got into you lately. You're perfect and anyone who doesn't think so can kiss my ass."

"I love you," Ashley said, emotion knotting her throat.

Pippa hugged her fiercely and then pulled away. "Are you pregnant or something? I swear you're not usually so emotional."

"Oh, God, I don't think so. I mean it's possible but I haven't even kept up with my periods. I just remember being thrilled it wasn't going to happen on my honeymoon. You know, the one I ended up cutting short."

"Well, take one of those home pregnancy tests. You're a mess, Ash. Hormones have to be the reason why."

She closed her eyes. No, she couldn't be pregnant yet. Well, she certainly could, but she suddenly didn't want to be. But it was a little too late for that line of thinking. When was the last time she and Devon had made love anyway? Definitely before the wedding. But it was still too soon to tell.

"I'll give it a little more time," she said firmly. "I'm just a wreck over this stupid party. I feel like it's my first big test as Mrs. Devon Carter. I don't want to humiliate myself or him in front of a hundred people."

"Stop it," Pippa chided. "You're going to be awesome. Now, do you want to try this sauce again?"

Ashley sighed. "I'm thinking I should start out with something even easier. Sauces aren't my thing apparently. I keep ruining them."

"Okay, then let's try something different. Name something else you love to eat."

Ashley thought a minute. "Lasagna. That sounds really good right now."

"Perfect! And it couldn't be easier. I'll give you the easy recipe. You can always graduate to fancier once you've mastered the kid-friendly version."

"That's me," Ashley said in resignation. "The kid-friendly version."

Pippa swatted her with a towel. "Grab the hamburger meat from the fridge. I think we're down to the last pack so you better nail this one, girlfriend."

Half an hour later, Ashley put her fist in the air as she and Pippa stood back and closed the oven door on a perfect, if somewhat beleaguered, lasagna.

"I can totally do that on my own," Ashley said as Pippa wiped her hands. "I'm so excited! Maybe I'm not a complete lost cause."

Pippa shook her head. "All it takes is a little time and patience. You're going to be a culinary genius in no time."

Ashley threw her arms around her friend and hugged her tight. "Thanks, Pip. I love you, you know. You're the best."

Pippa grinned. "I love you, too, you nut. Now go home and make your lasagna before your husband gets there. Call me tomorrow and let me know how it went. And take that damn pregnancy test. I'll want to know if I'm going to be an aunt!"

Ashley rolled her eyes. She started to walk toward the door when her cell phone beeped, signaling a received text message. She pulled it out and then frowned as she read it.

"What is it, Ash?" Pippa asked.

"There's a problem at the shelter. Molly is upset but she doesn't give any info. I'll hop over on my way home. It's not too out of the way. See you Friday afternoon at Tabitha's."

"Okay, be careful and call me when you get home so I'll know you made it. You know I hate you going down to the shelter by yourself all the time."

"Yes, mother," Ashley replied. "Later, chickie."

With a wave, she disappeared from Pippa's apartment and headed down to catch a cab to the shelter.

It was later than he'd have liked when Devon entered the apartment. His day had been long and full of endless meetings and his ears were still throbbing from the number of people who'd talked to him.

The only person he wanted to see was Ashley, and he was looking forward to seeing what disaster she'd come up with for dinner.

He grinned as he loosened his tie and headed for the kitchen. The past weeks had been hilarious. Oddly, he hadn't minded the sheer number of ruined meals he'd been served. It had become a contest for him to correctly guess what the meal was *supposed* to have been.

He sniffed as he reached the doorway into the kitchen and the delicious aroma of…something…floated into his nostrils. It didn't smell burned. Or even slightly scorched. It smelled like gooey, bubbly cheese and a hint of tomato.

His stomach growled and he scanned the kitchen area for Ashley. He frowned when he realized she was nowhere to be seen. Deciding he'd better check on whatever was for dinner, he hurried to the oven and pulled open the door.

Inside was what looked to be a perfectly put together and perfectly cooked lasagna. He snagged a potholder and then reached inside to take out the casserole dish.

After setting it on the stove, he turned off the oven and then went in search of Ashley. As he neared the bedroom, he heard the low murmur of her voice.

She was standing by the window overlooking the city and she was on her cell phone. He started to detour into his closet to change when he heard a betraying sniff.

He spun around, frowning as he zeroed in on Ashley. Her back was mostly to him though she was angled just enough that he could see her wipe at one cheek.

What the hell?

It took all his restraint not to walk over, take the phone and demand to know who the hell had upset her.

"I'll see what I can do, Molly. We can't let this happen," she said.

She wiped her cheek with the back of her free hand and then hit the button to end the call. Then she turned and saw Devon. Her eyes widened in alarm and then she closed them in dismay.

"Oh, my God, the lasagna!"

She bolted for the door, gone before he could even tell her he'd already taken care of it. He was more concerned with what had made her cry.

"Ash!" he called as he hurried after her.

He caught up to her in the kitchen to find her palming her forehead as she stared at the lasagna.

"I'm sorry," she said. "I just forgot it. If you hadn't come in, it would have burned."

"Hey, it's okay," he said. He walked over and slipped a hand over her shoulder. "It needs to rest a minute anyway. Let me grab some plates and we'll set the table. Then you can tell me what's got you so upset. Who was that on the phone?"

He steered her toward the table, parked her in a chair and then went back to retrieve plates and utensils. After setting the places, he went back for the lasagna and carried the still piping hot dish to the table.

He sat down, picking up a knife to cut into the lasagna while he waited for her to respond. To his horror, her eyes filled with tears and she buried her face in her hands.

He dropped the knife and bit out a curse. Then he scrambled out of his chair and pulled it around so he could scoot up next to Ashley.

"What's wrong?" he demanded. "Did someone upset you?" Obviously someone or something did but he wanted answers. He wasn't a patient man. His inclination was to wade in and fix things. He couldn't do that if he didn't have the story.

"I've had the most awful day," she croaked out. "And I wanted everything to be perfect. I finally learned how to cook that damn lasagna. But then Molly called. I stopped by the shelter and she had terrible news and I don't know what to do. We've been talking about it all evening."

He gently pulled her hands away, wincing at the flood of tears soaking her cheeks.

"Who's Molly?"

She frowned and lifted her gaze to meet his. "Molly from the shelter."

He looked searchingly at her. Clearly this was a person he was supposed to know, but he was drawing a complete blank.

"She's my boss at the shelter."

"Wait a minute. I thought you ran the shelter."

She shook her head impatiently. "I do, mostly, but she's in charge. I mean she runs it but I do most of the legwork and fundraising. She says I have more connections and am the natural choice to go out and pound the pavement for donations."

Devon scowled. It sounded to him as though this Molly person was taking advantage of Ashley. He wasn't certain of the salary that Ashley drew from her position at the shelter. He assumed that her parents still helped her financially since she didn't have a typical nine-to-five job and she'd been living in her own apartment for a while now. He hadn't concerned himself with her finances because he wanted her to be happy and he knew he'd fully support her once they were married. But he sure as hell didn't want her busting her ass in a job where she was being used.

"So what did Molly have to say?" he gently prompted.

"The grant the shelter had is being pulled and without it, we can't continue to stay open. It pays the basics like the utilities, food for the animals and the salary for the vet we have on retainer. We don't raise enough money to stay afloat without the grant."

Her eyes filled with tears again. "If we don't stay open, all the animals will have to be transferred to a city-run shelter and if they aren't adopted out, they'll be euthanized."

Devon sighed and carefully pulled Ashley into his arms. "Surely there's some way to keep the shelter open. Have you talked to your father about sponsoring it?"

She pulled away and shook her head. "You don't understand. Daddy's all business when it comes to stuff like that. He doesn't make emotional decisions. He's more interested in profit and return or it being a cause he sees the value in. He's not much of an animal person."

Ashley's view of her father was clearly wrong. William Copeland had made an emotional decision. A huge emotional decision when he'd opted to go with Tricorp because for whatever reason he'd decided Devon would be the perfect son-in-law and candidate to take over Copeland.

"How long can you continue running as you are now?"

She sniffed. "Two, maybe three weeks. I'm not sure. We're already at maximum capacity but it's hard to say no when a new animal comes in. We just got in a dog and it was so heartbreaking. The poor thing is the sweetest dog ever but he was horribly neglected. I don't understand how people can be so cruel. Would they dump their child out on the street somewhere? A pet isn't any different. They're just as much a family member as a child!"

Unfortunately, there were people who'd think nothing of tossing out their kid, not that Ashley needed to be reminded of that. It would only upset her further.

He smoothed his hand over her cheek and then leaned forward to kiss her forehead. "Why don't you eat something. The lasagna smells wonderful. There's nothing you can do tonight. Maybe a solution will present itself in the morning."

She nodded morosely and he scooted his seat back. He picked the knife back up and cut into the lasagna, spooning out neat squares onto the plates.

"This looks wonderful," he said in a cheerful tone. He wanted her to smile again. She'd been entirely too serious ever since they returned from their honeymoon and he was becoming impatient for her to return to her usual, sunny self.

He handed her a plate and then took his own. When he bit into the gooey cheese and the perfectly al dente noodles, and the savory sauce slid over his tongue, he moaned in pleasure.

"This is awesome, Ash."

She smiled but it didn't quite reach her eyes. There was still deep sadness in those big, blue eyes and it was twisting his gut into a knot.

As good as dinner was, he was anxious to get through it. He had a sudden urge to comfort Ashley and wipe away her pain.

She picked at her food and it was obvious she had no interest in eating, so he hurriedly gulped his down and then collected their plates to dump into the sink. "Come here," he said, holding his hand out to her.

She slid her fingers into his and he pulled her to her feet. He took her into the bedroom, sat her on the edge of the bed and began taking her shoes off.

Crouching between her legs, he slid his hands along the sides of her thighs until his fingers palmed her hips. He held her there, staring intently at her, unable to believe he was about to make her a promise.

The business side of him balked and demanded to know if he'd lost his damn mind. But the side of him that cringed upon witnessing Ashley's distress was urging him on.

"Listen to me," he said, before he could talk himself out of it. "Let me see what I can do, okay? Don't give up hope just yet. We have a few weeks. I may be able to help."

To his surprise she threw her arms around him and hugged him fiercely. It was the first spontaneous show of affection he'd been treated to since before their marriage.

"Oh, Devon, thank you," she whispered fiercely. "You have no idea how much this would mean to me."

"I have an idea," he said wryly. "You love those animals more than you love people."

She nodded solemnly, not in the least bit abashed to admit it. Then she kissed him full on the mouth.

It was like baiting a hungry lion. He didn't wait for her to pull back in regret. Didn't offer her the chance to change her mind. He'd suffered three long weeks wanting her with every breath and knowing she was emotionally out of reach.

If this was his chance to have her back in his bed without a wealth of space between them, he was going to grab the opportunity with both hands.

He kissed her back, his hands going to her face, holding her there as he fed hungrily on her lips. Tentatively her arms circled his neck and she leaned into him with a soft, sweet sigh that tightened every one of his muscles and made him instantly hard.

He had to force himself to exercise some restraint because what he really wanted to do was tear her clothes off, haul her up the bed and make love to her until neither of them could walk.

"You have far too many clothes on," he said, near desperation as he fumbled with the buttons on her blouse. It was expensive. Probably silk. But ah, hell, he'd buy her another one.

The sound of the material rending and the buttons popping and scattering on the floor only spurred his excitement. He fumbled clumsily with the button on her pants and then began pulling to get them off her. She lifted her bottom just enough that he could slide the material down her legs and then there she was, sitting so dainty and beautiful, clad only in her pale, pink lingerie.

She was the most beautiful sight he'd ever seen. Hair tousled just enough to make her look sexy. Her lips swollen from his kiss. Eyes glazed with passion instead of deep sadness. And her skin. So soft, glowing in the lamplight. Curvy in all the right places. Generous breasts, straining at the lace cups, and hips and behind just the right size for his hands to grip.

He stood only long enough to strip out of his clothes. It wasn't practiced or smooth. He felt like a fifteen-year-old getting his first glimpse of a naked woman. If he wasn't careful, he'd be acting just like one, too.

She stared shyly up at him and he nearly groaned. "Baby, you have to stop looking at me like that. I'm holding on to my control by my fingertips and you're not helping."

She smiled then, an adorable, sweet smile that took his breath away. He forgot all about trying to maintain an air of civility. His inner caveman came barreling out, grunting and pounding his chest and muttering unintelligible words.

He swept her into his arms, hauling her back on the bed.

They landed with a soft bounce and he claimed her mouth, wanting to taste her again and again.

"Love the lingerie," he said hoarsely. "I'll love it more when it's off, though."

She wiggled beneath him and he realized she was trying to work out of her straps.

"Oh, no, let me," he breathed.

He pushed himself off her and then maneuvered himself upward so he straddled her body, his knees digging into the mattress on either side of her hips.

Her gaze slid downward to his groin and her eyes darkened. Tentatively she moved her hands slowly toward his straining erection. Color dusted her cheeks and she glanced hastily upward, almost as if she was seeking his permission to touch him.

Hell, he'd give her anything in the world if she'd touch him. He'd buy her twenty damn shelters if that would make her happy. Right now, it would make him delirious if she just wrapped those soft little fingers...

He closed his eyes and groaned as she did exactly what he'd fantasized about. Her touch was gentle. Light and tentative. Like the tips of butterfly wings dancing over his length.

She grew bolder, stroking more firmly, running the length of him with her palm until he was little more than a babbling, incoherent fool. He was supposed to be in control here. She was the innocent. He was the one with more experience. But she literally and figuratively held him in the palm of her hand.

If he didn't put an end to her inquisitive exploration, he'd find release on her belly and he wanted to be inside her more than he wanted to breathe.

Leaning down, her kissed the shallow indention between her breasts and then nuzzled the swell as he reached up to slide the straps over her shoulders.

He loved the way she smelled. It was one thing he missed about the apartment now. Before she had little bowls of potpourri and little scented candles haphazardly arranged throughout. The entire apartment had smelled like…her. Fresh. Vibrant. Like spring sunshine.

Now that she'd gone through in a mad cleaning rush, it was as if her very presence had been expunged.

The cup of her bra slipped over her nipple, exposing the puckered point to his seeking lips. He sucked lightly, enjoying the sensation of her on his tongue. Underneath him, she quivered and her breathing sped up in reaction.

He slipped one hand beneath her back, reaching for the clasp of her bra. Seconds later, it came free and he pulled carefully until it came completely away. Tossing it aside, he eyed the feast before him.

She had beautiful breasts. Just the perfect size. Small and dainty, much like her, but there was just enough plumpness to make a man's mouth water. Her nipples were a succulent pink that just beckoned him to taste. He knew enough about her now to know her breasts were highly sensitive. And her neck. Up high, just below her ear. It was guaranteed to drive her crazy if he nibbled either spot.

Tonight he wanted to taste all of her, though. He wanted her imprinted on his tongue, his senses. He wanted to be able to fall asleep smelling her, the feel of her skin on his.

Palming both breasts, he caressed, rubbed his thumbs across the tips before lowering his head to suck at one and then the other. He nipped lightly, causing the peak to harden even further. Then he slid his mouth down her middle to the softness of her belly, where he licked a damp circle around her navel.

Chill bumps rose and danced their way across her rib cage. She stirred restlessly, murmuring what sounded like a plea for more.

He thumbed the thin lace band of her panties and carefully eased the delicate material over her hips then down her legs and over her feet. Finally, she was completely naked to his avid gaze.

He moved back over her, his head hovering over the soft nest of blond curls between her legs. Then he stroked his hands over her hips and downward. He spread her thighs with firm hands, opening her to his advances.

All that pink, glistening flesh beckoned. He lowered his mouth, pressed his lips to the soft folds and nuzzled softly until she strained upward to meet him.

"Devon," she whispered.

It had been a while since he'd heard her husky sweet voice murmur his name in what was a blend of pleasure and a plea for more. It made him all the more determined that before he was finished, she'd call out his name a dozen more times. She'd find her release with his name on her lips. There would be no doubt in her mind who possessed her.

He licked gently at the tiny nub surrounded by silken folds, enjoying every jitter and shudder that rolled through her body. She was more than ready to take him, but he held back, enjoying his sensual exploration of her most intimate flesh.

Slowly he worked downward until he tasted the very heart of her, stroking with lazy, seductive swipes of his tongue. She began to shake uncontrollably and her thighs tightened around his head. He pressed one last kiss to the mouth of her opening and then moved up her body, positioning himself between her legs.

He found her heat and sank inside her with one powerful thrust. Her chin went up, her eyes closed and her lips tightened in an expression that was almost agonizing.

He kissed the dimple in her chin and then slid his mouth down her neck and to the delicate hollow of her throat. Her pulse beat wildly, jumping against her pale skin, a staccato against his mouth.

Her slender arms went around him, gripping with surprising strength. Her nails dug into his shoulders like kitten claws.

"Put your legs around me," he said. "Just like that, baby. Perfect."

She crossed her heels at the small of his back and arched into each thrust. Her fingers danced their way across his back, sometimes light and then scoring his flesh when he thrust again. She thrust one hand into his hair, pulling forcefully until he realized she was demanding his kiss.

With a light chuckle, he gave in to her silent demand and found her mouth.

Breathless. Sweet. Their tongues worked hotly over each other, dueling, fighting for dominance. She had suddenly become the aggressor and he was lost, unable to deny her anything.

She was wrapped around him, her body urging him on, arching to meet him and finding a perfect rhythm so they moved as one.

Sex had never been this…perfect.

"Are you close?" he choked out.

"Don't stop," she begged.

"Oh hell, I'm not."

He closed his eyes and thrust hard and deep. And then he began working his hips against hers in rapid, urgent movements. She let out a strangled cry and he remembered his vow.

"My name," he said in a breathless pant. "Say my name."

"Devon!"

She came apart in his arms. Around him. Underneath him. He was bathed in liquid heat and he'd never felt anything so damn good in his life.

"Ashley," he whispered. "My Ashley. Mine."

He unraveled at light speed, his release sharp, bewildering and beautiful. His hips were still convulsively moving against her body as he settled down over her, too exhausted and spent to remember his own name. The one he'd demanded she say just moments ago.

He became aware of gentle caresses. Her hands gently stroking over his back. He was probably crushing her but he couldn't bring himself to move. He was inside her. Over her. Completely covering her. She was his.

He knew this moment was significant. Something had changed. But his mind was too numb to sort out the meaning. Never before had he been so undone after making love to a woman.

It was supremely satisfying and scary as hell.

Sixteen

Ashley surveyed the guests as they filtered into the upscale restaurant she'd rented out for the night and felt the ache inside her head bloom more rapidly. She was so nervous she wanted to puke. She wanted everything to be perfect and for things to go off without a hitch.

She'd spent the afternoon at Tabitha's getting hair and makeup done. Her friends had been skeptical of the look she wanted but in the end they hadn't argued and then told her how fabulous she looked.

Ashley wanted…sophisticated. Something that didn't scream flighty, exuberant or impulsive. This was her night to prove to Devon that she was the consummate hostess and perfect complement to him.

Her dress was, as she'd been assured, the perfect little black dress. Ridiculous as it sounded, it was the first such dress that Ashley had owned. For Ashley, wearing black was the equivalent of going to a funeral. It made her feel subdued and swal-

lowed up. Somber. She much preferred brighter, more cheerful colors.

As for her hair, she never paid much attention to it and wore
it down more often than not, or she just flipped it up in a clip
and went on her way.

But Tabitha had spent an hour fashioning an elegant knot,
without a hair out of place. Pippa had grumbled that it made
her look forty and not the young twenty-something she was.

Carly had applied light makeup using muted shades and
Ashley wore pale lip gloss instead of her usual shiny pink. The
perfect accompaniment to the dress and hair were the pearls
her grandmother had given her before she passed away two
years ago.

She wore a simple strand around her neck and a tiny cluster
at her ears.

Ashley thought she looked perfect. She just hoped everyone
else did as well and that she could pull off the evening with a
smile.

Across the room, the jazz ensemble played. Waiters circled
the room, offering hors d'oeuvres and a choice of white and red
wines. Two bartenders manned the open bar and in addition
to the appetizers offered by the waiters, there was an elegant
buffet arranged by the far wall.

Lights were strung in the fake potted trees, making the
room look festive and bright. Flickering candles illuminated
centerpieces of fresh flowers on each table.

Ashley had fretted endlessly over all the arrangements until
she was sure she was spouting menu choices in her sleep. She'd
tasted each and every one of the appetizers, wrinkling her
nose at some, loving others. She'd made Pippa accompany her,
though, because Pippa's tastes were more refined. Ashley was
pickier and more apt to turn her nose up at fine cuisine.

Now the moment had arrived and though she kept telling
herself that these people didn't matter to her and that they were
her father's and Devon's associates, she couldn't shake the par-

alyzing fear that she'd make some huge mistake and embarrass herself and her husband in front of everyone.

"Ashley, there you are," Pippa said as she made her way through the growing crowd.

"Oh, my God, I'm so glad you're here," Ashley said. "Thank you for coming. I'm a nervous wreck."

Pippa frowned. "Ash, there's no reason for you to be so worked up over this. It's a party. Loosen up. Have some fun. Let your hair down from that godawful bun."

Ashley let out a shaky laugh. "Easy for you to say. You aren't facing a hundred of your husband's closest business associates."

Pippa rolled her eyes. "Come on, let's go get a drink."

Ashley let Pippa lead her over to the bar but when they got there, Ashley ordered water. Pippa raised an eyebrow and Ashley sighed.

"I have a doctor's appointment tomorrow," Ashley whispered. "Don't you dare say a word to anyone, okay? I haven't told anyone I even suspect I might be pregnant. I took one of those damn home pregnancy tests and it was inconclusive but I haven't had my period yet and I'm sure I'm late. So until I know, I don't want to drink anything."

"What time is your appointment?" Pippa demanded.

"Ten in the morning."

"Okay, then here's what's going to happen. Carly, Tabitha and I are going to wait for you at Oscar's and you're going to come straight over for lunch after your appointment so you can tell us the news one way or another."

Ashley nodded. "Okay. I'll need the support regardless of the outcome. I'm kind of undecided about this whole thing."

Pippa blinked in surprise. "You mean you aren't sure you want to be pregnant?"

"Yes. No. Maybe. I don't know," she said miserably.

"Ash, what the hell is going on with you lately? All you've ever wanted is to have children."

Ashley bit her lip in consternation as she saw Devon making his way toward her. "Look, I can't talk about it now. I'll see you at lunch tomorrow after my appointment. And don't breathe a word! I haven't told anyone. Not even Dev."

Pippa looked at her oddly but went silent as Devon approached.

"There you are," Devon said when he got to the two women. He kissed Pippa's cheek in greeting and then tucked Ashley's hand in his. "If you don't mind, Pippa, I'm going to steal my wife for a bit. There are some people I want her to meet."

Pippa leaned over to kiss Ashley's cheek. "See you tomorrow," she whispered softly. "Take care of yourself."

Ashley smiled her thanks and allowed Devon to lead her away. For the next hour, she smiled and quietly listened as Devon introduced her around and discussed things she had no clue about. But she pretended interest and glued herself to his every word, nodding when she thought it was appropriate.

Her headache had worked itself down her neck until it hurt to even move it. Her cheeks ached from the permanent smile and her feet were killing her.

The old Ashley would have kicked off her shoes, pulled her hair down and found someone to talk with about things she understood. Finding or starting conversation was never difficult for her.

The new Ashley was going to survive this night even if it killed her.

Devon seemed appreciative of her effort. He'd told her she looked beautiful and he'd smiled at her often as he took her from group to group. Maybe she had imagined it or maybe it was wishful thinking on her part but she'd sworn she saw pride reflected in those golden eyes of his.

"Stay right here," Devon said as he parked her on the perimeter of the makeshift dance floor. "I have to find your father. He's announcing his retirement tonight."

She nodded and dutifully stood where he'd left her even

though her feet were about to throb right off her legs and her head hurt so bad her vision was fuzzing.

She was careful to wear a smile and not let her discomfort show. Instead she turned her thoughts to the possibility of her being pregnant.

It was true she'd lived the past week in denial. She hadn't entertained the thought. Hadn't wanted to think about it because if she acknowledged the possibility, then she had to consider the reality of her marriage and whether she was ready to bring a child into such uncertainty.

The previous night with Devon had been… Her smile faltered and she quickly recovered. It had been wonderful. But what was it exactly? Sex? Lust? It couldn't be considered making love. Not when he didn't love her.

He'd been exceedingly tender. She was still embarrassed that she'd lost control of her emotions and cried in front of him. It felt manipulative and she still worried that the only reason he'd had sex with her was because she'd been upset and he wanted to comfort her.

He'd left for work this morning before she'd awakened. She'd overslept—another reason she suspected she was pregnant. She was so tired that some days it was all she could do to remain upright. Twice she'd succumbed to the urge to take a nap simply because she would have lapsed into unconsciousness otherwise.

So she hadn't been able to gauge his mood after they had sex. She had no idea if it changed anything or nothing at all. And she hated the uncertainty. Hated not knowing her place in the world or in this relationship.

Devon had been good to her. He'd been kind. But she didn't want good or kind. She didn't want him to feel sorry for her because he'd broken her heart. She wanted his love.

She could feel the anxiety and rush of anger and confusion crawling over her skin, tightening and heating until the sensation reached her cheeks. She curled and uncurled her fingers at her sides, the only outward reaction she'd allow herself as she sought to calm the turmoil wreaking havoc with her mind.

Maybe it was best she didn't dwell on her possible pregnancy. She was already uptight enough without causing herself full-scale panic.

Her father stepped up onto the elevated platform along with Devon. Ashley's mom stood—just as she always had—by her husband's side. But Devon hadn't wanted Ashley there. He'd wanted her here. All the way across the floor from him. She didn't know if there was any significance to that. Her ego was bruised enough to conjure all sorts of pathetic scenarios that spiked the self-pity meter.

For half an hour her father talked, fondly recounting memories, thanking his staff and his family. She smiled faintly when he singled her out and gave her an indulgent, fatherly smile. Then he went on to say that he was stepping down and that Devon would be succeeding him.

There were surprised murmurs from some. Nods from others who obviously suspected such a thing. A few raised eyebrows but most notably, she noticed that people's gazes found her. There were knowing smiles. A few whispers. Nods in her direction.

Her facade was starting to crack. Her smile was beginning to falter. It was as if the world had put two and two together and said, "Aha! Now we get it."

She just wished she did. She stared around, looking for a possible escape path, but she was surrounded by people. All looking at her. Or between her and Devon. Those damn knowing smiles. The smirks of a few women.

It was the worst night of her entire life. Worse than even her wedding night.

Devon found himself surrounded by a throng of people offering their congratulations. He had only taken one step away from William before everyone had descended. Family members. Staff members. Some offering sincere congratulations. Some clearly wary and uncertain. But that was to be expected. Any time change was announced, fear took hold. It was too early to be offering anyone reassurances. Who knew what would happen over the course of the next few months when a changing of the guard would take place and Devon would be at the helm of what would now be the world's most exclusive line of resorts and luxury hotels.

Tonight, though, Devon was celebrating his own victory of sorts. He'd cornered William before the party had begun and told him that Copeland was going to sponsor Ashley's animal shelter.

William had been opposed until Devon threatened to refuse to take William's place in the company. Devon wanted full sponsorship with a yearly budget allocated to the shelter. He was determined that Ashley wouldn't shed another damn tear over her beloved animals.

His father-in-law grumbled and told Devon he was a besotted fool, but he'd given in, telling Devon he'd just do as he damn well wanted when he took over anyway. Which was absolutely true, but they didn't have that much time and he needed William's cooperation to fund the shelter now so it wouldn't have to close.

Now he just needed the right opportunity to tell Ashley the good news. Tonight in bed after the party seemed perfect. Then he'd make love to her until they were both insensible.

He was yanked from his thoughts when he saw Cam pushing his way through the crowd. He grinned when Cam got to him and he slapped his friend on the back. "Well, we did it. Everything. Copeland. The new resort. Oh, ye of little faith."

Cam ignored Devon's ribbing. His expression was grim and his gaze was focused over Devon's shoulder across the room. "What the hell have you done to her, Dev?"

Devon reared his head back. "Excuse me?" He turned, looking for the source of Cam's attention, but all he saw was

Ashley, standing where he'd left her so she wouldn't be swallowed up by the crowd.

Cam shook his head then turned his gaze on Devon. "You don't even see it, do you?"

Devon's eyes narrowed. "What the hell are you talking about?"

Cam made a sound of disgust. "Look at her, Dev."

Again, Devon followed Cam's gaze to Ashley. He studied her a long moment.

"Really look at her, Dev. Take a long, hard look."

Devon battled a surge of irritation. He was about to tell Cam to go to hell when Ashley rubbed her hand over her forehead. The gesture seemed to make abundantly clear what perhaps he'd missed before. Maybe he'd been missing for a while. Or maybe it just took Cam drawing his attention to it.

She was pale, her face drawn. She looked tired and exceedingly fragile. She looked…different. Not at all like the vivacious, sparkling woman he'd married.

He frowned. "She probably has a headache."

"You're a dumbass," Cam said in disgust.

Before Devon could respond, Cam turned on his heel and walked away, leaving Devon baffled by the anger in his friend's voice.

But he didn't have time to figure out Cam's mood or what bug was up his ass. Ashley looked exhausted. Her forehead was creased in pain and she rubbed the back of her neck. He was more convinced than ever that she had one of her headaches.

He pushed his way through the few people standing between him and where William now stood with his son, Eric.

"I'm going to take Ashley home," he said to William. "Please give our apologies to our guests."

William looked up in concern while Eric frowned and immediately sought Ashley out in the crowd.

"Is something wrong?" William asked.

"Everything's fine," Devon said in an effort to calm the older man. "I think she has a headache."

Eric scowled, his blue eyes flashing as he stared holes through Devon. "She seems to be having headaches quite frequently these days."

Devon wasn't going to stick around to argue the point. He nodded at William and then went to collect Ashley.

He found her conversing with two of the people who worked in the Tricorp offices. Or rather *they* were doing all the conversing. Ashley stood smiling and nodding.

"Excuse us please, gentlemen," Devon said smoothly. "I'd like to steal my wife if you don't mind."

The relief on her face made him wince. She was obviously suffering and she'd had to stand here through her father's speech.

His plans for the evening melted away. His primary concern now was getting her home so he could take care of her. The news about the shelter could wait until tomorrow. They'd have dinner together—another of her experimental concoctions, no doubt—and then he'd tell her that her animals were safe.

He drew her in close, noting again the fatigue etched in her features. But more than that, it was as if the light had been doused from her usually expressive eyes.

He experienced a tightening sensation in his chest but he shook it off and focused his attention on her.

"We're leaving."

She looked up in surprise. "But why? The party will be going on for hours yet."

"You're hurting," he said quietly. "Headache?"

A dull flush worked over her features. "It's okay. I'm fine, really. There's no need for you to leave. I can have Pippa take me home or I can just catch a cab."

"The hell I'll have you leave here in a cab," he bit out. "I've done what I needed to do here. The rest is William's night. I won't have you suffering when you could be at home in bed after taking your medication."

Her shoulders sagged a bit and she nodded her acceptance. He put his hand to her back, noting again just how fragile she felt. It wasn't something he could even describe. How did someone feel fragile? But there was an aura of vulnerability that surrounded her like a fog. He wasn't imagining it.

He guided her toward the door, not stopping to acknowledge the people who spoke as they passed.

She was silent the entire way home. She sat in the darkened interior of the car, eyes closed and so still that he was afraid to move for fear of disturbing her.

Once back at their apartment, he helped her undress and pulled back the covers so she could crawl into bed. He leaned down to kiss her brow as he pulled the sheet up to her chin.

"I'll go get your medication and something to drink."

To his surprise, she shook her head. "No," she said in a low voice. "I don't want it. I hate the way it makes me feel. I just need to sleep. I'll be fine in the morning."

He frowned but didn't want to argue with her. She needed to take the damn medicine. She was obviously in a lot of pain. But her eyes were already closed and her soft breathing signaled that she was relaxing or at least trying to.

"All right," he conceded. "But if you aren't better in the morning, you're taking the medicine."

She nodded without opening her eyes. "Promise."

Seventeen

Devon woke Ashley the next morning long enough to ascertain how she was feeling. Ashley assured him she was fine even though her stomach still churned with humiliation and upset. In truth, she just wanted him gone. The last thing she wanted was a set of eyes on her when she was on the verge of cracking.

After he left for work, she shuffled into the shower and stood for a long time underneath the heated spray. Afterward she didn't linger in the bathroom long. She dried her hair because of the cold, but pulled it back into a ponytail. She was too on edge to worry over makeup and just made do with moisturizer.

She was in turns scared and dismayed over the prospect of pregnancy. At times she firmly hoped she wasn't expecting. Others, she held a secret, ridiculous hope that a pregnancy would… What? She laughed helplessly at just how naive she was. Even as she knew a child would in no way fix a doomed relationship, there was a part of her that wondered if Devon would grow to love the mother of his child.

It angered her that she could even entertain such a notion. Why on earth would she settle for a man loving her because she produced his offspring? If he couldn't love her before that, why would she even care what happened after she popped out a kid?

Unrequited love sucked. There were no two ways about it.

If she had it to do all over again, she'd put a definite "wait and see" on any childbearing. Or at least get through the honeymoon without any life-altering surprises.

She ate a light breakfast to settle her stomach. She couldn't be entirely certain if her queasy morning stomach was due to pregnancy or her rather fragile emotional state of late. Or maybe subconsciously she wanted to be pregnant and so had convinced herself of the possibility. Weren't there women who had false pregnancies?

Her nervousness grew as she got into a cab to go to the doctor's office. The only person who knew what she was doing today was Pippa. And well, now Tabitha and Carly would know as well, but she was counting on them to get her through either scenario. Pregnant or not pregnant.

At the clinic, she filled out the paperwork and waited impatiently for the nurse to call her back. After answering a myriad of questions, she was asked to pee in a cup. They drew blood and then she was asked to wait in the reception area.

For twenty of the longest minutes of her life.

She fidgeted. She flipped through a magazine. Finally she got up to pace as she took in the other women in various stages of pregnancy.

Finally the nurse called her back. Ashley hurried toward the door and was escorted to a private sitting area outside one of the exam rooms.

"Well?" she blurted, unable to remain silent a moment longer.

The nurse smiled. "You're pregnant, Mrs. Carter. Judging by when you say your last period was, I'd say maybe six weeks at most. But we'll schedule a sonogram so we can better determine dates."

Ashley's stomach bottomed out. She broke out in a cold sweat and her head began pounding until her vision was blurred.

"Are you all right?" the nurse asked gently.

Ashley swallowed rapidly and nodded. "I'm fine. Just a little shocked. I mean, I suspected but maybe secretly I didn't really believe I was."

The nurse gave her a sympathetic look. "It takes time to adjust. It can be a little overwhelming at first. The important thing is for you to rest, take it easy. Take a little time to let it sink in. We're doing lab work and will check your HCG levels to make sure they're in an appropriate range. If there's any cause for concern, we'll call you. Otherwise, set up an appointment with the receptionist on your way out for your first visit to the doctor. We'll do your sonogram then."

Ashley walked out of the clinic a little—okay, a lot—numb. Again, it wasn't a huge shock. She and Devon hadn't done anything to prevent pregnancy at all. In fact they'd openly embraced the idea—at her instigation—but now she wondered if he was even as open to the idea as he'd let on. How could she be sure he hadn't said whatever was necessary to get her to agree to marry him?

Her mouth turned down in an unhappy frown as she laid her head back against the seat of the cab. She should have asked the nurse what she could take for a headache now that she was pregnant.

But she doubted even the strongest pain medication would help the roar in her ears and the nerves that were balanced on a razor's edge.

The cab dropped her off half a block from the restaurant where she was meeting her friends and she bundled her coat around her as she pushed through people hurrying by. She ducked into the bright eatery and scanned the small seating area for the girls.

In the corner, Pippa stood up and waved. Tabitha and Carly both turned immediately and motioned her over with a flurry of hands.

Ashley nearly ran, desperate to be surrounded by the comfort of her best friends in the world.

"So?" Pippa demanded before Ashley had even had a chance to shrug out of her coat. "Tell us!"

"Are you pregnant?" Tabitha asked.

Ashley flopped into her chair, wrung out from the events of the past weeks. To her utter horror, tears welled in her eyes. It was like knocking the final stone from an already weakened dam.

Her friends stared at her in shock as she dissolved into tears.

"Oh, my God, Ashley, what's wrong? Honey, it's okay, you have plenty of time to get pregnant," Carly soothed.

Tabitha and Pippa wrapped their arms around her from both sides and hugged her fiercely.

"I *am* pregnant," she said on a sob.

That earned her looks of bewilderment all around. Pippa took charge, taking a table napkin and dabbing at Ashley's tears. Her friends sat quietly, soothing and hugging her until finally she got her sobs under control and they diminished to quiet sniffles.

"What the hell is going on?" Pippa asked bluntly. "You look like hell, Ash. And you haven't been yourself. What the hell was that last night with the weird hair and the dress you wouldn't normally get caught dead in?"

"Pippa!" Tabitha scolded. "Can't you see how upset she is?"

"She's right," Carly said in a grim voice. "Besides we're her friends and we love her. We can get away with telling her she looks like crap."

Tabitha sighed. "I think what they're delicately trying to say is you just don't look happy, Ash. We're worried about you."

"Everything's such a mess," Ashley said as tears welled up all over again.

"We've got all day," Pippa said firmly. "Now tell us what's going on with you."

The entire story came spilling out. Every humiliating detail, right down to the disaster of a wedding night and her decision to make Devon fall in love with her.

The three women looked stunned. Then anger fired in Pippa's eyes. "That son of a bitch! I hate him!"

"So do I," Tabitha announced.

"I'd like to kick him right between the legs," Carly muttered.

"You aren't going to stand for this are you?" Pippa demanded.

"I don't know what to do," Ashley said wearily.

Carly grabbed Ashley's hands. "Look at me, honey. You are a beautiful, loving, generous woman. You are perfect just like you are. The only one who needs to change in this relationship is that jerk you married. I'm so pissed right now I can't even see straight. I cannot believe his nerve. I wouldn't change a single thing about you and moreover he doesn't deserve you."

"Amen," Pippa growled. "You need to tell him to take a long walk off the short end of a pier."

Tabitha pulled Ashley into her arms and hugged her tightly. Then she pulled away and gently wiped at the tears on Ashley's cheeks.

"No one who truly loves you should ever want you to change. And no one who wants to change that essential part that makes you *you* deserves a single moment of your time."

"I love you guys," Ashley said brokenly. "You can't even imagine how much I needed you right now."

"I just wish you'd confided in us sooner," Pippa said. "Nobody should have to endure all of what you've endured alone. That's what friends are for. We love you. We would have kicked his sorry ass weeks ago if we'd known."

Ashley cracked a watery smile. "What would I do without you all?"

"Let's not even consider the possibility since you're never going to be without us," Carly said.

"So what are you going to do, hon?" Tabitha asked, her voice full of concern.

Ashley took a deep breath because until right now, at this very moment, she hadn't known. Or maybe she had but had pushed it aside, unwilling to accept the decision that her heart had already made.

"I'm going to tell him I can't do this," she said softly.

"Good for you," Pippa said fiercely.

"You're leaving him?" Carly asked.

Ashley sighed again. "I can't stay with him. I deserve better. I deserve a man who loves me and doesn't want to change me. I'm tired of trying to be someone I'm not. I liked myself the way I was. I don't like this person I've become."

"That a girl," Tabitha said. "And don't you worry even for a minute about the baby. You have us. You know your parents will support you. We'll be with you every step of the way. We'll babysit. We'll go to the doctor with you. We'll even coach you in the delivery room."

"Oh God, stop before you make me cry again," Ashley choked out.

"Do you want one of us to go with you?" Carly asked anxiously. "I don't want you to have to do this alone. Pippa would be awesome to take with you. She can be scary when people mess with someone she loves."

Pippa grinned.

"No," Ashley said, squaring her shoulders. "This is something I have to do on my own. It's time I regained control over my own life and future. I haven't had it since Devon walked into my life."

"I'm so proud of you, Ash," Tabitha said.

"We all are," Pippa said firmly. "If you need a place to stay until you get everything sorted out, any one of us will be more than happy to let you stay as long as you need."

Ashley looked at her three friends and some of the terrible ache in her chest dissolved at the love and loyalty she saw burning in their eyes. She really would be okay. Things would suck for a while, but she was going to be okay. She'd get through this. She had family and friends—the very best of friends—and now she had a child to focus on.

The moment the nurse had confirmed that she had a life growing inside her, Ashley's entire world had changed. Her priorities had shifted and she'd instantly known that she had to do what was best for her and her child.

It had been a powerful moment of realization.

Calm settled over her. Oh, she was still terrified—and heartbroken. That wouldn't change overnight. But now she knew what she had to do and she couldn't escape the inevitability of the path that for once *she* had chosen instead of it choosing her.

Eighteen

Devon was having a hard time concentrating. He'd already blown three phone calls. He'd sent an email to the wrong recipient and replied to another thinking it was someone else. His focus was completely and utterly shot and he couldn't even pinpoint exactly what had him so out of sorts.

He was concerned for Ashley, definitely. He hadn't wanted to leave her that morning, but she'd insisted she was fine and that he should go into work. Still, he had a nagging sensation tugging at his chest that wouldn't go away.

Something just wasn't right.

He picked up his phone to call Ashley's cell but was interrupted by his door opening. He looked up and frowned. His secretary hadn't announced a visitor and he knew damn well he didn't have an appointment now.

To his surprise, Eric Copeland strode into the room, his expression grim. He stopped in front of Devon's desk and planted his palms down on the polished wood.

"What the hell have you done to my sister?"

Devon pushed back and shot up out of his chair. "What the hell are you talking about? I'm getting damn tired of people asking me what I've done to her. If you're asking why we left the party last night, she had a headache and I didn't want her to suffer needlessly. I took her home and put her to bed."

Eric made a sound of disgust. "You may not know this about Ashley but the only time she gets these headaches with any frequency is when she's stressed or unhappy. I find it pretty telling that she returned from her honeymoon after only two days because of a headache and that since then, she's suffered them on a regular basis."

It was a fist to Devon's gut. He sank back into his chair as Eric stood seething over him.

"My sister looks desperately unhappy," Eric continued. "I don't know what the hell is going on, but I don't like what I see. She's changed and something tells me you have everything to do with that."

"Maybe she's finally growing up," Devon said tightly. "Her family hasn't done her any favors by coddling her and shielding her from the world around her."

Eric gave him a look of pure disgust. The cold fury emanating from the younger man slapped Devon squarely in the face. It pricked at Devon and aroused an instinctive need to defend himself. The idea that his marriage was being picked apart by this outsider roused his ire even as a voice in the back of his mind whispered to him to listen.

"Her family loves her just like she is," Eric bit out. "She is cherished and adored by us all. She is appreciated for the beautiful, warm, loving person she is and we'd damn well never try to change her. Anyone that would doesn't *deserve* her."

He spun around and stalked toward the door but then he stopped and turned back to Devon, his lips curled into a snarl. "I don't know what the hell kind of deal you struck with my father but he was wrong. Dead wrong. You weren't the right man for my sister. The right man would know and appreciate what a gift he'd been given. I'm putting you on notice right now. I'm watching you. If Ashley isn't more herself in very short order, I'm coming after you with everything I've got. I hadn't planned to take over the business for my father, but if the choices are having you as a part of the family and making my sister miserable or me sucking it up and taking over myself, I'll do it."

Devon's lips thinned but he acknowledged Eric's ultimatum with a tight nod.

With another dark look, Eric stalked out of the door.

Devon stared out his window in brooding silence after Eric's abrupt departure. Then he stared down at his phone, suddenly afraid to make the call he'd planned just minutes before.

It also occurred to him that she hadn't called him at work in weeks. Not once. No more silly Tinker Bell chimes that amused his coworkers to no end. Not even a mushy text message like she'd done so often before.

He hadn't given it much thought. Things had been so busy after the wedding, with William wanting to move into retirement and the new resort going up, as well as the endless planning sessions for the future.

He'd honestly just forged ahead, hoping that with time, Ashley would get over her initial upset and see that things really hadn't changed that much between them. But a sick feeling settled into his stomach as he realized—truly realized—that everything had changed. And most notably, *she* had changed.

A ping sounded, signaling the intercom, and Devon raised his head irritably. Now his secretary wanted to talk to him? Giving him a heads-up on Eric's arrival would have been nice. But he forgot all about his irritation when he heard what she had to say.

"Mr. Carter, your wife is here to see you."

Adrenaline surged in his veins.

"Send her in," Devon demanded, rising from his seat.

Ashley hadn't ever set foot in his office. Not even when they were dating. She'd called him. Texted him. Sent him sweet emails. But she'd never actually come into his building.

He was striding across the room, fully intending to meet her, when the door opened and she hesitantly walked in. He stopped abruptly, taken aback by the starkness of her features. She was pale, her face was drawn and her eyes were heavy and dull.

An uneasy feeling crept up his spine as she stared back at him.

"Are you busy?" she asked in a soft voice. "Have I come at a bad time?"

"Of course not. Come, have a seat. Would you like something to drink?"

He was suddenly nervous and he hated that feeling. Somehow she'd managed to completely upend his confidence. Much like she'd upended his life.

She shook her head but took a seat on the small sofa in the small sitting area of his office. "I needed to talk to you, Devon."

It was only natural that any man hearing those words from his wife would dread what followed. But coming from Ashley, they seemed so…final.

"All right," he said quietly. He took a seat across from her and studied the tiredness in her eyes. Those rich, vibrant eyes looked…bleak. Without hope. That was what he'd been reaching for. What had eluded him about the way she looked. He caught his breath, suddenly filled with an impending sense of doom. She looked…hopeless, and Ashley was nothing if not eternally optimistic. Had he ever considered such a thing a flaw? He was ashamed to say he had. Now he just wanted it back.

"I'm pregnant," she said baldly. There was no emotion. No

accompanying excitement. No flash of joy. Frankly, he was bewildered by her reaction.

"That's wonderful," he said huskily.

But her expression said it was anything but wonderful. She looked as though she was battling tears.

"I can't do this anymore," she said in a choked voice.

Alarm blistered up his spine and rammed into the base of his skull. "What do you mean?"

She rose and it was all he could do not to tie her to the damn sofa because he had a sudden sense that she was slipping away from him in more ways than one.

Her hands shook but she exerted admirable control over her emotions as she courageously faced him down.

"This marriage. You asked how long it would take to determine whether it would work. The truth is, it was never going to work. It's taken me this long to realize it, but I deserve more. We both do. You deserve to find a woman you can love and that you won't be manipulated into marrying. I deserve a man who adores me and wants to be married to me. Someone who won't try to change me. Someone who accepts me, faults and all. Someone who loves flighty, impulsive Ashley and isn't embarrassed by her."

Tears clouded her eyes and her voice grew thick with emotion. "I thought… I thought I could make you love me, Dev. It was a mistake from the beginning to even try. It was a hard lesson for me to learn but I can't be someone I'm not even if it meant you'd eventually love the new me. Because it wouldn't be Ashley you loved. It would be someone I made up and all the while the real Ashley would be standing there, unloved. I can't do that to myself. And I can't do it to my child. I want to be a woman and a mother I can be proud of first. Before anyone else. I have to love and be at peace with myself, and you know what? I am. I liked me just fine. Was I perfect? No, but I was happy in my own skin and my family and friends accept that person. Someday there'll be a man who'll accept me, too. Until then, I'd rather be alone and true to myself than with someone who places conditions on his ability to love and accept me."

So stunned was he by her declaration that he stood while she walked quietly toward the door. When he realized she'd already slipped by him, he whirled around, calling her name, the lump in his throat so huge that it came out as a mere croak.

But the door had already closed quietly behind her, leaving him standing there so numb...and broken.

Dread consumed him. The realization, the true realization of just what he'd done threatened to completely unravel him. Oh, God. What had he done?

His legs buckled and would no longer sustain his weight. He staggered back onto the couch and slumped forward, burying his face in his hands.

She was right and so very wrong all at the same time. The realization was as clear to him as if someone had hit him over the head with it.

He'd destroyed something infinitely precious and he'd never forgive himself for it. He didn't deserve forgiveness.

Dear God, was this what he'd done to her? She'd come into his office and delivered the news of her pregnancy in a dispassionate fashion, as if she were telling him that she had a dentist appointment or that she was buying new shoes.

Where she'd once jumped up and down and squealed her joy over her cousin's pregnancy and vowed she'd do the same over her own pregnancy, she'd related the news with dead eyes and a broken spirit.

He'd done that to her. No one else. Him and his high-handed, arrogant opinions of how she should act or not act. He'd taken something beautiful and precious and had spit on it.

He'd suffocated a ray of sunshine and sucked every bit of joy and life from her.

Cam was right. Eric was right. Ashley was right. He didn't

deserve her. They'd seen clearly what he'd blithely ignored. In his arrogance, he'd assumed he was right and that he knew what was best for Ashley.

He had tried to change her. And she was bloody perfect just as she was. He hadn't even realized how much he'd missed all the things he professed to be annoyed over. The random calls at work just to say she loved him. The sudden attacks of affection when she'd throw her arms around him. Her exuberance around others.

She hadn't cleaned and organized their apartment because she felt like it. She'd eradicated every hint of her presence there because she'd thought that's what he wanted. She'd tried to become this image of the perfect wife to please him. He himself had thought he wanted her to.

The cooking. The endless trying to kill herself to please him. She'd gone from a vibrant breath of fresh air to a subdued, beaten-down shadow of her former self.

She no longer sparkled. All because he was the biggest ass on the face of the planet.

His pulse ratcheted up and the sick feeling inside him grew as he realized just how long it had been since she'd said she loved him. Since she'd demonstrated any outward affection for him. Since she'd simply smiled and seemed happy.

Tears burned his eyelids. He'd taken something so very beautiful and he'd crushed it. He'd rejected her love. The very gift of herself. He'd arrogantly told her in essence that she wasn't good enough for him. That he knew better. That she wasn't worthy of him.

A low moan escaped him. Not good enough for him? He wasn't good enough to lick her boots.

In clear and startling detail, he realized what perhaps he'd fought from the very first moment he laid eyes on Ashley. He loved her. Not the new, subdued Ashley. He loved the impulsive, passionate, sparkly Ashley. And the very thing he loved the most was what he'd tried to kill.

Rafe and Ryan had nothing on him when it came to being complete and utter bastards to the women who loved them. Devon had surpassed any amount of sin a man committed against someone they claimed to care for.

How could he possibly expect Ashley to forgive him when he'd never be able to forgive himself?

She was pregnant with his child and she was leaving him.

He didn't deserve her. He should let her walk away and find someone who adored her beyond reason and would never ever treat her as he had.

But he couldn't do it. He couldn't be that selfless. *He* adored her beyond reason and if it took the rest of his damn life, he would make it up to her for every wrong he'd done to her.

But first he had to make damn sure she didn't walk out of his life forever.

Nineteen

Ashley tugged the coat tighter around her as she stepped from the cab in front of her parents' apartment building. She had no desire to face them today but she needed to get it over with and she wanted the comfort only her mother could provide.

Devon had already called her cell a dozen times until finally she'd shut it off so it would stop ringing. She'd expected resistance. She was fortunate that she'd caught him off guard enough that she'd been able to get out of his office without much fuss.

But now he would want to talk to her. No doubt he'd give her another lecture about being impulsive and reckless and whatever other adjectives he'd want to assign to her. Then he'd inform her that there was no reason they couldn't have an enjoyable marriage, blah blah blah.

She wanted more than some damn enjoyable marriage. She wanted…awesome. She wanted a man who loved her and celebrated her for who she was. Maybe she'd never have it. But she damn sure wasn't going to settle for someone her father had bribed to marry her.

Which was another reason she'd come to her parents' apartment. Because first she was going to tell her father to stop interfering in her life. Then she wanted a hug from her mother.

She walked into the apartment and took off her coat. "Mom?" she called. "Daddy?"

Gloria Copeland hurried out of the kitchen and smiled her welcome. "Hi, darling. What brings you over today? I wish you'd called. I would have made sure I had tea ready."

"Where's Daddy?" Ashley asked quietly. "I need to talk to him. To you both, actually."

Gloria frowned. "I'll go get him. Is something wrong?"

"You could say that."

Alarm flashed across her mother's face. "Go sit down in the living room. We'll be right there."

Her mom hurried away and Ashley made her way into the spacious living room. Instead of sitting, she went to the fireplace, grateful for the warmth. She was cold on the inside and it felt as though she'd never be warm again.

A moment later, she heard the footsteps of her parents and she turned slowly to face them.

"Ashley, baby, what's wrong?" her father asked sharply.

Both her mother and her father stood a short distance away, impatient and worried. She drew a deep breath and took the plunge. "I've left Devon and I'm pregnant."

Gloria gasped and put her hand to her mouth. William's eyes narrowed and he frowned. "What the hell happened?"

"You happened," she said bitterly. "How could you, Daddy? How could you manipulate us both that way?"

Her father threw up his arm in anger and swore. "Damn it, I told him not to tell you."

"He didn't. I found out on my wedding night. Can you possibly imagine how awful it was to find out on my wedding night that my father had all but bought and paid for my husband?"

"William, what on earth is she talking about?" Gloria asked in bewilderment.

It relieved Ashley that at least her mother hadn't known. She wouldn't have been able to handle the double deception.

"He made me part of the Tricorp deal," Ashley said with more calm than she felt. "He forced Devon to marry me or the deal was off the table."

"Damn it, it wasn't like that," her father bit out. "You make it sound like…" He dragged a hand through his hair and closed his eyes wearily. "I just wanted what was best for you. I thought Devon would take care of you. He seemed perfect for you."

"I can take care of myself. I don't need a man to do that. I want a man who wants me for who I am, not because my father waves a lucrative deal in front of him. I want someone who *loves* me."

"Oh darling," Gloria said, finally finding her voice. She rushed forward and enfolded Ashley in her arms. "I'm so very sorry. How awful for you. I had no idea."

Ashley closed her eyes, absorbing the love and acceptance she'd been denied with Devon.

Her mom pulled away and gently stroked a hand through Ashley's hair. "What about you being pregnant? When did you find out?"

"I went to the doctor this morning. Then I went to see Devon."

"Ashley, are you sure about this?" William asked. "I don't believe for a moment that Devon doesn't care about you. Think about what you're doing here, honey. Do you really want to throw everything away because of the way you met? I understand your anger and I take full responsibility. Devon never wanted to deceive you. It was me from the start."

She had to take a moment as she battled tears. "He doesn't like the real me. He thinks I'm flighty, irresponsible, impulsive, too trusting. He wants to change everything about me.

How can you possibly think this is a man I'd want to be with? Is that really who you'd want your daughter married to? What would that teach my daughter if I stay with a man who doesn't value me? How can I expect her to have any self-respect if her mother doesn't?"

Her mother wrapped an arm around her shoulders and glared her husband down with furious eyes. "I can't believe you did this, William. What in the hell were you thinking? You may as well have told your daughter that she doesn't matter. You've pulled some stupid stunts in your time, but this takes the cake."

William sighed. "Ashley, please don't be angry with me. I only wanted the best for you. You're my only daughter and I just wanted to see your future secured. I thought that you and Devon would make a sound match. I was wrong and I'm sorrier than you can possibly imagine."

"You aren't pulling the plug on this deal," Ashley said in a low voice. "You won't punish Devon because he can't love me. If you think he's the best choice for the business then leave me out of it. I'd appreciate being able to make my own choices in the future, free of manipulation."

"I do love you, baby. Please believe that. I never meant to hurt you. Devon tried to tell me but I wouldn't listen. I thought I knew better. He wanted me to tell you everything. He didn't want to deceive you but I tied his hands and for that I'm sorry."

Tears welled in her eyes. Who knew what may have happened if they'd just been left alone?

William hesitantly pulled her into his arms and hugged her tight. "You know you can count on me and your mother to help you with whatever you need, and we'll be here for the baby when it comes."

"I know," she whispered. "And I love you too, Daddy. Just let me make my own mistakes from now on. Your heart was in the right place but now I've fallen in love with a man who can never love the real me."

He slowly released her and her mom pulled her into another hug. "Do you want me to send someone over for your things? You know you can stay here as long as you like."

Ashley shook her head. "I'm going to stay with Pippa for a bit until I figure out what my next step is. I need to find a better job. I have a child to consider now. Devon is right about one thing. It's time to pull my head out of the clouds and grow up."

How long could she possibly avoid him? Devon paced his office, though he hadn't gotten any work done in the three days since Ashley had walked out on him. He hadn't slept. He'd worn out his phone trying to call her. He'd called her friends, her parents, every family member he had a number for.

The reception had been understandably chilly.

He didn't care. He had no pride where Ashley was concerned. He didn't care if he came across as the most pathetic, lovesick guy who'd ever lived. He just wanted her back. He wanted her stuff strewn all over his apartment. He wanted to be able to smell her as soon as he walked into a room. He wanted her to be happy again. He wanted her to smile.

When he wasn't at the office, he was at the apartment, waiting. She hadn't returned. Not even to get her things. All her clothes were still neatly hung in the closet. Her shoes—and there were a ton of shoes—were stacked in boxes on the shelves in his closet. Ashley never went anywhere without her shoes and the fact that she still hadn't returned to the apartment worried him.

If only she'd answer her damn phone. Or one of the hundreds of texts he'd sent her. He just wanted to know she was all right. Worry was eating a hole in his gut. She was pregnant. What if she had another one of her headaches? Who would take care of her?

Eric had said she had frequent headaches when she was unhappy. Devon had made her miserable. Her medication was also at the apartment but surely she couldn't take it now that she was pregnant. He could at least hold her, rub her head, make sure it was cool and dark in the room.

If she would just talk to him. Just give him a chance to tell her how much he loved her. He hadn't realized how much he missed the sunshine she brought into his life until it was gone. Snuffed out over careless, thoughtless words he'd thrown at her.

His cell rang and he scrambled for it, nearly dropping it in his haste to see if it was Ashley calling. Disappointment nearly flattened him when he saw it was Rafael. With a heavy sigh, he put the phone to his ear and muttered a low hello.

"It's a girl!" Rafael said in a jubilant voice. "A beautiful six-pound, twelve-ounce baby girl. She was born an hour ago."

Devon's eyes closed and he swallowed back the bitter disappointment. He was so envious of his friend in this moment that it took everything he had not to throw the phone at the wall.

"Hey man, that's great. How is Bryony doing?"

"Oh she's wonderful. What a trooper. I'm so damn proud of her. She breezed right through labor. I think she was a hell of a lot stronger than I was. I was ready to fall over by the time the little one made her appearance. But boy, is she gorgeous. Looks just like her mama."

Devon could practically hear Rafael beaming through the phone.

"Give her my love," Devon said. "I'm happy for both of you."

"Is everything okay, Dev? You sound like hell if you don't mind me saying."

Devon hesitated. He didn't want to dump on Rafael on the day his daughter was born, but he was at the end of his rope and he could use any advice he could get.

"No," he said bluntly. "Ashley's pregnant and she left me."

"Whoa. Back up a minute. Holy crap. I thought she was

head over heels in love with you? What the hell happened? And damn, you move fast. How far along is she?"

"I have no idea," Devon said in a weary voice. "I don't know anything. She came to my office three days ago, told me she was pregnant and then announced she was leaving me."

"Ouch. That blows, man. I'm sorry to hear it. Is there anything I can do?"

Devon sank into his chair and rotated around so he could watch the falling snow through the window. "Yeah, you can give me some advice. I have to get her back, Rafe."

There was a prolonged silence. Then Rafael blew out his breath. "Okay, well the first question. Do you love her? Or is this more of a 'you're not leaving me because you're pregnant and we should stay married' type thing?"

Devon swore. "I love her. I screwed up but I love her. Not that she'll ever believe me. I messed up so bad with her, Rafe. I make you and Ryan look like choirboys."

"Oh boy. That's bad. That's really, really bad."

"Tell me about it."

"Well, I'll tell you like a certain gentleman once told me when I was standing around with my thumb up my ass wondering how the hell I was going to get Bryony to forgive me. Either go big or go home."

"What the hell is that supposed to mean?"

"It means you need to pull out the big guns. Do something huge. Make a gesture she can't possibly misunderstand. And then get on your knees and grovel. Trust me. The first time on your knees sucks, but if she takes you back, you'll spend the rest of your life on them anyway so better get used to it now."

"If she'll take me back, I'll gladly stay on them," Devon muttered.

"It pains me that I can't even give you hell about falling hard like the rest of us poor schmucks you liked to rag on. You're too pathetic to pick on right now."

"Gee thanks," Devon said dryly. "Don't you have a daughter to go take care of? She probably needs a diaper change or something."

"She's sleeping with her mama, but yeah, I'm going to get back to my family. It's the best feeling in the whole world, Dev. Get your ass out there and get your family back where they belong."

"I will. And thanks, Rafe."

"Hey, no problem, man. Anytime."

Devon slid the phone back into his pocket and pondered his friend's advice. Go big or go home. Pretty solid advice. Now he just had to figure out how big to go. There was absolutely nothing he wouldn't do to convince Ashley to give him another chance.

Twenty

Ashley sat on Pippa's couch, curled underneath a blanket as she sipped hot tea and watched it snow. It had snowed for the last two days, leaving a heavy blanket over the city. She longed for the comfort of her own apartment...or rather Devon's apartment. She bleakly considered that it had never really been her home. But she missed it all the same. Nights like tonight she and Devon would have snuggled in front of the fire and watched a movie.

"Hey, chickie," Pippa said as she settled down the couch from Ash with a bounce. "How are you feeling? Nausea still a problem?"

It was probably the pregnancy hormones—that was what she was blaming anyway—but she got positively weepy over how protective and caring Pippa had been ever since Ashley had moved in. Or sort of moved in, since Ashley hadn't yet worked up the nerve to get her things from Devon's apartment. Instead she'd been borrowing clothes from Pippa. But soon—as in tomorrow—she was going to have to brave going.

"Yes and no. I honestly don't know if it's the pregnancy or the fact I'm upset. I've been so queasy and nothing sounds good. Even my favorite foods have suddenly lost their appeal."

"I'm sure neither is helping," Pippa said dryly. She hesitated a moment as if deciding whether or not to say what was obviously on her mind. But Pippa wasn't one to hold back. "Have you talked to Devon yet, Ash?"

Ashley put her cup down and sighed. "No. I'm a horrible coward."

"No, you aren't," Pippa said fiercely. "It took guts to go to his office and lay it out to him like you did. I'm so freaking proud of you. I so want to be you when I grow up."

Ashley's eyes got all watery again. "Oh my God. I've got to stop this," she said, sniffling back the tears. "Pippa, you're the most put-together person I know. You've got it all. You're smart. You can cook like a dream. You're gorgeous. And you're the best friend I could possibly hope for."

"And strangely I'm still single," Pippa drawled.

Ashley giggled. "Only because you're a picky bitch, as you should be. I could use some lessons from you."

Pippa shifted forward on the couch, her expression suddenly serious. "Ashley, you have no idea how truly special you are. When the rest of us were struggling to find ourselves, sleeping around and experimenting with all the wrong guys, you were so calm and centered. You knew exactly who you were and what you wanted. You've always known who you were. You valued yourself and you refused to settle for less. Just because Devon turned out to be a prick who tried to change you doesn't mean you did anything wrong. You may have lost your way for a very short time, but ultimately you didn't let him change you."

Ashley smiled but inside she wondered if Pippa was right. Devon had changed her. Irrevocably. No matter that she'd resisted and refused to become someone she didn't like, she'd never truly be who she was before Devon entered her life.

But maybe that was what life was all about. People and circumstances changed you. It was what you did with that change that mattered.

The door buzzer sounded and Pippa made a face. "I swear if that's another salesman I'm going to wet down my steps so they'll freeze and anyone coming up will bust their ass. We've had two already this week."

"Are you expecting a delivery? Maybe it's your groceries."

Pippa grew thoughtful. "No, I'm pretty sure I arranged it for tomorrow. But maybe you're right. I'll be right back."

"You sit," Ashley said as she pushed the blanket back. "You've been on your feet all morning. I've done nothing but sit around and feel sorry for myself."

Pippa rolled her eyes but flopped back on the couch as Ashley padded toward the door. Ashley grinned as she imagined Pippa watering down her steps so they'd become icy. It was something she'd totally do.

She opened the door to the street-level apartment and blinked in shock to see Devon standing on the stoop, snow landing on his hair and wetting it. He wore a coat but had no scarf or cap, and he looked like he hadn't slept in a week.

"Hello, Ash," he said in a quiet, determined voice.

She gripped the door until her fingers went numb. "Uh, hi. What are you doing here?"

He laughed. It was a dry, brittle sound that in no way conveyed true amusement. "I haven't seen my wife in a week. She won't return my phone calls or texts. I have no idea if she's okay or where she's staying and she asks me what I'm doing here when I finally track her down."

She swallowed nervously but she held her ground. It was mean-spirited to make him stand out in the cold, but she didn't want him to come in.

"I was going to come by tomorrow to pick up my things," she said in a low voice that barely managed to hide the tremble. "If that's all right with you."

"No, it's not all right with me," he bit out.

Her eyes widened and she took a step back at the vehemence in his voice.

"Can we go somewhere and talk, Ash?"

She shook her head automatically. "I don't think that's a good idea."

His lips formed a grim line. "You don't think it's a good idea. You're pregnant with my child. We're married. We've only been married a short time. And you don't think we have anything to talk about?"

She closed her eyes and put a hand to her forehead in an automatic gesture.

"Ash? Is everything okay?" Pippa called. Then she came up behind Ashley. "Who is it?"

Ashley turned. "It's okay, Pip. It's Devon."

Pippa's expression darkened, but Ashley held up her hand. Pippa reluctantly turned to go back to the living room but she called back in a low voice, "I'll be right here if you need me."

Ashley returned her attention to Devon. "I know we need to talk. I just don't think I'm up to it right now. This has been hard for me, Dev. I don't expect you to believe that, but this isn't easy."

His expression softened and he took a step forward, snow dusting off his hair as he moved. "I know it's not, baby. Please. There's so much I need to say to you. There are things I need to show you. But I can't do that if you won't talk to me. Give me this afternoon. Please. If you still don't want anything to do with me, I'll take you over to the apartment myself and I'll help you pack your things."

She stared back at him, utterly befuddled by the pleading in his voice. He almost looked as though he were holding his breath. And his eyes. They looked…bleak.

"I—I need to get my coat," she said lamely.

The relief that poured over his face was stunning. His eyes

lightened and he immediately straightened, hope flashing in those golden depths.

"And shoes," he said. "I brought some from the apartment. I wasn't sure you had any you loved here."

She gaped at him. "You brought my shoes?"

He shifted uncomfortably. "Six pairs. They're in the trunk of the car. I chose those I thought would be warm and would protect your feet from getting wet in the snow."

Something loosened in her heart and began to slowly unwind.

"That would be great," she said softly. "Let me go get my coat and my cap. If you brought a pair of boots, that would be perfect."

"I'll be right back. Wait here. I don't want you falling on the ice," he said.

He turned and sprinted back toward the street, where his car was parked. She stood there a moment, staring in bemusement as he popped the trunk and bent over to rummage in the boxes.

He rarely drove his own car. She'd only seen the vehicle once. They always used his car service or hailed cabs.

Realizing she was still standing in the wide open doorway, allowing the bitter chill inside, she hastily withdrew into the apartment and shut the door.

She hurried back into the living room, grabbed a brush from the end table and began pulling it through her hair in short, rapid strokes.

"Ash? What's going on?" Pippa asked cautiously.

Ashley stopped and frowned. "I'm not altogether certain. Devon wants to talk. Asked if I'd give him the afternoon and then he'd take me to the apartment and help me pack if that's what I wanted. He's acting…weird."

Pippa snorted. "Of course he is. You dumped him after telling him you were pregnant with his baby. That has a way of altering your priorities."

"I guess I'll go…talk," Ashley said as she put the brush aside.

"Call me later," Pippa said. "I'll want a full report."

Ashley blew Pippa a kiss and went to the closet to retrieve her coat and scarf. She pulled on a cap and tucked her hair carefully underneath before heading back to the door.

When she opened it, Devon was standing there holding a pair of fur-lined boots. When she would have reached for them, he bent over and said, "Here, let me."

She put a hand on his shoulder to balance herself and stood on one foot while he pulled her boot on the other. After he zipped it up, she switched feet and he put the other one on for her.

When he was done, he straightened to his full height and then took her hand to help her down the steps. He walked her to the car and settled her into the passenger seat.

"Where are we going?" she asked as he pulled away into traffic.

"You'll see."

She wrinkled her nose and sighed. He slid his hand over the center console and tangled his fingers with hers.

"Trust me, Ash. I know it's a big thing to ask and I totally don't have the right to ask it of you, but trust me just this once."

The utter sincerity in his voice swayed her as nothing else could. There was raw vulnerability echoed in his every word and expression. He looked as terrible as she felt, almost as if he'd suffered as much as she had.

It didn't make sense to her. She had no doubt that he wasn't exactly celebrating her departure from the marriage, but with the deal still intact, he was getting precisely what he wanted without the unnecessary burden of a wife.

When they pulled up outside the shelter, Ashley sat there, bewildered. "Why are we here, Dev?"

Devon opened his door, walked around to hers and held out his hand. "Come on. There's something I want you to see."

She allowed him to help her out of the car and they hurried toward the entrance of the older building. As soon as they ducked inside, the sounds and smells of the animals filled her senses. Her heart softened when she saw Harry the cat sound asleep on the reception desk. He was their unofficial mascot and the children who often filtered through the shelter in search of a pet loved to pet him as much as he loved being petted.

To her further surprise, Devon ushered her past the reception area and through the hallway lined with cages. He'd never been here before. How could he possibly know where he was going?

He stopped outside the larger room they used for animal orientation when they'd put pet and new owner together for a period of adjustment before the animal was released to his new home.

He gave her a quick, nervous smile and then pushed the door open. Inside, Molly and the other shelter volunteers stood beaming in a line, and when Devon and Ashley walked fully through the entrance, they let out a loud cheer.

"What's going on?" Ashley asked in bewilderment.

"Say hello to your new staff," he said. "You are now the acting director of the Copeland Animal Shelter."

Ashley's eyes went wide as she stared at Molly and then at the other grinning volunteers. Then she glanced back at Devon. "I don't understand. We aren't closing?"

Molly rushed forward and threw her arms around Ashley. "No, we aren't closing! Thanks to your husband. He gave us the funding we needed to stay running. Not only can we stay open, but we also have the money for improvements and for marketing so we can heighten awareness for the animals we need homes for."

She disentangled herself from Molly's embrace and then turned back to Devon. "You did this for me?"

"I did it before you left," he said gruffly. "I talked to your father about it the night of the party. I threatened to refuse to take his position if he didn't agree to fund the shelter."

Her mouth fell open in shock. She wanted to throw her arms around him so badly, but she knew it wouldn't be what he wanted. But he looked so nervous, as if he worried she wouldn't appreciate what he'd done. How could she not?

"I know how much the animals mean to you, Ash."

Tears blurred her vision and her heart ached. She loved him so much. "Thank you," she whispered. "I can never thank you enough for this. It means the world to me."

"You mean the world to me," he said softly.

Her eyes widened and her heart thumped so hard against her chest that she put a hand over her breast to steady herself.

But before she could question him, he turned to the others and said, "As much as we'd love to stay and celebrate with you, I have to take Ashley one more place."

After saying their goodbyes, Devon ushered Ashley out to the car again. She sat in her seat, bemused and a little hopeful, but for what she wasn't sure. Something was different about Devon. Something that went deeper than simple regret or guilt.

"What did you mean, Dev?" she asked softly as they drove away. "Back there when you said I meant the world to you?"

His hands tightened around the steering wheel and his jaw worked up and down.

"Exactly what I said, Ash. There is so much I need to say to you, but I'm asking you to be patient with me. This isn't a conversation I want to have in a car when I'm driving and I can't look at you or touch you. So I'm asking you to give me a little while. There's a place I want to take you and then I want us to talk and I want you to listen to everything I have to say."

Her mouth went dry at the intensity in his voice. He was tense. Almost as if he feared she'd refuse and demand he take her back. Wanting in some way to alleviate his obvious stress, she reached over to lay her hand on his leg.

"Okay, Dev. I'll listen."

Twenty-One

Devon continuously had to ease up on the accelerator as he headed out of the city. He was impatient and time was running out for him, but the roads were slick and the very last thing he wanted to do was endanger his wife and child.

His wife and child.

The words and the image were powerful. *His* wife and child. The woman he loved and had hurt so terribly. A child resting inside her womb. Their creation. His family. Something that belonged solely to him.

What would he do if he wasn't granted a second chance to make amends?

He couldn't—wouldn't—focus on that possibility. To do so would drive him insane. It was up to him to make her forgive him or at least agree to give him one more chance to make it all right.

She was so beautiful, but there was an aura of sadness that surrounded her. It was as if a light had been extinguished or a black cloud had crawled across the sun and clung stubbornly as the storms rolled in.

. He wanted her to smile again. He wanted her to be happy. But more than anything he wanted to be *why* she was happy. He wanted her to be happy with *him*.

The trip to Greenwich, Connecticut, took longer than he'd like. The drive was silent and tense. They both seemed nervous and ill at ease. By the time he turned onto road that would wind around to the front of the sprawling home he wanted Ashley to see, they only had an hour of daylight left.

He pulled to the curb just before the bend in the private lane and shut the engine off. Beside him Ashley's brow furrowed in obvious confusion.

He walked around to her side of the car and opened the door. He pulled her out, carefully arranged her scarf and cap so she'd be warm and then took her hand and tugged her onto the road.

Snow drifted in the ditches and spread out over the landscape, a pristine covering of sheer white. It reminded him of her. Magical, almost like a fairy tale.

He'd once told her that life wasn't a fairy tale, but damn it, she was going to have one. Starting right now.

"It's beautiful here," she said breathlessly.

Enchantment filled her eyes as she stared out over the rolling hills. Her face had softened into a dreamy smile and he felt a stirring in his heart. This was how he wanted her to look every day. Happy. Sparkling. So damn beautiful she made him ache to his bones.

He pulled her up short just as they reached the sharp bend in the road. He kept hold of her hand and pulled her to face him, his heart pounding damn near out of his chest.

Their breaths came out in visible puffs. Snowflakes began to fall again, spiraling lazily down, some sticking in her hair, some melting and absorbed by the splash of sun in the barren white of winter.

"Ash."

It came out as a croak and he cleared his throat, prepared to fight with everything he had to keep the woman he loved.

She cocked her head to the side and sent him an inquisitive glance.

"Yes, Devon?"

Her voice was sweet and clear in the silence that had settled over the area. Only the distant crack of a tree limb disturbed the calm.

He hated that he stood here, tongue-tied, unable to form a single damn word, his heart in knots. There was so much to say he simply didn't know where to start. Finally his frustration got the better of him.

"Damn it, I love you. I'm standing here trying my best to come up with the words to everything I have to say and all I can think, all that weighs on my mind, is that I love you so damn much and I can't live without you. Don't make me live without you, Ash."

Her expressive eyes widened in shock. Her mouth popped open and then snapped shut again. She shook her head wordlessly as if she had no idea what to say to his sudden declaration.

Then hurt entered her eyes, crushing him with the weight of her pain. Her gaze held the memory of all the terrible things he'd said and done. He couldn't breathe for wanting to drop to his knees and beg her forgiveness.

"Then why?" she choked out. "If you love me, really love *me*, then why would you want me to change? You don't love the real me, Dev. You love the image you have in your head of how the perfect wife should be. Well, I've got news for you. I'm not her. I'll never be her."

She was glorious in her anger. Her eyes came to life and sparked darts of fire. Color suffused her cheeks and her lips pinched together as she glared holes through him.

"Trying to change you was the biggest mistake I've ever

made or will make in my life. God, Ash, when I think of how stupid I was I just want to punch something."

He put his hands on her shoulders and stared intently into her eyes. "You are the most beautiful, precious thing that has ever barreled into my life. I didn't see it because I didn't want to see it. When your father suggested the marriage, I was pissed and I resented his interference."

"That makes two of us," Ashley muttered.

"But the thing was, I didn't mind the idea of marrying you. Even when I told myself that I was angry, there was a part of me that didn't at all mind the idea of marriage and settling down. Starting a family. With you.

"I was torn and I was an immature jerk acting out because I felt like marriage was being forced on me instead of when I was ready for it. Even though I didn't mind the outcome, I was resentful on principle. Which is stupid. And then on our honeymoon night I was gutted when you found out because the last thing I ever wanted was to hurt you. I felt cornered. Here you were demanding to know how I felt and my feelings weren't even something I could admit to myself. So I answered out of frustration and I said all that crap about how we could have a good marriage anyway because in my mind I wanted things to go on as they had before but without the vulnerability I felt every time the question of love popped up."

He sighed and released her shoulders, stepping back for a moment as he stared off into the distance. "Your entire family baffles me, Ash. I don't always know how to take them. I'm not used to having this big, huge loving family where dysfunction isn't a way of life. Your dad was always calling me 'son,' and he wanted me to marry you, and all I could think was that I don't fit here. I'm not good enough. I wasn't worthy. And that made me angry because after I left home, I was determined never to feel inferior again."

She was still staring at him like she had no idea what to say.

"You scared me, Ash. You barged into my life, turned it

upside down with your take-no-prisoners attitude. You were the one thing I couldn't control, couldn't put in its proper place, and I tried. Oh, I tried. I was determined that you weren't going to be a threat to me. I hated how rattled you made me feel and how I went soft every time you entered a room. I thought somehow if I covered you up that you wouldn't shine quite so brightly and that maybe I could better control my reaction to you or at least I wouldn't feel like my guts had been ripped out every time you smiled at me."

"Wow," she whispered. "I have no idea what to say, Devon. I had no idea I affected you so badly."

He shook his head. "Oh, God, no, Ash. Don't you see? You are the very best part of me. It wasn't you. It was never you. It was me."

No longer able to keep his hands from her, he stepped forward again and pulled her close so that their faces were almost touching and he could feel the warmth of her breath on his throat.

"You are the very best part of my world. You are my life. I cannot imagine an existence without you. I don't want to. What I did was unforgivable. It was the result of ignorance and stupidity of the highest magnitude. I can only tell you that if you let me back into your life that you'll never have cause to doubt me again. I'll spend every single day proving to you that you are the absolute center of my universe. You wanted a man who adored you beyond reason. Someone who accepted you for the beautiful, amazing woman that you are. Look no further, Ash. He's standing in front of you with his heart in his hands. No man will ever love you more than I do. It isn't possible."

Her eyes were huge in her face. Brilliantly blue, sparkling like the most exquisite gems. Her cheeks were brushed with rose and her throat worked up and down as she swallowed. Tears glittered like diamonds, clung to her lashes but didn't fall. He wouldn't let them this time. If she never cried again, it would be too soon for him.

When she opened her mouth to speak, he simply put his lips to hers and kissed her long and sweet. He was shaking as he crushed her to him. For the last week he'd despaired of ever getting this close to her again and now she was warm and soft in his arms and so very precious.

"Don't say anything yet," he whispered. "There's still something I want to show you."

He pulled away, gathered her hand in his and pulled her along the road. She walked with him haltingly, as if she were in a solid daze. As they rounded the sharp bend, she stopped in her tracks and gazed in wonder at the sprawling house on top of the hill.

In the distance, dogs barked and she turned her head, her brow furrowing as she searched for the source of the noise. And then over the hill, two dogs bounded, making a beeline for Ashley.

"Mac! Paulina!"

She dropped to her knees just as the dogs launched themselves at her, licking and barking excitedly as Ashley tried to hug them.

"Oh my God, where did you come from?" she whispered.

Devon glanced up the hill to see Cam standing there and Devon waved his thanks before turning his attention back to Ashley and the sheer joy in her eyes.

One of the dogs knocked her over and she went laughing to the ground, snow sticking to her coat as she lay gasping for air.

Devon carefully picked her back up and fended off the animals as they tried their best to lick her to death.

"They come with the house," he said solemnly. "Since you're the new director of the shelter, it only stood to reason that some of the animals find their home here."

She brushed herself off and then stared back at the house again. "Is it… Is it yours?" she asked hesitantly.

"No, it's yours."

She turned to stare at him, excitement flashing like fireworks in her eyes. "You mean it? Really? How? Why? When?"

He chuckled indulgently and then because he couldn't help himself, he pulled her into his arms so that he was wrapped solidly around her. They stood staring up at the house as her heart beat solidly against his chest.

"You wanted a home where you could envision children playing and you could be surrounded by your animals. I ignored that because I wasn't ready for anything in my life to change. My apartment was comfortable and I saw no reason we couldn't live there. But the simple truth is, I want to live wherever you are and wherever makes you happy. A good friend told me to go big or go home. I'm going big, Ash. Because I'll do any damn thing in the world to have you back in my life."

"Oh my," she whispered. "I don't know what to say, Dev. You're saying everything I've ever dreamed you saying. I want to believe you. I want it more than anything. But I'm afraid."

He tugged her even closer and rested his forehead on hers. "I love you, Ash. That isn't going to change. I was an ass. I just need a chance to prove to you that you're safe with me and a chance to show you that I'll love and cherish you every day for the rest of your life. You and our children."

"You're okay with the baby?"

"If I was any more okay, I'd burst wide open. I can't think of anything better than this house with you and our son or daughter plus the half dozen or so more we'll fill it with."

"Oh I love that," she said, her eyes lighting up like a thousand suns.

He stroked a strand of her hair away from her face and then he kissed her softly, lingering over her lips as he savored being this close to her again.

"I love you," he said. "I love you more than I ever thought it possible to love another person. I won't lie. It scares the hell out of me, but being without you scares me even more. Give us a chance, Ash. I'll show you that you can trust me again. I swear it."

She wrapped her arms around his shoulders and moved her

forehead down to nestle in the side of his neck. "I love you too, Dev. So very much. You have the power to hurt me like no one else. But you also have the power to make me happier than anyone else in the world."

He inhaled the scent of her hair and hugged her more fiercely. "I want you to be happy. I want you to smile again. I'll do anything to make that happen."

She pulled away and smiled mischievously up at him as the dogs danced around at their heels. "Then why don't you show me my new house?"

He relaxed, going suddenly weak as relief tore through him with the force of a storm. Oh, God. He couldn't even find his tongue because he feared if he tried to speak right now, he'd lose what was left of his composure.

It was several long seconds before he could pull himself together enough to speak.

"The sale isn't final yet but the house has been empty for six months and I've gotten the keys. I'll be happy to show you around."

She threaded her arm through his as they started up the rest of the driveway leading to the house.

"Can't you just imagine our children playing here?" she said wistfully. "And the dogs running after them?"

He pulled his arm loose and wrapped it tightly around her as he leaned down to kiss her temple.

"Know what the best part will be?"

She glanced up at him in question.

"Seeing their mother's smile light up their father's world each and every day of his life."

* * * * *

MILLS & BOON®
By Request

RELIVE THE ROMANCE WITH THE BEST OF THE BEST

0617/05

Join Britain's BIGGEST Romance Book Club

50% OFF your first parcel

- EXCLUSIVE offers every month

- FREE delivery direct to your door

- NEVER MISS a title

- EARN Bonus Book points

Call Customer Services
0844 844 1358 *

or visit
millsandboon.co.uk/subscriptions